A Novel

Eyes to See

JOYCE CORDELL

Name: Joyce Cordell
Title: Eyes to See
By Joyce Cordell
ISBN: 978-1-952369-74-2
Subjects: 1. Fiction/Christian/Biblical
2. Fiction/Christian/Historical

Cover Designer: Whitley Howlett
Photo Credits: Joyce Cordell, author

All scripture, unless otherwise noted comes from THE HOLY BIBLE, NEW INTERNATIONAL VERSION®, NIV® Copyright © 1973, 1978, 1984, 2011 by Biblica, Inc.® Used by permission. All rights reserved worldwide.

Published by EA Books Publishing, a division of Living Parables of Central Florida, Inc. a 501c3
EABooksPublishing.com

Dedicated
To
Jim Cordell
My encouraging husband

Contents

Acknowledgements

Thank you to Cheri Cowell for jumpstarting my wanderings with publishing, to Peter Lundell for an amazing transformation of my manuscript with his editing, and to EA Books Publishing for bringing it all together.

Thank you to Micah Fletcher for posing for the cover photo and to Whitley Howlett for the cover design, using this photo. Thanks also to Whitley for taking the author photo.

Thank you to Dr. Gerald Borchert for reading my manuscript with an eye for biblical accuracies.

Thank you to my dear friend Mary Gaskins, ever eager to read the manuscript, advise, and cheer me on.

Thank you to my loving husband who has encouraged me these many years and done helpful jobs around the house to give me more time for writing. He is the love of my life.

Praise and thanks be to God who called me to this task some twenty years ago and has helped me move forward with the three books he inspired.

Characters

*Alphaeus – Matthew's father
  Amos – Capernaum friend who sold Levi his house
*Andrew – Matthew's boyhood classmate, one of the twelve
  Ariah – Owner of balsam salve business in Jericho
*Bartimaeus – the blind beggar from Jericho
  Caleb – Seller in Jericho
  Carmi – Long-time worker with the balsam bushes
  David – gardener for Ariah's estate
  Delilah – The party hostess outside Capernaum
  Gaius – Roman censure who gathers tax money
*Jairus – synagogue leader in Capernaum
  James – Matthew's brother
*John – one of the disciples
  Lily – Zacchaeus' daughter
  Lucius – a Roman soldier
  Martha – Jairus' wife
  Meleke – A trader who recommends Levi to Ariah
  Meribah – Teacher of the law, troublesome helper to Jairus
  Myrah – Matthew's mother
  Rabomba – Caravan friend from Ethiopia
*Peter – one of the disciples
*Philip – one of the disciples
  Prisca – Jairus's little daughter
  Samuel – the tanner in Capernaum
  Susanna – Levi's friend in Capernaum
*Thomas – Matthew's partner when they go out two by two
*Zacchaeus – chief tax collector in Jericho

*Bible characters
  All others are fictional

The Calling of Matthew

As Jesus went on from there, he saw a man named Matthew sitting at the tax collector's booth. "Follow me," he told him, and Matthew got up and followed him.

While Jesus was having dinner at Matthew's house, many tax collectors and sinners came and ate with him and his disciples. When the Pharisees saw this, they asked his disciples, "Why does your teacher eat with tax collectors and 'sinners'?"

On hearing this, Jesus said, "It is not the healthy who need a doctor, but the sick. But go and learn what this means: 'I desire mercy, not sacrifice.' For I have not come to call the righteous, but sinners."

Matthew 9:1–13, NIV

As [Jesus] walked along, he saw Levi son of Alphaeus sitting at the tax collector's booth. "Follow me," he told him, and he got up and followed him.

Mark 2:14, NIV

Chapter 1

Young Levi

Levi skipped across the dusty road and down to the shore. He stared at the Sea of Galilee and loved the way the sun made sparkles of light across the water. Maybe someday, when older than five, he might learn to swim, but today he must gather his monthly supply of stones. Levi scooped them up into the folds of his tunic and wobbled back toward the house, making sure he lost not a one.

As he approached the house, the familiar crash of a piece of pottery sounded through the air. He stopped short; his eyes darted to the pottery shed next to his house. Would Papa toss out more pieces? Would he blurt out angry words?

Hearing no more sounds, he took slow steps, then squatted near the door as he dumped his morning treasures on the ground. How would he sort them today? Three piles of small, medium, and large stones? Maybe he would form squares or circles.

Levi's mother poked her head out the door. She smiled. "Oh, I see you're making circles today!"

Just then, another crash came from the pottery shed. Levi's baby brother cried out from where he had been sleeping inside. Mama sighed. "Oh well, it's time to feed him anyway."

After she fed baby James, she sat him on a blanket just inside the door where he could see his brother and play with his toys. She picked up his favorite toy, the wooden boat with soft edges, made even softer as James constantly chewed it to soothe his bulging gums. Mama tapped his little nose. "You will be showing us your first tooth soon, won't you?"

Suddenly, another crash of pottery came from outside, louder this time, accompanied with lots of bad words. Levi cocked his head to look at Mama through the doorway. She stared at the floor while she slowly wiped a bowl over and over.

Levi stopped his rock play and remembered the angry words his father used once when yelling at his mother. Now Mama had the same hurt look on her face. *Why is Papa always so angry?* He looked back again to see his mother still wiping the same bowl. A tear puddled in her eye and trickled down her cheek.

Last year she talked about Papa one day. "Your papa is a good man. He provides for us. He prides himself on doing good work. The people will know they have a good product when he gets through with it." But all her talk could not erase the pain of Papa's bitter, stabbing words.

Giving her tear a quick swipe, Mama busied herself with a broom, so Levi returned to organizing his stones.

*****

Two years later

Mama said she would teach Levi to count on past fifty to one hundred today, so he strolled down to the shore for more stones. When he returned, Mama and James walked toward Levi's stone pile.

Levi had lined up neat rows, ten stones in each row. Mama taught Levi to count to sixty, seventy, and on to one hundred.

A few weeks later, Levi had studied his rows of ten. "Look Mama, I figured out how I can use a shortcut to get to one hundred. Ten, twenty, thirty…" he said, as he pointed to each row.

Mama clapped her hands and laughed out loud. "Oh, that's wonderful, Levi."

James tried to pull away from Mama's hand and reach out for the stones. "No, no, James. No stones for you. They would go straight to your mouth." She picked him up in her arms. "Besides, we must go to the market today."

Levi stood. "May I go too?"

"You want to leave your stones?"

"Yes, I can play with them later."

Levi found a safe place to put his stones while Mama retrieved a basket from the house. Alphaeus, Levi's father, had a few bowls ready for sale, so Mama put them in her basket.

She tied the ends of a strip of cloth, then threw the circle over her head and under one arm so she could carry James when he got tired of walking. Off they went to the market. James' three-year-old legs had to do double duty to keep up, and he soon grew tired. She picked him up and snuggled him in her cloth pouch to finish the last stretch into Capernaum.

The smell of onions signaled that the market must be near. Levi eyed the fresh array of fruits and vegetables—some piled in big baskets, others lined up in colorful rows on flat trays. "What do you think about all these colors and shapes, Levi?"

His eyes brightened. "They would be fun to play with!"

Mama chuckled. She sold a few pieces of pottery while Levi watched the exchange of coins. *Hmm, coins would be more fun than stones.*

After Mama made her selections, she put James back in the sling around her neck while Levi carried the basket of food they had purchased. Mama put her arm around his shoulder. "Thank you for carrying the basket for me. When we get home, you can help me count our purchases and put them away." Perfect. Counting was his specialty!

As they drew near the house, the clatter of crashing pottery sounded louder and longer than usual. One piece came flying out from behind the kiln. Mama clutched James in fear. James held his mama's neck tight.

Ugly words came before every shattered piece.

Frozen in their tracks, they waited. Levi gripped Mama around her waist and buried his face against her back, his heart pounding. Should they turn and go away for a while or creep into the house? Would they be treated like pieces of shattered pottery as well?

James sniffled, then he whimpered. Likely that whimper would soon erupt into a wail. Mama held him tight.

Silence.

Then one more crash. Levi held his breath and finally released it.

At last, Mama spoke. "Come, Levi, let's go into the house."

James bawled with great heaps of choked cries as they rushed into the house. No amount of patting or soothing would console him.

Levi's frustration with his father mounted. He stomped to the shelves in the kitchen to put the food away. He plopped a basket of onions on the table and smacked the bag of lentil beans down so hard that Mama flinched. He heard her heavy breathing and realized she was shaking.

Alphaeus tromped in carrying a sharp piece of pottery, his face livid. "Myrah, can't you keep that child quiet?"

"And can't you keep from throwing your pottery everywhere?" she screamed. "It is your crashing and banging and yelling that causes James to cry and all of us to be terrified." She lowered her face into cupped hands, filling them with tears.

Bug-eyed, James stared at his mother and froze. Levi's lips quivered as tears spilled down his cheeks.

Another silence.

Papa squinted his eyes at her. "You will regret those words, woman." He stormed out the door, slamming it as he went.

Mama slumped to her stool in exhaustion. Levi had never heard her talk back to Papa. What to do now? Would Papa use the back of his hand to Mama? Worse yet, would he use a jagged piece of pottery on Mama instead of words?

"Where can we go, Mama?"

"Oh, we can't…" she started to say as though leaving was not something they should ever consider. She thought a moment. "Your Aunt Martha lives in Bethsaida, but that is quite a walk, and besides, she has less room than we do." She exhaled a deep breath. "Maybe Papa will calm down soon." Myrah wiped her eyes with her tunic and stood to her feet. "Levi, will you please put the beans in the jar?" she whispered. She picked up James and rocked him in her arms. He fell asleep quickly and she laid him on his mat for a nap.

Levi liked sniffing the raw, dry smell of beans and the strong scent of the onions, but he was distracted by keeping an eye on the door as he worked.

"I've put the food away, Mama."

She motioned to him to come near. "Thank you, Levi." She opened her arms wide and he willingly curled up in her lap, snuggling in her embrace like he did when he was younger.

They sat for a long time, finding comfort in each other. While James made soft sucking noises, Levi held Mama's arm and drifted off to sleep.

Later, when she tried to gingerly get up to fix supper, Levi roused. He crawled over to play with a couple of James' toys in the corner.

"Wouldn't you rather play with your stones?"

"No, this is fine."

Levi glanced at Mama several times while he played. "The soup smells good, Mama." Mama was too deep in thought to respond.

When Papa came in, they ate in silence and went to bed soon after.

*****

The next day Alphaeus walked out of his potter's shed toward Levi. Levi stiffened. Had he done something wrong? Why was Alphaeus coming to him?

"Levi," he said, "take your brother for a walk down by the shore. He would enjoy that." His father's voice sounded almost pleasant, at least civil.

Levi left his stones and went into the house. "Mama, Papa wants me to take James for a walk down by the sea."

"Oh?" she said, puzzled. Deep furrows crossed her forehead, but she added, "Then do as your father says."

Levi took James by the hand and they walked toward the shore, but Levi kept looking back every little bit. When they had almost reached the shore, he saw his father going into the house. He quickly tried to distract James by showing him how to skip a rock over the water. Levi continued to glance at the house until Alphaeus went back to the shed.

"It's time for us to go back to the house," he told James.

"Aw, do we have to?"

"Yes, it will soon be lunch time."

Why had Papa gone to the house? Did he do something to Mama? Was he making good on his word? Had he harmed her?

When the boys returned, James busied himself with his toys, but Levi watched his mother as she stood by the kettle, stirring a pot of lentils.

"We had a good walk, Mama."

"And I skipped the rocks!" James declared.

Without looking at them, Myrah forced a pleasant, "I see," but the slight quiver in her voice was telling. When she reached for the bread, Levi saw a round bruise mark on her arm.

She brought some fruit to the table, and that was when he noticed the red slap marks across her face. Levi's heart sank.

"Oh, Mama," Levi whispered, so as not to alarm James. As he hugged her, he could feel her muffled shaking. Levi held her tight.

She finally drew in a deep breath. "I'm all right," she whispered. "I must fill our bowls." Levi held the bowls for her as she scooped the soup, and he set each one on the table.

"Well, tell me more about this rock skipping," she said to James.

Levi kept his eye on Mama. When she came to the table, she positioned herself so that her slapped side was turned away from James. Oblivious, James rambled on about their adventures.

When Alphaeus came in, he asked about their trip to the sea. James babbled on again with his stories. "Humph," Aphaeus grumbled, not paying much attention.

Levi stared daggers at his father, but as usual, Alphaeus did not even notice him.

Chapter 2

Levi's Yeshiva

Levi enjoyed finding new ways to count and add. "Eight, sixteen, twenty-four, thirty-two…" Glancing at the potter shed, Levi realized that Papa had not had many outbursts of temper recently. He took a deep breath, grateful to breathe easy again.

Levi walked over to help four-year-old James, who was old enough now to have his own pile of stones.

"Let's make a pile of big stones and little stones." Levi started two new stacks on the ground. "See, James, those are big, and these are little."

Levi picked up a big stone from the general pile. "Is this one big or little?"

"Big!" James squealed, as he grabbed it.

"Where do you think it should go?"

"Here!" James shouted, plunking it down in the big pile.

Levi grinned. "Good work, James."

*****

One night, after the meal, Myrah approached Alphaeus. "I've noticed Levi's interest in our Jewish traditions and his questions when we walk to the synagogue. Maybe Jairus, the synagogue ruler, would be available to give him lessons," Myra offered.

"Humph," Alphaeus mumbled. "That would cost a lot of money."

"Your father did that for you, didn't he?"

"I'll think about it."

On the way to the synagogue the next Sabbath, Levi asked, "Why does the Scripture give directions about so many offerings?"

Myrah looked at Alphaeus. "Well," she said, "God wants us to be thankful and devoted to him in many ways."

The next morning, Alphaeus told Myrah, "Maybe it's time for Levi to have a yeshiva class. I'll talk to Jairus when we go to the synagogue at the end of the week." Myrah smiled.

Alphaeus followed up the next Sabbath and arranged a time and place for Levi's first lesson with Jairus, the synagogue ruler.

The following morning, after she had served up breakfast, Myrah also served up the good news. "Levi, you know how you are always asking questions about the Holy Scripture, and about the bema in the synagogue and the dress of the rabbis?"

"Yes?" he answered, with a slight question in his voice.

"Well, Papa and I have decided that it is time for you to have yeshiva lessons where you will learn all about the Holy Scriptures."

Levi's eyes sparkled. "Really? When do I start?"

"Very soon. The day after next Sabbath."

"Yi-pee!" Levi squealed, as he twirled around with his outstretched hands in the air.

Suddenly he stopped and wrinkled his forehead as though figuring. "That would be... seven days!" he shouted.

"Why, that's right."

"Oh, Mama, this is so wonderful. I can hardly wait." He squeezed her around the waist. "Thank you, thank you."

"Be sure to thank Papa too."

*****

The long-awaited day came at last. When Levi, Mama, and James arrived, Jairus greeted them along with Andrew, another new boy from Bethsaida. After introductions, Jairus told Myrah, "We will be here until the noon hour."

She ruffled Levi's hair a bit and patted him on the shoulder while lingering.

"I can find my way back home, Mama."

"No, we will come to meet you."

"Okay." And off he went, just like that.

During the lesson, Levi gave attention to every word Jairus spoke. He and Andrew asked many questions and answered some as well.

"Jacob's name was changed to Israel," Jairus explained. "And so, you see, his twelve sons became the twelve tribes of Israel. The tribe of Reuben, Simeon, *Levi* . . ." Jairus grinned at Levi. "Judah, and eight more sons—eight more tribes."

Jairus went on. "Now, eleven of the brothers were very mean to one of the brothers."

"Joseph!" Andrew called out.

"Yes, that's right, Andrew. Joseph had strange dreams. Dreams that caused the brothers to be filled with jealousy." And on Jairus talked, with the boys leaning into every word.

As the sun shone directly overhead, Jairus gave his closing remarks. When Levi and his new friend, Andrew, came bounding out of the house, Mama and James were waiting under the fig tree.

"Oh, Mama, we learned so many new things. We learned about Abraham, Isaac, and Jacob and his twelve sons!" He pointed his nose in the air and his thumbs to his chest. "And one of them was named 'Levi'— just like me. Then we learned about Joseph and his time in Egypt when he was a slave and had an important job in the house of Potiphar and then was thrown in prison even when he didn't do anything wrong."

When Levi took a breath, Myrah quickly jumped in. "Well, you certainly covered a lot of territory in these few hours." She hugged him and smiled at Jairus.

Levi continued to give other details all the way home. Myrah grinned at his enthusiasm and prodded him on with questions.

The next day, Levi was up and ready to go again. Each day he came out of Jairus' house full of reports about his lessons.

*****

One day when Levi met Mama after class, he had little to say.

"How were your lessons today?" Myrah asked.

Without his usual burst of excitement, Levi answered, "Today we had a halacha."

"A halacha?"

"Yes. Master Jairus asked us a question, but he did not give us an answer. Andrew and I had to discuss which answer we thought was best. I thought one way and Andrew thought another. Master Jairus encouraged us to debate our points of view." Levi lowered his head. "It was hard because it felt like we were arguing."

"Did Andrew shout at you?"

"No, not really. We just didn't agree."

"That's okay. People do not always agree with one another. Some think one way and some another way. It helps you to weigh your own opinion about things."

"That's what Master Jairus said, but it was hard to disagree with my friend."

Myrah put her arm around Levi's shoulders. "And what was the question for today?"

"We had been talking about Shabbat, the Sabbath, and the fact that we are to rest on the holy day. Master Jairus asked us if it would be lawful to help a sick man walk on the Sabbath. Andrew said no, but I said yes. I felt like it would be right to help someone in need on the Sabbath, but Andrew declared it to be work and we are not allowed to work on the Sabbath day. We debated for a long time back and forth."

"And what did Master Jairus say?"

"He never gave us an answer. He just said we had a productive Halacha."

"But this debate did not seem good to you?"

"No, I felt like Andrew was mad at me."

"I see."

Levi hastened on. "Do you think it is wrong to help a sick person on the Sabbath, Mama?"

"I'm not a student of the law like you are. What do you think?"

"I think the Lord would always want us to do good deeds at any time."

"Then you have good reasons for your opinion. Master Jairus wants you to think and reason about the law. He is trying to help you do that very thing."

"I guess so," Levi conceded and put his arm around his mama's waist as they walked home.

Chapter 3

Levi Grows

A few months later, Myrah, Levi, and James had finished their breakfast, but Levi dawdled a bit.

"Hurry along, Levi. It's time to go to your lesson."

Levi stood tall and aloof with a slightly upturned chin. "Mama, I don't think you need to walk me to and from Master Jairus's house every day."

"Oh, I don't mind. It is a good walk for me and James."

"I don't mean it is a bother, I mean it is… not necessary."

Myrah looked at Levi's broad shoulders and long legs and this independent spirit. "You would like to have that time alone to think?"

Relieved, he said, "Yes, to think. That would be good."

"Well, you know the way, of course." She took off her head piece. "Okay, I think that will be fine."

He enthusiastically kissed her on the cheek. "Thank you, Mama."

A tear formed in her eye. "Would you play with your brother for a while before you go this morning. He misses your company."

"Sure." He went outside and squatted beside James to show him a new way of counting his stones. James learned quickly, especially with his big brother's attention.

While James remained engrossed in his play, Levi bid good-bye to his mama.

*****

As Levi walked away, a grumble came from the pottery shed, a reminder of the strained relationship he still had with his father. *Why can't Papa be more like Master Jairus, kind and stimulating, or at least pleasant? Papa rarely speaks to me. Humph, he doesn't even seem to know I'm alive.*

13

Levi took in a deep whiff of the sweet-smelling blossoms from a flower bush along the way. A bird flew across the sunny blue skies. He took in another deep breath. *The first time to walk by myself. Free as that bird I am.* His steps grew broader and faster.

When he arrived, Jairus asked, "Where is your mother today, Levi?"

"I'm walking by myself now," Levi announced, his chest a bit higher, his back straight.

"I see. Come on in and we'll hear from the prophet Isaiah."

On his way home, he missed talking to Mama about the lesson. He could have told about the mighty calling of Isaiah to his work as a prophet with the sights, sounds, and smells Isaiah experienced in the temple. He would tell her about the hardness of heart of the people as Isaiah tried to prophesy to them. *Hmm, "hardness of heart," just like my father.*

*****

After a month of walking alone to his lessons, Levi popped in the house asking, "Mama, do we have a piece of leather I could use?"

"Leather? Whatever for?"

"I want to make a sling!"

"A sling?"

"Yes, I could use my stones and practice with the sling."

"Oh, like King David did when he was a boy?"

"Yes, exactly! Do we have some leather?"

"Well, no, but perhaps we can get some from the tanner. Your papa wants us to take some of his pottery bowls to the market today. Can you help me load them in the cart? We can talk with Samuel the tanner when we get into town."

"Great!"

Levi pulled the cart around and placed a few blankets inside to protect the pottery pieces.

Myrah gathered up her basket and took James by the hand. Levi was bent over in the cart with the blankets. "You do a good job with the packing," she said.

Levi straightened up. "Yes, but I remember the time I didn't pack so well and broke two bowls, *and* I remember the harsh lecture I got from Papa."

Levi pushed the cart near the pottery shed. "I'm ready to pack the bowls, Papa."

"Be careful," Alphaeus warned, as he carried out a stack of bowls. "I've worked hard on these, and I don't want any of them broken."

Levi's mouth pouted.

"Yes, Papa," Levi mumbled sarcastically when Papa was out of earshot. He packed the stack of bowls in the cart, padding them well.

Alphaeus continued bringing armloads of pottery. He neither looked at Levi nor spoke to him.

With all the pottery packed, Levi, his mother, and James began their trip into town. Mama patted James on the shoulder. "I'm so glad you can walk this whole trip now." James beamed a big smile at her.

They walked in silence. Levi huffed some audible breaths, but he said not a word. Finally he blurted out, "Why does he always mistrust me? The broken bowl accident was months ago. Can he not forgive and forget? Nothing seems to please him." He kicked a stone out of his path.

Levi was right, but Mama did not want to feed his temper. "Your father works extremely hard. We must be patient."

As they walked along, they passed a farm of goats, then a farmer plowing in his field.

"Mama, why don't we have a farm?" James asked.

"Your father wouldn't have time for a farm with his pottery business."

"But everybody has a farm," James insisted.

15

"Not everybody," Levi chimed in. "Samuel has his tanning business and Zebedee his fishing business. Many *do* farm, but not *everybody*."

"Oh," said James.

They walked in silence again for a while. Soon Levi's face brightened. "I have an idea, Mama."

"Oh?"

"I thought of a new way to display the pottery. Perhaps it will draw more attention from the shoppers."

"Okay, you can show me when we get there."

In his excitement about this new idea, Levi walked right past the tanner's shop without remembering the leather.

He unloaded the cart and deliberately placed the bowls in three short stacks in a triangular shape. He added more stacks in a circular shape around the triangle. Then he lined plates in straight rows across the bottom, top, and down both sides.

"What a lovely design!" Myrah exclaimed. She gave him a side hug.

Soon others came along and noticed Levi's display.

"Oh, how pretty!" exclaimed one shopper.

"Levi's design," Myrah said.

The woman called to another shopper "Look, Martha. Look what Levi did." Soon, two more came over to see what the excitement was about.

"You know, I'm about out of good bowls. I guess I need to buy a couple of these."

"Well, I broke a plate just last night. I will take one. I hope that won't mess up your design."

"Oh, no, I'll just rearrange it." Levi grinned. "Which one would you like?"

Others noticed all the action at the pottery stand and meandered over as well. Levi stayed busy rearranging while Myrah collected the coins or bargained for a batch of fruits or vegetables. After two hours, she and Levi packed the remaining

16

few pieces of pottery into the cart along with their own purchases and a good amount of coins in their bag.

"Well, that was a productive trip to the market, and we have more than enough coins to purchase that bit of leather you wanted from Samuel. Your new idea proved to be a great plan. Good work, son."

Levi beamed. "Oh, I almost forgot about the leather." He ran toward the tanner's stall and explained what he needed.

Samuel said, "I used to practice with the sling myself when I was a boy. I'm not busy, so I can make the sling for you if you like."

Levi's eyes brightened. "That would be a big help." After Samuel made the sling, he showed Levi how to use it.

Before they left, Samuel turned to James. "And I have something for you too." He gave James a little fish that he had fashioned out of a piece of scrap leather.

When they arrived home from their productive trip, Levi could hardly wait for his father to finish in the pottery shed so he could show him the sales they made for the day.

When Alphaeus finally came out of the shed, he noticed the almost-empty cart. He stormed into the house. "Where's all the pottery? Did you break more pieces? Here I even put in extra pieces today!"

Levi's face fell.

"No, Alphaeus, no pieces broken." Myrah explained. "Most of them were sold or bartered."

Alphaeus looked puzzled. "But you usually come back with half a cart full."

Myrah gestured toward their son, "Levi had a new idea of how to set up the pottery. Everyone was attracted to his display, and the shoppers just kept coming and buying."

Alphaeus scrunched up his brows. The proof lay in the coins on the table. Then he looked over at Levi who stared at the floor. The silence felt deafening.

Alphaeus cleared his throat and spoke gruffly. "Well... I guess Levi is a peddler rather than a potter!"

Levi did not move, but he rolled his eyes over to see his father fiddling with the coins. Alphaeus glanced over at Levi and then nodded his head in approval as he fumbled with the coins. Myrah slipped into the awkward moment. "Well, I guess we better have a meal to celebrate our good day of potters and peddlers."

Myrah chatted at the meal, telling about some of the comments that were made. "When Martha and Nevah noticed Levi's display, they babbled on until others came to see. Everybody talked about Levi's pretty design. With all the sales, he kept busy rearranging. Then when others saw their friends carrying pieces of pottery, they decided they needed a plate or bowl as well."

Levi noticed that Papa smiled just a bit. Indeed, it had been an exceptionally good day.

Chapter 4

Jairus the Synagogue Leader

Jairus studied the bent heads of his two prodigies as they pored over their parchments with quills and ink. He listened to his five-year-old daughter humming a happy Jewish folk melody in the other room. *A fitting tune for what I am about to do,* he thought. As the two boys completed their tasks, he spoke in a brighter tone than usual.

"You boys have done a masterful job of reading, writing, and speaking Hebrew. You have studied the Torah and learned much of the Mishnah, the oral law, in these last four years. Now I would like for you to challenge yourself with a project."

In unison, both boys lifted their heads, eyes wide open with anticipation.

"You will be memorizing selected passages, but I would also like for you to work on having a project of your own choosing and then memorize your work."

"What kind of project?" Andrew asked.

"That's for you to decide," Jairus answered, with a slight grin.

"Can you give us some ideas?" Levi asked.

Jairus gazed out the window toward the Sea of Galilee. "Hmm... let me see." He pushed his lower lip against his upper lip in thought. "Well, perhaps you would like to recount the nine plagues cast on Egypt or search out the prayers of one of our great ancestors." Knowing Levi's propensity for organization, he suggested something to do with genealogy.

The boys sat deep in thought. Andrew, with his elbow on the table and chin leaning on his clutched fist, while Matthew, with furrowed brow, stared at the upper corner of the room. Neither boy spoke.

Finally, Jairus broke the silence. "You need not decide today. You can think about this overnight, and we will discuss it tomorrow."

*****

Levi pondered the new assignment all the way home that day. What would make an interesting project?

Hmm, genealogy. I know the first descendants of Abraham. Perhaps I could trace the family line down to King David. Let me see, Abraham, Isaac, Jacob. David was from the line of Judah, so Judah would be next in line. Then I know David's father was Jesse, and his father, Obed, and Obed's father was Boaz, but I do not know all the ones in between Judah and Boaz.

Satisfied with himself for having made his decision, he was eager to share it with his mother. His fast walk turned into a run until he dashed into the house out of breath. James and his mother both looked up with anticipation.

"Guess what!" he said, gasping for breath. "Master Jairus," double breath, "wants us to have," double breath, "a project."

"Well, sit down and catch your breath," Mama said. She handed him a cup of water. After his breathing settled, Myrah went on. "Well now, tell us about this project."

"It needs to be something that we can study, then memorize. I've decided to do the genealogy of Abraham to King David and maybe even David to the exile."

She turned to the bread she had been kneading. "Oh," she responded, rather casually.

"Genealogy is very important. Our ancestors kept explicit records to be handed down. They wanted us to know these things."

His mother smiled kindly, but there was no sparkle in her eyes as he saw when he did something well or discovered something new. She just kept kneading the bread.

He tried again. "You know, Abraham was the father of Isaac, Isaac was the father of Jacob, Jacob was the father of Judah. See I already have a good start."

Her eyes lit up. "Oh, that's what genealogy means."

"Yes, Mama, and I know that David's father was Jesse, and Jesse's father was Obed and Obed's father was Boaz."

"How smart you are!"

"There's many more in between. I must study to find them."

With his mother's encouragement and Jairus' blessing, Levi dug in energetically to making his list of *begats*.

*****

Meanwhile, Jairus thought about his fine students then pondered the next meeting with his synagogue officials.

That afternoon, Jairus's daughter came skipping in the room where he was working. "What are you doing, Papa?"

"I was just waiting for my sweet daughter to come and see me."

"Here I am!"

He sat on a stool and pulled her on to his lap. "And what have you been doing this fine day?"

"I helped Mama bring in some onions from the garden. She has a big basket, and I have a little one. My basket was more fuller than hers!"

"That's because you are such a good helper, my little Prisca." Prisca hugged her papa around his neck.

Soon he stood, eased her down to the floor, and gave her a little pat. "Now off you go my little one. She skipped out of the room just as she had entered. He smiled as he watched her go, a smile that lingered until he thought of the confrontation he would soon have with the other leaders.

They could never agree on who would officiate each upcoming Sabbath. Elisha, the old resident priest of Capernaum always seemed expected to be the one to take the Holy Scrolls down and place them on the bema, the table for the weekly reading. Every week, Jairus held his breath, expecting the aging Elisha to drop the heavy load.

Jarius's wife walked in with a vase of flowers. "What's troubling you today?"

"I have a meeting with the synagogue committee again. They will argue whether the visiting Pharisee from Jerusalem should do the reading and teaching lesson, or should the scribe from Jericho have the honor? They seem to forget that I am the synagogue leader, not them! They think they have this position."

"Oh my, you do have your hands full with that group." She shook her head in sympathy as she left the room.

Jairus sat at his desk to look back through his book that listed those who had aided in synagogue worship the last few months. Soon he heard voices coming along the path. He looked out his window. Sure enough, he saw the short, bent over Elisha trying his best to keep up with tall, lanky Meribah with his bright-colored robe flying in the breeze. Meribah gestured this way and that as he made some point to Elisha.

Humph, Meribah means, "always running." Good name for him. Bringing up the tail was Jerome. *Steady, quiet, and slow,* Jairus mused.

He walked out to greet the entourage and invited them to sit on stone benches on the front portico. Jairus attempted to begin the discussion in good humor. "Ah, good breeze off the sea today, gentlemen. Please have a seat. Martha will bring us a cup of wine shortly."

Meribah was already off and running with his rhetoric and complaints. "Yes, well, I think it's time we give some attention to the crumbling seats at the synagogue. Can we not rub those edges, so they won't be so sharp and prickly?"

Patiently Jairus told Meribah that it could be done, knowing all the while that it would not be "we" tending to the task, but Jairus himself would have to see that it was done.

"And then there is the matter of the Pharisee and the scribe," Meribah went on, barely stopping to take a breath.

Jairus had already determined he would head off any lengthy discussion. "I have decided to invite the Pharisee. He is only here for a week and then will travel on after Sabbath, but the scribe will be here for two more weeks. We can have him teach the following Sabbath."

"But the scribe's family are great contributors to the treasury," Meribah protested.

"He will have his turn," Jairus said, determined to stick by his decision for a change.

Martha came with a tray of wine cups. It provided only a momentary pause as Meribah sipped his wine.

The man would not let it go. "We hardly know this Pharisee. We have never heard him speak at our synagogue before."

Surprisingly, Jerome spoke up. "But we know his *family*. Good people. Very faithful."

"Who will tend to the scroll this week?" Elisha interjected.

Not wanting to cause any further conflict, Jairus offered, "Why, Elisha, would you like to do that for us?"

"I would be honored," he answered with a nod, as though this was the first time he had ever been asked.

They chatted on about this and that around the town. Meribah made another slight attempt to dissuade Jairus about the Pharisee, but Jairus stuck to his decision. Then they were off.

There was still the matter of the rough benches at the synagogue. Jairus would need to consult with his servant about what could be done to smooth the edges—especially to the seat always occupied by Meribah.

Chapter 5

Alphaeus and the Tax Collector

Levi had etched the ancestors' names on scraps of pottery so he might memorize them at home. "I almost have the genealogy memorized," he announced to Mama one afternoon.

Just as he began reciting, he heard someone speaking to James outside the door. He turned to look and heard James say, "Just a moment."

"I think it's the tax collector," James mouthed the words as he came in the door.

His mother jerked her head in that direction. "Oh, no."

The man knocked on the door post. "I must speak with Alphaeus," he said gruffly.

"He's in the—" Levi began to say when his mother gasped and shook her head no to Levi. What was he to do? He had already made Alphaeus' presence known to the man. He looked back at his mother who shrugged her shoulders, lowered her eyes, and shook her head as if to say, "It's done now, but it isn't going to go well."

Levi took a deep breath, stepped out the door, and pointed to the shed. "He's in the potter's shed."

The collector went around to the shed and pounded on the door. No sound. He pounded again and shouted, "Alphaeus! Alphaeus, I know you're in there."

Alphaeus had been to the side of the shed at the oven kiln. He slid the last bowls into the hot kiln for baking. "Whose banging my door down?" he shouted as he came around the shed.

"You are hiding from me?" the tax collector accused.

"No. Some of us actually work for a living, you know."

"Yes, and you earn a mighty good wage for it, I hear. It is time you pay your fair share of taxes. The good roads to your business take money, you know."

Alphaeus spit on the ground. "Roman uniforms and boots take money too."

"Watch your tongue, man, or those Roman boots may come to your house to do away with your potter's wheel and kiln or put a sword to your throat. You owe forty denarii for the year."

"Forty denarii? You are crazy! I only paid twenty last year."

"Ah, but business is good, I hear. Since the potter in the next town died, your business has doubled. Keep complaining and your tax may double again. You have one week to get your fair share ready." The tax collector stomped through the yard to the road, his fancy sandals thumping on the hard, beaten surface, paved with Jewish coins.

"Roads indeed," Alphaeus grumbled, out of earshot of the Jewish betrayer.

Levi cowered inside the door. He dreaded the antagonistic mood his father would be in after this encounter. Glancing at his mother, he knew she dreaded the aftermath as well. She sat slumped on her stool, elbows on her knees, hands cupped on her forehead. How could he comfort her when, yet again, he was also torn up inside from his father's anger.

He will come in the house in a rage as though we are somehow at fault. Levi gazed at the sea, wanting to run away or at the very least escape to the shore—anything to get out of this house. He looked back at his mother. *But I cannot leave her.*

Levi laid down his pottery scraps and stared at the biblical names he had scrawled on the surface. Somehow ancient names seemed to have little importance in the scheme of things.

Shortly, Alphaeus returned to the house. "Finally, some place cool," he grumbled. He sat on the cool stone floor and leaned his head against the stone wall, while wiping his brow with the back of his sleeve. He kicked off his sandals and closed his eyes. "I should have built the kiln farther from the shed," he mumbled. "Makes the shed too hot."

Myrah scurried to complete the evening meal. Tension hung in the air as Levi quietly put his pottery pieces away in a box. These were cast-away pieces, but he had not really asked for permission to use them. Knowing his father's temperament, he may have gotten angry even over scrap pieces. All the while, Levi eyed his father to see if he was rousing.

Myrah called the family to eat. Alphaeus grunted as he got up off the floor. They sat in silence as they ate their stew and bread. Levi could not enjoy the hearty smell and taste for worrying what his father might do or say next.

"It isn't fair," Alphaeus finally declared. "I work all day and sweat over the kiln. We sell the pottery and what do we get? Taxes. Caesar comes in the form of a Jewish betrayer to claim that we owe a massive amount of taxes." He chomped down on a piece of bread. "Robbery, that's what it is," he spoke again, with another mouthful of bread. "Pure robbery. That collector goes house to house stealing poor people's money, only to fill his own bag and live in luxury. Meanwhile, Roman soldiers trot through our town on their high and mighty steeds like they are our masters." Alphaeus lowered his head. "Indeed, they do own us. When will we ever be free of Roman domination?"

Levi considered his father's plight and for the first time felt a twinge of sympathy. *Perhaps it would be helpful for Papa to know that I have been keeping records for the past three years and that we doubled profit the second year and nearly tripled the third year compared to the first.*

Alphaeus continued, "How can he claim we doubled our income? How would he know what we bring in? We *have* done better, but double? Never!"

Whoa. I guess this is not the time to tell him I have been keeping records.

"Levi!" Alphaeus startled him. "How much do we have in the money bags?"

Levi's fourteen-year-old voice cracked a bit. "Uh, I have been setting some aside each month in a separate tax bag. I'll count it."

Levi went to the back corner of the upper shelf in the kitchen where he had been keeping the bags. He made stacks of five denarii. "Twenty, twenty-five, thirty," he counted, "thirty-five, thirty-six, thirty-seven. We have thirty-seven denarii."

"So much?" Alphaeus questioned.

Levi weighed his words. "We have done much better this year, Papa. I was fearful that the tax collector might charge more, so I kept adding a bit to the bag each month." Levi held his breath, waiting for his father's response.

"Humph, thirty-seven you say?"

"Yes, thirty-seven denarii."

"And how much in the other bag?"

Levi separated the coins and counted a coin at a time. "Nine, ten, eleven, twelve. We have twelve denarii. And then, let me see," he mumbled, as he assembled the other coins, "Twenty, twenty-five, thirty, thirty-five. We have thirty-five ases which would be, uh, sixteen and sixteen is thirty-two, so that would be two denarii plus three ases."

Not given to numbers, Alphaeus gave a loud, exasperated sigh. "So what does all that mean?"

"Well, we have thirty-seven denarii in the tax bag and about ten plus two denarii in the other bag and a few ases. So that would be a little over twelve denarii."

Alphaeus' frustration was mounting. "So how much is that all together?"

"About forty-nine denarii," Levi quickly simplified.

"So, we do have the money, but it will take practically everything we have. Outrageous! Robbery, I say. Robbery!"

"At least, we have it," Levi offered, feeling proud that he had wisely been saving a good amount.

"And you're glad to give away my hard-earned money?" Alphaeus shouted. "I slave in that hot shed day in and day out, and you're glad to give it away to the Romans?"

"No, Papa, I didn't mean—"

"We give it away, and what do we have to live on? A few denarii? Must I work day *and* night to feed those filthy Romans?" Alphaeus stormed out of the house and into the shed.

Levi lowered his head to the side with a loud huff of resentment. Mama and James did not speak.

"How can he think he does all the work?" Levi suddenly exploded. "True enough, he fashions the pottery and bakes it, but it makes no money until I cart it off to the market, bargain and deal, and come up with all kinds of business plans to sell it."

Levi gathered up the coins and returned them to the money bags. "I carefully laid aside coins to take care of taxes, but is there even a hint of gratitude? No, just criticism. Always criticism!"

Levi slapped the bags back on the shelf, marched out the door, and down to the shore. He had a favorite large rock—his "thinking rock" he used to say. It had become a place of retreat and safety for him.

He slumped down on the rock while his mind played out the previous interchange over and over. He tried to be a good son. He helped his mother, he was obedient to his father, and took care of the selling and the money. He was dutiful in his Torah studies and well-liked by the townspeople.

Everybody likes me except the one person who should love me above all others. I have done nothing wrong. In fact, I have done many things right, and yet he makes me feel that this misfortune is somehow all my fault.

Levi listened to the waves gently splash on the shore. He sat spellbound for a few moments by the serenity and predictability of the water, moving in, bubbling, moving out.

It dawned on him that he may have repeated the same behavior he so despised in his father. Did he make his mother and brother feel the way he felt? Lashing out in anger. Did they feel betrayed by his actions, as though *they* were at fault?

He thought of his mother, *always kind and encouraging, knowing just the words to say. Caught in the middle of caring for James and me and protecting us from my father's wrath.* Then he thought of James, growing up in the fear of their father just as he was.

He gazed across the vastness of the sea, wishing he could swim for hours or jump in one of Andrew's fishing boats and sail away. He knew he could do neither, for although he lived by this sea all his life, he had never been in it. He was horribly afraid of the water.

He took a deep breath and skipped a couple of stones across the water before he turned back to the house. *I must apologize.*

*****

Levi had three good days of selling the next week and earned almost three more denarii. Mama said she had enough food on hand to last a while, so they could manage well.

In one week the tax collector returned just as he had said. Alphaeus cajoled and bargained until he had talked the publican into letting him pay only twenty denarii this week and the other twenty next month. "Not a day more," the collector insisted.

Chapter 6

Levi Gives Selling Lessons

Alphaeus had not broken out with loud bursts of anger since the tax collector left two weeks ago. Levi even heard him whistle a little tune on the way to the shed one day.

I guess he is proud of himself for putting the publican off for a month. Maybe he realizes that I have been a help with selling the pottery and saving up for taxes.

The next day his father asked, "How much in the money bag?"

"Well, when we paid twenty to the tax collector, that left seventeen denarii, but I transferred two more to the tax bag from the other bag."

"Yes. Well? How much do we have?"

Knowing better than to give any further detailed account, Levi summed it all up. "Nineteen denarii in the tax bag and thirteen in the other bag."

"So, one more denarius in the tax bag and we're done with the Roman Jew." Alphaeus clapped his hands and kicked up one leg as though he had outwitted the tax man. "I tell you what, Levi. I have enough pottery to fill up the cart. I think I will take off from pottery making this morning and go with you to market. I want to see how you bring all these coins home."

It occurred to Levi that he had not heard his father say his name in an awfully long time. Levi smiled with delight. "That sounds like a good plan."

Eagerly, Levi helped move the pottery out to the cart. Papa was about to stack the bowls too high.

"We need to pack more blankets between the bowls. We don't want to crack your hard work, Papa."

Alphaeus almost smiled, "Humph, indeed!" He brought more bowls, plates, and small pitchers, plus a couple of large water jugs, but he sat them down by the cart so Levi could do the packing.

As they pushed off down the road, Levi noticed that his father looked over at the cart and Levi every now and then, as though he was impressed with Levi's handling and balancing of the heavy load.

When they arrived, Levi headed to the vegetable stands.

"Aren't we going by the wheat?" Alphaeus questioned. "I used to always set up over there"

"No, many people grow wheat, and some grow two or three types of vegetables, but it's always busier here because they want other vegetables they don't grow. It's best to set up where the most people are—well, where the most women are, because it's the women who usually buy the pottery." Levi had a slight smirk as he rolled his eyes over at his father.

Papa slowly nodded his head with an ever so slight smile. "Hmm," he grunted. He started unloading stacks of plates on the table.

"Uh, Papa, if you don't mind, I'll arrange the pottery if you'll just set the stacks out here on the ground."

"Humph," Papa grunted again.

Soon Levi had everything displayed in one of his lovely designs. Alphaeus glanced over the table with a frown. "What's all this?"

"It is pleasant to the eye. It draws attention to your fine craftsmanship." Another grunt from Alphaeus.

About that time, a woman came to the table with some onions in one hand and a small basket of figs in the other. "I always like to come by and see what design you have for the day, Levi."

"Why, thank you, Dinah. You know you could make a nice display of vegetables yourself on one of these plates. Only six ases. It makes it easy to pass it around to all the family."

"What a wonderful idea. I could put lots of pretty colored vegetables together."

"Exactly!"

"Six ases, you say?"

"That's right."

She dug in her coin bag. "Oh, I don't have enough ases. Do you have change for a denarius?"

"Certainly. Here you are."

"I believe I'll take that one." She laid her onions on the plate and carried them off.

When she left, Levi explained. "You see, Papa, she had not intended to purchase any pottery, but she was here by the vegetables and liked the display. I merely planted an idea in her head, and she could not resist. Besides, money is not an issue for her."

Another woman lingered near Levi's table, glancing over it two or three times. "Good morning," Levi said. "I see you found some plump olives today."

"Yes, Michael has a new batch. He's over there," she pointed. "You must be the one Dinah was telling me about. She always goes on about your pottery."

"Well, actually this is my father, Alphaeus. He is the potter. I merely sell it."

"Lovely work, sir."

Alphaeus nodded.

"And it is displayed so nicely."

"Could you use a nice bowl for your olives?" Levi asked. "Four ases today."

She picked up a bowl. "Hmm, one can always use another bowl. Wonderful craftsmanship."

Alphaeus nodded appreciation again.

"How many children in your family?" Levi asked.

"We have two children."

"I'll tell you what, if you would like to have a whole new set of four bowls for your family, I'll give you four bowls for a denarius and one free bowl to go with it for your olives."

"Oh my. Well, our bowls are getting rather old." She looked longingly at the bowls for a moment. "I believe I'll do that."

"Great. Would you like to choose your set?"

"Yes, thank you." And off went another happy customer.

A poorly dressed woman with straggly hair and dirt smudges jerked her head this way and that. She cautiously made her way to Levi's table. She kept her head down most of the time, too nervous to look Levi in the eye.

She finally managed to mumble, "How much for the bowl?"

"Four ases," Levi said.

She fumbled with a wad of cloth where she had a few coins tied up. Her stained hands and dirty fingernails bore the evidence of hard work. "I'll take one," she said. "Can you count it out?" She laid three coins on the table.

"Perfect change," Levi declared. Alphaeus took a breath to protest, but Levi touched his arm to stop him. "Would you like this one?" Levi asked.

She nodded, took the bowl, and stuffed her empty cloth in it as she scurried away.

"Why did you do that? She cheated you out of a coin. Besides that, you gave away one bowl to that last lady. We can't make anything at this rate!"

"This lady was in desperate need. She gave all she could. The other woman was well off, but she did not really need anything. A little incentive spurred her on, otherwise she would have walked away, and we would have one less denarius."

Alphaeus wrinkled his forehead with another slight grunt, not really convinced.

An hour passed with only lookers, no buyers.

"Why is no one buying?"

"We must be patient, Papa. Some are too poor for such. Others simply don't need any pottery today."

Shortly, a talkative woman made her way to Levi's table. "Levi. Levi, my boy, what do you have today?"

"Finely made pottery, straight from the kiln. What catches your eye, Sarah? A new set of plates or bowls? Maybe a lovely pitcher?"

"Aye, the pitcher has a nice shape." She picked it up to examine further. "Hmm, smooth as lamb's wool. How much?"

"One denarius."

She frowned. "Too much. I'll give you ten ases."

"Fourteen," countered Levi.

"Twelve, that's my final offer."

"Sold! You have a beautiful new pitcher, Sarah." She counted out her coins and walked away, smiling over her bargain.

"And why did you come down?" Papa questioned.

"I usually charge twelve ases, but Sarah always wants to talk me down. I just set the price higher so we can bargain down to my intended price. I usually get what I want, and she feels as if she got a bargain."

"You know the people so well. I didn't realize."

Another woman came to the table. "I saw Sarah's pitcher and remembered that mine fell and broke last week. Do you have another?"

"Indeed we do, just one left."

As Levi bent over to pick it up, a man came to the table and spoke to Alphaeus. "My wife wants me to buy a bowl. She cracked one yesterday."

Alphaeus hesitated. "Uh, that will be, uh…"

He looked at Levi. "Four," Levi mouthed.

"Uh, four. Four ases."

"Well, I might as well get two of them. She may crack another soon."

Levi saw the panic on his father's face. He had begun to realize that Alphaeus could not add numbers together.

"Total of eight ases," Levi told the man. Meanwhile, he collected from the woman with the pitcher.

When they left, Levi attempted to cover Alphaeus' embarrassment. "Whoa, that was a busy time. Good thing you were here to help me."

"I didn't realize how much you did. You're good at this, Levi."

Levi could not believe he heard these words from his father's mouth. It was an awkward moment. "Thank you, Papa."

Levi looked around and said, "Well, it looks like most of the shoppers are gone. Let's pack these pieces back in the cart.

As they put the final stack back in the cart, Alphaeus asked, "How much did we make today?"

"Over three denarii. It was a good day!" And in Levi's mind, a good day in many ways.

Chapter 7

Learning to Make Pottery

Alphaeus caught up with Levi on his way home from his yeshiva lessons. Before Alphaeus could speak, Levi had exciting news. "Papa, Jairus says I'm doing so well with my studies that he thinks I should begin studying with Rabbi Hanan. The rabbi visits Capernaum frequently and said, with Jairus' recommendation, he could take on another student."

"Uh-huh," Alphaeus half-listened. "Levi, after last week's trip to the market, I was thinking that it is time for you to apprentice the trade of pottery making."

Levi's shoulders slumped with his father's lack of enthusiasm over the news. Now this. He and his father *had* been getting along better, but spending time with his father in close quarters for long periods of time? Not so good. He liked the selling and had no real interest in the making, but he saw the look of anticipation on his father's face, and apprenticing with your father *was* the expected thing for a son to do.

Levi tried to muster some enthusiasm. "Okay. When did you want to begin?"

"Well, I was thinking we could begin after lunch," Alphaeus responded.

So soon? Levi walked on into the house to share his good news about the rabbi with his mother.

"Studying with a rabbi. How wonderful, Levi! I knew you would do well with your studies. The Lord has given you a good mind and an obedient heart."

Hmm, speaking of obedient… "Mama, Papa wants me to begin an apprentice in pottery."

"Oh," Myrah said, hesitantly. She drew back, her shoulders slumped a bit, her eyes cast down. "Well, you are fifteen years old, I suppose it is time." A heavy moment of silence fell on them. She gently added, "And how do you feel about this, Levi?"

Levi took in a deep breath as he turned to look out the window. "I just hope I can continue to study the Scriptures and learn from the rabbi. Then there is the selling to do as well."

"I'm sure you will learn well at the potter wheel," she said. But Levi could feel that their hearts hung heavy as they both faced their fears.

Mama broke the awkward silence. "Well, I guess I better prepare some lunch for the potters."

*****

Alphaeus bound in from the pottery shed with an air of excitement. "And what have you cooked up for us today, Myrah?" he said as he touched her back.

Startled, Myrah looked around at him and answered, "Oh, just chicken soup and bread. Uh, would you like figs as well?"

"Sounds wonderful!"

Levi snapped a questioning glance at his mother. She looked at him with an I-don't-know look and a shrug of the shoulders.

They sat down to eat. Alphaeus asked Myrah, "Has Levi told you the good news?"

"You mean about the rabbi?"

"Well, yes that, but also about beginning his apprenticeship."

"Uh, yes, he told me about that," she said, with forced enthusiasm in her voice.

James had not been in the room when Levi mentioned it to his mother. "Apprentice at what?" he asked, grabbing a fig.

"At making pottery, of course!" Alphaeus exclaimed.

James looked wide-eyed at Levi.

Alphaeus rattled on with other comments that filled in the empty conversation. He seemed totally oblivious to the fact that no one else was saying anything.

Finally, he stood up and asked, "Well, are you ready, Levi?"

"Uh, sure. Do I need anything?"

"You may want to put on something older. Sometimes it can get very messy." And out the door he went.

"Levi, what are you going to do?" James blurted out.

Levi sighed. "I guess I'm going to learn to make pottery."

James kept letting out heavy sighs and grunts of disbelief as Levi changed into a worn-out tunic.

*****

The first thing that struck Levi as he entered the previously forbidden pottery shed was the damp smell of the clay. The dark room reeked of it, and the low ceiling made him feel as though he would have to duck a lot. He surmised that since the potter sits all day, he does not need a high ceiling, but the thoughts of sitting in this low, tight, smelly room for any length of time did not appeal to him. Levi sat and began to study the wheel, his eyes slowly adjusting to the dim room.

"Here, I brought another stool," Alphaeus offered. "I'll make one bowl while you watch." Levi stepped out so Alphaeus could get in, then he pushed the other stool into the remaining tight spot.

Alphaeus picked up a blob of clay and wet it with water. His hands moved mechanically, kneading the lump of clay this way and that. Once he seemed satisfied, he leaned his leg against a stick and set the wheel into motion while he sprinkled it with water, then slapped the clay onto the spinning wheel.

Amazingly, Alphaeus formed and shaped the blob into a bowl, constantly changing its form, then placing one hand inside and the other hand outside. First a squatty bowl, then taller, then fatter, constantly wetting the clay. At the end, he placed one finger around the lower edge of the bowl to form a small base while the bowl sat spinning, then the wheel slowed to a stop.

"There, my son, a fine bowl for your soup."

For those several moments, Levi forgot the smells and dinginess and sat spellbound watching this master potter form a lump of clay into this useful creation. He saw for himself the master craftsman at work.

"That was amazing!"

"Now it is your turn." His father grinned.

"Oh, no, Papa, I'm not ready. You have done this so many times, you probably don't even think about what you are doing. I have too many questions to try it yet."

"What are your questions?"

"Well, why do you use so much water?"

"Oh, if you don't keep it wet, the clay will dry out and become crumbly. One tiny crumb can spoil the whole. You must keep it wet to continuously shape it."

"How do you know when to put it on the wheel?"

"You learn when it is pliable by the feel of the clay."

Levi looked around and under the wheel. "When you start the wheel, do you keep pushing the stick out or do you move your leg in and out?"

"These are all good questions. The wheel must remain steady. Much of it comes as you practice. You become one with the clay, molding, bending, working together."

"How did you learn the trade?"

"From my father, of course. He was a tradesman in Sepphoris where we lived. Some of the finest pottery makers come from Sepphoris." For a moment, Papa seemed to be far away, thinking of his boyhood.

"Did you learn quickly, Papa?"

Alphaeus chuckled. "No, it took me a while to get the feel of it. I tell you what, I will do it again and I will try to explain each thing I'm doing. Would that help?"

Levi sighed. "Yes, I think it would."

Alphaeus picked up another blob of clay. "About this much for a bowl. Slather it with water and knead it the way Mama kneads bread, working all the air out, forming a smooth ball." Again, Papa worked the clay with artful hands and little effort.

"Now it is ready for the wheel. I lean my leg against the throttle to set the wheel spinning and wet the wheel and the clay." He reached over to collect water from a tray and flick it on the clay and wheel.

Immediately, he cupped his hands around the ball. "The spinning helps to form it all the way around to keep it smooth. Now I use my thumbs to begin scooping out the middle. Slowly, slowly." A shallow bowl-shape began to form.

"As I push in, the sides come up. See?" Thick sides emerged as the middle was hollowed out. Gradually Papa's wrists turned up, thumbs inside and long fingers hung straight down on the outside, gradually making taller sides.

"Now to form a better hollowing out of the bowl, I put my left hand inside and balance it with my right hand cupped on the outside. You can slant the side out." He demonstrated. "Or straight down. Or you can make it a squatty bowl." His inside hand made the bowl bulge out around the bottom.

Levi watched as the sides of the bowl gradually took on different shapes. When Alphaeus completed the second bowl, he said, "Now you try it. It's the only way to learn."

Alphaeus stood and Levi stepped outside. After Alphaeus stepped out, Levi maneuvered around the stools to take his place.

While Alphaeus sat on the new stool, Levi gave a big sigh as he looked at everything from this point of view: the wheel, the peddle, the side trays of clay and water.

"Okay, get a handful of clay," Papa urged.

Levi sunk his hand into the clay and picked up a handful. Of course, his hand was slightly smaller than Papa's.

"Hmm, a little bit more."

Levi pulled another small chunk of clay and began to work both pieces together into a ball.

"Don't forget the water."

Levi dipped the ball into the water and patted the ball all around.

"Knead the ball like bread."

Levi remembered the many times he had watched his mother knead bread. He flattened it on the wheel to fold it over.

"Oh, not on the wheel until you wet it! Just knead it with your hands." Papa grabbed the lump and demonstrated, then handed it back to Levi.

Levi tried to imitate the kneading.

"More water, Levi," Papa said, somewhat firmly. "No, don't dip it in, sprinkle it with your fingers!"

Levi sighed again and made every attempt to follow directions.

"Wet the wheel and put the clay on the wheel," Papa's voice sounded like he was forcing it to be calm. "Now start the wheel."

As Levi looked down to find the stick, he inadvertently lifted his right hand slightly. The wheel started spinning and his lump of clay flew off and skidded across the pan of water knocking it and the clay off to the floor.

"Oh!" Levi squealed.

"Levi, you have to pay attention to your work!"

Levi reached down to retrieve the pan and almost toppled his stool. He managed to get the tray and reposition himself on the stool.

"We'll have to fill the water tray again." Papa huffed. He picked up a pitcher of water and reached across Levi to fill the tray.

"What about the clay, Papa?"

"It has picked up fragments from the floor. Just leave it there. Let's start again."

Levi's hands moved nervously over the clay as he tried to pick up just the right amount. He sprinkled it with water and kneaded it with his hands.

"This time, when you put the clay on the wheel, be sure to keep both hands around the clay."

Levi hesitated. He dreaded starting the wheel. He barely touched the stick with his leg and held on tightly to the clay. He began to relax as the wheel spun, and the clay formed in his hands.

They both sighed with relief.

"Now slowly push your thumbs into the middle." So far, so good. "Bring your wrists up."

But as Levi brought his wrists up, the clay went out from under his hands and flew with a thud onto the wall.

"Stop the wheel!" Papa shouted, while water swished across his face. Papa knocked his stool over and stomped out of the shed in a fit of anger.

Levi put his hands to his face, as he was about to cry in frustration. Once again, he had failed to please his father. He walked out of the shed with his muddied face and saw his father walking toward the shore. Papa stopped with both hands on his hips and stared out across the sea.

Levi hung his head then looked at his dirty hands. *I can't do this. I just can't do this.*

He lumbered back to the house, washed his hands and face, and slumped down on a mat.

Soon James and Mama came in. Levi poured out his whole story, struggling to hold back the tears. James began to snicker. "I can just see that clay flying." Then he burst out with full-blown laughter.

Mama saw the humor in it as well and had to contain her smile, but when she looked at Levi, her smile faded. "Levi," she said, "I know you're disappointed with your first try, but learning new things takes time."

"It isn't funny, James," Levi blurted out. "I'd like to see you do it!"

"Easy as can be," James chided with no mercy whatsoever, and out the door he went, still chuckling.

*****

Begrudgingly, Levi went back to the potter's shed with his father and in the next several days managed to produce a few acceptable bowls and dishes among the many failures. Finally, one day Papa agreed that Levi was much better at the selling than the making and decided to release him from the potter's shed. "Better the peddler than the potter, as your mama said."

Quite willingly, Levi accepted this decision.

Chapter 8

Making Friends on the Trade Route

Levi took a load of pottery to the market the next day. He cheerfully displayed the pieces with ease. "This is what I do best," he told his mother.

"And you do it well, my son." Mama patted his arm.

"Hmm, this bowl looks like one I may have made." He turned it upside down and right side up.

"It looks like all the others to me," she said.

"I can tell the difference." He stared at it a moment. "I'll sell it for a cheaper price," he mumbled and set it aside.

The day moved slowly, not much business. He packed up more than usual to take back home.

"You go on back home, Levi, I'm going to see old Miss Hannah. She has not been feeling well. I brought some bread to give her." Myrah headed across town to make her delivery.

As Levi pulled his cart along, he saw a caravan stopped in the middle of the trade route road. Ten muscular, bare-chested, black men with turbans on their heads unloaded three large wagons with sacks of goods. The master of the caravan argued back and forth with the tax collector, but the tax man stood his ground as he demanded a certain charge. The trade route tax collector looked wealthier than the town tax man who had argued with Papa.

Levi figured that the tradesman relented and paid his tax for the *privilege* of using the trade route, because he knew full well that if he did not, he would have Roman authorities on his trail.

Off to the side of the road, a boy, just as black as the servants, squatted down, drawing in the dirt with a stick. Levi casually approached, wondering if the boy could speak the common Greek language.

"Hello," Levi said, in his best Greek. Then motioning to the goods, "Do all these bags belong to your family?"

44

The boy stared up at Levi. Then he looked down, wrinkling his forehead as though thinking hard. He broke out in a toothy smile and spoke in broken Greek, "Yes, belong to me."

"I am called Levi." Levi pointed to himself.

The boy stood. "I am called Rabomba from Ethiopia."

"Rabamba?"

"No." He shook his head as he slowly broke down his name. "BOm. Rah-bOm-ba."

Levi pronounced it again and received another big smile from the boy.

"You," Rabomba pointed, "You, LeVI." He accented the second syllable.

"LEvi," Levi accented the first syllable.

"What in your wagon?" Rabomba arched his neck to look inside Levi's cart.

"Pottery. My father is a potter."

"A pohtah?"

"Yes, he makes these." Levi pulled out a bowl, but Rabomba had a puzzled look on his face. "For food." Levi pretended to scoop out imaginary food to eat.

"Ah, yes. But not made of wood?"

"No, clay. Then baked in an oven. Your mama would like?" Levi found himself talking in Rabomba's broken Greek.

"Hmm, maybe so."

"What do you carry in your bags?" Levi asked.

"Spices. Myrrh. We grow from bushes in my country. You like some?"

"Yes, but..."

Rabomba was already walking toward a large bag that had been reloaded. Levi looked at his coins but did not know if Rabomba could use them.

Rabomba untied the top of a bag. The fragrance floated through the air, and Levi took a deep breath to catch the aroma. He had an idea.

45

"I know. Let us trade!" He gestured. "I give you a set of bowls and you give me myrrh."

"Excellent!"

Levi dug in his cart and took out four bowls. "How many in your family?"

"My mother and father, two brothers, one sister, and me, Rabomba!"

Levi retrieved two more bowls for the family of six while Rabomba filled a small sack with the fragrant myrrh.

"It is good to do business with you, RabOmba."

"And with you, my friend."

"Shalom, peace be with you."

Rabomba nodded his head and smiled another toothy grin. "Kwaheri."

Levi smiled all the way back home, remembering his exchange of goods and good will with his new Ethiopian acquaintance.

When Mama came home, she instantly looked around the room as she sniffed the fragrance. "What is that I smell?"

"Myrrh!" Levi said with delight.

Mama looked at Levi with a questioning wrinkle in her forehead.

"A trading caravan from Ethiopia came through. They carried myrrh and other spices. I traded a set of bowls for this bag of myrrh. Do you like it?"

"Oh, it's very expensive." She sniffed the bag he handed to her. "A set of bowls, you say? I think you got the better part of the trade." She grinned. Then her smile turned to a frown. You best not mention this to your father. He may not like you trading with foreigners."

She quickly took the bag of myrrh out back to a box where she kept special things. When she returned, she began sweeping and fanning the air to shoo the sweet fragrance out the door. Then she baked bread to absorb more of the odor.

46

When Alphaeus came in that evening, he also sniffed the air. "What's that I smell?"

Myrah darted a glance at her son. "Oh, we went to market today. Some of the vegetables, I guess." Before Alphaeus could question further, she had him to the table and engaged in conversation.

After the meal, Alphaeus would not let it go. He questioned Levi further about the smell. Reluctantly, Levi told about his friend and the exchange of goods.

Alphaeus frowned. "You traded our valuable pottery for that worthless spice? We'll never make money that way!" he yelled. He stood up and bent over Levi, pointing his finger in Levi's face. "Don't ever trade with those foreigners again!"

*****

One year later

Alphaeus decided it was time for James to apprentice pottery making. To Levi's surprise, James seemed eager to try it.

He is not good with numbers like I am, but he is good with his hands, Levi mused. *Maybe he wants to prove he can do something I cannot do.*

The first day did not go so well. He came in with wet clay and dried clay all over his tunic, even in his hair. He said not a word but splashed water over his face and washed his hands.

"It's harder than it looks, eh?" Levi could not resist.

"It will take some time," James said brusquely.

"Okay, you make 'em and I'll sell 'em!"

After a month or so, James finally made pieces that Levi deemed sellable and loaded them in his cart for market.

*****

To Levi's delight, on his way from Capernaum, he saw the Ethiopian boy again. *Oh, what was his name? Boba? Rabambo?* He wrinkled his forehead trying to remember. *Rabomba! That's it. Ra-bOm-ba.*

Levi stopped his cart. "Rabomba!" he called out, waving his arms.

Rabomba turned around at the sound of his name. "LeVI!" he yelled with enthusiasm. He jumped off the huge wagon and ran over to Levi. "LeVI, it good to see you again!" He gave Levi a big hug.

"My father like your pottery. He say, if Mama like it, we buy more next time."

"Are you on your way home?" Levi asked.

"Yes, we sell most of spices and buy other goods to take back to our country."

Rabomba's family wagon came to a stop as they once again had to pay taxes for using the Roman road. It gave time for Levi and Rabomba to sit by the roadside and talk. Rabomba explained how they grew the plants and extracted the spices to sell. He spoke of his tribal customs and the hot weather.

Levi shared how he sold the pottery and his fiasco with pottery making. Rabomba laughed. Levi told of his lessons with his rabbi, but Rabomba could only relate with the ancient stories told in his tribe about many gods

Levi knew the Romans had other gods, but for the first time, Levi realized there were others like that in the world. "You mean you worship more than one God?"

"Yes, we have the wind god, sun god, river god, many gods."

About that time, one of the servants called to Rabomba because they were ready to leave. "We come again in our rainy season."

Once again Levi's Ethiopian friend popped in and out of his life.

The next day he shared this experience with his rabbi. His rabbi warned him that his new acquaintance was a pagan and not a believer in Almighty God, creator of all the world. It brought new meaning to the Shema, which he had been taught to speak every morning, "Hear, O Israel: The LORD our God, the

LORD is *one*. Love the LORD your God with all your heart and with all your soul and with all your strength."

Every time he touched the Mezuzah at the doorpost, he recited the verse again, thinking of his talk with the rabbi and remembering his friend Rabomba.

Chapter 9

Caravan Business

In the next month, Levi became more aware of traveling caravans as they passed through Capernaum on the Via Maris trade route. He saw rug sellers from Persia, perfume merchants from the Orient, and wood traders from Lebanon.

He reasoned that if he could communicate so easily with Rabomba, perhaps he could sell to others. Papa said no trading, he did not say no selling. Surely, he would be glad to *sell* to anyone!

On the first day, Levi walked beside the wagons and carts stacked high with goods. The heavy loads caused the travelers to trudge slowly. He tried to talk to the men who walked along tending to the cargo, but they always pointed to the owners who rode in the front.

When he tried to talk to the owners, they just ignored him. This was not going to be easy.

Another day he noticed that if it were around the lunch hour, the caravans would stop to pay their custom taxes and then pull ahead to stop again and eat. That gave Levi an idea. He could hand each man a plate or bowl for his food. That would give them time to enjoy looking at the pottery and using it—come to feel like it was theirs.

He also brought water in pottery pitchers and pottery cups for drinking. "Your wives and families will love this wonderful pottery, brought to them from the beautiful shores of the Galilee." Before they knew it, Levi had clean plates or bowls or cups all wrapped up in bags, ready for them to purchase and carry safely in their carts.

When a boy around Levi's age would wander his way, Levi made friends much as he did with Rabomba. Then he let the boy persuade the father to purchase some pottery.

These business deals did not always work out, but with practice, Levi became a smooth, shrewd businessman. In fact, as months went by, his caravan business proved to be as profitable as his city market business.

With Alphaeus and James both spinning the potter's wheel, he could fill all the requests. Alphaeus did not seem to realize that the business increased so much, as it was a slow steady growth. Levi managed to hide the fact that much of the business came from caravan sales.

One day, he had a conversation with a man named Meleke. Meleke had purchased from Levi three times. "I will be coming back through here in two months," the man said. "I would like to take twenty sets of your pottery back to my country to sell. Can you have it ready?"

"Most certainly!" Levi exclaimed.

"By the way," he added, "I know a businessman in the balsam business in Jericho. I believe he could use a smart man like you to help him in his trade. I'll put in a good word for you next time I see him." And off he went.

Levi stood dumbfounded. Not only did he have the promise of a great sale, he received an admirable compliment from the man. As he walked on toward town, he reflected on the man's words. *"Smart man like you." He called me a man! "Put in a good word for you." Where did he say? Jericho? Wow, I never even thought about leaving Capernaum.*

Levi did his work in town, but his mind stayed fixed on the morning encounter.

He pushed his almost-empty cart home, eager to tell his father and brother the good news about the big order for twenty sets of dishes. *Maybe Papa will be agreeable now that I have more business for him.*

*****

When Levi pulled the cart up to the pottery shed, Alphaeus was just coming around from firing up the kiln. Levi may have *thought* Papa would be agreeable to the caravan business, but his assumption proved terribly wrong.

Alphaeus flew into a furious rage. "I told you, no dealings with those foreigners, and you deliberately went against my word! Why did you do this?"

"You said no more *trading*, not selling."

Alphaeus squinted his eyes in anger. "You mince my words. You knew exactly what I meant." He slapped Levi's cheek with the back of his hand. "Get out of my sight!"

Levi felt the bitterness of the contemptuous attitude his father had for him, but even more the sting of his slap. His father often lashed out with angry words, but never had he struck him. Levi rushed in the house and threw the money pouch on the table. He lapped water on his stinging face, which blended with burning tears. Myrah was at a loss for words.

Levi stomped out the door, slamming it as he went. He headed straight for his thinking stone by the seashore.

His red cheek matched the heated build-up going on in his head. All he could think of was that phrase, "You knew exactly what I meant!" Deep down, he did know what his father meant, but he justified it by the thought that if he had good sales, it would please his father.

"Please my father, ha!" he shouted at the wind. "Nothing can please that man. No person can please him. Not my brother, not me, not even my mother. He is an evil, wicked man. He does not deserve the money I have made for him. He does not appreciate the way I saved what was needed for taxes or how I kept good records or how I worked hard to sell his precious pieces of pottery. What good would all those pieces of clay be if I had not sold them? A pile of junk—that's what they would be—a pile of junk."

Levi plopped down on his stone; tears filled his eyes. The more he tried to defy his father by not crying, the more the tears coursed down his cheeks. He bent over in agonizing sobs. The built up emotions from the depths of his memories, wrapped in years of anger, rose and burst out. Bitterness and hurt poured out layer by layer. It felt as if the flow would never stop. Elbows on knees, he held his forehead in the palms of his hands, crying until he could cry no longer.

Finally, Levi looked out over the sea, mesmerized by the ebb and flow of the tide. He felt numb and totally drained of emotion. He stood, and as he walked along the shore, the sun's evening colors reflected in the water, casting a beauty that brought a welcome calm to his soul.

Fishermen trudged to the shore. Some were loading nets in their boats. One boat had already pushed out for night fishing. Even at a distance, he recognized Andrew and his brother Simon gathering their nets. He thought about the early years when he and Andrew had studied with Jairus.

It prompted him to remember that he had been so busy selling the pottery, he had not spent much time recently with his rabbi—a sacrifice he had been willing to make to help the family. *And look at the thanks I get.*

He stopped suddenly and turned toward the house with an idea, well, more like an emotional response. He marched with determination back to the house. The more he walked, the more he fine-tuned his idea.

When Levi entered the house, he said nothing, didn't even eat, but went straight to bed. Through the night, he mulled over his plan, calculating figures in his head. *Papa can never understand figures, but he can certainly understand piles of coins. I will let the coins do the talking. I have had enough of his yelling. It is time I stand up for myself. After all, I am eighteen. I am man now.* He smiled to himself, remembering the words of Meleke, the caravan owner.

*****

The next morning he heard his father go out the door. *Perfect.* He scrambled out of bed, dressed quickly, and checked his records, adding up columns in his head. He gathered the coins and put them into three piles on the table, a medium pile, a small pile, and a large pile.

"Levi, what in the world are you doing?" his mother asked.

"You'll see. Go ahead and prepare breakfast. There is plenty of room on the table."

James wiped sleepy eyes and sauntered over to the table. "What's this?" He yawned.

Shortly, Alphaeus came back in. He hung up his cloak and turned to see everybody staring at him. Then his eyes fell on the stacks of coins. His forehead furrowed and he frowned at Myrah as if asking, *what is this*? She shrugged her shoulders with an *I don't know* look on her face.

Alphaeus sat down. "What is the meaning of this?" he mumbled gruffly.

Still standing, Levi pointed to the medium pile. "This, Papa, is the money earned in the market place the past six months." Pointing to the small pile, "This is more than enough money for possible taxes." Pointing to the large pile, "And this is the money earned from caravan sales." Pointing again to each pile, he repeated, "Money from market sales, tax money, and money from caravan sales. Do what you want with it. Throw it away if you wish."

With that, Levi picked up a piece of bread and a chunk of cheese and walked out the door with a smile on his face.

I should have given the caravan money a swish to the floor as I had planned, but the look on Papa's face was worth it all. Levi knew that, for his father, money talks. And the visual would prove far more effective than a verbal list of numbers. *I think I will stay away most of the day to let it soak in.* He did not bring the cart to the door to load for another day of sales. *I will let the pottery build up and be in the way. Perhaps that too will open Papa's eyes to the value of my work.*

Levi felt a sense of freedom as he walked along the shore. He watched the fishermen coming in from their night of fishing. Some sat repairing nets; others sorted the clean and unclean fish, while some filled baskets to sell the fish.

We all have our work and our sales. Such is life. I wonder if Andrew and Simon have differences with their father, Zebedee.

With the thoughts of Andrew, Levi decided to see the rabbi to continue his training. *Hmm, but it has been awhile. The rabbi might be as disagreeable as my father.* He kept walking and observing people along the way—a farmer plowing his plot of land, a shepherd on the hillside. As he came into town, he waved at the tanner, the carpenter, and nodded at the women with their boiling pots of dye.

He felt a bit guilty not to be working, but he also found refreshment in stepping aside for a time of reflection. As he entered the busy marketplace, he pondered the words of the psalmist, "Be still and know that I am God."

Before he knew it, he was at the place where he usually set up the pottery. *Hmm, habit,* he thought with a sigh. *Maybe it is time that I branch out and seek new places, new ideas, new work.*

Chapter 10

Back to Routine

Levi rather dreaded going back to the house. What mood would his father be in now? Had he made things worse with his coin demonstration?

Levi meandered home and at a distance saw no action around the house. But as he walked closer to the shed, he heard pottery wheels spinning away. Papa had been wanting to build another shed so James would have his own place without crowding Alphaeus. *Maybe the thoughts of that extra money will be enticing.*

Mama made a sweep out the door with her broom just as Levi was about to enter.

"Oh, I'm sorry, I didn't see you coming!" she said.

"You're just going to sweep me away, are you?" They laughed. It was a good laugh, a needed laugh for both. Levi looked at the table.

"Your father stared at the piles of coins all through breakfast and grunted every now and then," Myrah reported.

The piles were still there where Levi had left them that morning. He sat down and scooped the coins back into the pottery pitchers where he kept them.

Myrah placed her hand on his shoulder. "You certainly made lots of sales to the caravan owners. It must have been hard to do."

Dear Mama. Always there to encourage me. "Yes, Mama. It was a challenge to overcome the language and their ways of doing things, but I learned how to navigate around it. Most of them can speak a little Greek, and I have tried to learn a few key words in their different languages."

Papa and James were now outside the door, washing off the clay from the day. They came in and both had surprised looks on their faces when they saw Levi. Papa took off his work tunic and hung it on the knob by the door. He sat at the table across from Levi and chewed on a few nuts and figs while Myrah stirred a pot of stew.

Finally, he spoke but did not look at Levi. "I've been thinking," he said. "If those foreigners are willing to let go of their money, we may as well have it as anyone else. Now I do not want any foreign coins, though. They don't give you foreign coins, do they?"

"No, they keep some of our money on hand for smaller purchases. I tell them that I have no way of exchanging their money."

"Humph." Alphaeus chomped on a few more nuts. After a long pause, he added nonchalantly, "How many sets did you say that man wanted?"

"Twenty."

Alphaeus played with his beard. "And when will he be back?"

"Two months, the man said."

"Hmm, I guess James and I can have that many ready by then. What do you think, James?" Alphaeus looked over his shoulder toward James.

"Sure we can!" James smiled and winked at Levi.

The coin demonstration had paid off.

Myrah triumphantly placed bowls of stew on the table. "Stew for all my hard-working men." An almost-visible veil of woe was lifted, and they ate in peace.

*****

Two months sailed by. Levi told James that he would need to help him with a second cart to carry twenty sets of pottery. Each day they pulled the carts to the spot where Levi always set up at mid-morning. This would be the place and time when the man usually came through. James watched as his brother communicated with the travelers who came by.

"How did you learn to do this?" James asked, during a slow time one morning.

"I just kept trying different ways to get their attention. I had to learn at least how to say, 'Hello there' or 'Whoa' or something like that in different languages." Levi proceeded to share some of his tricks of the trade with James who listened with amazement.

One familiar caravan came through. "They're from Persia," Levi whispered to James. "Those two are brothers," he pointed. His pointing turned to a wave when he caught their attention. They stopped their carts and greeted Levi in their language. Levi answered back.

One of them gestured toward James and asked, "Who?"

"James, my brother."

They frowned in question, so Levi touched each of them on the shoulder back and forth and said, "Brother." Then he pointed to himself and James and said, "Brother." He repeated the demonstration, two more times.

Finally, the brothers spontaneously said, "Oh, dadash!"

"Yes, dadash." Levi pointed back and forth to them. "Dadash," he said, pointing to himself and James.

"We buy more pottery," one brother finally said in broken Greek. "Mama likes," he added with a smile.

Levi packed up a set of plates. James questioned why so much packing. "They would be fearful of broken pottery by the time they load and unload for the tax collectors," Levi explained.

As the Persian brothers turned to leave, they nodded to Levi, "Thank you, Levi" and then to James, "Thank you, dadash." James nodded and smiled.

"Sounds strange to hear them call me 'dadash.'" James chuckled.

In the next several days, James continued watching Levi do his selling magic with caravan owners from all over the world.

He went into town and saw more selling techniques from his brother at the market.

Finally, one mid-morning, on down the road came the man who wanted twenty sets of dishes. "That's the man!" Levi shouted. Quick, let's start wrapping the pottery."

By the time the caravan pulled up, they had finished the last piece. Meleke waved as he came within earshot and called out, "Hello, Levi."

The caravan stopped right beside them. "I see you have my twenty-five sets ready," the man commented.

"Oh, I thought you said you wanted twenty. Just a moment and we will have five more ready."

"Excellent. And I have more news for you."

Levi asked James to finish the wrapping and then led the man out of earshot.

"Last time in Jericho, Ariah, the man with balsam business, he tell me you come. He have job for you. Pay good money. His business, inside city gate. You tell Ariah that Meleke sent you. You do well in Jericho." Meleke grinned with a twinkle in his eye. "Now, how much I owe you? I had to exchange much money for your denarii. Is fifty denarii enough?" Meleke asked.

Levi tried to hide the surprise he felt. He had been thinking twenty-five denarii. "That will be fine. Fifty denarii," he said, with forced calm.

Meleke pulled out a large bag of coins. He began counting out the denarii in his language. Levi mentally counted along with him. He glanced up at James, whose mouth hung open in amazement.

Meleke's men carried the two boxes of pottery to the caravan cart, and Meleke handed Levi a Persian bag filled with the fifty denarii.

The two young men stood watching the caravan travel on down the road. They waved when Meleke turned to wave at them.

"I can't believe we just got fifty denarii," James gasped. "Wait till Papa sees this."

Both walked back to the carts, slapping each other on the back, one arm around the other brother's shoulder.

*****

Alphaeus came out of the shed when they arrived. He looked in the empty cart. "Did the man come to buy the twenty sets of pottery?"

"No, Papa, twenty-FIVE sets of pottery!" James laughed.

"Twenty-five?"

"Yes, Papa, and here is the money." Levi held up the bag, shaking it.

When they went inside, Levi poured the coins out on the table. Papa's eyes grew as big as his bowls. "How many denarii is that?" he asked.

"Fifty, Papa. Fifty denarii," Levi proclaimed.

Myrah clapped her hands. "Praise be to God!"

"That's enough for half a year's earnings," Papa said. "Maybe now we can build that extra shed for you, James. Let's go out here and think where the best place would be."

Alphaeus put an arm around James shoulder and led him outside. Levi sat with the pile of money still on the table. There were no comments like "Good job, Levi." No "You are a great salesman" observations. Not even "Thanks, son."

Levi sat staring at the table. Myrah put her hands on his shoulders and massaged them. "You did a great job, Levi. All these months of selling to the caravan traders paid off big this time. You have a wonderful talent for selling and meeting people."

"Thank you, Mama."

While he appreciated her words, what he wanted most to hear were these words from his father, but it was not to be. *It never will be. Why does he hate me so? What have I done to deserve this? Maybe I will take the man up on his offer. What*

60

was his name? Ariah? Yes, Ariah. "Tell Ariah that Meleke sent you."

Chapter 11

To Leave or Not to Leave

James sealed the last stone in place for the new shed. Levi enjoyed helping with the project and grew closer to his brother as they worked together, but his mind kept imagining a new life in Jericho.

He loved his mother and James. It would be heartbreaking to leave them.

With both James and Papa spinning the pottery wheels, I will have to work twice as hard to sell everything, he thought. *I cannot leave them with all that work.*

So, begrudgingly, he fell into the routine. Market day earnings were good, now that he only went once a week. Caravan sales continued to increase since he had become more established and acquainted with the regular traders.

Life with Papa remained the same, no gratitude, no acknowledgement. Papa talked to James and inquired about his work but had no conversation with Levi. *It is as if I don't even exist in my father's eyes.*

If Levi *were* to leave, he would need to train James to take care of the selling. Slowly, Levi managed to pull James away to *help* him one morning a week. Gradually, Levi worked it into two mornings a week. Levi urged him on to learn words in each language and initiate sales. James learned well and was personable with the traders as well as the townspeople in the market.

One day, James made a big sale, like the one with Meleke. This trader wanted to buy thirty sets the next time he came through!

Alphaeus praised James for his great selling skills but reminded him that he needed to help with the production of pottery as well. Once again, Alphaeus seemed oblivious to the fact that it was Levi who trained James in how to sell.

Ah, but in Papa's mind, the making is more important than the selling. Just let Levi do that. Well, Levi is ready to go where he might be appreciated.

Levi now made up his mind. He would stay until the big order was filled, and then he would be off to new adventures, new challenges, new people.

As the days went by, he made renewed effort to sell more so that they would be set. The more he thought about it, the more he could taste the anticipation of getting away.

It occurred to him that he would need money for travel, lodging, and food. He never worried about those things at home. He had never taken a wage. Surely, all his work these years was worth a decent wage. After all, it could be possible that this man in Jericho, Ariah, might not have a place for him or it might be a low-paying job at first. He would need plenty. He chewed on that thought for a few days, trying to decide a fair price.

He would gather his things and put them in a safe place away from the house. Then that morning he would retrieve them and walk away. No wrangles with Alphaeus: no unbearable tears from his mother or attempts from James to stop him. He only needed to decide about the money.

At last the day came when the buyer arrived with coins in hand to make his big purchase. James was delighted to take the man's money bag back to the house to show his mother and father. They were equally excited to receive it with "well done" from both—especially Alphaeus.

This just sealed the deal for Levi. He decided that thirty denarii should be fair enough for the many hours of work and money he had brought into the family these last few years. A denarius a day for a day's work. That would last him a month.

Levi gave his Mama a long hug that night. *She probably thinks it is for a good sale day.* He wanted to remember her touch and her warmth. He would miss her.

He gave James a hug and a pat on the back. "Good work, brother."

Later, he wrote a note to the family on a piece of parchment paper he had gotten at the market. He would place it on James' bed the next morning after James went to the shed. He did not want them to worry that he had been injured or killed when he didn't return.

He had a hard time getting to sleep that night. Did he have everything he would need? Were James and Alphaeus able to keep the business going? Was he putting undue hardship on James? *And what about Mama? She will be devastated.*

Levi tossed and turned, but finally settled into welcomed sleep.

Chapter 12

Jericho, a New Frontier

Levi awoke. His first thought, *Today is the day!* He dressed, ate his breakfast, but delayed until James and his father were busy in their pottery sheds.

"Have a good day," Myrah said.

She does not seem to suspect anything. I feel so deceitful. He contemplated telling her but thought better of it. He tried to act as normal as possible, but he dared not look her in the eye. She knew him too well.

When she turned her back, he quietly rolled up the parchment and placed it on James' bedding. No more delay. He must go quickly before he changed his mind.

Out the door and on to the place where he had hidden his few belongings. He retrieved the bag and added a chunk of bread, a few figs, and a handful of nuts for the first part of his trip.

The morning sun shone in his eyes. It helped to warm the chilly morning air. Fishermen were busy mending their nets and dealing with the night's catch of fish. He thought of purchasing some dried fish, but he would not need that until later and did not want the smell of fish in his bag.

He saw Andrew carrying baskets of fish to a boat for selling down the shore. Levi waved, and Andrew waved back. He yelled something at Levi, but he could not hear and didn't stop to talk. He would have to explain and was not ready to talk to anyone just yet.

Levi made his way on around the Sea of Galilee and proceeded south, glad that the sun was no longer in his eyes, but he began to feel the merciless rays of heat.

He glanced at the boats sailing across the sea, wishing he could be sitting in one as his legs grew tired. *Why did I never learn to swim? Why am I so afraid of the water?* Probably because of tales of storms at sea he had heard from Andrew and his friends. The thought of being out in the deep water with rain pouring down and wind whipping a boat this way and that was terrifying.

He stopped part way down the shore and found a big flat rock to sit on and spread out his things. After a few bites of bread and nuts, he drank from a flask of water and was ready to move on.

Many times his family traveled this route on their way to Jerusalem during festival times, but it was the first time by himself. A tinge of loneliness crept into his soul, but he pushed it back with thoughts of Jericho.

He remembered going past Jericho before. Someone would always mention the story of Joshua leading the children of Israel across the Jordan and how they marched around Jericho's strong walls for seven days until the LORD brought the walls down with the shout of the people.

By noon, he found a place to stop again under a tree so he could enjoy lunch in the shade. A fisherman had dried fish he could purchase, and he bought some fresh fruit at a market stand.

As he ate, he thought of his family. They would see the empty cart and wonder where he was. They might figure he just went on to talk to travelers and would come back to get the cart, although he never did that before.

Shaking off thoughts of home, and now very thirsty, he gathered his things and began searching for a well as he walked along.

By the time the sun hung low in the west, Levi kept an eye out for a place to stay for the evening. He finally found an old place where his family had once stayed on the way to Jerusalem for Passover.

Hmm... not exceptionally clean, but at least a shelter.

As he lay his head down that night, he knew that by now his family would have realized he was gone. He imagined their responses. James probably found the note and read it to the family. Mama would cry. James would say, "I can't believe it!" Papa would grunt and complain that he had left them with all that work to do.

But Levi was too tired to dwell on it and quickly fell asleep.

The second day proved uneventful. Levi's leg muscles ached from all the walking. His growing beard felt hot and sweaty, his clothes damp and smelly.

By the middle of the third day, he caught sight of Jericho in the distance.

*****

Levi took a deep breath. Here I go, a new place, a new life.

A lavish palace stood to one side of the city. Jairus once told that Herod the Great had built his winter palace in that location, but it was torn down when Herod died. Jairus said Herod commanded it on his death so the people would have something that would bring them to tears since not many would mourn his death. Eventually, his son rebuilt it to its glory—palm trees, fountains, gardens, and all.

Those and countless other palm trees waved in the gentle warm breeze as lush, grassy plains lay all around the city. No wonder Herod wanted a winter home here.

The wide road leading to the city gate held several caravans. One line headed toward the gate to begin trade, Levi assumed; the other line led away with the owners having completed their buying or selling. Meleke told him once about the three major trade routes that led to Jericho.

It all feels familiar, like the caravan on the route by Capernaum. A lot more traffic here, though.

As he walked beside the wagons, he heard bits of languages he had come to recognize. Out of habit, he greeted occasional caravan owners, recognizing their ethnicity by their clothing, facial features, and skin tones. Already he had a sense that he belonged here.

A blind man sat inside the city gate, begging. Levi rarely saw beggars in Capernaum. Most of his people were too poor to give—yet another sign of the wealth of Jericho. He gave the beggar a small coin and squatted beside him. "Shalom," he said to the man. "I'm new in town. This sure is a busy place."

"You are a stranger in town, but you give poor Bartimaeus a coin?"

"You're in need. Besides, no one else stops long enough for me to talk to them." Levi chuckled at his own comment and Bartimaeus joined in.

"True enough. Yes, it is a busy place, but I sit in this one spot day after day. You are from Galilee perhaps?"

"Yes. Yes, I am."

"Bless you, my good man."

Levi smiled as he left the blind man. *Blessing is what I need. Now, the first thing I must do is to contact the man named Ariah, but how will I find him? Can I trust that Meleke was telling me the truth? What would I do if I came all this way and found out there is no such man? Papa would say, "Foolish boy!"*

Casting aside the negative remembrance of his father, Levi moved farther inside the city past the gate; the strong smell of balsam hung in the air. A man up ahead stood on a stone block, talking with a caravan owner. Maybe that's Ariah. When the man finished his transaction, Levi stepped over to him.

"Shalom, I'm looking for a man named Ariah."

The man looked Levi up and down with a stern sideways glare. "What do you want with him?"

"I've come seeking a job with him."

"Do you know anything about harvesting balsam?"

"Well, no."

"Do you know how to grow balsam bushes?"

"Uh, no, but I'm actually here to—"

"He doesn't have any work for you." The man turned away and began talking to someone else.

Who does he think he is to speak for Ariah? Levi searched out the scene and finally saw a worker bringing a new box of jars to the man who seemed to be in charge. The worker helped wrap the jars for protection and packed whatever amount the travelers wanted to buy. Later another worker came with a second box-load of jars filled with the valuable salve. The second worker began to do the wrapping duties while the first worker walked away.

Levi decided to follow the first worker. Maybe that fellow will be more agreeable.

"Looks like business is good today," Levi said, trying to be friendly.

"Always good this time of the year." The man continued to walk.

Levi got in step with him. "Do you help make the salve?"

"No, just deliver it."

"I see that it keeps you quite busy."

"That's for sure. Good pay, though."

Ah, an opening. "So, Ariah is a good master?"

"He treats us well."

"Actually, I'm looking for Ariah. Where might I find him?"

"He's gone. Won't be back until the day after Sabbath." With that the worker went into a stone building, apparently where the jars of balm were stored.

The day after Sabbath? That is five more days! Now what will I do?

Levi plopped down on a bench under a palm tree and heaved a frustrated sigh. *I suppose I need to learn all I can about the process. That would make me seem like an asset to Ariah and might help me be a better salesman.*

Shortly, the first worker came back out with another load.

"Excuse me," Levi got in step with the worker, "I'm interested in seeing how the salve is made. Whom should I see?" He remembered that the gruff man mentioned balsam bushes. "Where are the balsam bushes?"

The worker nodded off to the left. "Over there on the hill."

Hill? This is a flat plain. He squinted his eyes as the sun interrupted his view. Finally, off in the distance he spotted rows of bushes on a slightly elevated field. He calculated the distance and decided by the time he got there and back; it would be nightfall.

Catching up to the worker, he asked, "Sorry to bother you again, but where might I find a night's lodging?" The man pointed him in the right direction. "Thank you, you've been very helpful." The man nodded, and Levi made his way to the inn.

Having secured a place to stay, he sought out a few remaining market stands where he could get food. Wearily, he turned in for the evening to rest from his exhausting day.

*****

The sun lit Levi's meager room the next morning. For a moment, he had to reorient himself. *Ah, yes, Jericho. No Ariah. Balsam bushes.*

After he dressed and ate a few bites of the bread he had saved from the night before, he launched out, searching for a well.

He found one where three young women were drawing up a bucket of water. "May I share a drink of water this morning?"

The three turned to see this handsome young man. They smiled shyly and glanced at each other. The youngest giggled. The oldest, barely older than Levi, spoke. "There's water in the bucket. Help yourself."

Levi picked up the bucket to fill his water jug and drank deeply from it. He poured a bit into his hand and splashed it over his face. The young girls tucked their heads and smiled

70

again as they turned away from him, but still eyed him. He refilled his jug.

"Thank you kindly." He nodded and walked off, ready for his new adventure. He overheard the giggly girl ask why he talked so funny. The other girl answered, "He must be from Galilee."

After a long morning walk, he made it to the "hill," where he saw the bushes that apparently held the valuable salve he had heard of. If the vision of all these bushes had not drawn him, the aroma certainly would have. Several workers squatted at their bushes, working at one bush for some time. He sauntered over to one worker. "I see this is a slow process."

No response.

"Have you worked the bushes for a long time?"

"Two years."

"I see. Uh, I'll be working for Ariah soon, and he wanted me to learn the whole process of making the salve and selling it."

"You need to see Carmi. He is the overseer." Levi stood there a bit frustrated for a moment. The worker made no attempt to direct him to this Carmi fellow.

"Where would I find Carmi?"

The man finally stood up and looked around. "Over there," he pointed. "The one standing up."

Levi tromped between a long line of bushes to the man who had been standing, but was now bent over a worker, pointing out something on the bush.

Levi paused until the conversation ended. When Carmi straightened up, Levi approached him.

"Excuse me, my name is Levi." He consciously tried to sound more Judean than Galilean. "Ariah wants me to learn more about the process of retrieving the balsam since I'm going to be selling it to the tradesmen. I wondered if you might instruct me."

Carmi thought a moment, nodded his head, and said, "If you come from Galilee, I suppose you know nothing of the balsam." *Caught.*

"No, nothing," he confessed.

"We must guard the bushes with the same kind of care the vine growers give to their vines." Carmi launched off into a lengthy discussion of the treatment and care of balsam bushes.

"And how do these workers retrieve the sap?" Levi asked, with genuine interest.

"This is prime time for collecting the ointment from the rind before it produces fruit. Come." By then, the worker had moved on down the row. They walked that way. Carmi bent over the harvester again and Levi leaned in. "You see how he uses a sharp knife to slit the rind?"

Levi watched as the worker made a slight incision. The man collected the whitish balsam with wool as it trickled out then dribbled it into a horn.

"Ah, yes," Carmi whispered, as though seeing these precious drops for the first time. Levi smiled at this expression of the devoted balsam grower, caring for his valued bushes. Carmi continued talking as they walked down the field of bushes. He instructed Levi about how they later pressed the seeds, rind, and even stems to make resin, inferior to the salve, though.

"Ah, but the harvest this time of the year is the best, the finest, the most valuable. The balm helps with breathing, coughs, aches and pains, dizziness, stomach cramps, nearly anything that ails you."

"I see," Levi nodded.

With a twinkle in his eye, Carmi added, "But watch the young ladies; they like to use it as perfume to seduce young men."

Levi grinned. "I'll take note, sir."

They walked on a bit farther, then Carmi stopped and looked out over the field of bushes. He gazed into the sky as though his thoughts were far away. "It is said, you know, that the Queen of Sheba brought the first roots of the balsam to King Solomon long ago. We are renowned for this precious plant and must take good care of the bushes."

"Yes, very valuable," Levi agreed. "And what happens after the oil is collected?"

"It is stored in new earthen jars where it becomes hard and reddish. And then, my friend, you must sell it."

"Indeed!" Levi smiled. "You have been most helpful. Thank you for your time and patience in teaching me today."

"Come back any time." Carmi said.

Chapter 13

Meeting Ariah

The days dragged on as Levi tried to entertain himself and learn more about the balsam trade. He made another trip to see Carmi asking more questions. *Wouldn't it be wonderful to have a father like him?*

Levi observed those who transported the precious balm from one place to another and ended up back in the trade area. He learned a few names, like the worker named Jeho.

"How did you get that name?" Levi questioned.

"My mother named me 'Jehoshaphat,' but that's too long. So I shortened it."

"Sounds good," Levi agreed. "By the way, what's *his* name?" Levi pointed to the seller he met the first day, the one who was so brash and made him feel worthless.

"Oh, that's Caleb."

"Hmm. Caleb, meaning bold."

"Humph. Caleb also means 'dog!'" Jeho said under his breath.

Levi caught Jeho's distaste for the man and silently agreed. Yet, despite Caleb's attitude, it all seemed to be like a well-run operation. *Why would Ariah need me?*

He decided to spend one day watching Caleb, who frequently snapped at the workers and even treated the traders with practically the same disdain.

Jeho came with a boxload of jars but waited to wrap them until a caravan finally rode in ready to buy. When the last of the jars finally sold, Jeho sauntered back to the storage building.

Levi caught up with him. "Business seems slow today."

"Usually slow the day before Sabbath."

"Why should that matter to these pagan travelers?"

"It takes a while to get into town. I guess they're afraid they won't make it here before we close business due to Sabbath."

"I see. Is it always slow on this day?"

"Yes, especially in the afternoon."

"So, more workers are needed through the week and less on this day."

"You could say that."

Levi walked back to the inn for the night and heard families singing and laughing as they observed the beginning hours of Sabbath. He saw candles lit through the windows and smelled chicken soup wafting through the air. He thought of home, Mama, James, and the sea, Capernaum, Jairus, Andrew, and friends in town.

Life felt different here. No set routine. No real job, no place to call home. He looked in his money pouch. The thirty denarii had dipped to twenty. He spent the Sabbath evening alone in his room.

On Sabbath morning, Levi sought out the local synagogue and found a place to stand against the back wall. It would not be a good idea to sit on a bench that is usually used by someone else. Jeho and a few other workers stood across the room. The familiar chants, Scripture readings, and teaching encouraged him. *May I find my way in this new place.*

*****

The next day he stepped outside, closed his eyes, and turned his face to the sunshine, basking in its warm rays. *A new day. Perhaps this is the day I will meet Ariah.*

A few caravans had already come into town. As Levi walked past the city gate, he saw the blind man sitting in the same place begging. "Well, Bartimaeus, I hope this is the day I get my job."

"I hope so too. Maybe then you will have a few coins for your friend," he said, with a mischievous grin.

"Yes, my friend, it would be good news for both of us." He laughed.

Levi walked past several caravans in line, greeting each owner. As he approached one wagon, a boy stood bent over

75

with his hands on his knees. Just before Levi got there, the boy heaved whatever he had had for breakfast. He moaned and groaned, holding his stomach. A man came and held him.

Levi arrived at the wagon. "Looks like he's in pain."

"Yes, my son has been hurting this whole trip."

"Have you tried the balm sold here in Jericho?"

"I've heard of it but never tried it."

"I'll go ahead and get you some."

With that, Levi took off in a run passing several wagons. He soon found Jeho and asked for a jar.

"I can't just give you a jar," he said.

"Okay, how much does it cost?"

"You'll have to get it from Caleb."

"Oh, great." Levi rolled his eyes.

He took a deep breath and approached Caleb. "I need one jar of balm."

"For what?" Caleb asked gruffly.

"A boy in one of the caravans is having stomach pain."

"So, let him come and purchase a jar himself."

"I told him I would get one for him."

"And you have a denarius to give for the stranger?"

Levi realized there was only one possible way to get through to Caleb. "Well, let's consider this. Suppose the boy begins to feel better. The father, who owns the caravan, might decide to buy a boat load of jars. Give one, sell many."

Caleb chewed on that thought for a moment. "And suppose he doesn't buy any, then what?"

Levi had had just about enough of Caleb and his bad attitude. "Sometimes it is worth it to try new ideas. Besides that, the boy is in great need. Oh, I'll buy it myself." Levi pulled out one denarius and handed it to Caleb.

Caleb grabbed the coin out of Levi's hand and barked orders to the worker. "Give 'em a jar."

76

Levi ran back to the caravan and gave the jar to the father. "Rub this on his stomach. It is very healing."

The grateful father looked at him in surprise. "How much do I owe you?"

"Nothing. I am just trying to help."

"Thank you. We will try it. We trade in wheat." He turned to his foreman. "Give him a bag."

"No need."

"I insist."

Levi nodded and accepted the bag of wheat. As he walked on back to the trading area, he hoped the balm helped. He trusted Carmi's advice that the balm would "heal all that ails you."

Jeho met Levi as he came back. "Thought you might like to meet Ariah. He's the big man over by the building."

"Thanks, Jeho."

Jeho had that right. Ariah was a big man, tall and broad-chested. He started walking Levi's way. The closer he came, the taller he seemed. Levi's medium-tall stature and thin frame dwarfed next to this burly balsam company owner.

Levi gathered his wits and courage to call out. "Ariah?"

The man turned Levi's way. "Yes?"

"Shalom. I am Levi from Capernaum. I have dealt with traders on the Via Maris. One trader, Meleke, said he talked to you and you had interest in giving me a job here in Jericho."

"Meleke?"

"Yes. I believe he is from Persia."

"Oh, of course, the rug seller!" Ariah threw his head back into a hearty laugh, his bushy beard wiggling up and down. "Yes, Meleke. He talked me into buying three rugs." He leaned down as if sharing a secret. "The wife loves them. They do look smart in the house." He looked up, pursing his lips as though thinking. "Capernaum, you say. Yes, I do seem to remember him talking about you. Said you were a good seller. Say, was that you I heard talking to Caleb a while ago? Something about taking a jar of salve to a sick boy?"

"Yes, sir, that was me."

"I liked your thinking—give one jar, sell many. How is the boy doing?"

"I don't know. I just instructed the father to rub it on him. They are back in the line waiting to get into town—from Egypt, I think. Selling wheat."

"You conversed with the man, the Egyptian?"

"I have learned to speak a few words in several languages, enough to get by."

"You know about our good balm?"

"Carmi filled me in on the many uses and showed me the bushes and the process of extracting the precious fluid."

Ariah smiled. "Yes, Carmi loves those bushes the way a father loves his son. He is a good man and a faithful worker. It takes patience and knowledge to work the bushes, much like a vine grower with vines."

Ariah studied Levi with admiration. "So, you have been exploring the balsam business?"

"I wanted to understand how things work in your trade."

"I see," he said, with a serious expression. "Well, we have a good business. It is steady, but we don't seem to be growing. Perhaps some new blood, new ideas would be helpful. Let's talk more this afternoon after lunch. My office is over in that building."

"Yes, sir, I'll be there."

As Ariah walked away, Levi thought his heart would go flying out of his chest. He wanted to shout to the wind, "He likes me! He wants to know more of my ideas. Rejoice, oh my soul, rejoice!" He thought of Mama. She would be so proud. She would hug him and tell him she knew he could do it. But she was not here. No one to hug. No one to rejoice with him.

Jeho came out of the storage building, and Levi caught his eye. Jeho raised his eyebrows as if to question how the conversation went. Levi hurried over to him.

"Do you have a job?" Jeho asked.

"I think he liked me. He wants me to come to his office after lunch."

"That's a good sign. I hope it works out."

"Thank you. I do too."

"Here, Jeho, take this bag of wheat to your wife. I have no need of it." Jeho trudged back to the building carrying the wheat and his empty box. *At least one person to share in my good news.*

Levi noticed that the wheat caravan was almost to the city gate. He walked over to the father to inquire about the son.

"He rested and seems much better," the father reported. "Where can I find that salve? I'd like to buy more to take back to my city."

"Do you see the man up there in the green turban? He can help you. Better yet, I'll take you to him." *I want to see the look on Caleb's face when the man buys several jars.*

"Thank you."

When they made it to Caleb, Levi said, "This is the father whose son had need of our salve today. He would like to buy more jars." Caleb rolled his eyes at Levi and Levi gave him a smirk.

"How many jars for you, sir?"

"How many are in that box?"

"Fifteen."

"I'll take three boxes."

Caleb's eyes bulged in disbelief. "Jeho," he shouted, "tell the men to bring three more boxes."

"Three *boxes*?"

"Yes, three boxes." He growled, almost begrudgingly.

Levi could not help but gloat inside over this huge success despite Caleb's negative perspective. Jeho gave a quick smile and winked at Levi.

Now Levi had more news to share with Ariah.

*****

After lunch, Levi hurried to Ariah's office, his mind brimming with ideas. He knocked at the open door.

"Come on in, Levi".

Levi was overwhelmed when he stepped into the luxurious office. A vibrant Persian rug lay in front of a heavy wooden desk. Rich-looking fabrics covered the benches on each side of the room. The walls were covered with exotic hangings—trades or purchases, no doubt, from other countries.

"Pull over a stool." Levi moved a covered stool in front of Ariah's desk, a bit overwhelmed by it all.

Ariah still had quill in hand from working on one of many stacks of parchment papers. Levi had never seen so much parchment in one place.

"There's always a mountain of work when I return from a trip. Ordering more jars, wrapping cloths, boxes, earthen jars to store the sap, horns and wool to gather it, records of payments to workers."

"While setting aside money for taxes." Levi finished his sentence.

Surprised, Ariah looked up. "Yes, that too. You know about such things? Tell me more of what you did in Capernaum."

"My father is a potter. I took the pottery pieces to market each day to sell. One day I made acquaintance with a boy from Ethiopia who came through the trading route. I offered him a set of pottery, and he gave me a bag of myrrh. His mother liked the pottery so much that they bought four sets the next season. Others in their city liked it as well. So the next time my friend came through, his father bought twenty sets to sell.

80

"The experience taught me that I might do well with others on the trade route. I learned enough of each country's common phrases to communicate on a more personal level and devised creative ways to get pottery pieces in their hands. Eventually, we were making more money with the caravan business than at the city market. I took care of the money and allowed a certain amount each week to go toward taxes. That way we had the money ready at tax time."

"Amazing! I can see why Meleke recommended you. Perhaps you can do your tricks of the trade with the caravans in the balsam business."

"You might like to know that the father with the sick boy came in this morning and bought three *boxes* of salve. The one free jar paid off!"

Ariah clapped his hands with joy. "Ha, ha, I love it! If you grow my business like that, I may have *you* in here organizing these papers!"

"I would be glad to do that, sir."

"Where would you like to begin?"

"Perhaps I could work the line of caravans, begin to talk with the travelers, one by one, but you will need to be sure they have an extra stock of boxes in the storehouse." Gathering his confidence, he added, "You may need to start another field of bushes. When the business grows, the fields must grow as well."

"Hey, hey. I like the way you think, young man," he grinned. "I tell you what, let's start your pay with ten denarii a week, and we'll go from there."

Levi wanted to jump up and down in victory, but he restrained himself. "That sounds like a good plan." Emboldened further, he added, "I wonder if you could tell me of any lodging that might be available. I've been staying in an inn since I arrived here five days ago."

"Hmm." He leaned back and looked up at the corner of the room. "I have a little cottage near my house where a worker stayed temporarily. He built a house and moved out last month. You can stay there if you like."

"That would be wonderful. Thank you." Then wondering how much that would cut into his pay, he asked, "What is the charge?"

"No charge. It sits there empty. Better to be used than to fall into disrepair. Just keep it clean and repaired."

"Where can I find the cottage?"

"It's behind my house over there on the hill." Ariah pointed out the side window. Levi spotted the house right away as it stood tall and sprawling right before the land turned upward to form a slight hill.

"I'll move in this afternoon, if that is suitable with you."

"Agreed." He stood, indicating the conversation was over.

"Thank you, sir. I won't let you down."

Levi nearly floated from Ariah's office. Jeho was the only one he could think of with whom he could share his good news, so he practically flew back to the city gate where he saw Jeho making his regular walk to Caleb.

Levi caught his eye and shared his news. "Good for you, Levi. Welcome to the business." Off he trudged to retrieve the next box. *Is that it? Just "good for you?"* Levi stood there a moment to gather his thoughts and feelings. He could not tell about the good pay he would receive or brag about how impressed Ariah seemed to be with him. That would not have gone over well with the low pay Jeho likely received.

Levi longed to see his mother, to share his good news and receive her loving enthusiasm and pride in him. Even though this position fulfilled his hopes and dreams in coming to Jericho, he felt lost and empty. He meandered back to the inn, trying to reclaim his enthusiasm.

On his way, old Bartimaeus sat in his usual spot, begging. Levi dropped in a coin. "That's a victory coin!" he mused.

"Ah, so you got the job!"

"Yes, indeed. Now we'll both be the richer."

Bartimaeus chuckled.

Nice to have one friend, even a blind beggar. After collecting his few belongings, he made the trek back across the city, past the trading area, and on to the hill. *Will there be other buildings behind the house? Will I know which one?*

Chapter 14

Starting a New Life

Ariah's mansion loomed even larger as Levi approached. Flowering bushes lined the long pathway to the house with gardens and a fountain off to the side. *Must be a miniature of Herod's old palace.*

Should he alert Ariah's wife that he was moving in? But the house seemed too austere to go knocking on the door, so Levi proceeded to hunt around behind the house, keeping a respectable distance away. He saw three out-buildings— probably storage sheds. Only one appeared to be what could be called a "cottage."

Bushes and vines had overtaken the front, nearly hiding the two windows. He cautiously opened the creaky door, his eyes not yet adjusted to the dim light inside. It smelled a bit musty, but a little airing out would probably take care of that, so he left the door open.

As his eyes adapted, he found a bed pallet, not on the floor but raised up on a wooden frame. The other part of the room had a table with a bench and a few shelves lined the wall, apparently the kitchen. A couple of bowls and plates and other utensils sat on the shelves, and a broom stood in the corner. The floor seemed to have been swept, at least at one time.

Glancing back to the "bedroom" side, he spotted a small stand with a water pitcher, a bowl, and a lantern. *Well, all the necessities and no charge. Sounds like a good deal to me.*

Shortly, he heard steps coming up the walk and arched his head to look through the window. The man called out. "Hey there."

"Yes, Shalom," Levi answered, poking his head out the door.

A thin, slightly bent man ambled up the path, loaded with a jug and cloths draped over his arm. "Shalom to you," he said.

"I'm David—like the king," he added with a smile and kind eyes.

"Well, hello, King David."

The man smiled. "I brought you a jug of water and some cloths. When you need more water, the well is over there." He pointed in the direction of the well, part way between the cottage and the house. *Impressive. Ariah has his own well!*

"Thank you, David, it is good to meet you."

"I take care of the gardens, so I'm out and around much of the time if you should need anything else."

"Thank you. You are truly kind. The gardens are beautiful. Have you been working them for a long time?"

"Hmm. Coming on forty years."

"You are a master gardener then."

David chuckled. "I worked for Ariah's father before him. They have been good to me."

"I appreciate you bringing me these things." Levi smiled as he watched the old man trudge down the path. *Nice to have a friend.*

He placed the jug on the floor by the bed and arranged the cloths on one end of the table. He thought about the vines around the windows and ran out the door to catch up with David. "David, do you have a sickle I might use to trim the vines around the windows?"

With sickle in hand, Levi went about trimming the vines and cleaning out and around the cottage.

As he swept, he could not help but think of his mother again. He could see her sweeping away as she did so often. A pang of heartache hit him. Oh, how he would love to see her, hug her, and tell her all the things that have happened. He swept harder, forcing any would-be tears from his eyes.

Looking at the bare shelves, he decided to go back into town to buy some food at the market. On his way, he returned the sickle and waved at David. All would be in readiness for beginning his new life the next day.

*****

The next morning, Levi launched out with brisk, sure steps as he made his way past the garden; the flowers seemed especially vivid and fragrant. He breathed a prayer of adoration to God for the quiet beauty around him. "The LORD reigns, he is robed in majesty and is armed with strength," he quoted from the Psalm. On to the trading area.

In contrast to the stillness of the countryside, the busyness and noise of the market stirred an excitement within Levi. He managed to talk Caleb into giving him three jars of salve. Jars in hand, he passed those who were already engaged in business dealings and on to those who waited in line.

The first wagon he approached carried wheat. *Egypt*, he made a mental note, like the sick boy from yesterday. Remembering a few Egyptian phrases, he greeted the man who seemed to be in charge. The man's eyes brightened hearing his own language. He responded in kind.

"How is your health today?" Levi inquired.

"It's been a long journey. Two of my men have stomach trouble."

"Ah, I have just the cure for that. You can find more over there." Levi pointed toward the Caleb.

The Egyptian frowned, not understanding. Levi pretended to scoop out the salve and rub on his stomach, then he sighed out loud as though he had received relief. He pointed to the salve and then to the area where Caleb stood.

"Oh, I buy there?"

"Yes, yes," Levi nodded his head. "You may have this jar to try."

The man reached in his money bag to pay. "No, no, it is yours." Levi handed the jar to him and walked to the next wagon. When he glanced back the Egyptian was explaining it

86

all to his men. He demonstrated just like Levi had done. Levi smiled as his plan worked.

The next caravan had rolls of rugs. A few hung from the side of the wagon displaying their brilliant colors. *Hmm. Persia.* He thought about the large Persian rug in Ariah's office. Levi knew only a few Persian phrases. He greeted the owner and tried to demonstrate the salve and its healing properties.

The man broke into a big grin as he recognized the jar. He spoke in his broken Greek. "Ah, yes, salve from Ariah. Good."

Well, looks like Ariah already beat me to this customer long ago. Levi grinned and nodded his head.

On to the next wagon. No interest, as the helpers shooed him away.

When he started toward the following wagon, he smelled a familiar fragrance—myrrh. His eyes darted around the caravan, looking for his old friend. "Old" indeed. In two years, his friend had matured, but Levi still recognized him. "Rabomba!" he called.

Rabomba jerked his head this way and that, searching for the one who had called his name. Levi waved, "Rabomba!"

Rabomba frowned in puzzlement, but then he recognized his long-ago friend. "LeVi," he shouted. Rabomba jumped down and ran around the wagon, giving his friend a big hug.

"Why you here, not Galilee?"

"I moved. Bigger business!" Levi spread his arms out to emphasize his words. "Sell salve," he pointed to his jar.

Puzzled, Rabomba looked at the jar.

Levi groaned and bent over holding his stomach as though it hurt. Then he pretended to scoop out the salve and rub it on his belly and sigh with relief as he did earlier.

Rabomba smiled and nodded his head as he said something in his Ethiopian language. He understood, then turned to Levi. "You sell here?"

"Yes, you can buy, over there," Levi pointed.

They talked further. Rabomba had become his father's assistant. He had gotten married and seemed happy. Levi gave Rabomba the second jar and bid him goodbye.

Soon Levi had given his last jar away, complete with the demonstration he had perfected. He headed back to the trading area and found Caleb busy with new customers. It seemed the Egyptian had become an assistant salesman because of the good recovery of his men and had brought three other caravans to buy boxes and boxes of salve.

*****

A month later, Levi stopped to get his morning jars of salve. Caleb grumbled. "I'm not going to give you any more jars. We're about to run out of salve."

Levi did not say a word and did not look at Caleb, but just stood there thinking. He finally nodded his head to himself as though he had his next idea; he turned around and walked away.

Levi knocked at Ariah's office door and walked in when Ariah spoke to him.

"Levi, my young man, what can I do for you today? I hear business is good, more than good, great!"

"That is true. Caleb tells me that we are about out of salve. That is exactly what I predicted. I remind you that you must find new fields and grow more balsam bushes."

"Ha, Ha, yes I remember you said that." Ariah chuckled a bit more, but Levi stood firm and did not smile.

Ariah noticed. "So, you are very serious about this idea."

"The sooner, the better," Levi stated flatly. "If you have no salve to sell, the customers will not ask again. It takes a long time to plant and to harvest. We must be ready when these new customers return the next year."

Ariah stood and sauntered over to the window. He gazed toward the hill where his bushes grew. "Hmm," he grunted. "Hmm."

When he turned around, he focused sternly on Levi. "I believe you are right. The stock has diminished quickly since you have done your magic with the caravans. It will take some time for me to make all these arrangements, so I will need someone to take over these records. You say you are good with numbers?"

"Yes, sir, it is my specialty." Levi's eyes brightened with the prospect.

Ariah nodded his head. "You seem to have many specialties," he smiled. "Let me sort through these piles to get things together. When you come back this afternoon, we will go over the records."

Chapter 15

New Ventures

In the following months, Levi conquered the written page of numbers. He streamlined the way records were kept at the building where they stored the balsam, and where the jars were boxed and sent out to the trading area. Much to Caleb's chagrin, Levi also restructured the way the money was handled, not that Levi did not trust him, but, well no, Levi did not trust him.

During one of Ariah's meetings with Levi, he complimented the vast work Levi had done with the records. "And we have gotten quite organized around here. Things seem to be running smooth as can be."

"Thank you, sir."

Ariah stood and gazed out the window. "I have been investigating new land over in Gilead. Your advice to take Carmi with me proved to be a good idea." He turned toward Levi. "Carmi knows everything there is to know about growing balsam bushes and the ground to put them in."

'Yes, sir, you did a good day's work when you hired him."

Ariah smiled and nodded his head. "Indeed." Ariah took a deep breath and looked out the window again. "And now I must pull some of my workers to go to the new fields to prepare the soil and begin the new plantings. That means hiring new workers for the old fields."

"Fortunately, your assets are adequate to afford these new workers until the new fields bear fruit."

Ariah turned back to Levi. "Hmm, yes," he said, thoughtfully rubbing his beard. "Yes, that's good to know. Keep up the good work, Levi."

*****

Months later, tax time drew near. Levi had been saving back an estimated amount due. Unfortunately, he had not allowed for the inordinate charge that was accessed. He asked Ariah about the tax system in Jericho.

"Zacchaeus *is* the tax system here," Ariah exclaimed. "He would squeeze the very marrow out of your bones if he thought he could find a few coins there. He is a chief tax collector and ruthlessly rules in this area. Besides that, he is jealous of my estate. His house is more elaborate than mine, but his is in town. He envies the land that goes with my estate. He certainly enjoys the fruit of my labor or maybe I should say, the *salve* of my labor." Ariah chuckled at his own comment.

Levi refused to give in to this power seeker. *Maybe I have more of my father in me than I would wish, but I believe I can show that this new field expense should come into account.*

The next day, Levi gathered up pertinent parchment papers to take to this Zacchaeus. He would confront him head on.

As he went through town, inquiring where Zacchaeus could be found, people shook their heads, frowned with scorn, and refused to talk about Zacchaeus. *Looks like I need another approach.*

Levi bought a piece of fruit from a seller in the market and sat on a stone wall nearby with his bag of papers carefully out of sight. Soon a merchant sat beside him, munching on a few dates.

"Looks like a good day for business," Levi offered.

"Yes, rather steady, I guess. Keeps food on the table."

"Hmm. Until Zacchaeus sends his tax men around," Levi rolled his eyes over to the merchant.

"Isn't that the truth. He raises taxes every year whether you earn more or less."

"I hear he has a luxurious house to live in with our money," Levi led him on.

"House? Palace is more like it!"

"Where does he live?"

"Down the main road there. Do you see that sycamore tree way over yonder? A turn to the right and he lives out that way."

"I'll have a look sometime."

"Not me, I don't want to go anywhere near that scoundrel. Well, back to work for me."

"Have a good day."

The merchant returned to his business, so Levi picked up his bag and proceeded down the main road. When he turned at the sycamore tree, he easily spotted the sprawling house on down the way. A lump formed in his throat. Was it a bad idea to move forward with this plan? Would he jeopardize the "due" taxes more?

He took a deep breath and prodded on, practicing his speech all the way. As he approached the fenced property, the gate appeared to be locked. *Now what will I do?*

Just then a young woman unlocked the gate and opened it. She nervously looked back toward the house and then stepped through the opening. By this time, Levi approached her. Her beauty overwhelmed him for a moment, taking his breath away.

Startled, she stared at him.

"What—what do you want?" she blurted out.

"Uh... uh, I came to see Zacchaeus."

"He's inside. Do you have an appointment with him?"

"Well, not exactly. I have a matter I need to discuss with him."

"He probably won't see you. He doesn't see anybody," she lowered her eyes. "Not even me," she said quietly.

"Is he related to you?"

She raised her sad eyes to Levi, "He's my father."

"I..." Levi didn't know what to say but sensed she was hurting. "He ignores you?"

She looked into Levi's eyes as though someone finally understood her feelings. Slowly, she looked down again. "Yes."

How did this happen? I came fully prepared to make my case to this bully, and here I am dealing with old feelings I thought I had buried. I wish I could take this helpless, beautiful girl in my arms to comfort her, but that certainly is not an option.

"I'm sorry," he finally managed to say. "I've dealt with the same thing." *What am I saying?*

"You have? Your father?"

Levi took a deep breath, looked up at the elaborate portico of the house, and blurted out, "Yes, my father ignored me. He was irritable and cared only about himself." *There, I said it.*

"You do understand," she said, looking at him again with those beautiful eyes.

"Yes, I do, but I'm sure your father cares about you. He is only distracted with... with all of this." Levi motioned with arms wide open to the house.

"Perhaps you're right." She fiddled with a pendant on her neckless. "I'll see if I can find him and bring you in."

As quickly as she came out, she was gone again. Levi stood there, stunned by what had taken place. He shook his head. This certainly was not what he had expected—a helpless, wounded daughter stirring up the pain of his own past.

He doubted the girl would come back, but to his surprise, she appeared at the door and walked to Levi, confidently wearing a smile.

"Come with me," she said.

I am finally going to meet this powerful man.

*****

"Come this way," barked Zacchaeus, as he rushed into the spacious room. Levi tried to take in the elaborate furnishings and décor while this wiry little man scurried down a long hall. As Levi hustled to keep up with him, Zacchaeus kept mumbling something about the roof and leaking.

Other beautiful rooms jutted out from either side of the hall; tall columns bordered the openings. Toward the end of the marble-floored hall, grand windows exposed views of a beautiful garden. Levi finally caught up with Zacchaeus but could hardly concentrate on his babbling because of the full view of this lovely courtyard, complete with flowers, greenery, carved stone benches, even a full sycamore tree sprawling out to one side. A stone wall surrounded the courtyard with vines crawling up its surface, forming curled patterns.

Zacchaeus raved on and on about a leak from the overhang at the entrance. Standing next to this short man, Levi was suddenly aware of his own height. He stood taller than most men, but he towered over this tax man.

"So, can you fix it?" Zacchaeus demanded, hands on hips.

"Huh?"

"The roof. You're a repairman, aren't you?"

"I'm sorry, I'm not here to repair a roof, but about an unfair... uh, a mistaken charge of taxes."

Zacchaeus' scowl pushed his eyes into two slits. "Sit," he demanded.

Levi sat on a bench that he could feel next to his leg. Now Zacchaeus could tower over him.

"You deceived me into thinking that you were here to repair my roof, so you could talk about your tax?" he shouted, shaking his finger at Levi.

"No, no." Levi shook his bent head. He paused. Using a quiet, deliberate tone, he went on. "You see, sir, I told your daughter that I needed to see you. You assumed that I was a repairman, but I am not. I have come because of the circumstances of my owner's affairs concerning his taxes, circumstances of which your assistants may not be aware."

Zacchaeus straightened up and folded his arms in defiance. "And who is this *owner*?"

"Ariah, owner of the balsam plants and balm business."

One of Zacchaeus' brows arched, and a sly smile began to form. "So, Ariah sent you to come begging." His smirk grew wider.

"No, Ariah doesn't know I came."

Zacchaeus tilted his head, a bit perplexed. "You came here on your own?"

"Yes, I handle the finances and the records." Levi quickly pulled out his papers, showing the added expenses this year. "You see, the assets have been altered by the expense of acquiring new fields to plant more bushes and additional workers, so the income has been greatly reduced, thus the taxes should reflect that. I had figured the probable taxes based on previous years and set that aside to have ready, but you can see that assumes the expenses figured in as well."

"Let me see that," Zacchaeus grumbled, grabbing the papyrus scrolls. "Hmm. Uh-huh." He grunted as continued to examine them. "Yes, I see."

Levi wondered if showing these figures was a mistake. Probably better that this tax monger not be in the know of Ariah's business. *I guess it wasn't too smart of me to come on my own without Ariah's approval. Zacchaeus may turn on me and charge even more.*

Then he had an idea. "One way to look at it is that while the tax should justifiably be less this year, it will be much greater next year when sales increase."

Zacchaeus kept murmuring over Levi's work. He was not even sure the man had heard him. Finally Zacchaeus spoke. "Excellent records, well kept, attention to the numbers. You have a fine head with the figures." Then peering at Levi over the papers, he added, "Ariah has given you great authority in these matters. I could use someone like you to work in the tax business. You come back tomorrow, early afternoon, and I will have one of my men here to work out the details of your *proposal*."

He handed the scrolls back to Levi. "And bring those with you. I want my man to see how it's done in a clear way."

With that, he walked down the hall and out of sight. Levi packed up his scrolls and moved on through the long hall at a slower pace, taking in all the extravagance of this palace, especially the opulence of the spacious entry room.

When Levi opened the front door, he saw the daughter sitting on the bench in the front yard. She stood, anticipating a response.

He walked toward her. "Well, I had my say and it went better than I had expected."

"I'm so glad." She smiled.

"I am to come back tomorrow, early afternoon, to talk with one of your father's assistants."

Her eyes brightened. "That rarely happens. Few are allowed in and none are invited to return."

"Thank you for making it possible for me to see him." He could not suppress a grin. "Actually, he thought I was here to repair his roof."

"Oh!" She gasped. Putting her hands to her mouth, she broke out in giggles. "No wonder he was so willing to see you."

Levi joined her in laughter, loving to see her happy. Her smooth skin and long dark hair cascaded in gentle waves over her shoulders. Most young women he saw wore headpieces tied around their hair, but it was her brown eyes that captivated him most.

He stood there transfixed by her beauty. As her laughter slowly subsided, she noticed him staring. She shyly lowered her eyes. Catching himself, Levi turned to leave. "Well, I must be on about my business. Perhaps I'll see you tomorrow."

"Yes, tomorrow," she smiled.

He had to force his feet to move on to the gate. He looked back to see her one last time. She had not moved and gave a slight wave as he turned again to leave.

What is this going on inside of me? I have never felt like this before. He passed young women here and there and noticed them as for the first time. They had plain faces. One looked like the other. None of them compared to... *I don't even know her name!*

Chapter 16

What to Do with Zacchaeus

The longer he walked among the humdrum of people and places, the more he faced reality. *If these people knew where I have been, they would cry "traitor" or "unclean!"* Ariah might feel the same, and now Zacchaeus knows all the details of Ariah's business. *How might Zacchaeus use that against me?*

Levi arrived at his own humble, drab abode. He laid his bag of documents on the table and stretched out on his bed, staring at a cobweb on the ceiling.

"What have I gotten myself into?" He closed his eyes, but instead of focusing on the affairs with Zacchaeus, his thoughts drifted to the beautiful daughter. Why didn't he ask her name? What does she do all day? No doubt all her needs were met with handmaids at her side.

But she was so sad, almost fearful, as she confided in him about her father and their relationship. It brought back unpleasant memories of his own father. He held his own arms, wishing she were there so he could hold her and comfort her.

His mind swirled with thoughts of Ariah, numbers on the page, balsam bushes, Zacchaeus, and his beautiful daughter.

Levi woke up with a start when he heard David, the gardener, poking around outside. How long had he been asleep? He jumped up, not wanting David to think he had been lying around all day.

Levi grabbed a pen so it would look as if he had been working. "How are you on this fine day, King David?" he said, as he flung open the door.

The gardener grinned. "Sorry to disturb your work. I was about to trim the bushes over your window and remembered that you had done it the other day. I'll just trim around the side here if it doesn't bother your work."

"Oh, not at all. Truly kind of you. I'm sure this big place keeps you busy."

"Oh, yes, always something to do. The master has a large property here. Are you finding your cottage to be comfortable?"

"It's sufficient." Levi tried to sound positive. "Do you live close by?"

"Just beyond the ridge over there." He pointed. "Let me know if you need anything."

"Thank you."

David continued to prune the bushes around the cottage. He trimmed around a side window, swept out the brush, and hauled it away. The room was noticeably lighter. David's service proved to be a blessing, and his presence brought a sense of comfort to Levi.

Dare he share the good news of lower taxes with Ariah when he knew that he had probably revealed way too much of Ariah's business? Was his desire to hear accolades about his work clouding his good judgement?

And what of the daughter? He had no idea what to make of that. What he did know was that he had an appointed time to meet with Zacchaeus and his "man" tomorrow, which meant he would see *her* as well. Would she be there when he arrived? Would she be glad to see him?

*****

The next morning, Levi opened his eyes and thought immediately of her pretty face. He imagined her waiting for him in the lovely garden area, smiling with those big brown eyes.

His revelry faded when he thought about meeting with Zacchaeus, for though the short man was very complimentary of Levi's work and ideas, he appeared an abrupt, sly man.

An uneasiness came over him as he got up and readied himself for the second visit. *If Zacchaeus makes his daughter feel afraid and sad, is he like my father? Will he flare at the least thing? Will he turn on me?*

Soon Levi reached the big sycamore tree and turned down the street that led to Zacchaeus' house. Through the tall, pointed rods of the fence, he saw her. She was in the outside garden, bent over gathering flowers and placing them in her basket. When she rose, she turned to see him and started his way. But she abruptly stopped.

Levi frowned. Why did she stop?

Then he saw a servant at the gate, ready to let him in. *Hmm. This time he is expecting me.*

Levi followed behind the servant and gave a nod to the daughter, reminded again that he did not know her name. She gave a slow nod in return. Perhaps when he finished his business, she would be waiting for him.

The spacious entry room and long hall felt familiar now, but instead of going all the way to the courtyard, they turned to a room off the hall. It appeared to be an office with a table edged in intricately carved designs and a throne-like chair, padded in purple velvet. *The king's throne, I presume.*

The servant gestured for Levi to sit on a bench behind another table, not quite as elaborately adorned. Levi slid across the bench behind the table and laid his bag beside him.

"Master Zacchaeus will be with you in due time," the servant said, with a slight bow.

"Thank you," Levi responded.

Levi rubbed his hands over the smooth table. Having seen many a caravan carrying goods from all over the region, he assessed the room: a huge tightly woven rug from Persia spread across the floor, a wall hanging from Phoenicia, small round mahogany tables from Lebanon topped with decorated vases from Sepphoris. So this is how a tax collector uses all the money he sucks out of the poor, hard-working people who barely eke out a living.

Levi caught a whiff of the beautiful flowers in the vases and realized they came from *her* garden. He closed his eyes and took in a deep breath trying to smell the sweet fragrance of the flowers to match his remembrance of her.

His eyes popped open when he heard low voices and footsteps coming down the hall. He took his papers out of the bag and placed them neatly on the desk table.

Zacchaeus hurried into the room with his "man" trailing behind him. The man made no eye contact with Levi. He pulled a stool over at the end of Levi's table and sat subserviently waiting for further instructions from "the Master."

Zacchaeus did not greet Levi or introduce his helper but went straight to work.

"Pull out those records. I want Ramel to see the straight columns and the clear figures that you can *actually read*," he emphasized as he glared at his tax man. "That's how it should be done!"

Levi glanced out the corner of his eye to see Ramel's reaction. Ramel stared at the table unflinching. *He is probably brow-beaten like this all the time.* Levi identified with the man. Nothing is ever good enough. The same hasty, demeaning tone he remembered from his father.

"Go on, show him your figures!" Zacchaeus demanded.

Levi slid one sheet over to the end of the desk. Ramel glanced over at it and then stared again at the floor while Zacchaeus ranted on about people who complained about their taxes and Rome's pressure on him to produce, sliding by the fact that he fared lucratively in the process. He rambled about the many records he had to keep, the thousands of people he had to deal with, and the collectors he had to manage.

Finally, he mentioned Ariah's taxes. "As for Ariah, I see your point that he has had additional expenses so that he may expand his business. We can reduce the tax a bit," then with a cunning gleam in his eye, he added, "but I will expect a substantial amount of tax due next year. "Bring me a *proposal*," he emphasized, "tax expected this year, tax projected for next year. See me tomorrow at the same time."

Levi felt a throbbing rush in his head. What had he gotten himself into? Had he made matters worse? "But, sir, how can I possibly know the income for next year?"

"Estimate!" With that, Zacchaeus sprung from his throne and marched out of the room with Ramel tottering behind him.

Levi sat stunned. What had been the purpose of this meeting? To intimidate him? To show Ramel proper record keeping? To show Levi who is in control?

Once again, he was left alone to find his way out. He placed his worksheets back in his bag and walked to the hall. At least he had the hope of seeing the daughter as he went out.

As he stepped out in the warm sunlight, he glanced to the left. Sure enough, she walked from the garden to meet him. They met by the Rose of Sharon bushes. "How was your meeting today?" she asked.

"Well, I'm not sure. He wants me to submit a proposal for my tax issue."

"A proposal? I'm not sure he has ever done that before. He must like you."

"He likes my record keeping and readable figures. Poor Ramel. Your father was very, uh…"

"Demeaning to him?"

"Yes, exactly."

"Come, sit on the bench."

Levi very willingly followed.

"You see, Ramel is his cousin. When Ramel's father was on his deathbed, he made my father promise to take care of Ramel. Unfortunately, my father regrets the promise and treats him poorly."

Trying to change the subject to more pleasant conversation, Levi commented on the vase of flowers. "I noticed the flowers in the room. I knew you had been there. They were quite lovely."

"Oh, I love my flowers. My mother always kept flowers in the house."

"She no longer does that?"

"She passed five years ago." Looking down at her lap, she added, "I was fourteen years old."

"I'm sorry. You have no brothers or sisters?"

"No, just me."

"So your father keeps you in."

She looked at him with tender eyes. "Once again, you understand."

Levi's heart swelled with emotion.

"You said that you had difficulty with your father as well?"

"Yes. In many ways, your father reminds me of my father, stubborn and very controlling. Does your father have a bad temper as well?"

"Yes, yes, he does," she said in surprise. "They really are quite alike."

"Except for one thing. One is a tax collector and the other hates tax collectors!"

She chuckled.

Then he remembered his burning question. "Oh, I almost forgot, I don't know your name."

She smiled. "Lily," she said. "The lilies had just bloomed when I was born. Mama loved those lilies. And your name?"

"I am Levi, son of Alphaeus from Capernaum on the northern banks of the Sea of Galilee."

"Ah, I thought I detected an accent."

"Well, if you were in Galilee, it would be you who has the accent."

She laughed. "Perhaps you're right." She looked across the garden and then up at the sky. "The truth is, I've never been anywhere. Oh, we used to ride the wagon to grandfather's house, but that was long ago. Mama soon put those visits to a stop because grandfather acted so gruff and had me in tears half the time."

"Was he your father's father?"

"Yes."

"Maybe that explains your father's actions."

"Hmm. Could be. What about your grandfather?"

"I never knew either of my grandparents. We escaped from Sepphoris when I was quite young. The Romans came through and destroyed property and people alike. I believe my grandparents died in the revolt."

They both sat quietly for a moment. Levi broke the silence. "I just realized that I have never asked my mother about my grandparents. Perhaps both of our fathers imitated their fathers. I can only hope that I will be able to break that chain in my family."

"We have much in common," she said, gazing into his eyes.

He drank in the beauty of her eyes. "Yes, it seems we do."

After another awkward moment of silence, he said, "Well, I must be on my way. It was good to see you again." She smiled but did not move. Finally he stood. "I'll be back tomorrow at this same time."

Lily walked with Levi to the gate and watched him walk on down the street. They waved when he looked back.

"Lily, Lily," he repeated under his breath. He raised his face to the summer sun and closed his eyes. *I know her name. Lily, the loveliest flower in the garden.*

His steps were light and airy as though floating through the air. He smiled and nodded at everyone he passed. "I'd like this bunch of grapes," he said to the market vendor, as though he were making a great purchase.

He passed by blind Bartimaeus. "A big coin for you today, my friend."

"Levi, is that you?"

"Yes, yes, it's me, and life is beautiful!"

"You must have come upon a fortune, or else you're in love."

Levi squatted next to Bartimaeus. "In love, my friend. She is beautiful. Her name is Lily."

Bartimaeus smiled and shook his head. "Oh my. Be careful, women can distort your mind."

"My mind is soaring. Want a grape?"

Bartimaeus took full advantage of Levi's jovial mood. "Why thank you, my good man."

As Levi stood and bid him Shalom, he heard Bartimaeus's blind friend comment, "That man is in for trouble."

Nothing could cloud his joy. He saw her again today and learned her name, Lily!

As he passed the caravans coming into the city, he spied Caleb, who had his usual frown. It reminded him that he had to write a proposal of this year's taxes and next year's estimate.

Instead of floating on air, his feet plodded up the incline, across the grassy land, and into his humble abode. He plopped his bag on the table and ate the last of the grapes before he warmed his soup for supper.

He thought about his discussion with Lily concerning grandparents. Why had Mama never told him about them, especially about his father's father? Could he have been one of those who led the revolt against the Romans back then? Is that where Papa inherited his angry, bitter attitude about life?

"Help me, oh Lord, not to continue a pattern of bitterness and anger."

*****

After an agonizing night of dealing with the figures until he came up with what he thought was a reasonable proposal, Levi dressed and went into his office next to Ariah's.

"Good morning, Levi."

"Good morning, sir. How are things with the new land?"

105

"The ground has been prepared and the new starts will be planted every day this week." Ariah's forehead wrinkled with worry.

"You don't sound pleased. Is that not good news?"

"Yes, but Carmi tells me it may be two years before the bushes will be able to produce sufficient sap for the salve."

"I see." It certainly was not a good time to tell Ariah what he had been doing. He must wait for a better time.

After taking care of his work for the morning, he headed toward Zacchaeus' house. The only pleasant thing about the whole situation was Lily.

Levi dropped a coin in blind Bartimaeus' cup.

"Thank you, kind Levi."

"How did you know it was me?"

"I recognize the sound of your walk. When one sense is taken, the other senses gain strength. But I hear worry in your walk today."

"You are an amazing man, Bartimaeus."

"Thank you, sir. May your steps improve."

As before, the servant waited at the gate for Levi. He glanced over at the garden, but no sign of Lily. Disappointed, he followed the servant in. Just as they passed the first room off the hall, Lily came out of the office carrying a basket. She looked as startled as Levi felt.

Quickly, she stopped and bowed slightly to Levi and the servant. Levi smiled and winked at her as he followed the servant to the office door. Inside, he sat at "his" chair and laid his proposal on the table. When he caught a fragrance in the room, he immediately looked at the vase of fresh flowers—lilies.

Shortly, Ramel entered.

"Do you have the proposal?"

"Yes, I have it here." Levi held it up.

As Ramel took it from Levi, he said, "Master Zacchaeus will review it and send a collector to your business."

Ramel took the scroll and left the room. Levi sat stunned. *Is that it? No greetings, no shalom, no consultation with Zacchaeus?*

Levi picked up his bag and walked to the front door. *Will Lily be in the garden? Is this it?*

He closed the front door and immediately looked to the left. Yes! There by the Rose of Sharon sat Lily. He hurried to her and sat beside her. "That didn't take long," she said.

"I was afraid you wouldn't be here."

She smiled. "Did you see the flowers?"

"Yes, lilies, picked by your sweet hands." He slipped one hand under hers and laid his other hand on top. She willingly squeezed his hand. "Lily, I think this is the last time I will be coming. I wasn't invited back."

She lowered her eyes, her forehead wrinkled with worry.

"Can you come out for a while?" he asked.

"No, I'm never allowed to leave. Someone watches the gate regularly. We often have intruders who wish to retaliate because of taxes."

"I would protect you. We could just walk to the market then find a quiet place to talk." She looked doubtful. "Is there another way to leave?" he asked.

"Well, there is a slight opening around the bush at the back of the garden." She glanced that way.

Levi stared at the bush and thought for a moment. "I could leave from the main gate and then you could go out the opening and meet me at the sycamore tree at the end of the street. You would just be gone for a short time." She still looked worried. "I'm sorry," he continued. "I don't want to cause you trouble. I want to be with… uh, I want to talk with you more."

She squeezed his hand again. "I know. I love talking to you. I never get to talk to anyone my age, anyone who understands."

"Would people recognize you?"

"No, I'm never on the street."

He eyed her hair and clothes, remembering the women of the town. "It would be best if you could retrieve a wide strip of cloth to cover your hair. All the women have their heads covered." He looked at her gold shoes. "Uh, do you have a pair of sandals? Plain sandals?"

"Only the old ones I use to work in the garden."

"Perfect!"

She snickered slightly, then hesitated.

"Okay, I'll do it," she said, squeezing his hand once more.

His smile reflected hers. "It will be difficult to hide your beauty, but maybe a head piece will help." She shyly looked down. "So, it's settled. I will meet you at the tree at the end of the street, right?"

She nodded her head. He patted her hand and stood to leave. After he closed the gate, he looked back and saw her scurrying into the house. He tried to walk steady, but his heart pounded with excitement and anticipation. Would she follow through? Would a servant in the house get suspicious and foil their plan?

Levi arrived at the tree to wait. Thankfully, not too many people passed by since this location was a bit removed from the busyness of the marketplace. Still, he paced up and down waiting and trying not to look suspicious as a few locals passed by.

"How long does it take to grab a headpiece and put on a pair of sandals?" he muttered to himself, with a heavy sigh. He found a large stone bench of sorts on which he could position himself so that he could see down the street to watch for Lily.

Maybe she changed her mind or was afraid. Maybe she got caught, was questioned, or received punishment.

Finally, he spied her in the distance, looking convincingly common, but as she drew near, her beautiful face still set her apart. Levi stood in anticipation, smiling with great delight.

"How do I look?" she whispered.

"Common as can be!" he grinned. He leaned over to whisper, "But I knew it was you." She snickered. "Did anyone see you," he asked.

"I don't think so. Everything was very routine today, except for your visit."

"Well, shall we shop at the market?"

"I suppose we can. I don't know exactly what to do."

"Just follow me."

As they passed shoppers on the way, no one seemed suspicious. Occasionally, a man gave her a second look. Levi leaned over to suggest she pull her headpiece forward a bit and look down when they passed young men.

When they stood in front of the fruit stand, Levi made a purchase, but she stood slightly behind him. After he bought a small bag of nuts and fruit, he led her to an area outside the marketplace where they would have privacy and a place to sit in the shade.

He pulled out a piece of fruit. "An apricot for my lady." He swirled his arm with a flourish and a bow.

"Oh, thank you, kind sir," she grinned, with an equally dramatic bow.

They quite forgot the time with all their conversation. Shortly, Lily kept looking back over her shoulder toward her street.

"You're thinking we should return to your house?" he offered.

"You know me so well. Yes, I think so. I don't want to overdo the time."

"I understand." He helped her up.

They walked along in silence. Was she as sad as he to know their time together was almost over?

"I enjoyed this adventure today. I felt like one of the people, not someone isolated. I think I know better how to fix my headpiece after seeing the women in town."

"Then you would like to meet me again? Tomorrow?"

"If you would like."

"I would like that very much."

She smiled. "It's so easy to talk with you. It seems we always have something to talk about."

By that time, they reached the tree. "When do you have your lunch?" he asked.

"Oh, exactly at the sixth hour, without fail. Father insists on it. It is the one time I see him each day."

"Shall we meet one hour past lunch then?"

"Perfect," she said, looking up at him with her dancing eyes in full view. "I had a wonderful afternoon."

"I did as well."

After another awkward pause, she said, "Well, I must go. I will see you tomorrow."

"Tomorrow," he said.

His heart soared as he watched her walk away. Halfway down the street, she turned to wave. He waved back and lingered until she was out of sight.

Chapter 17

From Ecstasy to Agony

Every day, Levi and Lily planned their escapades. He took her to the balsam fields to show her the precious oils that the balsam released. On another day, they visited the new fields to see how freshly planted sprouts were progressing.

Another time, Levi showed her the caravans bringing in goods and trading for other treasures. She watched Levi at his best, selling and persuading foreigners to purchase the salve.

Lily asked about the man who kept staring at them, the one up there on the crate. Levi followed her gaze and spied Caleb glaring in their direction.

"He is not a man to be trusted," Levi said, and turned his back to Caleb. He quickly escorted Lily through the crowd, behind loaded caravans, and off out of the sight of Caleb.

"I haven't shown you where I live, have I?" he asked, when they were alone again.

"No. May I see your house?"

"I have to warn you, it isn't anything like yours."

"Mine is extravagant and unnecessary."

"But mine is exceedingly small, too small. The owner of my business is quite wealthy. His palace is spacious like yours. He provided me a small cottage on his land. I'm hoping to build my own house soon, one with more than one room."

"One room?"

"I told you it was small."

Soon they were walking across Ariah's expansive estate. "Oh, this is beautiful. So much land, and look at the garden," she exclaimed with delight.

"The gardener, David, tends the flowers." Levi grabbed a flower from the garden and looked at his own tiny cottage, glad that David had kept the bushes back. At least it looked slightly larger. Still, it could pass for a gardener's shed. Levi glanced around to be sure no one saw them. They walked on to his little cottage.

"Well, here we are, the mansion of Levi. Enter Queen Lily!"

Lily smiled, but cautiously stepped inside as though afraid something might jump out at her.

"To your right is the dining hall, enhanced by a well-supplied kitchen, managed by the head bread-maker, cook, and wine-taster." Levi spoke with the voice of a proclaimer as he gave his "tour." He grabbed a bottle, poked the flower in it, and set it on the table.

Lily relaxed as she enjoyed the fun, with, "Oh!" and "Ah!" and "I see!" coupled with deep, dramatic nods of her head. "Lovely vase of flowers."

"As you turn down this hall, you will find the bedrooms, er… ah… bedroom of the master of the house, equipped with a massive bed from King Herod's previous palace. To your left, a nightstand imported from Lebanon and porcelain pitcher and bowl from Phoenicia."

"So elegant," she joined in.

Suddenly, they were facing each other, aware for the first time that they were alone, totally alone. The light from the window lit her radiant eyes. He gently removed her headpiece as she looked up to his handsome face.

He stroked her hair. "Your hair is so beautiful." His hand caressed her cheek. "And your eyes." Slowly he leaned down, and she willingly welcomed his gentle kiss.

Something stirred in him that he had never felt before. They gazed in each other's eyes and smiled but were speechless. They kissed again, tightly embracing each other.

Over and over they embraced and kissed, overwhelmed with the surge of first love. Before they knew it, they were lying in bed together, making passionate love. It was as though they could not get enough of each other.

Finally, they lay in exhaustion side by side.

A noise outside the cottage startled them. They each grabbed the blanket to cover themselves and froze in terror.

A knock came. "Master Levi, are you home?"

Levi looked at Lily and put his fingers to his lips.

"Yes, David. What do you want?" Levi stalled for time as he threw on his tunic.

"You know that leak in your roof that you mentioned?"

"Yes?"

"I thought I might work on repairing it in the morning while you're at work. Would that be okay with you?"

Levi had his tunic on and ran his fingers through his hair before he opened the door slightly.

"Yes, David. That would be fine."

"It looks like we might get some rain soon. Just thought you'd want to stay dry."

"Very kind of you. Tomorrow morning will be fine. Thank you." He slowly closed the door and held his hand out for Lily to stay while he looked out the window to watch David walk to the garden, then on toward his own house. He gave a loud sigh. "I think he's well out of sight now."

Lily quickly gathered her things and began to dress. Levi turned his back, so as not too embarrass her. When she had dressed, she said, "We better be going."

"Lily, I… I'm sorry."

"I know."

"He held both her shoulders at arm's length. "Lily, I love you. I would not want to do anything to hurt you."

She looked down, then slowly raised her head to look in his eyes. "I love you too, Levi."

He drew her in and hugged her. She hugged him tight for a moment, then said, "We must be going."

They walked along in silence. How could something so wonderful and passionate suddenly feel shameful? When anyone looked at them in the slightest, it was as though he felt everybody knew.

Storm clouds gathered overhead. A clap of thunder made them both jump. Soon, a gentle sprinkle turned into a torrent of rain. Everyone retreated to their homes or businesses. Levi and Lily were almost to the sycamore tree and sought shelter under its boughs.

Levi held her in his arms, gathering his cloak around and hovering over her to protect her from the torrent of rain and raging wind that whipped around their legs.

"Lily, I'm sorry," he shouted against the wind. "Please forgive me. I would never do anything to use you. I just feel so in love with you and want to share all that I am with you. It was wonderful."

She pressed the side of her face into his chest and squeezed him tightly under his cloak. Slowly, the rain began to subside; the wind died down.

"Can we meet again tomorrow?" he asked.

"Let's wait for two days."

"Two days?" he questioned.

"I don't want to arouse any suspicions."

"I will wait," he relinquished. He kissed her forehead and held her for one more moment.

She slipped away, fully drenched.

*****

Unknown to Levi, Caleb had been in Ariah's office earlier that afternoon and had glanced out the window when Levi and Lily tripped through the grass on their way from Levi's house.

"Hmm, seems that your boy, Levi, has other interests here."

"What do you mean, Caleb?"

"Have a look."

Ariah strolled to the window.

"I see. And you have never had those kinds of interests?"

Ignoring Ariah's insinuations, Caleb went on to plant a thought in Ariah's mind. "They are seen together quite often, perhaps to the neglect of his work."

"Who is this girl?"

"I don't know, but I can find out."

"I'm sure you will, Caleb, I'm sure you will."

"Good day, sir."

Chapter 18

Who Is this Girl?

Delighted with his new self-appointed assignment, Caleb went to work immediately to check about Levi's *friend*. The torrential rain brought on the perfect opportunity. While the caravan owners found refuge under tent material they kept on their wagons, the balsam workers hurried to the storehouse to seek shelter.

Caleb sat on a crate next to Darthus, one of the workers. "I guess Levi and his *friend* are getting caught in this rain."

"Probably so," Darthus responded. "She has been everywhere with him."

"Oh?"

"He had her up in the balsam field last week, showing her the plants."

"How *lovely*," Caleb said.

"They're together just about every day."

"So you've been keeping an eye on them?"

"Just happen to see them. She *is* pretty, easy on the eyes." Darthus raised his eyebrows and rolled his eyes over at Caleb with a sly smile.

"I've been wondering where she came from. Do you know where she lives?" Caleb pressed on.

"No, but I could probably find out."

Just what Caleb wanted to hear. "I tell you what, I'll give you a couple of afternoons off this week to do some investigative work. Report back to me."

With a partially toothless grin, Darthus agreed to the deal.

*****

When Levi returned home drenched from the afternoon downpour, he was greeted with a good-sized leak dripping onto his kitchen table. He grabbed a bucket to catch the drops.

As soon as he dried himself, another dripping leak started over the washstand. He figured the wash bowl could just as easily double for a leak bowl and shifted it to accommodate the leaky roof.

He had just sat to have a cold bowl of soup when another drip started near the door. "What next?" he sighed. He found an old cloth and plugged up the hole.

Weary from the rain, the leaks, and the shock of being startled by David earlier, he decided to go to bed, but even there he tossed and turned. The only thing that brought comfort was the delight of holding Lily in his arms, the tenderness of her kisses, and the passion he felt in making love to her. He held the pallet of his bed imagining it to be her.

Somehow he had ignored the fact that they were not married, until the knock had come at the door. The thought of feeling "caught" made him toss and turn in frustration and guilt.

What had he done to her? Would she want to be with him again? What would her father say if he knew? This could be scandalous, even deadly. Questions, questions, all through the night.

Finally, the sun lit his room. He no longer heard the splash of leaks in the bowls, but they were all nearly full. After he dressed, he took the bowls outside to empty. This time he was delighted to see David coming up the path.

"Good morning," David shouted from a distance. "I imagine you are ready for leak repairs."

"Yes indeed!" Levi called back.

"I guess I should have taken care of that roof yesterday." David breathed a heavy sigh after his brisk walk up the path.

"Well, I'm glad you're here. Now I can show you where to find the leaks."

After he pointed them out, David went to work, and Levi tromped off to the office.

*****

"Levi, come in here," Ariah called out, as Levi passed the window. When Levi entered, Ariah looked up from his desk. "The tax collector just came by. The tax assessment seems surprisingly low this year."

I guess now is the time to tell him. "Well, sir, the original charge was almost twice that."

"You saw another charge and didn't tell me?"

"I thought you would want me to take care of it, sir."

"And how do you know what it is now?" Ariah stood.

"Well, you see, I felt the first charge was way too high considering you have had great expenses this year to purchase more land and bushes, not to mention more workers, so I presented the case to the assessor."

"The assessor?" Ariah raised an eyebrow.

"Yes sir, the one who is fully in charge, like yourself, sir."

"Do you mean Zacchaeus?" he asked with a frown.

"Uh… yes, sir."

"You went to see that snake in the grass without consulting me?"

"He listened to what I had to say and as you see, I was able to convince him to lower the tax."

Ariah leaned over his desk squinted his eyes at Levi. "At what price?"

Once again, Levi had that feeling of being caught in the act. "Uh, well, uh, of course next year, uh, the tax will be more, because the business will increase, maybe even double." Levi tried to be positive.

Ariah leaned over a little farther. "Remember, Carmi told me that it may be two years before the bushes will begin to produce. I don't look for any great increase yet."

No, Levi had not remembered that small detail. He must think of a response and quick. "Meantime, I thought you would be pleased that I took the initiative to reduce the unreasonable taxes."

"Yes, that's good for now, but you should have talked to me about this first." Ariah eased down in his seat. "I don't trust that conniving old fool. He's been a thorn in my flesh for as long as I've known him." Then, as if talking to himself. "Working for the Romans. Humph, he sold his soul!"

He studied the tax paper as he settled down. "Levi, be sure you check with me before you talk to anyone about the business."

"Yes, sir, I certainly will." Levi left to go to his adjoining office and felt like he could breathe again.

With all the visits to Lily, he had gotten behind in his work. He made great effort to concentrate on his figures, but every time he tried to add a column, he had to do it again.

At last, he caught up with his work in time to check on something at the balsam salve storage building, eat a quick lunch, and meet Lily.

*****

Levi paced back and forth by the sycamore tree. No sign of Lily.

It must be an hour since I arrived. Where is she? Is she having trouble getting away under watchful eyes? Does she regret our passionate time together yesterday? Is she ashamed? Or did she come early, and I missed her? Does she think I have abandoned her?

Finally he decided to walk down the street, far enough to be able to see in the garden, but no Lily. Then he remembered. *Oh, she said to wait two days.*

Feeling foolish and dejected, he sauntered on toward home. He passed Bartimaeus and dropped a coin in his cup. "Your feet carry a heavy load," Bartimaeus told him.

"Yes, you might say that, but the load is inside rather than outside."

"The worst kind."

119

Levi considered Bartimaeus. *He is blind but has eyes to see better than most men.*

*****

Caleb found a break in the late afternoon and strolled over to see Darthus. "And how was your investigation today?"

"Not so good. Levi went way over to the other end of town, but he stood around one corner for way over an hour. It was like he was waiting, but she never came. Not much news to give."

"What street was it?"

"The main street."

"You said he was at a corner. What was the other street?"

"Aw, I don't know them street names. It's the one where Zacchaeus has his big house. Oh, yeah, Levi did walk down that way one time, but he didn't go far."

"Levi walked toward Zacchaeus' house?" Caleb asked in anticipation.

"Well, he kind of walked that way, but I couldn't say exactly to the tax collector's house."

"Good work today, Darthus. Follow him again tomorrow. Maybe she will meet him this time. Be sure to watch where she comes from and where she returns."

"Yes, sir, I will do it."

Chapter 19

Doomsday

The next morning, Levi went through the motions of working with the records in his office. After lunch, his feet automatically took him through town, down the main street to the familiar tree. He arrived earlier than usual and found a spot to sit and wait and watch.

After a short wait, and to his delight, he spied her coming down the street. He stood, constraining himself from running to meet her. He waved so she would see him. She smiled but stared at the ground as she hurried down the street. He reached out for both her hands. She responded instantly but with serious, weary eyes and held his hands briefly.

"Let's go to our special spot to talk," she said as she led the way.

When they sat on the stone ledge, she nervously fingered her headpiece and took deep breaths.

"Lily, what is it? Has something happened at the house?"

Tears began filling her sad eyes. "Oh, Levi," her voice caught. She took in another great breath, attempting to control her emotions.

He held her hand. "Take your time, my sweet love."

She looked up to the sky and released a deep sigh. "When I ran in the house during the rain, two of the women servants were waiting for me. They scolded me for being out in the rain and being gone so long. They had searched the house and garden for me, but thankfully they had not told Papa yet. I had to make up a story to try to ease their worry and irritation. They fussed around more, helping me get dry and warm."

She took another big breath. "They were being very protective—well, suspicious." She rolled her eyes and tilted her head at him with a half-smile.

"Oh, my dear Lily, I'm so sorry you have had to go through this. I should never have kept you away so long, and then the rain."

She put her hand on top of his. "Levi, you can't control the rain." She smiled into his eyes for the first time.

He placed his other hand on top of hers. "I missed you so much. I could hardly stand being away from you for one day."

"I know. We have been together every day. My heart was lost without you. The day was so long." She looked away. "I felt imprisoned."

"What can we do?" he asked.

"I don't know, but I knew I had to see you, even for a few moments. I must go back now. The servants were busy cleaning up the dishes from lunch. They'll be checking on me again."

She stood and started to walk away. "Lily, so soon?" He hastened after her.

"Yes." When they reached the tree, she turned. "We will need to wait a while. I'll meet you again in two days." And off she went, hurrying down the street. He watched as she rushed to the end of the street and around the bushes. Another two days. How could he bear it?

Levi plodded along, unaware of anything or anybody around him. He found himself sitting in his office, still in a daze. At least he knew that she still wanted to be with him, but at what price?

*****

Darthus had arrived for his investigation just as the girl met Levi. *Ah-ha, I caught them.* He grinned. When they moved to their special spot, he carefully followed and watched as they looked deep in conversation.

Before he could get settled, the girl jumped up and started in his direction. Darthus scrambled to get out of the way and not be noticed. Then off she went down the street. Thankfully,

Levi's eyes were fixed on the girl, so Darthus slowly slipped a short way behind Levi to watch where the girl went.

As Levi turned to leave, Darthus quickly turned the other way as if going further down the main street. When he looked back, Levi had sauntered on into town. This was his chance! Darthus walked down the street where he had watched the girl. After passing a few houses, sure enough, there stood the stately mansion of Zacchaeus.

Darthus saw the main gate up ahead but noticed the slight opening by the bush where the girl had slipped through. A servant came out a side door and looked around. Darthus ducked behind another bush.

When the servant went inside, Darthus scurried on back to the main street, pleased with his discovery.

*****

"You actually saw her go into Zacchaeus's house?"

"I watched her go to the end of the street and disappear into the bushes. The house of Zacchaeus is the only one at the end and I discovered the opening where she could come and go from the garden."

"So, is this a servant girl?"

"How should I know? She is a pretty one. Dresses like any other girl, I guess. What else would she be, coming from that big house?"

"Could she be a daughter?" Caleb asked with a sly smirk, practically licking his lips at the possibility.

"I don't know." Darthus shrugged his shoulders.

Caleb pressed further. "Ask some of the women who have seen them out together. They can tell a servant girl from a rich daughter, no matter how she dresses herself."

"Aw, I don't know who to ask. You just asked me to find out where she lives."

"Oh, I'll do it myself."

Caleb figured that the next time they came around, he would have one of the women take a good look at her and help him know if she was a servant or a relative.

*****

Two days dragged by, and finally Levi set out to meet Lily. He sat waiting only a short time before he caught sight of her hurrying toward him. She looked up several times as she made the jaunt and willingly smiled at him with outstretched hands when they met. Her eyes kissed him, even if her lips were prohibited in public view.

His eyes kissed her back as he squeezed her hands. "Oh, how I missed you," he whispered.

They quickly walked to their special place. "How are things at the house," he asked, as they sat together.

"So far, so good." Her voice sounded more relaxed. "Things have settled a bit. Sarah is protective, but kind. She is just a few years older than me, and we talk easily with each other. I know she cares about me." Then Lily sighed, "But Eldrah is her usual disagreeable self. I think her back pain might be the thing that makes her so irritable. She walks bent most of the time. Papa expects too much of her, and then I think she takes it out on me," she said with a grimace.

"You seem more settled."

"I discovered that Eldrah sits down to "rest" about this time of day, but then she falls asleep." Lily chuckled. "What about you? How are things with you?"

"Well, my roof did leak with all that rain, but David came the next morning and fixed it." Levi thought a moment, leaned his elbows on his knees, and ran his fingers through his hair. He took a deep breath. "Ariah received the revised tax notice, and he was surprised."

"Did your talk with Papa work? Was the tax less than before?"

Levi looked at the trees. "Yes, but I made the mistake of telling Ariah that it was much better than the first notice, which he had not seen, then I had to explain that I had come to meet with your father. Ariah didn't like that at all."

"You mean, Ariah didn't know you had come to meet Papa?"

"No, I thought I could take care of it."

"I'm sorry." She reached over to touch his hand.

"The one good thing about it is that I met you."

Levi looked around. "I have an idea." He grabbed her hand and hurried her off through the grass to a tall, stout olive tree. Its branches curled around making it appear even thicker.

Levi whisked Lily around to the backside of the tree. "Alone at last," he grinned. He pulled her into his arms and she willingly kissed him. They held an embrace for a long time before he kissed her again.

"Levi, I must go now."

"So soon?"

"Yes, and I think we will have to meet only once a week."

All the joy drained from his face.

"Just to be safe," she added. "Now I must go." She started to leave but turned to give one more embrace and tender kiss.

*****

Meanwhile, Caleb wasted no time in trying to find out the status of the girl. But every woman he talked to either hadn't seen the girl or hadn't paid any attention to her. Caleb complained to Darthus.

"Well, the girl hasn't been around here for a few weeks," Darthus observed.

"Hmm, that gives me an idea," Caleb's face brightened. "We need to ask a woman who lives over that way, where Levi and the girl meet."

"What do you mean, *we*?"

125

Ignoring Darthus's comment, Caleb said, "I've been keeping an eye on Levi. He seems to leave only about once a week now. I think it's the second day of the week. If you—"

"Oh no you don't. I told you, I'm not good with women."

"All right, I'll do it myself."

Caleb arranged for someone to fill in for him. Sure enough, on the second day of the week, Levi headed across town. Caleb caught up with him, keeping a sensible distance.

Just as Darthus had told him, he saw Levi hanging around the corner, waiting. Caleb glanced around to find a woman who may have observed the couple before. One woman sat behind a tub of dye, dipping a cloth up and down in the green stuff. *Hmm, perfect!*

"I see that you do good work with the dye," he commented to the woman.

"Why, thank you, sir."

"I would like to have one of my tunics dyed in that color. Could you do that for me?"

"Certainly, bring it by any time."

Caleb chatted away, uncharacteristically. "You have a good shady spot to work here."

"Yes, it's quite pleasant."

As if on cue, Caleb saw the girl coming down the street from the direction of Zacchaeus' house, just as Darthus told him.

Caleb talked on with his captive audience as he watched the couple all but embrace.

"Looks like that young man and woman are glad to be together."

"They used to meet every day. Only about once a week now."

"I see. She is extremely attractive. A servant girl from down the way?"

"Oh no, she's no servant girl. She tries to dress herself humbly, but her fair face and hands are not that of a servant girl. Her headpiece and dress are plain, but the fabric is expensive."

Another woman taking dried cloths off the rack turned. "She doesn't speak like common women. Her voice and words are of the higher class. Comes from the line of Zacchaeus, she does."

Neither would declare her a daughter, though, because "No one has ever seen his family. Haven't even seen Zacchaeus much. He knows how much everyone hates him. I suppose he's afraid of being killed except when the Roman soldiers come calling. He probably thinks they would protect him. But they're about as deceitful as he is."

"It is good to talk with you fine women. I will be back with my tunic later." With a nod, Caleb ambled on down the street, relishing in his great victory, and eager to share his news with Darthus.

*****

Meanwhile, Levi and Lily proceeded to their usual spot. Levi watched her nervously because she had that troublesome demeanor once again. "What is it, Lily? Has Eldrah or Sarah upset you again?"

"No, it's that I..." Lily broke down in uncontrollable tears this time. He held her hand; he patted her shoulder, and rubbed her arm up and down, trying to help her. She tried again to speak, but her emotions would not allow it.

"Lily, please let me help you."

She closed her eyes and took several deep breaths. "I've not been feeling well for the last few weeks. Very few foods taste good to me, and I have been throwing up what little food I eat. My stomach churns over and over."

"You must see a doctor. I hate to see you so upset."

She held up her hand. "No, let me finish," she said. "I talked to Sarah one day. She has three children. I managed to move the conversation around to her giving birth, and then I asked her how she felt when she first knew she was going to have a baby."

Levi felt ill. He caught his breath, slowly shaking his head. "No, no, this can't be happening."

She grabbed his arm, "Levi, Sarah described all the symptoms I'm having."

Levi leaned over with elbows on knees, forehead in hands, still shaking his head. Then he looked over to her. "Maybe you just have an illness."

"I've never had anything like this. I... I also missed my monthly time." A sob caught in her throat. "Levi, if I am with child, my father will know I have been with a man. He will be furious that I have disobeyed him and furious when he finds the man. And he *will* find the man. He has his ways. Levi, I would never see you again. We would never be able to be together again!"

"Come with me," he said, and he took her behind their olive tree and held her in his arms until her sobs subsided.

He stepped back and held both her shoulders as he looked her straight in the eyes. "Lily I have an idea, but I will need to meet you again tomorrow. Can you do that?"

Her questioning eyes searched his face. "What is it?"

"I'll tell you tomorrow," he said, with earnest voice. "Can you meet me again?"

She paused, struck by his change of tone, then looked up at him. "Yes, I can do that."

He held her once more. "We'll work it out."

Chapter 20

The Solution

Levi went straight to the new fields of balsa in search of Carmi. He could see the hills of Gilead from Jericho, but they were farther than he remembered.

Along the way he tossed his idea over and over in his mind, finally deciding this was the only possible solution to Lily's problem, well, *their* problem.

He spied Carmi among the late afternoon workers. He remembered a conversation he had one time with Carmi about the values of the salve. But how could he manage the conversation to find out what he needed without being too obvious?

He waved his arm with vigorous sweeps to get Carmi's attention. Carmi recognized him and waved back.

When he finally reached his friend, they grasped each other's arms with warm greetings. "Levi, I haven't seen you in a while."

"It's good to be with you again. I hadn't seen the new fields for a while and thought it was time I have a look."

Carmi spread his arm across the field. "Welcome to my new domain," he said, with smiling eyes.

Levi looked across the field, admiring the bushes. "It looks like you and your workers have made good progress."

"It's *slow* progress, planting roots one by one, but yes, we are moving forward now."

"Many people will benefit from your work," Levi assured him.

Carmi surveyed the field. "Hmm, perhaps that's a good way of looking at it."

"I remember that you told me one time about all the benefits of the salve. That is helpful to know when we are trying to sell the product. I remember that the salve helps with stomach

129

problems, as well as aches and pains. What were some of the other benefits?"

"The salve is good for all those pains and of course the women like it for the sweet fragrance as well as cramping. Some have been known to even abort a pregnancy."

Ah, just what Levi wanted to hear. "That's quite extreme! How would they do that?"

"I've heard that they rub the salve on themselves twice a day for two weeks. Never knew anyone who did it. Only heard about it."

Just what Levi needed to know. He went back to asking about the plants. "Will the plants be ready soon?"

"I didn't think the new shoots would take hold this quickly, but several plants look like they might bare sap next year. Time will tell."

Better than Ariah had thought. That would be good. Levi brought the discussion to a close and walked away feeling confident about his idea.

*****

The next day, Levi headed to the salve storage building to pick up two jars. On his way, he passed Caleb, who stared down at him from the platform where he always stood. Caleb had an unusually sly grin on his face. He nodded to Levi, but Levi had too much on his mind to worry about Caleb today.

When Levi met Lily the next day, they went immediately to their stone ledge to talk. Lily looked at Levi anxiously for him to reveal his idea.

He held out the jar of salve. "Lily, this is the salve we sell. It is good for aches and pains." He opened it and held it to her nose. "You can smell its sweet fragrance." She sniffed it, then looked at him with questioning eyes.

This was not going to be as easy as he thought. "Another use of the salve is for pain that women have." Oh, this was not going well. Lily cocked her head and frowned as though totally bewildered with what he was trying to say.

He might as well just come out with it. "If you rub this on your lower abdomen two times a day for two weeks, it may take care of your problem."

"Do you mean the nausea I'm having?"

"Uh, well, no. I mean the baby."

She looked stunned and lowered her head. "Do you mean it would kill my baby?"

Levi's face flushed. It sounded so final, so evil. He suddenly realized how cruel it must have felt to her. She placed her hand on her stomach, rubbing it gently.

"You were upset with what your father would say, even fearful. I just wanted to help you, protect you, try to find a solution."

With sad eyes, she stared at a nearby garden, but she did not seem to see it. Finally, she spoke with no emotion in her voice or her face. "If this is what I need to do, I will do it. I will not return for two weeks."

He wanted to protest, but she seemed so determined and so withdrawn. He did not know how to bring her back. She reached out to take the jar.

"Here's another jar, if you need it."

She clutched the jars and walked away.

"Lily…" He started to go after her, hold her, ease her shock, but she kept walking without turning back. No good-bye, no touch, no caress.

He watched her walk the long street. Had he done the right thing? What else could he have done? *Mama would know how to talk to her, ease her burden.*

Levi watched until Lily walked out of sight.

As he trudged back to his house, he heard one voice in his head—Papa. *You broke the dishes. Why are you so careless? Can't you do anything right?*

Suddenly, he heard a crash. He jerked around but realized someone had dropped a flowerpot in the market as he passed by. He heaved a sigh of relief. It was not Papa.

He walked past the office and Ariah called him. When he went in, Ariah sat with his arms crossed and a scowl on his face. "Have you been hard at work?" he asked.

"Uh, yes, sir, the records are all in order."

"That's amazing with all the trips I hear you've been making across the town."

"Trips?"

"It seems that a young woman has occupied most of your time these days, a wealthy woman at that."

"I'm not sure what you mean, sir."

"Has Zacchaeus used this girl to draw you into his schemes?"

"No, sir, nothing like that. When I went to his house to confront him about the taxes, I met his daughter and..."

He leaned forward on his desk. "So, she *is* his daughter."

"I had conversation with her outside the house. Zacchaeus knows nothing of this."

"Are you telling me that you and this girl have been together, and her father knows nothing of it?"

"Yes, sir. She is careful to disguise herself and slip away without his knowing." As soon as the words were out of his mouth, he wanted to draw them back in.

Now Ariah stood. "Do you realize the trouble you could be causing me? If that thief knew one of my men was meeting his daughter behind his back, he would not only slit your throat, he would tax me for all I'm worth!"

The reality of Ariah's words hit Levi like a slap on the face. In fact, he closed his eyes and turned his head as though he felt it. "I'm sorry."

"You're sorry all right. I demand that you never see this girl again and that you put that wasted time in on your work, not a dead-end relationship. And if you ever see her again, it will mean the end of your employment with me."

"Yes, sir."

Levi turned to leave, but Ariah handed him a papyrus note. "Oh, I almost forgot, here's a letter a messenger brought in today." Levi took the letter and went back to his cottage.

He collapsed on his bed, his mind and emotions completely exhausted; his world torn in two. How could he go two weeks without seeing Lily, or worse yet, never see her again if Ariah had his way?

How did Ariah know about Lily? And how did he know that he was away many afternoons? Caleb. That is why he had that smirk on his face.

Levi beat his fist into his pillow. Why? Why did I allow this to happen? Why? Why? Why? With every beat of the pillow, more tears poured out.

When he rolled over, there was the letter lying on the floor. It looked like some of the old papyrus he used to have at home in Capernaum.

> To Levi, son of Alphaeus of Capernaum
> Jericho

He pulled the seal and carefully unrolled the letter.

> Papa is gone under difficult circumstances.
> We buried him yesterday. Mama is terribly upset.
> She misses you. I do as well. I am not sure how
> I will hold the business together.
> > James, son of Alphaeus of Capernaum

Chapter 21

What next?

Buried him? My father? Gone? Dead? Levi stared out the window to see the streaks of yellows and pinks reflecting off the clouds from the sunset. A page of his life concluded just like that. Relief mixed with sorrow and regret. Was it the same feeling for his mother?

He looked at the page again. "Under difficult circumstances." *What does that mean? A lengthy illness? Accident? What?*

"Mama misses you." Just the mention of her name moistened his eyes. "I miss you too, Mama," he whispered. And brother James "holding on to the business."

Levi took a deep breath. More worries. He reread the letter, then rolled it and held it to his chest as he reclined back in bed.

His mind tossed from Lily to Ariah to his father and home. His father's words and actions throbbing in his head. "Don't break that pottery again!" Selling thousands of pieces could not make up for those few broken dishes.

Levi could picture Papa's cold stare into the air, never looking at him, back turned to him just like Lily, walking away. He saw Ariah leaning over his desk, shouting at him. Caleb, smiling that derisive smirk.

"Caught!" Caleb called out. *"Caught,"* David whispered, through the half-opened door. *"Caught,"* Lily cried as she held her fertile womb. *"Caught,"* Ariah's booming voice implied. *"Caught,"* his father called from the grave.

"No!" Levi shouted, as he sat up from the fitful dream. He swung his feet to the floor and wiped his sweaty face and neck with a corner of his cloak. How could he go on? Why should he go on?

Then, a psalm Jairus used to quote, came into his head.

In you, O LORD, I have taken refuge;
  Let me never be put to shame.
Rescue and deliver me in your righteousness;
  Turn your ear to me and save me.
Be my rock of refuge, to which I can always go;
  give the command to save me,
  for you are my rock and fortress.

"No," he shouted. "I'm not worthy to approach the heavenly throne. I'm not worthy to approach anyone. What am I to do?"

The next day, Levi moved methodically through his work, faithfully executing his responsibilities to Ariah. He glared at Caleb only to receive that knowing smile. From that point on, Levi determined not to make eye contact with Caleb ever again.

For two weeks he would not see Lily, but he determined, one way or another, to see her again, so he studied Caleb's routine patterns: who he talked to, what time he had his lunch, how long, and when he quit working in the afternoons.

When Levi worked the caravans in the afternoon, he started where Caleb could see him, but each day he moved farther out of Caleb's sight, and then ended up within sight again.

As the two weeks wore on, he knew he had to face a decision about whether to go home or stay in Jericho.

Several scenarios played out in his head. Continued visits with Lily offered a constant threat to her, and to him for that matter, as Ariah so aptly pointed out, speaking of "a slit to the throat." And what about the baby? Then there was the tax issue. Eventually Ariah would find out that Zacchaeus planned to tax him dearly the next year, whether the new crops produced or not.

A caravan owner interrupted his thoughts. Levi explained to the traveler the many values of the salve. As another wagon was stopped by the publican, Levi watched the father and son unload their goods to be taxed. The two worked together in harmony, but then the son picked up a bag of the salve and accidently dropped it. The father patted his son's shoulder and helped him pick it up.

Why couldn't Levi have had that kind of relationship with *his* father?

In another caravan, though rare, the mother had come along on the trip. She tended to two younger boys. The older boy sat near his mother with his arm around her waist.

Warm memories flooded in as his heart ached to see his mother. He was reminded that the first-born son's duty is to care for his widowed mother. Since Ariah provided Levi's cottage at no cost, he had saved much of his pay and had accumulated a sizable amount. He could be of great help to James and Mama.

*****

By the end of the second week, Levi had made up his mind what he must do. He moved down the caravan line and on to see Lily. Did she still suffer pain? Had the salve worked? How would she take his news?

With the familiar sycamore in sight, his heart pounded. He noticed a couple of women across from the tree, dipping cloths into their vats of dye. One woman nudged the other and pointed her head at Levi. The other woman immediately stared in Levi's direction. The two of them leaned into each other to whisper.

"Nosey old women," he muttered to himself. He purposely ignored them as he passed by. Why had he not noticed them before?

As soon as he arrived at the tree, he glanced down the side street, but no Lily. He crossed over the main street to sit on the stone ledge, purposely placing himself next to an old tree trunk blocking his view of the women.

He practiced what he planned to say to Lily, scooted a few pebbles with his sandaled feet, gazed up at the sky through the tree branches, and watched for any sign of Lily. Nothing. Had she lost tract of the days? Was she delayed? Had *he* miscalculated the days? Was she ill?

He walked to their special spot and leaned against the tree where he always held her. The memory lingered, but he pushed it out of his mind. He had to do what he had to do. Best to go back to the rock ledge.

The empty street now in view, he fingered a fig leaf he had plucked from the tree. Where is she?

Finally, he squinted his eyes and caught a glimpse of someone. She resembled Lily, but the walk was different—slow, labored. When she drew nearer, he recognized her face, though her head was bent.

Finally, she was within reach. She raised her soulful eyes when he grasped her hands, her face drained of color. "Lily, are you not feeling well?"

"I lost my baby two days ago," she said, with a catch in her voice.

"Then, the salve worked!" Levi said with enthusiasm.

She looked up at him in disbelief and turned away.

He frowned. Wasn't that the goal? Why is she so sad?

"Lily, are you in pain?"

She looked out over the field beyond their tree. "It was bloody, a small mass. But it was my baby." Her voice sounded devoid of emotion, but obviously she had been devastated by this experience. She reached for him. "I'm weak. So weak."

Levi grabbed her arm, hardly knowing what to do. "Lily, sit here." He helped her to the stone ledge. "Did you have anyone to help you?"

"Yes, Sarah stayed by my side. She realized what I was going through with my questions and behavior and all. I don't know what I would have done without her." Lily looked at Levi. "Now she knows about us."

Levi stared at his lap. What could he say?

"Lily, my father died."

"Your father?"

"Yes, and as you know, the first-born son is expected to care for his widowed mother. Lily, I feel I have greatly interfered in your life. I have put you in danger with your father and caused you to deal with constant secrecy and now, the pain of losing a baby. Though it breaks my heart, I think it is best for both of us if I go back to Capernaum."

"Levi, you have not interfered. You have been the greatest joy in my life."

"Oh, Lily, I love you too." He stood and paced back and forth rubbing his hand across the back of his neck. "This so hard." Lily could only respond with questioning eyes. Levi sat beside her again. "Lily, I feel I must do this, for you, for me, for my family." He took her hand. "I know this comes at a terrible time for you, but I fear for you. You see, the man who oversees the balsam trade sales is mean and underhanded. In his devious ways, he found out about us and even knows that you are the daughter of Zacchaeus."

Lily gasped.

"Now the man who owns the business has declared that I am never to see you again. He fears what your father would do to his business if he found out about us. When the letter came from my brother about my father's death, it seemed that leaving Jericho was the thing I had to do. Lily, I hope someday I can come back and take you far away where neither your father nor any of his men could ever find us, but for now, this is all I know to do."

Lily thought for a moment. "Whatever you think is best," she said, with tired eyes. "I must get back now."

"I wish I could help you, you're so weak."

"I'll be all right," she said, standing with effort.

He started to lead her in the direction of their special tree for one last embrace, but she said, "I must go."

Slowly, with slight limp and slumped shoulders, she managed the walk, the last walk, back toward her house. She didn't look back.

Tears filled his eyes as he watched with aching heart. He sunk to the ledge, elbows on knees, clasping his hands, fingering the fold of his tunic.

How could he let her go? Should he run to her, scoop her up in his arms, and escape with her? Why did he ever come here in the first place? It was not his place to talk to Zacchaeus. If he had talked to Ariah about it, he would have told him no. Then he would never have met Lily. He would not be sitting here mourning this terrible loss.

Levi glanced down her street. She was almost to the opening and would soon be out of sight—forever. *Lily, Lily, how I love you. You taught me the tenderness of a caress, the gentleness of a kiss, the passion of making love to you. You loved me for who I am, without criticism, with total acceptance, and now you are gone.* More tears flooded his eyes as he buried his face in his hands.

At last, he stood as if in a bad dream and walked back to the trading area. Would Caleb know he had been gone? It did not matter; he would be leaving soon. It did not matter. Nothing mattered.

*****

Early the next morning, Levi's work lay spread across his desk when Ariah approached the office. "You're up bright and early," said Ariah, poking his head in the door.

"Yes sir, much to do."

Ariah gave a slight chuckle as he strolled on passed the door.

Levi worked steadily all morning, detailing a report that covered the year he had been there, showing the income before he came and the monthly growth since he had started work. The gradual increase was obvious.

Regrettably, the purchase of the new fields and workers did negate much of the increase, but in his mind, it showed progress and future growth. He hoped Ariah would be pleased.

Shortly before lunch, Levi walked to Ariah's office. When he knocked at the open door, Ariah invited him in.

Levi handed Ariah the long list of numbers and summaries. "This will show you the income and expenditures for the year. Everything is up to date."

Ariah glanced at the figures, but before he could begin to take it all in, Levi asked if this would be a good time to talk about some important matters.

"What is it, Levi?"

Levi sat on a stool across from Ariah. "Do you remember that you handed me a letter two weeks ago?"

"Yes."

"It was from my brother. He informed me that my father died.''

"I'm sorry, Levi."

"My mother and brother are having trouble managing. I feel I must go home to take care of my family. And besides, I must not see the young lady again."

Ariah leaned back. "Well, of course. How long do you think you will be gone?"

"Uh, this is a permanent arrangement, sir. I plan to leave tomorrow."

"Tomorrow?" He leaned forward. "Permanent you say? Are you sure you have thought this through?"

"Yes. I have decided that this is the best decision."

"I see." Ariah looked down at the numbers. "You have done good work for me. I have wrestled with these figures before; I guess can do it again, but not as well as you."

"Thank you. And thank you for giving me this opportunity." Levi stood.

"Wait." Ariah went to a crate of jars and pulled out a money bag, handing Levi several coins. "For your journey back home."

"That is very kind of you." He accepted the coins and left.

Chapter 22

Going Home

Levi gathered his bag of clothes. He came with few items and was leaving with few. He bid shalom to David as he passed the garden but opted not to see Ariah again.

With delight, he cocked his head at Caleb and stared directly at him. He gave Caleb a sly smile and marched on by. *Good riddance!* he wanted to shout but found consolation in that he would never have to deal with Caleb again.

He continued past the caravans and saw Bartimaeus sitting at the gate. Digging into his money pouch, he pulled out a coin and dropped it in his cup.

"You're here early, Master Levi."

"Yes, Bartimaeus. I'm on my way home."

"Home?"

"Back to Capernaum."

"But what of the young woman?"

"Some things have to end, Bartimaeus."

"I will miss you. No one talks to me like a real person the way you do."

Levi knelt beside him and touched his arm. "Good-bye, my friend."

Bartimaeus clasped his hand over Levi's hand. "God's peace with you."

With the genuine warmth of that touch, Levi set out on his journey home. The all-day walk provided more than enough time to think back over his months in Jericho. Memorable moments flooded his mind—pleasant and not so pleasant. He fought most to release thoughts of Lily. He tried to see her happy smile greeting him at each visit, but only her tired, sad face appeared in his mind.

The second day and third day dragged on, but the closer he came to home, the more he welcomed the thought of seeing

James, Mama, friends and neighbors. He touched his money bag from time to time to be sure the coins were there.

What would they think when they saw him? Surprise? Excitement? Or would they be angry with him for leaving without telling them good-bye?

At last he reached the sea. Ah, the smell of the water, the fish, the wind. He closed his eyes and breathed it in. *Home. I'll soon be home.*

If he rode partway in a boat with some fishermen, it would cut off half a day. But could he bear the thought of being on the water? How could he live by the sea his whole life and be so fearful of it?

Then he remembered the time when he was eight years old. *I thought I was so big, old enough to walk into the water. It felt refreshing on that hot day and I loved the way it flowed when I ran my arms through the water, getting deeper and deeper. But then, with that one more step, the bottom dropped out. Oh, the frantic feeling when I flailed my arms and legs about until my feet finally touched bottom again.*

Levi shook his head to get rid of the memory. When he looked up, two fishermen sat mending their nets after a night's catch, but two others looked like they were preparing a boat for sailing. "Where are you headed?" he called to them.

"Capernaum," they shouted back.

The sun shone across the water, beckoning him. The wind blew with gentle breezes—no sign of storms. He could be home by afternoon.

"Mind if I ride along with you?"

"If you're ready to leave now."

"I'm ready." And he gave them four ases for the ride.

Levi steadied himself in the deepest part of the boat and tried to persuade himself that he must overcome this fear. If he looked at the sky or the mountains—anything but the water—then maybe he could make the journey.

His stomach began churning; he felt light-headed. *Think of something. Concentrate on home, Mama, James, the house.* He purposely took deep breaths and focused on calming himself. He held on to his desire to see Mama as he held on to the side of the boat.

But what about James? Would James be angry with him? He may have resented being left with the business and having to deal with Papa by himself. How did James know where he was in Jericho? Maybe word got back to him through the traders. Probably Meleke told him. Then there was the matter of Papa's mysterious death.

At last, Levi looked out to see the shore, *his* shore. Familiar homes and shops came into view. With mounting excitement, Levi sat up straighter, craning his neck this way and that around the fisherman, as he strained to find his own house. He thought he could see James walking in front of the house. His heart beat fast with excitement, completely forgetting about the water and the boat.

They landed close to the city. The familiar aroma of fresh fruits and vegetables, onions cooking, and bread baking in and around the marketplace overpowered the fishy smell of the sea.

He closed his eyes and sniffed the air as though sampling a rare perfume. "Ah, home," he said out loud.

He hurried along the familiar path toward his house, a path he had traveled many times, carting loads of pottery. He smiled as he remembered the day Papa went with him and how amazed Papa was with Levi's selling skills, at least one happy memory of him.

His pace slowed as he drew near the house. His memory turned to childhood days when he carried a lap full of stones to the house for counting.

Just then his mother came out the door, sweeping the last of the house dust. She glanced in Levi's direction, cocked her head, and squinted her eyes. Her mouth opened in surprise.

"Levi," she mouthed. Her broom fell to the ground. "Levi," she called, as she walked in his direction. He hurried to meet her outstretched arms. "Levi!" she cried.

"Mama." They held each other in a tight embrace. He felt her shake with sobs of joy.

She reached her hands up to hold his face. "I missed you so much, Son."

"I missed you too, Mama. I'm sorry I left without saying good-bye. I knew how hard it would be to leave you, but I, uh, I had an opportunity and felt like I had to leave."

"It's just so good to see you. I can hardly believe you are here." She hugged him again. "You must be hungry. I was fixing some chicken soup."

"Sounds wonderful, Mama."

Arm in arm, they walked back to the house. The house felt larger to Levi after being used to his tiny cottage. A faint tinge of myrrh mixed in with the familiar smell of fresh bread.

"Mmm, smells good," he said, taking in a deep breath. Mama busied herself with the soup.

"Do I also smell the myrrh I traded last year?"

His mother's countenance fell. "Yes," she said softly. "We had it out to use…" Her voice quivered. "To use for the burial." She stopped stirring; a tear slipped down her cheek as she stared at the pot of soup. She wiped the tear with the back of her hand.

Immediately, Levi laid his bag down and went to her side. "I'm sorry, Mama." Once more, they embraced. Her audible sobs broke Levi's heart. "I'm so sorry I wasn't here to be with you." He held her until she was able to breathe steadily again. "James wrote to tell me about Papa."

She looked up at him with tear-stained eyes. "He did?"

"Yes."

"How did he know where you were?"

"I guess he heard from one of the traders."

"Where have you been all these months?"

145

"In Jericho, Mama. I had learned of a job opportunity there and felt it was time to seek new roads in my life."

Mama looked down and went back to stirring her pot of soup. "Running away from your father?"

She knew him well. "Yes. That was part of the reason." He pulled extra tunics out of his bag and put them away.

"The soup is ready," she called.

He had not had anything as good as his mother's soup in a long time. How familiar to be eating out of his father's pottery once again. He had to keep reminding himself that Papa was not there. No need to fear Papa coming in with his demeaning attitude, demanding to know where Levi had been, why he left, and why he was back home.

While his absence brought relief, the mystery of the "difficult circumstances" brought anxiety. What could it mean?

"I remember toting many of these bowls to the market," Levi said.

"Yes, and all your arrangements," she smiled. Her smile quickly turned into a melancholy stare at the table.

"Has James continued to make the pottery?"

"Yes, he does his best." Her wistful tone left many unanswered questions.

"Perhaps I need to be the peddler again while he is the potter," Levi offered, trying to lighten the conversation.

"Perhaps," she said, with a faint smile, not looking up from the table. She sipped slowly from her bowl as though in another place.

Was this the time to bring up the circumstances of Papa's death? She seemed so fragile. "Has James had his meal?"

"No, but he will be in soon."

Levi tore off a piece of bread. "I don't know how long it took for James' letter to reach me. He mentioned Papa's passing."

"It was well over three months ago," Mama shot back. Her quick response rather took Levi back. She quickly picked up her bowl and took it to the water basin, her back to Levi.

"I'm sorry I wasn't here to be with you, Mama."

"I had James," she muttered softly. After washing and drying her bowl, she clutched the towel, her head bent.

Levi did not think it best to address the circumstances with her at this moment. It seemed that fresh wounds were re-opened, and he did not want her to go through it again.

She went to her broom and began sweeping. She used to do that frequently when the floor was already clean, but she needed to release frustration with Alphaeus.

Levi thought it best to go outside and have a talk with James.

"I'm going to see James," he told her.

"Okay," she said, without looking up.

Maybe James will tell me about these "difficult circumstances." Mama certainly cannot manage it.

He passed the quiet, empty shed that was once his father's. Something dark and foreboding seem to hover around it. He hastened on to the new shed they had built for James. In the dim light, James was spinning away. Once James stopped the wheel and set the piece over on the shelf, Levi knocked and called out his name.

James emerged from the shed a taller man with more mature features in his face. "Brother," James said, with straightforward sincerity. James embraced Levi with the same tight grip as his mother had and with shaking sobs that seemed to come from deep within his soul.

Even with the smell of damp clay on this brother, this was a sacred moment, and Levi welcomed it. "I'm sorry," he whispered in James' ear. "I'm sorry for everything."

When they finally released, James' face was streaked with tears and mud. He started to wipe his face with the back of his hand, then his tunic but everything was smeared with the morning clay. Levi offered the tail of his cloak. James smiled slightly. "I'm a mess."

"You were always a mess," Levi poked him in the side.

James grinned. "Come over here. I made a stone bench." James led him to a stone bench on the other side of the shed where they sat together.

"James, I'm sorry I left the way I did. I had more than I could take from Papa. One of the traders said he had talked to a businessman in Jericho about me, and the businessman was interested in hiring me. It seemed like a good idea. Still, I should have at least talked to you about it rather than just leaving a note."

"Was it?"

"What?"

"Was it a good idea?"

"Hmm." Levi pondered a moment. "Yes, I believe it was. I experienced many new things. We will have plenty of time to talk about all that."

"You will be staying for a while?"

Levi looked him in the eyes, "I'm here to stay, James." James heaved a sigh of relief. Levi went on. "In your letter, you mentioned difficult circumstances surrounding Papa's death."

James leaned over, elbows on knees, running his fingers through his hair, much like Levi always did. "It was a nightmare, Levi." He heaved another sigh and stared at the ground, searching for words and the strength to say them.

"One evening, the tax collector came around. You know how Papa always acted with that man. They were outside yelling and arguing. The tax man was trying to charge Papa more tax than he had paid last year. Papa kept trying to tell him that we had not made as much money this year with you gone, but the man refused to accept his "excuses" and demanded payment by the next week. When the tax collector left, Papa came in the house still cursing and fuming about it. I told him I had saved out some tax money just like you did the year before, but nothing satisfied him."

James sat up, gazed at the sky, and heaved another big sigh. "We went on to bed. I did not hear anything else. The next morning, we heard that the tax collector had been stabbed to death and left out on the street all night between here and town.

"That afternoon, two Roman soldiers came to Papa's shed, grabbed him up, and took him away. Of course, Papa was yelling and questioning them all along the way. We didn't know what was going on or where they were taking him. I followed at a short distance, then one of the soldiers shouted at me to go back home. I turned but looked back every now and then, but finally they were out of sight.

"What else could I do?" James said, as though talking to himself. "Who am I against two Roman soldiers with swords?"

Levi waited patiently, giving James time to finish his account as he was able. It was obvious why James struggled to tell what would inevitably grow worse. Levi also hung his head, staring at the ground alongside the brother who endured all this by himself. A wave of further regret swept over Levi as he pictured James walking home that afternoon, alone.

James could speak no more for a few moments. He rubbed the back of his neck and blew out air. He grasped his knees, looked to the side away from Levi and blew out air again, trying to get control of his emotions.

"Papa was gone all night. The next morning, one of my friends came running to the shed, looking white as a sheet. He told me to come quickly. All he said was, 'It's your father.' I dropped everything and ran after him. I yelled back at Mama to stay in the house." James' voice broke, his face grimaced as he looked up to the sky. All the pain and pent-up memories came pouring out in uncontrollable sobs.

Levi put one arm around his brother's shaking shoulders and a hand on his arm, tears streaming down his own face. Oh, that he could take this pain for him.

After a long spell of sobs and heaving, James gave one deep sigh. Totally depleted, he sat up and continued with a dead-like stare at the sea and a steady, unemotional voice. "Those bastard soldiers had stabbed and whipped Papa until he was hardly recognizable except for the potter clothes he wore. They hung him over the branch of that big olive tree just outside of town for all to see. My friend helped me take his body down. Someone had brought a sheet for us to lay him in. I wrapped him and carried him to that little cave up behind the house that we used to play in. I went to the well to get water and wash the blood off me before I came to see Mama. I did not tell her about the beating and stabbing or that they hung him over the tree branch. I just told her that the soldiers had killed Papa and that I had taken his body to the cave."

James looked at Levi for the first time. "Mama cried some, but I don't think she was surprised. She wanted me to get some of that myrrh you traded a while back." Levi nodded his head.

James turned back to the sea. "I washed Papa's body, tucked a fresh tunic around him, and put the myrrh over him. I found a large stone that covered most of the opening. Jairus came that afternoon to recite verses of Scripture at the tomb, and a few friends gathered to support Mama. I think many were afraid to come near for fear of the Romans."

Emotionally spent, James stopped. They sat in silence for a time as Levi thought about this younger brother and all he had faced, alone. He had truly matured and certainly needed support at this challenging time.

Finally, Levi spoke. "James, I regret that I wasn't here to help and that you had to endure all this heartache by yourself. You have proven yourself to be a caring son and a remarkable man. I pray that together we can pick up the pieces and start anew."

"That will be harder than you think, Levi. The people of the town have been shaken by these two deaths, the tax collector and now Papa. They fear the Romans even more, which is exactly what the soldiers intended. The townspeople have been reluctant about buying from us."

Levi thought a moment and finally voiced what neither had said out loud. "Do you think Papa killed the tax collector?"

"I," he paused, "I don't know, but the Romans certainly thought so."

Chapter 23

Trying to Recover

Levi felt sure he could use his selling skills once more and get the family back on their feet, but as he pushed the cart of pottery into town, he decided to first stop and visit his old-time mentor, Jairus.

The walk to Jairus' house gave Levi time to reflect, not only about the situation with his father, but also his own life. He saw the house in the distance, just outside of the city. Jairus had the luxury of a small yard with grass and a lovely olive tree.

Jairus sat on the portico of his house with a young girl. Could that be his little daughter? Everybody seemed to have aged in this past year. Prisca, as he called her, strained to recognize him coming down the path. When she finally did, she waved enthusiastically in her typical, happy way. She ran to give him a hug, and he leaned over to willingly accept it.

"Where have you been?" she asked. "I haven't seen you in a long, long time."

He looked up at Jairus who stood and smiled at them. "I've been working in a city called Jericho," he told Prisca.

They walked to the portico where Jairus persuaded her that he and Levi needed some time to talk. She reluctantly went in the house.

"She's turning into a lovely young lady," Levi commented.

"Yes, she's been the joy of my life these past eleven years."

Levi sat on the bench next to Jairus. "I want to thank you for being with my family at the funeral. It has been a trying time. I regret I wasn't here to help them."

"They have had much heartache and little support. The Romans not only repress us individually, but they also thrive on turning us against each other in fear." He observed Levi a moment. "And you, you also have turned into a grown man. Tell me more of this Jericho stay."

152

"I had opportunity to work for a man in the balsam trade. His workers produce and sell the balm from the balsam plant, a salve that has many healing properties."

"Ah," as the prophet Jeremiah said, 'Go up to Gilead and get balm.' And your part in the business?"

"First, I did the selling, but later I kept the records of products sold, business expenses, wages, and so forth."

"Hmm. Sounds impressive. And you had opportunity for study and worship at our Holy Temple?"

Levi squirmed a bit. "Well, I kept so busy with the business, I had little time for any further study in the ancient Scriptures. I went to the synagogue in Jericho. However, it seemed that the rabbis and teachers of the law who came on Sabbath placed so many heavy burdens on the people that even the best worshipper would have trouble keeping up with all their rules."

Jairus nodded his head. "Indeed, the Pharisees who come here are particularly burdensome. They forget that they are talking to poor, hard-working people."

They talked on about the leaders in the Capernaum synagogue, the people, the Romans, and touched on the holy Scriptures, but nothing said about Alphaeus and his possible connection to the tax collector's murder.

As they parted, Jairus did comment on the relationship of the people with the pottery business. "Levi, you may find things strained in your family business. The people are very wary about buying James' pottery since the Romans killed your father. It isn't your fault, but be aware."

"Thank you. So good to be with you again and to see your little Prisca. Shalom."

*****

As Levi strolled on to Capernaum, he considered Jairus' question about the Temple. No, he had not been there, and only a few times to the synagogue in Jericho. In fact, he had given little thought to things of the Lord. All his attention—his worship—had focused on Lily. The very thought of her filled him with longing, love, and regret all at the same time. One minute he wanted to be with her; another, he wished he had never met her. Then, there were the issues with Zacchaeus. That was the start of his downward spiral.

The marketplace came into view. Now, on to fixing the family income. He felt sure, with his expert selling skills, that he could build the business back up.

The place he used to set up was taken by a woman with her array of vegetables. He started for another empty spot, but the man next to it said that the olive oil vendor always set up there. No one made eye contact with Levi and others barely acknowledged him when he addressed them.

Some people stared at him as though they thought he was familiar but were not quite sure. *Guess I have changed too.*

He finally found a spot where he could set up the pottery. The seller beside him looked at Levi with a suspicious side glance. Levi attempted to make conversation with him, but the man grumbled only an answer or two.

Two women started his way. One whispered to the other who turned and looked at Levi. Quickly, they scurried in another direction. Others seemed to noticeably skirt around Levi's booth.

One woman slowly approached his display, examined the pottery, then looked directly into Levi's eyes. She had attractive features and smiled at him. "You have lovely pottery," she said, in a rather beguiling way. "I would like to purchase these two bowls. How much are they?" She seemed more interested in Levi than the bowls.

He did not remember seeing her before. "Uh, that will be eight ases," he said, almost forgetting what he used to charge. She continued looking at his face and hair with a most alluring expression as he accepted her coins and wrapped the bowls. He felt a slight flush filling his face. "I hope you enjoy these," he said as he handed her the bowls.

"I'm sure I will." And she smiled once more. He watched her walk away, spellbound.

Other than *her* purchase, he had no others the rest of the morning. People seemed to be avoiding him, especially those he knew well. He would see three or four clustered together talking and one would glance his way and immediately turn back to the group.

He had not committed murder. *He* had not suffered the shame of Roman discipline, yet he now had to bear it as much as his father. Even from the grave, Alphaeus' wrath affected Levi. Frustrated, he packed up the pottery and headed back home.

When James saw that Levi had returned with a full cart, he shook his head. "They wouldn't come to your pottery stand, would they?"

"No. You were right. They didn't even give me an opportunity to sell anything."

"I don't know why I bother to keep spinning the wheel." James sighed.

"I have money that I saved from the business in Jericho. That will help us for a while. I may try the caravan business again. I used to do well with the traders who came through, and I have learned many new words in their languages from my work in Jericho. They wouldn't know about the things going on here locally."

The next morning, Levi pushed the cart down to the trade route. He had gotten used to a steady stream of caravans in Jericho where three major trade routes converged, but not so here.

When he returned, James peered in the cart. "You sold some pieces!" he said, with excitement.

"A few, but not what I expected. Traffic was slow today." It was no better the next day or the next.

His mother greeted him each day when he came in. "I see you sold a few more," she said, with excitement in her voice.

"A few," Levi conceded with no enthusiasm.

On the fourth day, traffic picked up. "I sold a large set of dishes, bowls, and cups," he announced. James and his mama cheered him on. The next week proved to be no more profitable than the first week. James had used almost all the money he had, so they had to dip into Levi's savings.

One morning, Levi went into town to buy a few items Myrah needed. While he purchased vegetables, a young woman approached him—the one who had bought two bowls a few days earlier.

"I like the bowls I bought from you. Do you have two plates I could buy?"

"Uh, well, uh, yes." he blubbered. "But I don't have any with me. I could bring them to you. Where do you live?"

"I live down this main street," she motioned with her hand, "then you turn right at the second street. I'm in the last house."

"Right at the second street, last house," he repeated. She nodded with the same captivating smile. "I'll be there in the early afternoon."

"I'll be ready," she said, gazing deep into his eyes as before. Long dark curls hung loose beneath her head piece. Her garment flowed smoothly over her trim body, swaying gently as she walked.

He stood paralyzed for a moment, but finally made his body turn and walk away. "This afternoon, two plates," he mumbled, trying to remember the order.

Levi meandered through the marketplace clutching the vegetables in a daze. An onion slipped out and fell to the ground. Picking it up, he remembered that James wanted a round piece of leather to put on the top of his stool since the old covering had worn down to the wood. Levi stopped by the tanner shop to see Samuel.

Two men were just about to leave. One man looked at the other and nodded toward Levi. They left without acknowledging him. Samuel noticed the exchange. "Hello Levi, I heard you were back. I'm sorry you had to come back to such difficult circumstances."

"You're about the first one who's not afraid to speak to me."

"We haven't had anything like this before." He picked up a piece of leather and shook his head. "So many rumors. The people don't know what to make of it." He brushed a few stray fragments into a container. "What can I do for you?"

"James needs a piece of leather to cover his potter stool."

"How about this one?" He held out a circular cut of leather.

"That looks about right." As Levi paid, he added, "Do you remember that sling you made for me years ago? I still have it."

He smiled. "One never knows when he might have to face a Goliath."

"Thanks for the leather, Samuel."

A Goliath indeed, Levi thought as he walked home. *Thanks be to God for Samuel and Jairus, the only people who will speak to me. Oh, and the lady.* The thoughts of her brought on all kinds of thoughts and emotions he still did not know how to handle. *Two plates, early afternoon.*

Levi hurried to make his deliveries to James and his mother. He quickly pushed the cart to the trade route and had a bit more enthusiasm selling the pottery to the caravan tradesmen. The morning proved profitable. He ate the lunch he had packed and pushed his cart under a tree out of the way. After he wrapped two plates, he rushed back to town for his *delivery*.

Down the main street, second street, turn right, last house. With his fast pace, he had worked up quite a sweat. He paused, reached for the tail of his cloak to wipe his face and took a deep breath. His heart was pounding not from the hasty walk but the lure of this adventure.

He knocked at the door. She opened it wide and flashed a smile. With her headpiece off, thick black curls cascaded over her shoulders. A touch of color applied to her cheeks and lips highlighted her beautiful face.

"Come in," she spoke with a rich, still alluring tone.

For a moment, Levi stood as in a trance, unsure if he should enter this place.

She strolled on toward the table. "Perhaps you would like some grapes and a sip of wine on this warm day?"

Levi followed her on in. After all, he was quite thirsty after his brisk walk. Her house felt welcoming, clean and tastefully decorated, a double bed in one corner, a kitchen and small table with grapes and two flasks for wine. He suddenly remembered the plates. "I have the plates for you."

"Yes, of course. How much did you say?"

"Uh, twelve ases."

She motioned for him to sit on a stool. He nibbled on the grapes, trying to keep his focus. Without her head piece that had draped over the arms, her arms were now bare and graceful as she poured the wine.

"You live here alone?" he asked, wondering how she could afford this place.

"Yes, just me. My parents died two years ago. This is what I have left," she motioned around the room.

Figuring that he had probed enough, he offered to share about his family. "My father died recently, but I have my mother and brother. He's the one who makes the pottery, following after my father."

"You are not a potter?"

"Oh, no," he chuckled. "I tried it a few times, but it was a disaster."

She smiled with her alluring eyes. "Tell me about it."

"Not much to tell. I soon learned that working with the clay was not my talent."

"And what *is* your talent?"

"Selling. That is my gift. And working with numbers. I did very well with the trade, then went to Jericho and did even better."

"How exciting. I have never been outside of Capernaum. Why did you come back?"

He took a few more grapes and sipped more wine, trying to think how much to tell her. Apparently, she had not heard about the *death* or at least had not connected Levi to the situation.

"My father's death."

"Oh."

He decided that was as much as he wanted to say, so he stood to leave. "I must be going. Thank you for the grapes and wine."

"Yes, well let me get the coins." She pulled down a jar and counted out the coins. "I have the bowls and the plates; I guess I should have cups to go with them. Will you be at your booth again this week?"

"Uh, no, I'm not selling in the marketplace now, mostly on the trade route." He hesitated. "But I can bring them by next week. How about the first day of the week?"

"That would be fine, and if you come in the evening, I'll plan to make you a fine meal to eat on those plates."

"Just before sundown," he said. "Two cups?"

"Two cups."

"You know, it occurred to me that I don't even know your name."

"I'm Susanna. My name means Lily."

He froze. "Lily," he whispered under his breath. How could this be?

"And you are?"

"What?"

159

"Your name."

"Levi." He did not want to tell her that it meant *someone pledged for a debt* and certainly not a *wild cow*. "Well, I will see you next week."

He felt a bit clumsy as he staggered away, whether because of the wine or the renewed thoughts of Lily or perhaps Susanna herself. She was the most positive thing that had happened to him since he had returned. He looked around though, to be sure no one had noticed him going into the house of a single lady. Her inherited house was one thing, but how did she live? No garden for food, and how could she afford to buy pottery?

Chapter 24

An Unexpected Opportunity

Levi sat on the edge of the road after another draining day in the sun with very few coins in his bag. He noticed the new customs tax collector on the trade route, a temporary replacement for the man who left the previous week. The thought crossed his mind that the new man certainly must have had more to show for his day than Levi did. He dreaded hearing the complaints from James that Levi was not selling enough.

Sure enough, as he trudged home, James came out the door, ready to pounce on him. James glanced inside the cart.

"I'm doing all I can, James. The travelers are fewer this time of the year and the ones who come are just not buying." His voice grew louder. "Don't forget, we're living off the money *I* saved. I would try to sell at the marketplace, but you know how it is in town. Well, no you don't know; you never go into town to see all the rejection. It's as if *we* are the murderers being tortured."

About that time Levi saw his mother standing at the door. Her face looked tired and weary. She turned and went back inside. His harsh words must have cut deep in her soul. He looked at James and let out a loud, exhausted sigh. "I'm sorry, James. I'm doing all I can."

The only bright spot for Levi was what had become a once-a-week visit to see Susanna. James began asking questions about where he had been when he came in late on those evenings. Levi tried to put him off as he was not ready to tell James about her.

One afternoon, two Roman officials approached Levi while he was peddling his pottery. At first, he thought they might be coming to tell him he was intruding on the collection of trade route taxes, but they were acting too congenial for that.

"Are you Levi, son of Alphaeus?"

161

"Yes," Levi said, with a half question in his voice.

"As you may know, the trade route tax collector moved to Jericho last week. We are in search of a new man to take his place. We have been in touch with the chief tax collector in Jericho, who gave you high recommendations."

"Zacchaeus?"

"Yes, I see you know him. He says you are exceptionally good with numbers and record keeping. We have observed that you have a way with the traders and even know how to speak some of their languages. We have been given authority to offer this position to you." Then tipping his head down, he rolled his eyes up at Levi. "It can be quite lucrative, you know."

Levi stood there stunned. *A tax collector? What Jew in his right mind would lower himself to such standards?* The family had pretty much hit the bottom of their income, but a tax collector? A publican?

"May I have time to consider this?"

"We'll be back tomorrow. Have your answer then." And off they went.

Levi watched as they walked away, overwhelmed by the offer. He could never have imagined such a thing. He turned and rolled his cart along the shore and found himself at his "thinking rock." It looked smaller than he had remembered.

He sat down and bent over to pick up a few stones much as he had as a child. Memories of counting, sorting, and adding flooded his mind. *Was all that to lead me to this moment?* His father would be cursing him from the grave to even entertain such an idea.

Did these men not know what my father was accused of doing? Did they not know that my father was killed and hung over a tree branch by the Romans? Perhaps not. They did not have a "Galilean" accent.

What would his mother and brother say? At least he would not be in the position of collecting taxes from his own people.

162

This would entail collecting port duties and taxes from the travelers on the trade route. He knew many of them and could communicate in their language. It seemed like a good fit.

Still, what would the people of Capernaum say? Hmm, it didn't really matter anymore. They had already marked him for disrespect. Could it be any worse? Besides, his family was becoming the poorest of the poor. In this new position, he could finally take care of the mother he loved, but at what price?

Did he dare desecrate the memory of his father by walking into the company of those his father so despised? On the other hand, what did he care about his father's memory? His own memory of his father was so tarnished with bitterness, fear, and anxiety. Must Alphaeus continue to control him even from the grave? It wasn't Levi's fault that his hate-filled father struck a Roman tax collector.

He dropped the stones and held his head. What to do? Finally, Levi decided he had to talk to James.

*****

James was livid. He jumped up from the stone bench where they sat and clapped both hands over his ears as if to shut out this nonsense. "I cannot hear this. I cannot believe you would even consider such a thing!" He paced about, huffing and puffing. Finally, he stopped beside Levi and cast a sideways snarl down at Levi as he threw out the words. "You, the righteous one, the learned one, Jairus' pet student of the law; you would degrade yourself with the filth of the Romans." He let out another loud huff and turned away to spit on the ground.

Levi was stunned. James paced again. "You think you're so smart with numbers and we're not good enough for you, so you go off to another city and have a big high-paying job. Then you come back here thinking you can get everything going again. Well you saw what we had been living with. Shame! Now you want to bring more shame on us!"

James' voice began to crack, his back turned, but Levi felt the heartbreak. Levi had no idea that James had been living with jealousy and hostility against him all these years.

In his deliberation, Levi had managed to push down the gut feeling that this offer went against every grain in his Jewish upbringing. He knew the disgust God had for the children of Israel who fell at the feet of foreign idols, but he rationalized that he was not agreeing with the Romans, just collecting their money and the money of those who, for the most part, were not Jews.

Levi waited for a few moments until James calmed down. "Come, sit with me, brother, we have much to talk about."

James took a deep breath and reluctantly returned to the bench.

Levi began in a quiet, caring tone. "James, I'm sorry you have been living so long with these feelings. I never intended to lord it over you or act as though I were greater or better than you. I envied you for the ways Papa treated you better than he did me. We all have our gifts. Making pottery is definitely not one of mine."

James smiled a bit.

"I ran off to Jericho, not because I thought I was better than anyone else, but because I could no longer stand Papa's anger. It ate away at me every day. It paralyzed me. I needed to find my own way." Levi paused. He picked up a small pebble, rolled it around with his fingers, then tossed it aside.

"Strange, isn't it? You thought I felt high and mighty, but to tell the truth, I was struggling to find worth. How you managed to continue living with Papa and under such close conditions in the shed, I will never know. You had to do double duty, selling and molding the clay. I regret that I left all that to you." Levi turned his head and looked up to the sky with a sigh. "I was selfish."

164

He continued. "You made valid points about associating with the Romans in this way. It is something I'm struggling with. But, James, I look at our situation. We are down to our last bit of money, and there is hardly any food in the house. The people have closed us out even though we did nothing wrong. Papa's anger still enslaves us. If we are not careful, we will become just like him. At least the job does not require me to take money from our own people, only the travelers on the route."

"Then you are going to accept this offer?"

"I see no other way, James. Perhaps, after I make enough money, we can move elsewhere and start all over."

Chapter 25

Life as Tax Collector

Before he could think any further, Levi found himself sitting in a booth as a tax collector. He paused from totaling a column of figures to gaze out at the sea. He had been a student of the law, then a peddler, a would-be potter, a businessman of Jericho, and now a despised tax collector. How did all this happen in his twenty years?

Out of the corner of his eye, he could see another caravan approaching. Thankfully, the owners did not appear to be tradesmen he recognized. It was always harder to deal with men he had come to know as friends. When he went through their pack of belongings to tax them, he could see the accusation of *traitor* written on their puzzled, frowning faces.

A tax man had to pay Rome a basic price, and everything above that would be his. The previous tax collector used to go through every single pack and find additional things to tax, even letters and other papers. *Now I realize why the people hate tax collectors so much.* Levi determined to tax only the bulk of goods. This practice proved to bring in an adequate salary, enough to generously provide for James, his mother, and himself.

The days went on in one monotonous groan as Levi removed bundles and bags and goods for inspection, dealt with begruntled tradesmen, collected their taxes, weighed their coins, and recorded the transactions. *At least it's an income.* He sighed as he waited for the next caravan.

James complained less and less now that they had plenty to eat and money left over. He talked to Levi about adding on another room to the house, "a room to give Mama more privacy," he said.

Levi agreed. Besides, the project would be good for James since he did not have much to keep himself occupied these days.

James shuffled in each evening moaning and groaning. "Now I know how the slaves in Egypt felt lugging stones from one place to another. Even pushing that heavy cart is exhausting. It must be nice to just sit at a table all day."

"I do have to lift heavy bundles and bags off the wagons to be sure I have counted everything, you know."

"Oh, those servants do all the work!" James chided as he splashed water on his sweaty face, then he playfully splashed a few sprinkles at his brother.

With James' flair for design and his eye for balance, he arranged the stones and filled them in with ease. Levi delighted in being able to praise James' work.

Another day, Levi came home and found several things moved out of the house. James had been knocking a hole in the wall to create a doorway into the new room. Mama stood outside with her broom shaking her head.

Levi peeked in the house. "What is *this*?"

James stood up, dust all over his face. "A fine work in progress."

"Looks like a mess to me."

Stone chunks and crumbles lay covered with dust all over the floor. "You *could* help me clear all this out so we can sleep tonight."

Levi wondered what James would come up with next to occupy himself, but for several more days he worked on smoothing out the inside walls.

Meanwhile, Levi sat day by day at his table, counting coins, recording totals, and baking in the hot sun as he dealt with traders of all sorts, some with sweet smelling spices, some with colorful rugs, others with arts and crafts from their native countries.

At times three or four were lined up back to back, leaving those toward the back very disgruntled. Other times one came from the east and one from the west, arriving at the same time and each expecting to be served first.

Most aggravating were the ones who paid their tax, then left their wagons in the way while they went into town to buy supplies. Levi had to get the next caravan to move around.

At times, the local fishermen caused congestion as well. Each morning when they brought in the night's catch, they had tables set up with tubs of water filled with squirming fish. Traders could buy fresh fish to cook later in the day. Levi had to constantly remind them to move on rather than leaving their wagons in the way.

Usually, by mid-afternoon, he had less traffic and more time to catch up on his figures.

The hardest part came when the townspeople passed by. They talked to each other as though he did not exist, gossiping about this one and that. Several commented about some man down the Jordan River they called John the baptizer. This John apparently preached while standing in the river and then called the people to come and be baptized.

No one talked to Matthew, though. Even those who knew him well made a wide path around him, never making eye contact, or if they did, they looked away immediately. Shunned and shamed, he felt their disapproval. Better to bury his head in his writing or look away himself.

At least Galius, the Roman censor, talked to him, only because he came to pick up the month's payments. He also had an occasional visit from Lucius, a Roman soldier assigned to check on things.

The only social life he had at all was occasional visits to Susanna. He planned to see her tonight. She had invited him to a dinner at a friend's house. At least it gave him something to look forward to.

*****

Levi arrived at Susanna's house to accompany her to the dinner. She greeted him in a colorful festive outfit, her cheeks blushed with something that made them rosy and her eyes outlined in black.

"Perfect timing," Susanna said, as she flashed a smile at Levi and threw a shawl around her shoulders. They walked a short way to the edge of town to a spacious house compared to most in Capernaum.

Susanna said the house belonged to a lady known as Delilah. *Delilah?* Levi thought. *Hmm.*

Delilah looked about like Levi had expected, her face was made up even more colorfully than Susanna's. A string of gold coins dangled from a band around her forehead. Her dress looked like something Roman women would wear, with a scooped neck and a gold necklace with a ruby stone.

Levi noted the three plush couches in the large gathering room and trays with wine flasks on three small tables, along with fruits, cheeses, and breads. Two musicians plucked their stringed instruments while another blew enchanting melodies with his flute.

Levi recognized another tax collector he had met before, but the other three women and six or eight men were new to him. A few lounged on the couches, drinking wine and nibbling on the pre-dinner foods. Others stood in clusters of two or three, talking. All seemed elegantly dressed, leaving Levi ill at ease with his plain clothes, though he had felt better dressed than most people before he came.

Susanna introduced him around to this one and that. "Levi is a tax collector with the foreign traders," she said, making it sound almost important. Each guest nodded and smiled, not seeming to be bothered in the least with the words "tax collector."

169

When they ended up by the platter of food, Levi picked up a handful of grapes and asked Susanna about some of the people.

"The man holding the wine cup is a landowner farther north. The one talking to him inherited his wealth from an uncle. I don't know about the man behind them."

Levi leaned around slightly to see the last one. He seemed familiar, but Levi could not place him. Kind of sneaky looking.

Susanna nodded her head toward a couple in the other corner of the room. "He's a Roman businessman. I think Delilah purchased her couches from him. The one to his left is a tax collector west of here."

"Yes, I recognize him. We were at a meeting together. Where is Delilah's husband?"

About that time, a servant brought a tray of wine to them. "Oh, do have some wine, Levi. Delilah has the best," Susanna said, as she picked a cup off the tray.

Levi sipped the wine. "Ah, yes, it is good."

By night's end, Levi had indulged in a sumptuous dinner and way too much wine. He felt a bit light-headed and stumbled a time or two as they made their way back to Susanna's house. He could hardly keep his thoughts straight. When they got back to her house, she insisted he lay down for a while on her bed until he felt better. It did not take any more coaxing, and he willingly collapsed on her bed.

The next morning when he awoke, he tried to think where he was. He turned toward the kitchen and realized he was still at Susanna's house. She stirred around preparing breakfast. When he pulled the covers off, he saw no clothes on his body. He pulled the covers back over himself and looked around for his tunic and cloak, which lay on the floor by the bed.

His mind raced to reconfigure what had happened. Dinner party, wine, stumbling to Susanna's, but that was as far as he could remember. How did he get to bed? And why did he not have his clothes on?

He pulled his tunic over his head when Susanna's back was turned. That is when the throbbing headache began. He held his head and groaned. Susanna glanced around. "Oh, so the lazy man is awake!"

He moaned. "What happened?"

"I think you enjoyed Delilah's wine a little too much. Come, I fixed you some warm porridge. That will make you feel better."

He struggled to get to his feet and put on his cloak. He sat in puzzled stupor, staring at the food in the familiar pottery bowl. How would he explain to his family where he had been all night? And what about his job? What time was it, anyway?

"What time is it?" he finally asked.

"Maybe two or three hours until noon."

"I've got to get to work!" He gobbled down the rest of his porridge and put on his headpiece. "Thank you for breakfast," he said on the way out the door.

He glanced around to be sure no one saw him coming out of this single woman's house at this hour of the morning. He did not have time to ask her anymore questions about it and was not sure he wanted to hear anyway.

He looked around at people he passed in the market, but they were too busy to notice him, and even if they did, they would have ignored him as usual. Right now, with a heavy dose of guilt-laden feelings and a headache that pounded at his temples, he was glad to be ignored.

At last he made it to his booth, but he did not have his log or money pouch or scales or anything, and he spied a caravan coming down the road. Would he have time to retrieve all his needed tools before the caravan arrived?

He took off in a run, pounding head and all, knowing full well he would be bombarded with a thousand questions from Mama and James.

Sure enough, there stood James, hands on hips. "Well, here's the long-lost son, returning at last!"

"We were so worried, Levi." Mama's voice sounded broken.

Levi quickly gathered up his tools as he spoke. "I'm sorry, Mama. I cannot explain right now. I will have to talk to you later. I must get to work; a caravan is coming." Out the door and off in a run again. He barely reached his post before the caravan arrived. Out of breath and sure he was about to pass out, he panted until he could breathe normally and have some composure. He laid his things out on the table, counted his coins, ready for work.

Two more wagons were behind the first one. About the time he recorded all those, another wagon approached. And so it went all day. By early evening he was exhausted.

Again, he had to face what had happened last night. What did he do? What did *she* do? What would he tell James and Mama?

He gathered his tools, put them in his bag, and pulled the strap over his shoulder. First things first, he told himself. He was satisfied with the story he made up to tell the family. Sorry for the concern he caused them; went to a party with a friend, it lasted longer than he thought, decided to spend the night with the friend, overslept. After all, that was mostly the truth.

James and Mama seemed satisfied with his explanation, though recently, James had continued questioning Levi's late evenings.

But what to do about Susanna. He had to talk to her, of course. He would go after work the next day.

She was watering flowers when he approached the house late afternoon. She smiled knowingly. "Well, I wondered when you would return."

"I'm sorry I left in such a rush, but I was very late for my work."

"Of course. I have a pot of stew simmering. Come in."

She chatted as though this were just another day, altogether avoiding the night before. As they sat and ate, Levi asked about that last night at her house. She smiled again, that beguiling smile.

"It was a lovely evening at Delilah's. You did have a bit too much of her famous wine, though. You really couldn't have made it back to your house." She snickered. "I was barely able to get you to my house."

"So I passed out on your bed?"

"Well, not totally passed out." She raised her eyebrows in a most beguiling expression.

"I don't remember anything." He looked away. "I'm sorry if I was aggressive."

"Not at all, my love." She caressed the top of his hand and slid her hand up his arm under his cloak. "You were wonderful."

A tingle darted through his body, much like he felt with Lily, but this was different. It was not sparked by love, only a physical impulse. He had dismissed Susanna's strange ways because he needed friendship, someone besides family to talk to. She was a friend, nothing more. He had to get out. He jerked his arm out of her grasp. "I have to go," he said. "Thank you for the meal." And off he went.

Levi rushed away from her house in a flurry as one who was fleeing disaster. *Did I overtake her? Or did she overtake me? Did I envision Lily? Or did Susanna take advantage of my condition? I was satisfied to be friends, but that does not seem to be her intent. How could I be so naïve?*

When he saw his house, his emotions remained unsettled, his mind still troubled. He talked to Mama and James briefly and went to bed. Yes, he had a job, and money was no longer a problem. But nothing in his life really mattered anymore.

Chapter 26

New Man in Town

Levi added totals from yesterday's taxes and updated the entries that he had so far that morning. He sat waiting for other traders to come into view, but none were in sight. Along the shores of Galilee, waves swept in and out with regularity, his mind in neutral.

He thought of a segment from one of the psalms.

> *My soul is downcast within me;*
> *Deep calls to deep*
> *in the roar of your waterfalls;*
> *all your waves and breakers*
> *have swept over me.*

As tax collector, the law banned him from the synagogue. Even family members were not permitted to attend.

> *As the deer pants for streams of water,*
> *so my soul pants for you, O God.*
> *My soul thirsts for God, for the living God.*
> *When can I go and meet with God?*
> *My tears have been my food day and night,*
> *while men say to me all day long,*
> *"Where is your God?"*

An animated group of men approached Levi's booth, talking loud enough that he heard them. Of course, as always, they were oblivious to his presence.

The men talked about John the baptizer again. "How do you know all this?" one asked.

"Elias told me. He was there, just a few feet from the water. He could hear John's voice."

"Exactly what did Elias see?"

"Well, he said that this other man went down into the water by John like all the other people had done and asked John to baptize him, but John didn't want to baptize the man."

"Why?"

"He said he wasn't worthy to baptize him, not even worthy to untie his sandals. The man insisted that John must baptize him, so John finally did."

"So?"

"When John raised him up from the water, they both looked up to the sky. Elias said he heard something like a roaring sound, not really thunder. There weren't any dark clouds, but he said it was very eerie."

The men's voices faded. Levi glanced over his shoulder and the friend of Elias motioned with his hands as he continued talking.

Levi thought about earlier descriptions of this John. Some described him as a rather earthy man, wearing camel hair clothes and a leather belt, eating locusts and wild honey, with a bushy beard. Sounded like someone out of the desert. He had said that one greater than he would be coming.

The thought of Isaiah's words came to Levi:

> I will send my messenger ahead of you,
> who will prepare your way—
> a voice of one calling in the desert,
> "Prepare the way for the LORD,
> make straight paths for him."

He remembered Jairus's telling that this quote was one of the prophecies of the coming Messiah. It had been a long time since Levi had thought about the Psalms or Isaiah or anything else based on the Holy Scriptures.

About that time, he heard the familiar sound of rolling wheels and saw another wagon coming. Back to work.

Something about the bundles and the wagon, even the servant helpers looked familiar. He finally made out the black profile of his friend from Ethiopia. "Rah-boh-bah," he whispered. "No, Ra-bOm-bah." As he practiced the correct way to say it, he smiled, remembering Rabomba's laughter and bright personality.

Levi's smile faded as he remembered that rather than selling or trading with Rabomba, he would be taking from him now. His heart sank. Of course, he had to do his job, but he certainly would not like it.

Out of routine, Rabomba stopped at the tax booth. Now he had a caravan with larger wagons. Business must be good. Even more taxes though, Levi calculated. Rabomba recognized him immediately and jumped off the wagon. "LeVi, my friend," he said, with outstretched arms.

Levi left his booth and greeted him. "Rabomba!" They embraced.

"You are no longer in Jericho?" Immediately, Rabomba noticed the booth. His smile faded; his face fell. "You no longer sell?"

"No, my friend. I have had unfortunate troubles. I now collect taxes."

"I see. Unfortunate indeed. I will have my men unload the bags."

"No need. I will charge only what I see."

Rabomba gave a low bow and made a dramatic gesture toward the wagons for inspection. Levi walked beside the goods and made a quick assessment, then told the amount due.

"Ah, you treat an old friend well." Rabomba counted out the coins in his African language.

Levi grinned. "It is good to see you again."

"Ah, perhaps next time you be a buyer!" They laughed together and slapped each other on the back.

"Shalom, my friend."

"Good-bye." He waved.

*****

Weeks turned into months with the same monotonous routine. Levi spent an early evening at Susanna's on the second and fifth day of each week, showing her that they were *just friends*. He liked the well-organized routine if nothing else. They attended more parties with Delilah's friends, though he did not particularly like the companionship of possible thieves, pridefully wealthy landowners, women of the night, other tax collectors, even an over-zealous zealot. Quite a host of misfits.

More snippets of storytelling came almost daily now about the man whom John baptized. The man's name was Jesus. Some claimed that John declared him the Anointed One. Some said this Jesus fellow came from Nazareth, then others said, "What good could come from Nazareth?"

One day two women were passing by and he caught the words, "miracle at the wedding in Cana." Levi noticed that Simon and Andrew no longer tended their fishing boats, as well as James and John, sons of Zebedee. Others had taken over the fishing but did not fare as well. Apparently, the better fishermen had gone off following this Jesus, who evidently attracted large crowds. Levi told Susanna about it, but she just passively said, "Uh, huh," finding no interest in the subject.

The day before Sabbath, everyone in town seemed excited about the fact that Jesus was going to teach at the synagogue in Capernaum. Levi mentioned it to James. "Well, we can't go," he said.

"I know," Levi conceded. "But it would be interesting to see the man and hear what he has to say."

"What do you know of him?" James asked.

"Oh, plenty. Not only does he teach, but he also healed a lame man the other day. Others said he even healed a leper!"

"How do you hear all these things?"

177

"People forget I have ears. They think that since I don't talk to them—because they don't speak to me—that I also don't have ears. No ears to hear, no eyes to see."

"Just sounds like made-up stories to me."

"Maybe so, but I'd at least like to see whom they're talking about."

"I thought you didn't have any eyes to see." James grinned. Levi poked him in the shoulder.

Sabbath morning Levi walked toward the synagogue. The crowd overflowed all around the outside, waiting to hear the teacher. Levi stayed beyond the outer edge, hoping to at least get a glimpse of the man. Soon the crowd parted a bit for Simon, Andrew, James, John, and a couple others to come through. Levi decided that the one he did not recognize must be Jesus. *Fairly common looking*, Levi observed.

Once they were inside, the crowd grew quiet through the reading of Scripture and chanting of the psalms. Levi smiled with joy at hearing the psalms again, even at a distance.

Then Jesus spoke, his voice ringing out in rich tones, explaining the Scripture as Levi had never heard before. No litany of rules and boring rhetoric as usual with the rabbis or Pharisees who came to town.

Suddenly, a man ran into the synagogue, shrieking and waving his arms about. The people around him drew back. Even at a distance, Levi could hear his loud voice.

"What do you want with us, Jesus of Nazareth?" the man roared. "Have you come to destroy us?" Everyone looked at each other, not sure what to do or what to make of this outburst. The man was known for acting rather weird at times, but not this.

"I know who you are, the Holy one of God!" he shouted again.

Levi could hear Jesus call out sternly, "Silence!" Then he heard Jesus say, "Come out of him!" Levi stretched to peer through the crowd. The man shook violently then let out an unearthly shriek and collapsed to the floor. All stood in stunned stillness. Levi could not see him very well, but it looked as if the man were reaching up toward Jesus, maybe in praise or thankfulness. A collective release of air seemed to come spontaneously from the crowd and immediately all responded to what they had seen and heard.

"His teaching is so clear," one woman said. "It is amazing," her friend agreed.

A man near Levi commented, "He speaks with such authority." And the man next to him, "He even gives orders to evil spirits and they obey him!" Soon the whole crowd was roused with excitement. Levi kept his eye on the man with the evil spirit. He walked out smiling and thankful, seemingly cleansed and transformed.

Levi slipped away lest he be noticed. The crowd would likely not be so happy to see him in their midst.

He tried to explain to Mama and James all that happened, but it was difficult to remember everything Jesus taught and to capture the unbelievable transformation that occurred in the man with the evil spirit.

Levi could see from their blank faces that Mama and James had trouble taking in the crowd's reaction to Jesus. They had not been around crowds for a while. Levi realized anew what his position as tax collector had done to all of them. Once again, he faulted his father for the whole miserable situation. Anger always just a breath away.

The next day the chatter he heard was all about Jesus and the man he had healed. Levi also learned that all evening people brought their sick and lame to Simon's house where Jesus was staying. Many received healing.

As the days passed, Levi did not hear anything more about the teacher-healer.

*****

Still making his weekly trek to Susanna's house, Levi wanted to share about the exciting day at the synagogue, but he figured she would not be interested. To his surprise, she had heard shoppers at the market talking about it and was eager to hear more of the details.

He gladly shared from his perspective. Susanna liked the drama of the demon-possessed man's turnaround. Then she took a turn to tell about the marketplace. "You know the woman who has the vegetable stand close to where you used to be?"

Levi thought a moment. "You mean the one who is kind of short and stocky?"

"Yes, that one. Her son has been ill. She took him that Sabbath evening to see Jesus and said that Jesus had completely healed her son. She kept telling her story over and over to each one who came by."

Susanna had a bright look as she relayed two other stories of healing she had heard that day. She seemed more alive than she had been in weeks. They had worked past the incident the evening of the first party. Whatever had happened that night, he made it clear that their relationship was purely friendship.

On this evening, however, she began her alluring looks again, touching his hand and arm. Their warm conversation had softened him. Her sensual touch drew him in. His body reacted to her beguiling ways. Was it the extra cup of wine, her animated story telling, or his own sexual impulses? He did not know, but he soon found himself sinking deeper and deeper into her enticing ways. She drew him to her bed, and he willingly succumbed to her passionate caresses.

When he came to his senses, he felt that she had used him, and he had used her to satisfy purely physical desires. He felt he had betrayed his love for Lily.

"I must go now," he told her.

"Do you have to? Stay with me. Stay with me all night."

"No, I can't."

He quickly dressed and fled into the evening air, inhaling it, wishing he could cleanse himself. What he had declared to himself that he would not do—he did. "Lily, oh Lily, I have betrayed you. I have made a mockery of our love," he cried out. How had he let his life turn out like this?

He did not want to return to the house. Even with the extra room for his mother, it felt crowded sharing a room with James. After all, he had plenty of money and could easily buy a big house for himself. If he paid James to build it, that would give James an income and something to do.

Levi walked on to the sea, basking in the fresh breeze. The moon shone on the water. A few fishermen's boats bobbled along with their lamps dotting their nighttime fishing. Oh, to be a fisherman or a tailor, a silversmith or anything but a tax collector. *A tax collector, humph, exactly what Lily was used to, a tax collector's big salary and spacious house.*

He walked slowly into the night. "What am I thinking?" he said out loud. "She would never come to live with me, the man who caused her to give up her baby. The man who left her alone and had now betrayed their love." He sat on a flat rock and buried his face in his hands.

Finally, he trudged back home and slipped into the house, careful not to wake anyone.

Chapter 27

Jesus Returns to Teach

Levi returned to his tax collector's booth the next morning, routinely going through the motions as he checked goods, collected taxes, and recorded the amounts.

Galius, the censor, would soon come to collect. Galius often commented that the records Levi kept were far better than the previous tax collector.

Lucius, the Roman soldier, often came along with Galius to be sure there was no trouble with anyone who might like to get their hands on a large amount of tax money. Sometimes Lucius would linger to talk. He was not like the other Roman soldiers who seemed to always be ready to pick a fight or make demeaning remarks.

Last night's fishermen had counted their fish and were preparing them to sell. Everything was business as usual. Then a man appeared on the road, surrounded by a group and coming toward Levi.

"It's Jesus!" one man called to another, and they rushed past Levi to join the group. Jesus continued along the shore not far from Levi's booth.

When Jesus stopped and sat on a large rock, everyone else sat to hear him teach. With Jesus' back to the sea, Levi could see and hear clearly.

"How do you have true happiness, you ask?" Jesus' strong voice drifted across the crowd. "Blessed are those who have poverty of spirit, who realize their sinful condition, for only then will they receive the Kingdom of Heaven. Blessed are those who therefore mourn over this sin, for they will be comforted. Blessed are those who humble themselves with meekness before God, for they will inherit the earth, the new promised land."

Levi sat mesmerized. How timely these words of conviction after last night's episode with Susanna. Thoughts of the evening would not be suppressed. He lived it over and over, trapped in lustful memory. What should he say to Susanna? Did he even want to see her again? Did she really care for him as a person or was he just an object? His mind distracted with Susanna, Levi did not hear the next few teachings of what would bring happiness.

Out of the corner of his eye, he noticed a movement. Jairus had come with two others from the synagogue, the elder Elisha and the scribe Meribah. They stood at the edge of the crowd and mumbled something to one other, then Meribah folded his arms in disgust as he glared at Jesus.

Jesus raised his voice a bit as he spoke—to the crowd, yes—but with obvious intentionality to the religious leaders.

"Do not think that I have come to abolish the Law or the Prophets; I have not come to abolish them but to fulfill them. I tell you the truth, until heaven and earth disappear, not the smallest letter, nor the least stroke of a pen, will by any means disappear from the Law until everything is accomplished." A few listeners looked back toward this threesome.

Meribah and Elisha raised their eyebrows and gave one nod of approval.

"Anyone who breaks one of the least of these commandments and teaches others to do the same will be called least in the kingdom of heaven, but whoever practices these commands will be called great in the kingdom of heaven."

Meribah lifted his nose in the air in assurance that he was one of the *great* ones. Jairus' face showed a serious expression, his eyes deep in contemplative thought.

"For I tell you that unless your righteousness surpasses that of the Pharisees and the teachers of the law, you will certainly not enter the kingdom of heaven."

Meribah and Elisha audibly gasped. Their mouths dropped open in disbelief at the audacity of this mere Nazarene to speak in such a way. They immediately turned and left the group. Jairus lingered a moment, evidently wanting to hear more, but the other two motioned to him. He briefly made eye contact with Levi, then turned to follow his friends.

All eyes had turned in their direction, so Jesus paused.

He went on. "You have heard that it was said to the people long ago, 'Do not murder, and anyone who murders will be subject to judgment."

Levi felt the sting of a few eyes from the back of the crowd staring at him. *Must I constantly be accused for the sin of my father?*

Jesus continued, "But I tell you that anyone who is angry with his brother will be subject to judgment."

Who is this man? He seems to see straight into the heart. Papa was full of anger and acted upon it, but I cannot deny my own anger at the townspeople and my life situation, an anger that constantly eats away at me.

"You have heard that it was said, 'Do not commit adultery.'" *Are Jesus' eyes looking above the crowd and focusing on me?* "But I tell you that anyone who looks at a woman lustfully has already committed adultery in his heart." Levi had to turn away. Those eyes—too penetrating. *He knows. But how? How can he possibly know?*

Levi opened his tax records and refigured the last column of numbers. Anything to take his mind off these words. He turned to see if any caravans were coming. Nothing. Nothing to distract him from Jesus' teaching.

"You have heard it said, 'Love your neighbor and hate your enemy.' But I tell you: Love your enemies and pray for those who persecute you, that you may be sons of your father in heaven."

These words, these strange words and ideas, so different from the teachings Levi had heard growing up.

"He causes his sun to rise on the evil and the good and sends rain on the righteous and the unrighteous. If you love those who love you, what reward will you get? Are not even the tax collectors doing that?"

Several heads swiveled toward Levi, but Jesus went on to make his point.

"And if you greet only your brothers, what are you doing more than others? Do not even pagans do that?"

Jesus continued teaching, but Levi was stuck on the point of loving your enemies and being singled out as one of those "enemies." He looked away, wanting to run from his post, but to do so would bring more attention to himself. He looked down at his page, hoping something might take his mind off the teaching of this man.

"And when you pray," Jesus said, "do not be like the hypocrites, for they love to pray standing in the synagogues and on the street corners to be seen by men. I tell you the truth, they have received their reward in full."

How true, Levi thought, as he had observed some of the Pharisees who came to visit Capernaum from time to time, even his own religious leaders liked to spout off loud flowery prayers.

"But when you pray, go into your room, close the door and pray to your Father, who is unseen. Then your Father, who sees what is done in secret, will reward you."

Humph. Pray? How long had it been since he had prayed anything, anywhere? This Jesus made prayer sound like a very personal thing, a private discussion.

Jesus gave an example of a personal prayer which included asking for forgiveness. Then he said, "For if you forgive men when they sin against you, your heavenly Father will also

185

forgive you. But if you do not forgive men their sins, your Father will not forgive your sins."

Levi hung his head then looked around, observing that many others were deep in thought as well. Quietly, with slow steps, Levi walked away. He had to get away from this man and process all the thoughts and emotions that stirred inside him.

He moved out of hearing distance and around the seashore, away from fishermen, away from food stands, houses, and people. He picked up a long stick and absently poked at stones as he sauntered along the shore. He rested on a ledge and gazed out at the sea, listening to the consistency of the lapping waves.

Prayer. "Go into your room and close the door," Jesus had said. *So intimate.* Dare he be that way with his maker? Weren't prayers to be done in the synagogue?

Forgiveness. "If you do not forgive men their sins, your Father will not forgive your sins." Levi looked up at the sky and took a deep breath. Forgive men their sins. How could he even think of forgiving his father? He had pushed his father's anger deep in his soul, and on top of that, he piled on the belittlement he felt from the townspeople. Layered over that was his own anger and bitterness. How could he deal with all that, much less find a way to forgive?

He shook his head and stared at the rocky sand beneath him.

In the distance a teacher of the law was passing by with the steady gait, the straight back, and the air of assurance and self-righteousness. *Yes, standing in the synagogue to pray, receiving their full reward. Jesus has that one right.*

But loving enemies? *That is going too far.*

The evening sun cast a sparkling beam across the sea. Too many thoughts rattled around in his head. Too much to take in. The distant crowd had now dispersed, and no more travelers came through to be taxed. He suddenly remembered that he and Susanna were to go to another party tonight.

Levi returned to his table and picked up his tax records, then walked back to the house to wash his hands and face. Water would not wash away the worry, fatigue, or "sins" as the teacher might say.

"Are you eating with us tonight?" his mother asked.

"No, I'm invited to a, uh, to eat with some friends."

"I never see these friends," she said, fishing for more information.

"Well, they live north of town." He tried to evade any more discussion.

"Why not have them come . . ."

"I have to be going," Levi interrupted. "Don't wait up for me." He pecked a kiss on her cheek and dashed out the door.

Chapter 28

More Complications

Levi trudged to Susanna's. "Ready to go?" he asked, with little enthusiasm.

She raised her eyebrows. "Well, I wasn't sure you would be here after your hasty departure the other night."

He made no comment.

She turned. "I will get my cloak."

Levi rushed along the road leading to the edge of town and on up to Delilah's big house. Susanna huffed along behind him, trying to keep up. "Are you in some kind of hurry?" she finally called out, hardly able to breathe.

"Oh, sorry," he said, finally aware of her heavy breathing.

"Are you in a hurry to get there or to get through with it?"

He answered with a grunt. *Good question.*

When they arrived, he mingled in the crowd and had a drink but promised himself only one. Amos, the wealthy landowner, lounged in one corner by himself long enough that Levi had an opportunity to talk to him alone.

"You're interested in a big house, you say?"

"Yes," Levi replied. "I want enough land to build a sizeable place."

"Uh-huh." The large man straightened up and stroked his beard. "Well, I have the ideal place for you, and it will save you quite a bit of work. I own a large house northeast of here. Hasn't been used for a couple of years. Needs a little repair, but it would save you from building from the ground up." He quoted a very reasonable price.

"I'd like to see it. How about late afternoon tomorrow?" They agreed on a place to meet.

Levi celebrated the idea with one more drink, but only one. He noticed Susanna in deep discussion with Delilah. Somehow that did not seem like a good thing, but his mission had been accomplished.

"Are you ready to go?" Levi asked Susanna.

"So soon?" She raised her eyebrows.

"I have a lot to do tomorrow."

"My, aren't we all business tonight? How about one more drink?"

"I'm ready to go, Susanna."

Delilah gave Susanna a knowing smile and flashed an alluring nod to Levi. What had they been talking about?

Levi headed for the door. If Susanna were going to be escorted, she would have to move quickly. Once outside, Levi scurried at the same pace as he did before.

"You sure are in a hurry tonight," She complained.

"Sorry, I have a lot on my mind."

"I saw you talking to Amos."

"I'm thinking about buying some property."

"Oh?"

"It just feels crowded at home. I'd like some space to breathe."

"You mean build a house?"

"Amos has a house he's willing to sell. Needs some repair though. I'm going to have a look tomorrow."

"Sounds interesting." Her tone sounded too interesting to Levi. Was she thinking of moving into the house with him?

"Just something I'm thinking about," he said, trying to sound casual.

As they came near to her house, she opened the door wide for him to come in, but he declined and headed home. Immediately!

*****

Levi could not wait to get through with his work for the day. Fortunately, he stayed busy which made the day pass quickly. Soon he was on his way to meet Amos.

The house sat in a beautiful location on the upper edge of town, high enough to see part of the sea over the other houses and trees. In fact, he could see his mother's house from there. Strange that he had never noticed this house up on the hill before.

However, when he went inside and looked around, "repair" was a mild word to describe it. It smelled of wild animals; the roof needed repair, and the walls had begun to crumble on the floor. It needed more than a broom. Levi surmised that James could work on it and make it livable. At least James would not have to carry heavy blocks of stones as he had done with their mother's house.

Obviously, Amos wanted to get rid of it, so Levi offered a lower price, emphasizing the many repairs needed.

Amos stalled a bit, trying to test Levi. "Oh, I don't know," he said, slowly shaking his head and frowning. Levi did not say a word. Finally, Amos consented, "Well, I suppose I can agree to that price." They decided on the payments and Levi would have a house, such as it was.

Levi walked away with a wide stride. A landowner, king of his castle—well, potential king of a house at least. He wanted to share his good news. So on the way home, he decided to stop by Susanna's.

As he approached, he noticed that the house was dark. Where could she be this time of the evening? Suddenly a lamp lit up the dark. Perhaps she had been resting. But then a man came out the door and turned back to say something. As he left, Levi tried to make out his features, but he did not recognize the man.

Levi sat on a nearby stool by the tailor's shop. *Puzzling. What was this man doing here, and why was the house dark, then light?*

Levi waited until the man was down the street. Just then, he could tell by the shadows behind the curtain that Susanna carried a candle and set it in the window. What in the world was going on? Levi sat there in a daze trying to figure it out.

Shortly, another man came walking down the street. Levi scrunched up against the tailor's shop behind a bush so as not to be seen. The man walked hesitantly, constantly looking around. He did not see Levi, but Levi felt his heart throbbing inside his chest as though he were going to be caught any moment.

As the man passed by, Levi recognized his brisk, jerky movements, his tall height, and the robe. It was the scribe, Meribah! What was he doing on this street at this late hour?

To Levi's utter surprise, Meribah went to Susanna's door. She immediately let him in. In a few moments, the candle was blown out as well as the lantern in the house.

In stunned silence, it became all too clear to Levi what was going on. How could he have been so blind? He had assumed her enchanting ways were meant only for him. In her deception, she had convinced him that seeing her on the second and fifth day of the week was his idea. Little did he realize the other days were for other "visitors."

So that is how she was able to afford her house and food. How could he have been so dense? But why did she never expect him to pay her? That was a mystery. Did she feel something more for him than the others? No matter, he would not be further deceived by this harlot.

Even Meribah the scribe comes to defile himself. Self-righteous Meribah.

Levi felt sick. He could hardly breathe. He had to get away from this house of sin before Meribah came out from his sexual spree.

Stumbling through the darkness, Levi made his way home, hardly conscious of where he was or where he had walked. Misled, blinded, deceived, how could he have been so naïve, so foolish? Then, he thought of the teacher's words. Not only had he lusted in his heart, but he had also acted on those feelings.

191

"Unless your righteousness exceeds that of the Pharisees and teachers of the law…" *Jesus even knew the actions and hearts of men like Meribah.*

"How do you have true happiness?" Jesus had asked. *But I ask, "What is happiness at all?" I have not known happiness in a long time, if ever.*

Jesus' words rang in his ears, "Blessed are those who have poverty of spirit, who realize their sinful condition, for only then will they receive the kingdom of heaven."

Levi dragged himself into his house, grateful that Mama and James were asleep. Tossing and turning, he finally drifted off and dreamed that Jesus was standing next to his new house. Instead of a dilapidated roof and crumbling stones, it looked fresh and new with bushes and budding flowers by the door. Jesus motioned to Amos to come in, as well as Delilah, Susanna, the man who was always drunk, the thief, the zealot.

*****

When Levi awoke, he still had all the happenings of yesterday in his head and wondered about that unusual dream.

"You're rather quiet this morning," James commented. "Another long night?" he added suspiciously.

Levi rubbed his forehead and took a deep breath. "In some ways."

"Porridge?" Mama asked.

"Yes, thank you, Mama."

Mama went outside for a moment. While she was out, Levi told James, "I have something I want you to see late this afternoon. I'll tell you more later."

"Why can't you tell—"

Levi held up his hand to stop James and nodded at Mama who was getting ready to come back in the door.

"We heard the teacher you were talking about the other day, Levi," Mama said as she came in the door with her broom. "He certainly had a crowd gathered around him."

"What did you think of him?" Levi asked.

Mama stood with her chin propped on the broom handle. "He speaks with deep emotion and authority. Everyone seemed amazed at his teaching." When Levi stood to collect his things for the day, she asked, "Will you be coming in for tonight's meal?"

"Yes, but make it late." Out the door he went before any further questions ensued.

All day, Levi tried to focus on the house, but in his quiet moments the thought of Susanna kept haunting him. Over and over, he could see that scoundrel Meribah sneaking down the street to Susanna's ready arms. When the light went out, so did Levi's spirit. How could she be so deceitful? How could Meribah be such a fraud? But then how could he avoid admitting his own secretive behavior. Gone to parties with people on the lowest moral rung of society; succumbing to the wiles of Susanna himself, leaving Mama and James to fend for themselves. Oh, he worked to provide for them, but he was not fully present for them.

Once again, he could hear his father's voice crying out from the grave, "Foolish boy, you can't do anything right. Look what you have done with your life."

Just then the Roman, Lucius, trotted in on his regal horse and dismounted to check on things. He said he had just gotten back in town. Evidently his home base was somewhere around Capernaum. He commented that Galius always spoke of the good work Levi did. Then he mounted and trotted off.

The only encouragement I receive is from a Roman. Not a positive situation.

Chapter 29

Under Construction

Levi found James in the field behind the house. James stopped his work long enough to respond to the questioning look on Levi's face. "I decided to have a garden," James shouted.

Levi stood for a moment, watching James plow a new section of field. He could not help but think of that day long ago when they were children walking to the market, and James had asked, "Why don't we have a garden?" Levi smiled. *Well, James, now you have your garden.*

Levi went on to the house to wash the dusty sweat from his day's work and chatted with his mother. She beamed at finally receiving his attention.

When James came in, Levi figured it would be better to first talk to him about the new house before he mentioned it to his mother, so after the evening meal, he asked James to show him the fruit of his labor.

On the way out to the field, James explained, "I know we have plenty of money for food, but Mama doesn't like going into town to shop at the market. No one will talk to her. Besides, I like having something constructive to do since we lost the pottery business."

"You've done a masterful job plowing for the garden, James." James grinned. "I want to talk to you about another project."

"Oh?" James looked at him with interest.

"You did an excellent job with the additional room for Mama. Now that we are grown men, it would be nice to have more space for yourself and for me, as well. I have purchased a house way up the hill there." Levi pointed in that direction. "Do you see that clump of olive trees, then a few houses beyond that?"

"Almost at the top of the hill?"

"Yes. Then just beyond that, can you see part of another house."

"The very last house?" James squinted.

"Yes, that's it."

James looked down, scrunched his mouth to the side like he always did when he was thinking. He looked to the side, took a deep breath and released it quickly. "So, you're leaving us again."

"No, James, I would come often to share a meal. I would still be here in Capernaum. This will give you more space as well."

"So, what's the project?"

Relieved, Levi told him about the condition of the house and his desire to have James do the repairs. "After I finish my work tomorrow, let's go up to the house and I'll show you what's needed. You won't have to carry stones to the house like you did here, but there is much work to be done."

"The next task will be convincing Mama that it is a good idea." James smirked.

*****

The next day, Levi could tell James was reluctant about this wild move. James lingered in the garden when Levi arrived, then sauntered leisurely to meet Levi.

"Are you ready to go?" Levi asked, trying to be enthusiastic.

"Why don't we just build another room on our house?"

"I've already bought the house, James. At least, I'm in process. Besides, remember how you complained about lugging all those stones to the house? Let's head up there before it gets dark."

"Let me take these tools back to the house."

Finally, they were on their way. Levi took the back way around town to get to the house, totally avoiding Susanna.

After some convincing, James agreed to the job. To soften things, Levi promised that he would take Mama and James to the next festival at the Temple in Jerusalem, "just like we used

195

to." Papa had stopped taking them after he grew increasingly angry and bitter. "Mama would like the opportunity to see her sister in Jerusalem."

*****

Levi looked forward each day to seeing what improvements James made. "You are truly doing a masterful job with the house. You work with such ease at repairing and shaping the walls. I guess it is those potter hands."

"That will cost you extra," he teased.

Levi gave him a poke in the arm. "I have to give you something to do to keep you out of trouble."

Occasionally, Amos came by to check on the progress. "A good workman you have there, Levi."

"Yes, indeed, Amos." Levi put his hand on James' shoulder. "This is my brother, James." Turning to James, he said, "Amos sold me this house."

"Hello, sir," James nodded, as he stood there covered with stone dust.

"Nice to meet you, James. You have done some fine work. I would be interested in employing you for other jobs when you're finished here."

James smiled and nodded again.

*****

By the time Passover drew nigh, James had completed his work on the house. Mama gathered a few cooking utensils Levi might need, and James constructed pieces of furniture for him. They celebrated with a meal in the new house, Mama doing most of the cooking, of course.

Chapter 30

Off to Jerusalem

Mama scurried around the house, washing clothes and packing. "Oh my, it has been so long since I've made the trip to Jerusalem, I have about forgotten what all to take."

Still forbidden to enter the synagogue, they waited until the day after everyone else left so as not to attract scorn for something so audacious as going to the Temple. Though they would not be permitted into the court of men, they would be allowed into the outer court of the Gentiles.

At last they were packed, and Mama had her last sweep out the door. Levi smiled. "Put that broom away, Mama. Let's go to Jerusalem!"

On the way they stopped at a well to pull up water to drink. When they found the cool shade of a tree, they ate their lunch. For some reason, Mama began talking about Papa.

"We first lived in Sepphoris. That is where your father learned the pottery trade from his father. They made beautiful, fancy pieces like the fine craftsmen of that area. We were happy there." Mama had a faraway look.

"What caused you to move to Capernaum?" James asked.

Mama looked off in the distance with a frown as though wanting to push that part of her memory away. She sighed. "Many young men felt like Rome was too heavy handed and that they were invading our city more and more with their demands."

She turned to look at James and Levi. "Your grandfather, Papa's father, stirred the young ones up. He encouraged their rage with his own anger. It caused an uprising. In retaliation, the Roman soldiers marched into the city, ransacking the shops and houses, setting fires, and taking the rebels captive. Alphaeus' parents were killed. Your father and I escaped, but he never forgave the Romans. That bitterness constantly raged in his soul. He could never rid himself of it."

Mama looked at her hands, rubbing them this way and that. Levi slipped over to sit beside her, his arm around her shoulder. "I'm sorry, Mama. Sorry you have had to bear this grief so many years. It does explain many things."

She touched Levi's hand and laid her cheek over on his shoulder. James sat on the other side of her. "God blessed me with two fine sons," she said, as she patted each of their knees. "And now, we must move along. We still have a journey ahead of us."

As they walked beside the Jordan River, a crowd gathered up ahead. A man, standing in the water, waved his arms and shouted as though he was preaching.

"Must be the one they call John the baptizer," Levi told James. "They say he came out from the desert."

"He *looks* like it—bushy beard, camel-hair clothes." James crinkled his nose. "I'm sure he smells too."

Levi mumbled, "A voice of one calling in the desert, 'Prepare the way for the Lord, make straight paths for him.'"

"What did you say?" James asked.

"Just remembering a verse I studied with Jairus."

They both turned when John shouted, "Repent for the kingdom of heaven is near. I baptize you with water for repentance. But after me will come one who is more powerful than I, whose sandals I am not worthy to carry. He will baptize you with the Holy Spirit and with fire."

A group of Pharisees congregated to one side. Levi elbowed James. "Looks like they are gathering their forces to complain," he said as he nodded their way.

"Let's go around this crowd," James suggested. That suited Levi. He felt burdened by John's words, but he noticed the smiles and joy of those who had come out of the water.

They walked in silence for a while until Mama wanted to stop to rest and have a drink of water at a nearby well.

The next day they traveled farther along the river. In the distance, they saw another crowd. "Look, I think that's Jesus," James said. "He must be on his way to Jerusalem for Passover. Let's go listen to him."

Levi was not too sure about that, but Mama was eager to see Jesus as well and hear him teach. Again, a few Pharisees stood at the edge of the crowd.

Jesus' voice rang out, "Be careful not to do your 'acts of righteousness' before men, to be seen by them. If you do, you will have no reward from your Father in heaven. So, when you give to the needy, do not announce it with trumpets, as the hypocrites do in the synagogues and on the streets, to be honored by men. I tell you they have their reward in full."

James rolled his eyes over to Levi, nodding toward the Pharisees, the breeze ruffling their long robes as well as their attitudes.

"But when you give to the needy, do not let your left hand know what your right hand is doing, so that your giving may be in secret. Then your Father, who sees what is done in secret, will reward you."

Levi looked around, fidgeting with his cloak. The thought of God seeing what is done in secret did not set well.

Jesus paused, then he told a parable: "Two men went up to the Temple to pray." He motioned toward Jerusalem. "One was a Pharisee and the other a tax collector."

Levi lowered his head with this unexpected mention of a tax collector. His eyes jerked in every direction to see if anyone noticed him, but all eyes were on Jesus. He slowly released a pent-up breath. *It is good to just be one in a crowd, unknown.*

"The Pharisee," Jesus went on, "stood up and prayed about himself: 'God, I thank you that I am not like other men— robbers, evil doers, adulterers—or even like this tax collector.'"

Again, Levi flinched at the mention of his acquired profession, feeling the hate. Jesus concluded the Pharisee's prayer. "'I fast twice a week and give a tenth of all I get.'"

Jesus continued his parable, "But the tax collector, stood at a distance. He would not even look up to heaven, but beat his breast and said, 'God have mercy on me, a sinner.'"

Tears welled up in Levi's eyes. He looked at Jesus in disbelief that he would acknowledge a tax collector in this way. "I tell you this man went home justified before God."

Jesus' eyes scanned the crowd and then to the Pharisees. "For everyone who exalts himself will be humbled, and he who humbles himself will be exalted."

Jesus went on to say many other things, but one phrase played over and over in Levi's head. "God, have mercy on me, a sinner."

Levi eased back further to the edge of the crowd and James and his mother followed. But as they slipped away, Levi saw Ariah straight ahead. Levi froze in his tracks, causing James and Mama to bump into him. "What is it, Levi?" James asked.

It was too late. Ariah spotted him, waved, and began heading that way. Had the new balsam bushes failed to produce? Had Ariah received an overloaded bill from Zacchaeus? Had something happened to Lily? Levi's heart about thumped right out of his chest.

"Levi, my friend, I thought that was you." Ariah gave him a big hug and a slap on the back. "And this must be your dear mother."

Levi could hardly believe such a greeting. "Uh, yes, this is my mother, Myrah, and my brother, James."

"So good to meet you, my friends. You have a fine son, dear woman. He encouraged me to plant more balsam bushes and now they flourish all over Gilead. Oh, listen to me. I must convey my sorrow for the loss of your husband."

"Thank you, sir," Myrah mumbled, not sure how to respond to this stranger.

"You must have come for Passover. I insist that you come and stay at my house. We have this big house and no one to fill it."

Levi's mind flooded with a hundred thoughts and questions. How special it would be to stay inside the house he never got to see. Would he come across Caleb? Did Zacchaeus ever find out about him and Lily? Would Ariah probe to know what Levi was doing now? His mother's face had a helpless look.

Levi quickly said, "Ariah, that is kind of you, but we already have other plans. In fact, we are on our way now to meet family, but thank you for your gracious offer. So good to see you again."

Levi scurried James and Mama on down the road and did not say a word until they were well out of sight of Ariah.

"Can we go a bit slower. I'm out of breath," Mama complained.

"I'm sorry," Levi conceded. "A stay at Ariah's huge mansion would have been an exciting treat for you, but I don't think he would have been happy if he found he was taking in a tax collector. People here in Jericho don't take kindly to tax collectors any more than they do in Capernaum. And, of course, you want to stay with Aunt Sarah."

"What did he mean about balsam bushes?" James asked.

"I worked for Ariah, selling balm from the balsam plants and later keeping the records for the whole balsam trade. We had tradesmen ready to buy more than we had to sell. I encouraged Ariah to invest in more bushes to boost the company's profit. Evidently, the bushes are producing well now."

Mama shook her head and looked down. "And you gave this up to come back to help us." She searched Levi's face.

It must have appeared that everything here seemed wonderful. "It was what I needed to do, Mama." Truth be known, going back home was his escape from what he had brought on himself. Levi walked beside his mother with an arm around her shoulders. The circumstances of Alphaeus' life, his anger, his relationship with the family, and his death had certainly taken a toll on all of them.

Levi looked toward Jerusalem. Thoughts of seeing the Temple once again gave him a sense of anticipation. At the same time, there he was, hiding in the crowd from those who knew him, whether they be villagers of Capernaum or Roman soldiers. He did not belong to either. Added to that were the gnawing words of this Jesus.

After climbing the long, steep, winding, and exhausting road to Jerusalem they came to the house of Mama's relatives. She fell gratefully into the arms of her sister, whom she had not seen in several years. The husband, Levi's uncle, greeted her warmly, but barely spoke to Levi. *He knows I am a tax collector*, Levi concluded, so he avoided any further discussion.

Talk at the evening meal felt awkward, so James and Levi took a walk after they ate.

"I don't think our uncle is very happy to see us," James observed.

"You mean, not happy to see *me*."

The next morning, Levi busied himself with purchasing a lamb. His eyes darted here and there, constantly on the lookout for anyone from his hometown. They would not accept that their town customs tax collector should participate in the sin atonement, much less Passover. He was certainly not an upright Jewish man.

He pulled out plentiful coins to purchase an unblemished lamb for sacrifice.

James caught up with Levi later that morning and saw the lamb that he carried. His eyes locked with Levi's. James' questioning eyes glanced down to the lamb and back to Levi.

"For the sacrifice," Levi said.

James raised his eyebrows and looked away as if to say, "You? Offering a sacrifice?"

"I'll be back," Levi stated flatly, not to be delayed from his task.

Levi went through the motions of taking his lamb to a priest who methodically took it to another who carried the lamb up the steps for slaughter. It all seemed so methodical and left Levi feeling more dissatisfied than when he came. Neither his money nor this lamb could bring a sense of atonement for his sin.

As he came down a path, two Roman soldiers came strolling through the crowd, keeping their eyes on the pilgrims who had come for Passover. Then he realized that one of them was Lucius. Their eyes met, but neither wanted to acknowledge the other in the presence of the crowd, so each went his own way.

Levi caught up with James, and they returned for the evening Passover meal at their aunt's house. That too felt methodical. What little comfort he found in the family tradition, disappeared when it became marred by the looks of disdain from his uncle.

Levi was ready to return home the next morning.

"Must we leave so soon?" his mother pleaded.

"I must get back to my work, Mama," he whispered.

Disappointed, Mama's eyes were cast down as she began to get her things together to travel back home.

James pulled Levi aside. "Why don't you go on if you must? I'll stay here with Mama for a few more days so she can have more time with the family."

"Well, I suppose that would be all right. Here are some coins."

Mama clapped her hands with delight when she heard she could spend more time with her sister. Thankfully, the uncle had gone out before Levi left. He thanked Aunt Sarah and hugged his mother.

On his way, he spied the stout vegetable stand woman from the Capernaum market. He quickly turned and walked the other way. Once she passed by, he pulled his headpiece further over his head and hurried on out of town.

When he passed Jericho, he had a sudden urge to go into the city, maybe go by Zacchaeus' house. Perhaps he would see Lily out in the garden, but he thought better of it and stayed on the path back home. He did gaze at the hills of Gilead and sure enough, balsam bushes covered the hillside. *Well, at least I did something right.*

Levi mulled over the story his mother told of his father and his family. Evidently, his grandfather had the same raging temperament his father had. That explained many things, but it did not change the hurt he felt for so many years.

He dreaded going along the Jordan for fear the baptizer would be calling people to repent, or Jesus might still be teaching, but he did not see either one. The rest of the trip home was thankfully uneventful.

His new house, though quite well repaired, did not feel comfortable or welcoming. The bed, however, *any* bed, was most welcome.

Chapter 31

Assessing

The Jerusalem trip had turned out to be a disappointment like most everything else in Levi's life.

After returning, he dragged himself to the tax booth and went through the motions of the day. His mind kept returning to the night he saw the men going to Susanna's house. *I must confront her about this.*

He plodded into town and on to her house, rehearsing what he would say. It was his usual day of the week to see her, so maybe there would not be any other "visitors" at her house.

When he arrived, she opened the door, looking surprised. "Well, I wondered when I would see you again. Come in."

"I took my family to Jerusalem for Passover."

"I did not cook anything tonight. Would you like some bread and cheese?"

"That is fine."

She cut slices of cheese. "Did you have a good trip?"

"The travel takes a long time." Determined to get through this, he moved on. "Susanna, I must speak to you about a matter."

"Sounds serious." She continued slicing the cheese.

"The last time I came to your house, I had news to share with you, but it wasn't one of my usual days to come."

She stopped slicing but did not turn around.

"As I approached your house, I saw a man coming out the door. I waited until he left and saw you put a candle in the window."

She still had her back to Levi but raised her head.

"Another man came to your house, and shortly you blew out the candle *and* the lantern. I came to the only possible conclusion that… that you have followed the path of Delilah."

Susanna slammed her knife down and whirled around facing Levi. "And how do you think a single woman can survive without a husband, without a family? How do you think I can manage to have food on the table for you and keep this house?"

Levi's eyes opened wide. "Well, uh…"

"How do you think I can buy your precious pottery and have clothes to wear?" Her eyes began to squint. "So, you came snooping around my house, hiding and spying on me."

"I…"

"Did you notice that I never charged you? I thought you were different. I thought you cared." She covered her face with her hands and sobbed.

Levi sat startled and unable to move or speak. He had come to chastise, but instead he was the recipient. His impulse was to hold her and comfort her, but that would send a mixed message. Finally he managed to say, "I am sorry, Susanna. I had not come to spy. It, uh, it just happened. I suppose I have been totally naïve, and maybe insensitive to your condition, but I felt horribly disappointed. I do care about our friendship, but I think I better go now."

Susanna lowered her head, staring at the floor. "I'm sorry," she spoke softly. "What were you going to show me?"

"Show you?"

"You said that when you came before, you had planned to show me something."

"Oh, yes, I was going to show you the house, the house I bought from Amos. My brother repaired it, and it looks good now."

"May I see it?"

"Uh, well, I guess so."

"I'll get my cloak."

Levi tried to remember if he left it messy. When they arrived, the house looked presentable. Susanna commented on every little thing and seemed impressed. Just then they heard music coming from way over at Delilah's house.

"She's having another party. Would you like to go? They would probably like to come see your house as well." Reluctantly, Levi agreed to go.

A few guests were sprawled out on the sofas from drinking, but several agreed they would like to see his house.

One of the other tax collectors lifted his cup for another swallow and slurred. "Sure, take us to see yur bootiful hawse."

"Les go now," the thief managed to say as he nearly fell over, wine dripping down his chin.

The longer they stayed at the party, the more they drank until most were practically passed out. Levi kept his one-drink rule and was ready to go home and be done with the whole lot of them.

He walked Susanna home and left immediately.

Chapter 32

"Follow Me"

"I may as well have gotten drunk last night. That way I could have gone to sleep," Matthew grumbled to himself. But after he dressed and packed his tax bag, he stepped out the door to see the sky, particularly blue today, which cast a slight bluish hue on the sea. He loved these days and breathed in a slow, intentional breath of morning air, enjoying the panoramic view of town, sea, and hills. "A new day," he said to himself, trying to forget last night's troubles.

After three caravans came through, he walked back to his booth and glanced up the hill. He stared at his house as though noticing it for the first time. *Never thought I would have a house so big. But then, what is a big house when it is empty? Empty, like my life.*

When Levi heard more than the usual chatter, he realized a crowd had begun forming. Evidently the teacher was back in town. Three men behind him talked about a healing incident the previous day.

"A leper you say?"

"Yes, all bandaged up and smelly as could be."

"He didn't send him away?"

"No. In fact, Jesus walked to him and talked to him, then he actually *touched* the man."

"Heaven forbid!"

"But that's not all. Jesus healed the man."

"A leper?"

"Yes. I saw it with my own eyes."

"Unbelievable! But then, come to think of it, I talked with my friend Jeremiah last week. You know, the one who could not hear or speak? He talked clearly and heard every word I said after Jesus healed him. It's amazing!"

A boy passed in front of Levi's booth. He pointed in the direction of a clump of people. "Look, there he is!" he shouted back to his friends, and off they ran toward the gathering crowd.

Levi stretched his neck to see Jesus, but he was hidden in the crowd. Levi sat on his stool, trying to dismiss thoughts of the teacher. Maybe another caravan would come to distract him, but none was in sight.

"There he is, down by the sea!" another man shouted to his friend. They headed that way. People seemed to appear from every direction. Jesus got in a boat. Was he going to leave? No, he turned to the crowd and motioned for them to sit.

At first, Levi could not hear very well, but as a hush fell over the crowd, Jesus' projected voice came through. His words clear. Too clear. He talked about being merciful. He talked about fasting. "Do not fast to be seen of men like the hypocrites do, but do it in secret."

Jesus said the same about prayer. "Go into your closet and pray privately."

Is he suggesting we have a private relationship with the Almighty? How can this be? So different from our thinking and teaching.

Levi turned to see Meribah and his friend standing a few feet away. They wore skeptical faces as they had before.

"Do not store up for yourselves treasures on earth," Jesus said.

Humph, what treasures do I have? All this money and what do I have to show for it? Well, my house, I guess. I put my all into that, such as it is. But what does it really mean to me? What does anything mean to me?

"For where your treasure is, there will your heart be also." Levi looked down at the stack of coins. *Roman money. Is that where my heart is? In Roman money?*

Jesus paused. His eyes scanned the crowd and turned toward Levi's direction. "The eye is the lamp of the body. If your eyes are good, your whole body will be full of light. But if your eyes are bad, your whole body will be full of darkness. If then the light within you is darkness, how great is that darkness!"

Tears formed in Levi's eyes. Oh, that he could have eyes to see clearly. But he knew, deep within himself, that his eyes reflected the darkness of his soul. *I am lost in a world of bitterness, regret, dependency on Rome, and now, "a life of sin," as John the Baptist would say.*

"No one can serve two masters," Jesus continued. "Either he will hate the one and love the other or be devoted to one and despise the other. You cannot serve both God and money."

How do you know my heart? Levi wanted to cry out. He hung his head; his chest sunk in. He tried to breathe despite his shaking body.

"Ask, and it will be given you," Jesus said. "Seek and you will find; knock and the door will be opened to you."

Levi lowered his forehead on his arm at the table. He could hear no more. He was aware that the people began talking among themselves. He no longer heard Jesus voice, only the words that kept ringing in his ears.

"If then the light within you is darkness, how great is that darkness."

"You cannot serve both God and money."

"Ask and it will be given you."

Tears flowed uncontrollably. He could hear the crowd dispersing. He must get control of himself. He swiftly wiped the tears off his cheek, took deep breaths, reached for the coins on the table and slowly put one coin at a time in his money bag. Anything to keep his eye's lowered and his hands busy. People passed by, talking about Jesus' words. For once, he was glad to be ignored.

After he had put the coins in his pouch, he glanced up and became aware that Jesus and his followers were moving in his direction. He tried to remain busy with packing his tools, but he had a growing sensation that they were heading straight toward his booth.

Jesus' followers lagged behind, but Jesus kept walking directly toward Levi. His heart pounded. He glanced up to see that Jesus was indeed focused on him as he continued to approach.

Levi started to gather up his belongings, but he could only stare at his bag. What was he to do? Why would Jesus come to him? He sat frozen, unable to move or breathe.

Then he saw Jesus' cloak right in front of him.

Slowly Levi lifted his face to Jesus, tears puddling in his eyes. Jesus looked at him with a kind, gentle expression. "Levi," he said, "follow me."

What? Levi lowered his eyes, his forehead wrinkled as questions raced through his mind. *Why? Why would this man of God purposely come to me? And then invite me, sinful as I am, to follow him?*

He looked up, searching Jesus' face.

"Come, follow me," Jesus said again.

Something inside Levi broke. Like the shattered pottery he'd heard for years. But this time it was a jar that contained his whole miserable, foolish life. And from what he'd heard from Jesus so far, the man probably knew how badly Levi had conducted his life.

And here Jesus was presenting him a radical change.

Do I keep collecting taxes? Or do I walk away from all this? He had not one single reason to carry on his life the way he had been.

He stood, broken open and yearning to be free.

He picked up his tax bag, if only to spare him the wrath of the Romans, walked away from the tax table, and followed Jesus.

Gasps and derogatory remarks came from the crowd. But he did not look at them or concern himself with their criticisms. His attention focused purely on Jesus.

Levi was not sure where Jesus and his small band of men were going, but he followed behind Jesus just as he had been invited to do.

He would certainly get himself fired. But he couldn't convince himself to care.

The band of followers gathered on the hillside not far from Levi's house and sat on the ground to hear more teachings from Jesus, but Levi's attention was fixed on the words Jesus had said earlier and the thought of Jesus' coming directly to him. The words, "Follow me," echoed in his head.

Levi looked around at the other men in the group. He sat slightly apart from them, but none of them pushed him away or made demeaning remarks like everyone else. But then, neither did they speak to him. Regardless, he still smiled at the thought that Jesus wanted him to be one of his followers.

When Jesus finished his teaching, the men each went their way back to their homes.

Chapter 33

Walking with Jesus

Levi tossed in his bed that night, remembering the events of the afternoon, the stark condition of his soul, the words of truth from Jesus' lips, the emotions as Jesus stood before him, compelling him to "Follow me."

Even at that moment, tears welled up in his eyes. He rolled over, wiping the tears with his covers.

What to do now? The other followers clearly did not welcome his presence. He was not "one of them." But Jesus welcomed him with open arms.

What of his job? The Roman money in his pouch? His own money and money for Mama and James? He could not possibly go back to the booth and follow Jesus at the same time. "You cannot serve both God and money," Jesus said.

Morning came. Where would he find Jesus and the others? When he came outside, they were gathered on the hillside not far from the spot where they were the day before. Though reluctant, he joined the group again.

Fortunately, the fifteen or twenty men were turned toward Jesus. Maybe they would not notice him moving in behind them.

"Remember," Jesus was saying, "I have not come to abolish the law or the Prophets; I have come to fulfill them. I tell you the truth, until heaven and earth disappear, not the smallest letter, not the least stroke of a pen, will by any means disappear from the Law until everything is accomplished."

Jesus paused and looked at the men intently. With slow, sincere words, he said, "I tell you that unless your righteousness surpasses that of the Pharisees and the teachers of the law, you will certainly not enter the kingdom of heaven."

The men's attention stayed fixed on Jesus, but as soon as his penetrating gaze left them, they looked down. Perhaps they were thinking as Levi did that to surpass the piety of the teachers of the Law and the Pharisees was a tall order, but Meribah's actions and attitudes made Jesus' words understandable.

"You are the light of the world," Jesus went on. "A city on the hill cannot be hidden. Neither do people light a lamp and put it under a bowl. Instead they put it on its stand, and it gives light to everyone in the house. In the same way, let your light shine before men, that they may see your good deeds and praise your Father in heaven."

Levi turned toward Jairus' house. Now there was a leader who cast a light in Levi's life. Memories of loving God's Word washed over him. He smiled as he remembered his ancestry project—the strong men of faith who carried the promises made to Abraham down through the centuries. Even the women who were outside the Hebrews had a part: Tamar, Rahab, and Ruth.

Jairus had taught him much. How could he have turned away from these things to follow Roman money? Jairus cared about him and talked to him when others shunned him on his return to Capernaum. Jairus had been a light in so many ways.

Levi looked past Jairus' house to the trade route. A caravan headed toward his tax booth. He automatically started to stand, ready to do his work, but remembered his decision to follow Jesus. Still, he could hardly take his eyes off the caravan. He had to deal with the issue of tax collection because Galius would be coming soon to collect.

And what of Lucius? *What can I say? How can I explain a religious matter to a Roman soldier? Then the other burning question—how can my family live with no income?*

"Therefore," Jesus was saying, "do not worry about your life, what you will eat or drink; or about your body, what you will wear. Is not life more important than food, and the body more important than clothes?"

How does he know my thoughts, my concerns?

Two birds flew over. Jesus looked up and raised his hand. "Look at the birds of the air; they do not sow or reap or store away in barns." The men looked up at the birds, then smiled at each other with the thought of birds having barns. "And yet," Jesus continued, "your heavenly Father feeds them. Are you not much more valuable than they? Who of you by worrying can add a single hour to his life?"

"And why do you worry about clothes? See how the lilies of the field grow." Jesus gestured toward a nearby field. "They do not labor or spin. Yet I tell you that not even Solomon in all his splendor was dressed like one of these."

Levi glanced over at the field Jesus pointed out. How many times had he seen that field but hadn't really seen it? The flowers in full bloom covered the field in beautiful clusters of reds, whites, and purples. *What other things have I not seen around me?*

Jesus continued, "If that is how God clothes the grass of the field, which is here today and tomorrow is thrown into the fire, will he not much more clothe you, O you of little faith?"

Is that what I lack? Faith? O that I could release my doubts and questions to trust him more.

"So do not worry about what you will eat or drink or wear. For the pagans run after these things, and your Heavenly Father knows you have need of them. But seek first his kingdom and his righteousness and all these things will be given to you as well."

After a slight pause, Levi still struggled with these words. He had to know how it could be. "Sir, how do we do that?"

Several turned to look at him—stern expressions showed their disapproval of his presence.

Jesus answered without missing a beat. "You will find that it is more about being than doing." Levi needed time to think about this saying. He wasn't used to this kind of teaching from the rabbis.

"Another teaching I have for you, my friends; do not judge or you too will be judged. For in the same way you judge others, you will be judged, and by the measure you use, it will be measured to you."

Jesus pulled a long, fallen branch over and pinched a fragment from it. Rubbing the fragment between his fingers, he said, "Why do you look at the speck of sawdust in your brother's eye?" Pulling the heavy branch up by one end, he added, "And pay no attention to the plank in your own eye?" The men smiled again, some even chuckled at his extreme illustration.

But Jesus was serious. He threw the branch on the ground. "You hypocrite, first take the plank out of your own eye and then you will see clearly to remove the speck from your brother's eye." The men had nervous expressions as they glanced at Levi. *Perhaps they realize that this was a rebuke of their disdain toward me.*

Levi stared at the ground, discouraged. Would he find a place of acceptance among them?

Jesus went on, "You ask how you seek God's kingdom and his righteousness. I say to you, ask, and keep on asking, and it will be given you; seek, and keep on seeking, and you will find; knock, and keep on knocking, and the door will be opened to you."

Jesus paused, looked out over the sea, and spoke again. "Your Heavenly Father gives good gifts to those who ask him."

He turned back. "So in everything, do to others what you would have them do to you."

Jesus stood up and left the group. What was Levi to do now? He sat there trying to think what was next. Follow Jesus for the next teaching lesson? Figure out what to do about the Roman money and his job? Get reacquainted with his friends? Go off to ask, seek, and knock?

The rest of the men were slow as well to get up and do anything. A few finally stood and talked among themselves. Two walked on to the seashore. Some followed where Jesus went. But Andrew came over to Levi and sat beside him.

"It's been a long time since we've been together," he offered.

"Yes, several years since our studies."

Andrew smiled. "Those were good years with Master Jairus."

Levi nodded, then turned away. "He's about the only who would speak to me when I returned."

"You went to Jericho?"

"Yes, I had a good job with the balsam business."

"Why did you come back?"

Levi shifted a bit and told only part of the truth. "When I got word that my father died, I felt like I had to return to care for my family."

Andrew sat silently beside him. Neither man seemed to know what to say next. *It is complicated,* Levi wanted to say. Andrew's brother, Simon, stood with one group at a distance. He turned and motioned Andrew to come.

"Maybe we can talk again, Levi." Off he went with his brother and the others.

It was not lost on Levi that Simon's motion did not include him. As he sat a few moments watching Andrew walk away, he smiled, grateful for Andrew. *I guess he took Jesus' words to heart. "Do to others what you would have them do to you."*

Ask, seek, knock. Levi lifted his head up to heaven. "O, Holy God of Israel, I come asking, asking for help, seeking direction, knocking to find an open door."

When he looked down the hillside, he saw Lucius and his horse trotting along in the direction of Levi's tax booth. This was not exactly the door he had hoped for, but it was one he had to face.

He reached over to touch the bag he brought with his tax records and the tax money, knowing full well that if he followed through with this new life, his own money would soon be depleted.

Feeling a surge of determination, he grabbed the bag and raced to his booth shortly before Lucius arrived.

Chapter 34

First Steps

The Roman dismounted his horse and strode toward Levi as all Romans do, as though they owned everything in sight, which in a way they did.

This would not be easy. Levi breathed another prayer. *Lord, give me the words to say.*

"Good morning," Levi began.

"Hello, do you have your report ready for Galius?"

"Yes." He hesitated. "It will be my final report."

"Final?" Lucius eyes widened in surprise.

"I have decided to no longer collect taxes."

Lucius straightened and wrinkled his forehead in concern. "And what would cause you to make this decision?"

"Keeping records is fine. I have worked with numbers all my life. The income is plentiful, and I've learned to get along with most of the travelers." Levi turned away. "But I have decided to go another direction."

Lucius studied Levi. "Another direction?"

"There is a teacher in our town, and, well… I have decided to be his follower. To do that, I have to give up this job."

Lucius looked to the sea with his nose pointed in the air. "I see," he said. Then turning again to Levi, he asked, "Is this teacher named Jesus?"

"Yes. You have heard of him?"

Once again Lucius turned away, staring out over the sea. He told the story of a centurion. "This centurion had a long-time servant who had become terribly ill, so ill in fact, he feared his servant would die. The centurion had heard about the miracles of healing that this Jesus had performed. He contacted the healer to ask if he would heal his servant. He insisted that Jesus need not go to his servant but merely give the command." Lucius leaned toward Levi, a slight smile in his eyes. "You know that centurions are used to giving commands and expecting them to be followed."

Lucius gazed back over the sea and finished his story. "Jesus was most impressed with my friend's faith that Jesus could do such a thing. When the centurion headed back toward the town where his servant lay suffering, other servants came running to report to him that at the very hour he had talked with Jesus, his servant was made well again."

Lucius stood in silence.

Levi handed him the bag. "Then perhaps you understand. You will find the money and reports in there. Will you give them to Galius?"

"It will be difficult to replace you," he said. He accepted the bag, mounted his horse, and rode away.

Levi stood stunned. Not only had the Lord given him words to say, he had gone before him to pave the way for this departure. As he glanced at the empty table, he felt the impact of this closure in his life.

Telling his mother and James might be even harder.

As he walked along the path to his mother's house, he wondered. *How will they take to yet another turn in their lives because of the choices I make? Lord, please open the way; give me direction, help me to trust you.*

James came walking from the garden toward the house with an armload of vegetables. *Probably going in for lunch. This will be a good time to catch them both.*

"James," he shouted and waved. They met at the house. Mama busied herself with preparing lunch, excited to have both of her boys. As soon as they finished eating, Levi got to the business at hand. "You know about the teacher, the healer, Jesus?"

"Of course," James said. "I heard the townspeople talking about his amazing teachings yesterday from the boat. I was able to get there in time to hear some of his last words and hear from others about his miracles of healing." He paused. "You remember that day, Levi, when you told us about Jesus' healing the man who was demon possessed in our synagogue? Well, that was old Jonas. I remember him. He was kind of wild and talked strangely. They say he's been quiet and sane since that day."

Just the opening Levi needed. "And do you remember the day we went to Jerusalem and saw John the Baptizer in the Jordan River?" Mama and James nodded. "He talked about repentance of sin. I have thought about that over and over. My life has gotten way out of hand. I have heard Jesus' teachings by the shore each day as I sat at the booth. I felt like he was speaking directly to me." Levi's body started to quiver, and he couldn't stop it.

He turned away, fighting the tears. James and Mama looked at each other in concern. Finally, Levi continued with a husky voice. "Yesterday, when Jesus finished teaching, he walked to my booth and stood right before me. He said, 'Follow me.'" Levi could not fight back the tears.

His mother reached over to place her hand on his.

"I cannot follow him and work for the Romans at the same time, so I have turned in my records and the money. This will affect the finances for our family."

Mama squeezed his hand. "Don't you worry about that, son. The Lord will provide."

"I'm making good money with the building projects," James said. "And Amos has another job for me. We'll manage."

More tears came to his eyes as he saw the ready acceptance of his family. How could this be? He had asked and it was given to him. *Blessed be the name of the Lord!*

*****

Levi left his mother and brother to walk along the sea. The sun shone brightly across the calm waves, creating a wide path of sparkles that seemed to dance across the water. How full of life and hope this happy scene was. But would it last?

What next? He remembered Jesus saying, "Don't worry." *Ah worry, a first lesson in trusting.*

He had conquered the discussion with Lucius and found acceptance with his family, but what of the other followers of Jesus? Were they willing to take him in? *One step at a time.*

Levi kicked off his sandals and buried his feet into the sandy, pebbly shore, allowing the waves to wash over the tops of his feet, and feel the draw of the sand.

"Draw me into your plan, O Heavenly Father. Lead these feet into the next steps," he whispered as he closed his eyes and tilted his face toward the brilliant sun.

He walked along the shore barefooted, just as he did as a child, and recalled his mother's words, "Only to the shore."

Reaching down to pick up a few pebbles and squatting by the shore, Levi formed a circle and a square. He smiled, aware how this simple pleasure had led him to excel with numbers. Even numbering off the generations from Abraham to David—fourteen, then the generations from David to the exile—fourteen, double perfect sevens each.

On his way home, he glanced toward Susanna's house. She and her friends were another matter. What to do about them?

*****

The next morning, he awoke, ready to hear more of Jesus' teachings. Would they still be in the same place? Sometimes they went off on trips.

Thankfully, when he stepped out of his house, he saw Jesus a short way off, talking with his followers.

"Blessed are you when people insult you, persecute you, and falsely say all kinds of evil against you because of me. Rejoice and be exceedingly glad for great is your reward in heaven, for in the same way they persecuted the prophets who were before you."

Well, that is a jolt first thing in the morning!

"You are to be the salt of the earth. But if the salt has lost its saltiness, how can it be made salt again? It is no longer good for anything, except to be thrown out and trampled by men."

Jesus paused, focusing on each man's eyes in the group. "You are to be the light of the world." Jesus glanced up the hill beyond Levi's house. "A city on a hill cannot be hidden." Then he turned to the men. "Neither do men light a lamp and put it under a bowl. Instead, they put it on its stand, and it gives light to everyone in the house. In the same way, my friends," Jesus said with a yearning look at Levi, "let your light shine before men, that they may see your good deeds and praise your Father in heaven."

Jesus had taught these same things yesterday. They must be important. He went on with more teaching, but Levi was stuck on the conviction that he must be salt and light to Susanna and her friends—quite honestly, the only friends he had known in the last several months. *But I am so incapable of talking to them about spiritual things.*

Then he had an idea. These *friends* were used to parties. What if he invited them all to his house for a dinner and had Jesus as the main guest? They all wanted to see his new house the last time they were together but got too drunk to follow through. They would surely be ready to come.

He could hardly wait until Jesus finished his lesson to ask him if he might be interested.

As the others were leaving, Levi approached Jesus. Jesus smiled his approval. The day and time were set.

Susanna was glad to hear from Levi again and offered to help him get things ready for the dinner and issue invitations. When they discovered that several of Jesus' disciples were also coming, they realized that they would have to spill outside to the porch with more mats for seating.

Chapter 35

The Dinner

Levi's excitement mounted when the day finally came. Now these friends might come to know Jesus as well. But would they understand? They were not synagogue goers. Their lives were as bad or worse than Levi's had been, but surely Jesus' influence and words would win them. *Perhaps, in this way, I can be salt and light.*

As each group arrived, Levi showed them his house. They complimented the structure and spaciousness, and at one point or another each asked, "Who is this special guest you have invited?"

"Wait and see," he baited them each time. After the last one arrived, he looked out the front door and saw Jesus with the disciples trailing behind him. "Ah, here he comes now."

Everyone cocked their heads around each other, straining to see who was coming. Levi ushered Jesus to the head of the circle of mats, while Susanna motioned the disciples to the mats on the porch.

Once the guests were in place, Levi began his introductions.

"I am glad to have all of you here tonight to enjoy my new house. I also welcome the followers of our special guest.

"I invited all of you this evening to introduce you to the man who has changed my life. This is Jesus of Nazareth, who has words of truth to share with us. God has sent him to show us the way to live in relationship to God."

His guests glanced at each other with questioning frowns as if to say, *what has happened to Levi?*

Jesus smiled and nodded to Levi, "We thank Levi for his invitation. He who was walking in darkness has found a great light, along with the cleansing power of forgiveness."

The guests fell silent as they listened. His kind manner, his gentle tone, drew them in immediately.

"All who sup together at this meal know the dark places of their lives," he said. "You grow weary following the ways of this world, searching for meaning when you know better than anyone else what lures you to discontent. Those places can be made clean when sin is confessed. No longer do you need to long for peace in your soul, for God provides a place of peace for you.

"We might think about life in the way that we think of Levi's new house." Jesus motioned toward the ceiling. "It had walls and a roof, but it had been standing a long time, and inside, the walls had crumbled, and animals had invaded, bringing their filth with them. Now, this house has been restored and cleansed."

The thief hung his head. The zealot frowned but listened attentively. A fellow tax collector stared at the floor. Amos sat aloof; one eyebrow raised. Others gazed in space with solemn, thoughtful expressions.

"You too can be restored and cleansed. I have come that you might find rest for your souls. No longer do you need to do it all on your own. You may fall before God's holy throne in confession and find peace that surpasses all understanding. As we eat together, I welcome your questions and your comments."

Levi asked, "Master, will you bless the food, please."

After Jesus' prayer, servants, who Levi had hired, brought in the food. Soft chatter gradually built, but no one commented to Jesus or asked questions. Levi watched his guests while they ate. Many glanced often at Jesus.

One of Levi's tax-collector friends, who had heard of Levi's departure as a publican, nervously looked from side to side and hovered over his food, looking down most of the time. Delilah chatted away, oblivious to Jesus' opening remarks. Amos ate with a questioning eye on Jesus.

While Levi smiled with delight at having brought Jesus to his friends, he could not help but notice the disapproving looks from the disciples. One subtly pointed with his head toward a man well known for being a zealous zealot, while the disciple next to him scowled and nodded his head in agreement. Seemingly unable to accept their being stuck in this house with all these sinful misfits, most hung their heads, casting occasional glares.

When Levi walked close to the porch to say something to a servant, Simon and James were looking down the path that led to Levi's house. He could hear their conversation.

Simon whispered, "Who is it?"

"I don't know. It's too dark."

"More of Levi's 'friends'?"

"I think it's Meribah."

"Is Jairus with him?"

"I can't tell. No, I think it's those Pharisees who have been visiting this past week."

"This should be interesting."

"Who invited them?"

"Probably no one."

Meribah ushered his "guests" to the edge of the group just behind the disciples. "You see. Just as I told you. This Jesus not only enters the house of a tax collector, but he eats with him and his friends of questionable repute."

One of the Pharisees scanned the crowd with judgmental eyes. "Thieves and drunkards, did you say?"

"Indeed. And a zealot, an unscrupulous landowner, as well as women of ill repute, not to mention other tax collectors like Levi."

"Scandalous!"

The uninvited visitors were unaware that Levi stood nearby. Simon and James and the other disciples were also privy to their comments as the Pharisees spoke out amid the noisy diners.

Soon, Amos, Levi's landowner friend, spoke. "Jesus, you said you welcomed questions and comments." The crowd quickly ceased their chatter.

"Yes, go on."

"I own many houses and have great wealth. I have men under me who obey my commands. I have all my needs met. Does that sound as if I need anything else? Maybe you need to stick with taking your message to people in poverty, the ones who are needy."

Others around the table muttered grumbles of approval.

"It is true," Jesus spoke with calm assurance. "Many of you have plenty of coins in your money belts, but you cannot serve both money and God. You will love the one and hate the other. If your wealth is ill gotten, it brings you no lasting comfort. It is illusive. You must constantly strive for it by any means possible—thievery, trickery, denouncing allegiance to your own people, offering your souls or your own body for it. But that wealth can be here today and gone tomorrow. What I bring you is rest for your souls, forgiveness for your sin and an inner peace beyond all understanding."

Susanna sat directly across from Levi. He saw tears filling her eyes. *Praise God, Jesus' message is penetrating her heart.*

Just then one of the Pharisees, who apparently did not know how to whisper, spoke to the disciples, "Why does your teacher eat with tax collectors and sinners?"

Levi watched the disciples as they reacted with nervous shifting of positions and refusal to look the Pharisees in the eye. Not one of them seemed to be able to defend the unusual, life-changing work Jesus was doing in the lives of Levi's guests. *Can they not respond because they agree with these accusers?*

Jesus came to their rescue. He stood and spoke to the Pharisees. "It is not the healthy who need a doctor, but the sick. For I have not come to call the righteous, but sinners to repentance. Go and learn what this means: 'I desire mercy, not sacrifice.'"

The accusers pointed their noses in the air, whisked their robes around them, and left.

Levi quickly focused again on Susanna. Her eyes were wide in alarm; her whole demeanor had changed from thoughtful and engaged to disturbed and angry.

Levi lowered his head in regret. Things were not going well. Why did the disciples not defend their own teacher? Why were the religious leaders so blind and heartless? Now it appeared he would lose most of the few friends he had.

Jesus continued to speak with care and urgency, but the damage had been done. A few seemed to listen with open hearts, but Susanna's emotionally drained face and distracted attitude indicated that she had closed her feelings. Levi could only hope that some of Jesus' words would penetrate her heart.

As the evening concluded, Jesus quietly gave parting words of assurance to Levi. "You have done well, Levi. You chose to share your new-found faith in this way with those in need of it. Seeds were planted that will grow to fruition, but you must be patient."

One by one, the guests gave awkward parting words of thanks for the dinner. Amos talked about how well James had fixed up the house and added, "Nice dinner." Susanna stayed a bit to help gather the dishes but quickly left.

*****

Levi sat forlorn on the porch of his house looking down the hillside. The lights of the fishing boats were all that penetrated the darkness.

"Lord," he said as he looked into the dark sky. "I had such high expectations. Even Jesus acknowledged my efforts, but I feel totally defeated. The men whom I am to serve alongside don't like me or want me. The religious leaders, who should have your love in their hearts, have shown their bitterness and

228

hatred. I no longer have a job, and now no prospect of work with my apparently former friends. How am I to live?"

Jesus' teaching came immediately to mind. "Do not worry, seek first the kingdom of God and his righteousness, and all these things will be added to you."

Worry versus trust. "Be patient," Jesus had said.

"Holy Lord, help me to be patient, patient in all things. I have so much to learn. You gave me grace in dealing with Lucius and talking with Mama and James. Help me now to trust you with the challenges I will face."

Chapter 36

Adventures to Come

Levi dressed the next morning and found Jesus and his followers already sitting in the field nearby as before.

Once again Levi slipped in behind them. Andrew nodded with a slight smile. Simon, whom Jesus was now calling Peter, glanced but quickly gave his attention back to Jesus. Thomas was toward the back but made no effort to acknowledge Levi. John, James' brother, moved over slightly to make room for Levi. As was his custom—he could not help but count—Levi counted the group of men who gathered for Jesus' teaching. He realized a few had dropped off and only twelve remained.

Jesus reminded them of the teaching about judgment from the day before. "We have talked about being judgmental, trying to examine the speck in another person's eye when there is a plank in your own eye. We certainly saw an example of that last night with the Pharisees. Bitterness and hatred do not bring people into the kingdom, only love."

Jesus nodded toward Levi. "Levi knew the weary condition of sin in his own life. He also discovered the cleansing power of God when he came to repentance. His desire was to share that same forgiveness with his friends, much like many of you did when you began to follow me. John, you went to tell your brother James. Andrew, you went to tell Peter. Philip went to Nathaniel. May we learn from all these examples. Love—this is the heart of the good news that we bring."

Several of the other followers glanced at Levi and smiled.

"The eye is the lamp of the body. If your eyes are good, your whole body will be full of light. But if your eyes are bad, if they see only evil, your whole body will be full of darkness. If then the light within you is darkness, how great is that darkness!"

These were the very words that had convicted Levi just a few days ago. Must he say them again? Did the other disciples not hear them? Or not pay attention to them?

Jesus looked directly at Levi. "'Levi' means 'a person pledged for a debt.'" The others also turned to look at him. "The debt is paid, Levi. You have now become Matthew, 'a gift of God.'" The others nodded. Finally some affirmation.

Levi's eyes moistened. Overwhelmed, yet embarrassed with this attention, Levi lowered his head.

Jesus spoke of loving others with the kind of love God has for his people, for it is the motivation of the heart that governs a person's actions. He emphasized faith, faith that God would protect and guide.

Jesus stood. "Come now, we are going to take a trip." He walked down the hillside with his students following behind. Levi ambled down the hill, excited to now be accepted among some of them, off on an adventure together.

Jesus headed straight to the sea.

Oh, no, not the sea. Please not the sea. Regardless of Levi's fears, Jesus insisted that they all get in the boat. Levi stuffed himself as deep in the hull as one possibly can in a fishing boat. Jesus settled in also and laid his head on a pillow of nets.

The boat moved in smooth sways with the rolling water. So far, so good. He was mainly happy to be part of the group. They were different from most people, more casual. Several fished for a living and bantered back and forth as he imagined they might do on a night's fishing trip.

But shortly, the wind picked up and the waves grew deeper and stronger. Water splashed up to the edge of the boat as Levi grabbed hold of the side. Soon streams of water ran over his hand, down his arm, and into the boat. The next wave splashed in his face.

"Grab the other bucket!" Peter commanded someone. Two of them scooped buckets of water out of the boat as the wind blew in a fury. The force of the sea water nearly blinded Levi. He was half aware of others who were scooping water out of the boat with their hands, but he was too frightened to let go as the boat rocked back and forth. His sandals slid across the slippery side, plunging his feet into the boatful of water. Another strong wave hit the side of the boat nearly turning it over. Levi grabbed that side, thrusting himself against it to try to bring it back down. *I knew I should never have come on this trip!*

One of the disciples shook Jesus who still lay sleeping. "Lord, save us! We're going to drown!"

Jesus sat up and shouted over the roar of the wind and water, "You of little faith, why are you so afraid?" Then he stood, raised his hands in the air, and rebuked the wind and the waves. "Quiet! Be still!"

The wind died down and in no time, it was completely calm.

Though Levi had not worked like the rest, his heart pumped so hard he still felt the pounding. The men who had been heaving water panted heavily, but finally were able to catch deep satisfying breaths of air as they all sat amazed at the power of Jesus' words over the wind.

Philip pushed the wet hair from his face and whispered to Levi. "What kind of man is this? Even the wind and waves obey him."

Peter and James picked up their buckets again and scooped up the water still left in the boat.

The men sat quietly the rest of the trip as the boat bobbed along. *What a living lesson of fear and faith!* Levi mused.

*****

They arrived at the other side of the lake in the region of Gerasa, a land of Gentiles. Near the town of Gadara they came to some hewn-out caves in the side of a mountain ridge that gave the place an eerie feel.

Compared to this dreary place, the boat of the storm felt more secure. These caves looked to be caves for the dead, yet two barely dressed men came out from the holes. One stared at the disciples but went back in his cave. The other came toward the boat.

"Shall we push back from the shore?" Peter asked.

"No, let's get out." Jesus already had one foot on the sandy rocks.

As they gathered on the shore, the grotesque-looking man came closer. Chains around his wrists clanked and dangled loose as he moved. Cuts all over his arms and chest betrayed the wild behavior of the man. But his massive build, bushy brows, and haunting eyes were the most frightening.

Worse yet, the man started running toward them. Thankfully, Jesus stood in front of the men. Though Levi's heart raced once again, Jesus' presence brought some security. Surely, if he could contain the wind and waves, he could deal with this man.

Instead of attacking them, the man fell at Jesus' feet. Then he burst out with a deep, thunderous voice that sounded like a frightening chorus of voices. "What do you want with me, Jesus, Son of the Most High God? Swear to God that you won't torture me!"

"What is your name?" Jesus asked.

"My name is Legion for we are many. Do not send us away! Do not send us out of the region. Please do not send us away. We don't want to go into the abyss." The voices were begging! Then they said, "See the pigs feeding on the hillside. Send us into them."

"Come out of him!" Jesus called. The man let out a loud shriek, writhed about and then calmed. Immediately his demeanor changed. The wild look out of his eyes transformed into a calm, grateful gaze. A slight smile warmed his face.

The man, still on his knees, looked up to Jesus. "Thank you," he said, now in a single, gentle voice. He lifted his arms, "Praise God, thank you." He buried his head in his hands, heaving great sighs of relief and crying, "Thank you. Thank you."

Jesus placed his hand on the man's shoulder. The man touched Jesus' hand. "Thank you," he said again. Jesus helped him stand and took off his own cloak to wrap it around the man.

Just then, the disciples' attention turned to a thunderous sound coming from the hill across the way. Hundreds of pigs went running down the hillside in a stampede. They formed a cascade off the cliff and into the sea, snorting and grunting as they fell.

Not long after, people came out from town to see what was going on. They had heard about the drowning of the pigs and saw the demonic man dressed and in his right mind. The man explained to the people what had happened, but instead of seeing him made well, all they could think about was the destruction of their neighbor's pigs and the costly worth of his livelihood, not to mention the loss of food for their Gentile bellies. They begged Jesus to leave. "And don't come back!" one man shouted as they all departed.

When the people left, the cleansed man asked Jesus to take him with them, but Jesus told him to go back into the town and proclaim what had happened to him.

"But they won't listen to me," he protested.

"Just share your story," Jesus told him.

The disciples said not a word, but one by one, they embraced the man who had been healed. Warmed by their touch and the miracle of his healing, he waved goodbye to them.

As they sailed back, no one spoke. Perhaps, like Levi, they were simply trying to process all that had happened during this day.

Fear and wonder wove in and out. A storm at sea, one of the reasons he feared the water, came to pass in all its fury, leaving him helpless and out of control. But Jesus was there, and the welcomed calm afterward was beyond comprehension.

The man at the burial caves was pitiful beyond imagination. Levi remembered hearing the man in the synagogue at

Capernaum who was demon-possessed. *Jonas? Was that what James called him?* Levi had never experienced a person like this nor seen this kind of healing up close.

Philip, who sat next to Levi in the boat, leaned over. "I'm telling you, the very sight of that man struck fear in my heart, but the transformation was glorious to behold."

"Yes," Levi nodded his head.

Their boat continued its course. Soon, Levi's childhood house came into view, and his eyes went straight to the pottery shed. Old memories of fear rushed to his mind. He closed his eyes and hung his head, his shoulders rounded in protection, a stance he automatically used when Papa shouted his anger and displeasure. When would he ever be rid of the memory that brought fear and condemnation?

Taking a deep breath, Levi determinedly straightened up. The boat had shifted slightly, and now Jesus, with his back to Levi, blocked his view of the shed. *Perhaps Jesus will be the one to block my fears as well. After all, I certainly had living lessons about fear this very day.*

Levi studied Jesus as the setting sun lowered in the west, thankful to have his mind on someone who brought joy and purpose to his life. Jesus' hair blew slightly in the breeze. *Who is this man? More than a teacher, more than a healer. He has command over the elements of nature and the demons within. Though he is powerful, he is gentle, kind, and caring. He demonstrates love as he teaches us faith. He knows our hearts, our sinful temptations—but also our potential. Will he block the view of my past? The pain of what was?*

Levi closed his eyes to the wind and prayed. *Holy Father, help me follow his teachings; help me love the unlovely as he does. Grow my faith.*

Chapter 37

Eyes to See

The next morning, Levi arrived earlier than most of the followers to receive Jesus' teaching. Andrew greeted him. "Up earlier today, I see." Andrew smiled.

"Yes, I don't want to miss a word."

Others joined with sleepy looks on their faces after the strenuous day before. Thomas made eye contact with him but looked away. Simon Peter was the last to arrive.

Peter sat and glanced around, not noticing Levi right behind him. "Where's the tax collector?" he muttered, just loud enough to be heard by all. James nodded in Levi's direction. Peter barely glanced over his shoulder.

The words cut deeply. Would he always be "the tax collector" to some of them?

Jesus began his teaching for the morning. "I have taught you many things these past weeks, teachings you will hear again and again as I teach the many who come to listen. We have talked about worshiping God, not money, the futility of worry, the importance of asking, seeking the Father, knocking, and the dangers of being judgmental."

Did Levi imagine it, or did Jesus' gaze linger on Peter at the word *judgmental*?

"Therefore, everyone who hears these words of mine and puts them into practice is like a wise man who built his house on the rock. The rain came down, the streams rose, and the winds blew and beat against that house; yet it did not fall, because it had its foundation on the rock.

"But everyone who hears these words of mine and does *not* put them into practice is like a foolish man who built his house upon the sand. The rain came down, the streams rose, and the wind blew and beat against that house, and it fell with a great crash."

Jesus paused to re-emphasize his beginning point. "It is important that you put my teachings into practice. It provides the foundation for further work."

After added teaching, Jesus led them down to the shore. As always, people gathered to hear him, but today, the crowd was larger than usual. They crowded in so close that Jesus had difficulty being heard and seen.

As before, he instructed Peter, "Bring in one of the boats."

Peter pulled a boat up to the shore. Jesus stepped in and pushed out a few feet so he might see the crowd better. They sat along the shore's edge to listen.

Jesus taught through parables much as he did with the disciples. A blind man came, one Levi had seen many times. It occurred to him that he had never talked with the man. His thoughts went back to Jericho and his conversations with blind Bartimaeus.

Levi sauntered over to the blind man. "Do you hear the teacher well?" he asked.

"No, not very well. He sounds far away."

"Jesus is teaching from a boat along the water's edge. Would you like to get closer?"

"Yes, that would be most helpful. I've heard that he is a great teacher and a healer as well."

"That is true."

The blind man held tightly to Levi's arm as he led the man in and around the listeners to an opening much closer. "Let's sit here." Levi helped the old man sit on the ground. At times, the man did not understand a concept, so Levi quietly explained. The man hung on every word of Jesus' teaching.

After Jesus finished and the crowd slowly dispersed, Levi turned to help the blind man up. He noticed tears in his eyes.

"His teaching is amazing," the man said, "not like the teachers of the law. You have been so kind to me. May I touch your face."

Levi hardly knew how to react. "Yes. Of course."

The man touched Levi's chest. "Oh, you are very tall."

Levi smiled as the man's hands moved up his neck to his cheeks. "You are a handsome young man and truly kind to this old man. Do you think I might touch the teacher's face?"

"I will take you to him. You can ask him yourself."

Jesus seemed to maneuver toward Levi's direction even as they moved toward him.

"Master, this blind man would like to touch you."

"Yes, Raspiah, you may touch me."

"You know my name?" Raspiah's hands were shaking as he reached up to touch Jesus' face. "Such a kind face. Lord, if you will, would you heal these tired eyes?"

Jesus took the old man's hands in his. "I will. Do you believe?"

"I believe you have the heart of God Almighty in you, and I believe you can heal me."

Jesus touched the man's eyes. "According to your faith will it be done to you."

Raspiah slowly opened and closed, and opened and closed his eyes. He blinked a few more times and the glassy stare was gone. His eyes looked healthy. He gazed at Jesus' face. As if by long-time habit, he once again reached up to feel Jesus cheek. "It is you, the teacher, the healer coming in mercy to bring sight to these blind eyes. Praise God! Now I can see you." He looked at the sea. "The water, the boats, the people, I see it all! And the young man who helped me, where is he?"

Levi held out his hands.

He reached up to touch Levi's face again. "Yes, it is you, the wonderful man who brought me to Jesus!"

Those standing around realized what had happened. A few knew Raspiah and rejoiced with him. A young woman came running and screaming. She flung her arms around him. "Oh,

Papa, I heard the good news. Can you really see? Is it true? Can you see me?"

"Lily, is this my Lily?"

"Yes, Papa. It is me, Lily! You can see my face at last!" She wrapped her arms around her father.

At the mention of her name, Levi stepped back from the gathering of astonished friends. His mind went straight to the Lily of his past. *How unworthy I am to be a part of this. I am not the wonderful man Raspiah thinks I am. He does not even know that just a few weeks ago I was the tax collector.*

The jubilant crowd moved on with the man who could now see.

Oh, Lord, may I have eyes to see as well.

Jesus stepped over to Levi and put his hand on his shoulder. "Well done, Matthew, gift of God. The Lord is using you for his purposes. You have been forgiven of your old life. Behold, he is making all things new."

Levi needed to think this through.

Making all things new, Levi thought as he wandered along the shore. *So many new things—the delight on the blind man's face, the peace on the demoniac's face, the calm of the storm. All things new.*

He looked up ahead to see the tax booth. *Hmm, a new tax collector.* He watched as the man walked down the way to meet a caravan, thankful that it was no longer his job.

Making all things new. *Matthew. He keeps calling me Matthew.* He smiled to himself. *I don't know that I am a gift of God, but I certainly have been given a gift of new life. Thank you, Lord. Matthew it is.*

Chapter 38

Teachings of Purpose, Miracles of Life

Jesus began his teaching for the morning. "The kingdom of heaven is at hand. It is like a mustard seed, which a man took and planted in his field. It is the smallest of all the seeds, yet when it grows, it is the largest of garden plants and becomes a tree, so that the birds of the air come and perch on its branches."

"Today, I am calling you." He looked at each man as he called their names. "Simon Peter and Andrew, James and John, Philip and Bartholomew, Thomas and Matthew, James and Thaddaeus, Simon and Judas Iscariot. I am calling each of you, to be that mustard seed. Though you feel small, you must plant that seed in many hearts so that people of all nations will find their rest in those branches.

"Matthew has given us an example with his desire to plant this new-found seed in the hearts of his friends who are far from the kingdom." Simon Peter squirmed a bit, moving his legs into a new position.

Jesus reached in his bag and brought out a piece of bread. "The kingdom of heaven is like yeast that a woman took and mixed into a large amount of flour until it worked all through the dough. You have been called to serve in the kingdom like that yeast, spreading the message, allowing the Spirit to work through the minds and hearts of the people."

Jesus smiled, "Take and eat my parable." The furrowed, thoughtful brows of his followers softened. They smiled at each other as they each broke of a piece and passed the illustration to the next man.

Matthew—formerly Levi—turned to Andrew in a whisper, "It is like the psalmist said, 'I will open my mouth in parables, I will utter things hidden since the creation of the world.'"

Peter inclined his ear toward Levi's comment but said nothing.

Jesus continued, "The kingdom of heaven is like treasure hidden in a field. When a man found it, he hid it again, and then in his joy went and sold all he had and bought that field."

Jesus paused, "You have found this treasure to be worth your all. Again, the kingdom of heaven is like a merchant looking for fine pearls. When he found one of great value, he went away and sold everything he had and bought it."

Matthew frowned in confusion. *Only Gentiles go after pearls. Does he mean the Gentiles are included in kingdom work? A Gentile like the demon-possessed man by the caves?*

"Likewise, you have all left your merchant work or a tax booth or fishing boats because you have found treasure in the kingdom. Once again, the kingdom of heaven is like a net that was let down into the lake and caught all kinds of fish. When it was full, the fishermen pulled it up on the shore. Then they sat down and collected the good fish in baskets but threw the bad away."

Matthew glanced at the fishermen in the group; all were nodding their heads knowingly, having done this countless times.

"This is how it will be at the end of the age. The angels will come and separate the wicked from the righteous and throw them into the fiery furnace, where there will be weeping and gnashing of teeth."

Jesus paused. "Have you understood all these things?"

"Yes," they whispered or nodded their heads.

"Therefore, every teacher of the law who has been instructed about the kingdom of heaven is like the owner of the house who brings out of his storeroom new treasures as well as old."

Oh, to be that kind of teacher! Ready to bring out new thoughts.

"We will travel to other towns today to share these treasures with the people." And just that quickly, they got up and headed down the road.

*****

In each town they were welcomed because the people had heard about Jesus' teachings and miracles of healing. From town to town, the responses echoed over and over, "His teaching is amazing." "We have never heard this kind of teaching." "He helps us understand." And many came asking for healing.

One healing made a powerful impact on Matthew. They had just left a village, with several following after them. Suddenly, they heard the cry, "Unclean! Unclean!" Instead of the leprous man moving away from Jesus and the others, the man came toward them, but he kept a little distance. Several turned their backs. The women gasped and instinctively cupped their hands to their faces, anticipating the smell.

Jesus moved toward the man. The leper hesitated but walked forward and knelt before Jesus. Peter and Judas took the first step to protect the crowd, but Jesus put his hand out to stop them.

Trembling, the leper called out, "Lord, if you are willing, you can make me clean."

The crowd took in audible breaths and stood frozen. What would Jesus do? He walked forward and touched the man's shoulder. He *touched* the leper. Touched an unclean, contagious leper. "I am willing," Jesus said. "Be clean!"

The leper's face slowly turned smooth. His missing nose had formed again. Rags fell off his hands where once there were only partial fingers. Now the man lifted healthy, fully developed hands in praise and thanksgiving. Matthew had heard about this kind of healing, but now he experienced it for himself. He would not soon forget the ecstatic cry that poured forth from this grateful leper.

The once-silent crowd uttered words of amazement and praise as well. Momentum grew as word spread back through the crowd to those who could not see what had happened.

242

Matthew turned to Philip, "If I had not seen this with my own eyes, I would not have believed it." Matthew heard Jesus say to the man, "See that you do not tell anyone. But go, show yourself to the priest and offer the gift Moses commanded as a testimony to them."

That night when Jesus and the disciples gathered around a fire to eat, Thomas asked Jesus why he told the man with leprosy not to tell anyone about his healing.

"I told the man to go to the priest to verify his healing and to be vindicated in his community in accordance with the law," Jesus answered. "Many who know this man will know of his healing, but it is better for the man to express his faith rather than broadcast sensationalism about the healing to others outside his town. I heal to meet the needs of those who place their faith in me, not to use them." Jesus paused. "Besides that, my time has not yet come."

Andrew and Matthew lay in a grassy area with the other followers that night. Matthew rolled over toward Andrew. "What do think Jesus meant when he said that his time had not yet come?"

"I don't know. I was wondering that myself."

*****

At last, back to Capernaum. Matthew and Andrew sat munching on their lunch together, as they watched the women who often followed them and graciously provided meals. Just then, Matthew froze in surprise. Susanna was among them.

"Andrew, look. Susanna is helping the women!"

"Susanna?"

"Yes. Uh, she was one of the friends at the dinner I had at my house when Jesus spoke to them. She seemed to be influenced by his words, but when the Pharisees and Meribah showed up, her attitude changed. I have not seen her since. Maybe one of the women came to talk to her."

"Was she more than a 'friend'?"

"Well, it's complicated. I'm glad she has received good influences from the other women."

Then Matthew spied his mother. He ran over to greet her. "Mama!"

"Oh Levi, it's so good to see you again." Matthew hugged her and smiled at hearing his old name. "Levi, I've been so busy making new friends, telling many about Jesus and his love for us. His mother, Mary, teaches us and we teach the younger ones. She told us that you and the others were coming back, so we were ready to provide food for you."

Matthew beamed with delight at her enthusiasm.

She grabbed his arm. "Come, I want you to meet a young woman who has come to be a new believer."

Mama whisked him over to a group of women who were scooping food onto plates. She led him to one who was bent over the kettle. "Susanna," Myrah called, "I want you to meet my son."

When Susanna stood, she and Matthew both looked surprised. "Levi!" she shouted. She looked from Myrah and back to Levi. "Myrah is your mother?"

"Yes," he laughed, "she certainly is."

"You know each other?" Myrah questioned.

"Uh, yes, we do," Matthew sputtered.

Susanna went on. "Your mother has become my good friend. She has taught me about Jesus and his love for us."

Matthew's heart soared. He remembered Jesus' words from the dinner about planting the seed, and now his own mother had watered that seed to fruition. "I'm so happy for you, Susanna. This is good news indeed."

Just then, a woman called her to come and help. Susanna smiled and held out the plate in her hands. "Here, have another plate of food," she said, as she hurried off.

Myrah grabbed his arm again, and she moved them away from the busy scene. They were able to share all the things that had happened to both of them since he was gone. One of the women finally called to Myrah, so she hugged Matthew and hurried off to help.

Matthew meandered back to Andrew to share all his news.

"It's good to be back home," Andrew mused. He looked toward Bethsaida to the east. "My father would not believe the things we have seen and heard. In fact, he probably would refuse to believe even if we told him. He is a stubborn old fisherman."

"I didn't realize you had a problem with your father."

"Humph, we could never please him."

"I know the feeling. My father was as rough as one of his pottery chips."

They sat in silence for a moment.

"Matthew," he said, then he chuckled before he went on. "I'm still trying to get used to calling you Matthew like Jesus does. And to call my brother Peter instead of Simon." He paused. "Matthew, I know Peter has been rather unkind to you, never letting you forget that you were a tax collector. Like our father, he's a bit rough around the edges as well, but he'll come around."

Matthew stopped in the middle of chewing his figs and stared at the ground. His shoulders humped over. "It isn't just Peter. Some of the others still have not accepted me. Thomas always seems to have a question in his eyes when he looks at me."

The two sat in silence for a moment, then Matthew spoke again. "But I have come to feel so much acceptance and care from Jesus that it makes the difference. He shows me our *Heavenly* Father's love."

"Yes, I know what you mean. We've been following him for some time now."

Matthew looked up. "It looks like he's about to teach again; the crowd is gathering."

*****

As they walked through the crowd, Matthew heard different groups telling what they had heard about the leper, the blind man, and a lame man. Some spoke of his teachings. They pressed in to get near him.

Just then Jairus appeared, walking in haste toward Jesus and pushing his way through. Another synagogue official trailed along behind him. Matthew squeezed in to see what was happening. Jairus fell at the feet of Jesus and pleaded earnestly with him. "My little daughter is dying. Please come and put your hands on her so that she will be healed and live."

Oh, no, not little Prisca. I still think of her as a small child, but she must be about twelve years old by now.

Jesus began moving toward the house of Jairus, but the crowd pressed in so, that he had trouble moving quickly. Suddenly Jesus stopped and looked around. "Who touched me?"

Someone questioned, "Don't you see the people crowding around you, Lord, and yet you ask, 'Who touched me?'"

"Power has gone out from me." Jesus kept looking around.

Then a woman came and fell at his feet, trembling with fear. "Sir, I have been subject to bleeding for twelve years. I have suffered a great deal under the care of many doctors and have spent all I have, yet instead of getting better, I have grown worse."

She raised her head to look at Jesus. "I had heard about you and thought if I just touched the hem of your garment, I would be healed." Her voice quivered. "Indeed, when I touched your cloak, I could feel my bleeding stop immediately, and I felt in my body that I had been freed from my suffering." Tears rolled down her cheeks as she bowed before him.

Jesus bent down and helped her up. "Daughter, your faith has healed you. Go in peace and be freed from your suffering." Two women took each arm to comfort her and stand by her.

When Jesus turned back to Jairus, Meribah and two others had pushed their way through the crowd. Meribah straightened his tall frame and announced with little remorse, "Jairus, your daughter is dead." Then he added with a dismissive air, "Why bother the teacher anymore?"

Ignoring what he said, Jesus told Jairus, "Don't be afraid, just believe." Peter, James, and John went with Jesus and the other friends. Andrew and Matthew trailed behind, concerned for their beloved teacher and his daughter.

When they arrived, mourners were already crowding around the house, weeping with loud wails. Three clusters of noisy flute players seemed to compete with one another, one nasal tune louder than the next which caused the mourners to wail even louder to be heard.

Jesus cried out, "Why all this commotion and wailing? The child is not dead but asleep." The mourners abruptly cut off their loud wails and laughed at him in ridicule. Jesus quickly put them out of the house. He went inside, taking Peter, James, and John with him.

Andrew whispered sideways to Matthew, "Some 'mourners' these people are."

Matthew nodded in agreement. "What would you expect when they were paid to do it?"

The crowd settled into low mumbling as all awaited the outcome.

Soon a cry went out from the house. Was it a cry of sorrow or gladness? Then a more audible cry, "Praise to the Lord!"

Matthew and Andrew immediately looked at each other with broad smiles. "She's been raised to life!" Matthew said.

"Praise to the Lord indeed!" Andrew shouted as he put his arm around Matthew's shoulder. As soon as they saw Peter, James, and John come to the door, they rushed to hear the news.

Peter was the first to speak. He looked at Andrew. "Young Prisca was lying lifeless in her bed, pale as death itself. The

Master took her hand and said, 'Little girl, I say to you, get up!' She opened her eyes to see Jesus, then looked over to see her parents. Immediately, Prisca stood up and walked around the room. Jairus and his wife hugged her with tears of joy."

Peter choked up with his own tears, so John picked up the story. "They thanked Jesus over and over for this blessed miracle. Once again, Jesus gave them orders not to let anyone know about this, then he told them to give their daughter something to eat."

Peter declared, "Our Master has dominion over life itself."

Chapter 39

Fishers of Men

Andrew and Matthew strolled along the shore. "You told me that Peter came to the Lord later than you," Matthew said. "How did that happen?"

"It's a long story. Let's sit here on these rocks." They settled in. "In the beginning, I had been following John the baptizer. Simon, as we called Peter then, constantly made fun of me and ridiculed me. It got worse when I decided to follow Jesus. I tried to tell him that we believed Jesus to be the Promised One, but he wouldn't listen. One morning, after we had an unsuccessful night of fishing, we sat along the shore, mending our nets, and Jesus began teaching as he had other days.

"Simon couldn't help but hear Jesus, though he pretended not to be listening."

"Yes, I know how that is. I sat at the tax booth, trying to focus on my numbers or hope for a caravan to come, but I still heard his words."

Andrew smiled in agreement. "Well, as the crowd grew, Jesus came directly to Simon and asked him to help him push out one of the boats so the crowd could see and hear him better. Reluctantly, Simon helped, and I went along as well."

Andrew chuckled. "Now, he was really a captive audience as he sat there in the boat with Jesus. When Jesus had finished speaking, he told Simon, 'Put out into the deep water, and let down for a catch.' But Simon said, 'We worked hard all night and didn't catch a thing.' Jesus continued to look at him, so he shrugged his shoulders and said, 'But, because you say so, I will let down the nets.'"

Andrew knowingly grinned. "After we rowed out farther, we threw the nets out, one on the right, the other on the left. Well, you would have thought all the fish in the sea had decided to come to our nets! We hauled up the first full net and emptied it into the boat. By that time, the other net was full, so we pulled it in. No sooner did we get that one emptied than the first one was ready again. When we tried to pull that one up, it was so full of fish the net began to break.

"We called to James and John on the shore to come and help us. When they came, we soon had two boatloads—so many fish! That's when it happened. Simon Peter fell at Jesus' knees and humbly said, 'Go away from me, Lord; I am a sinful man!' Simon realized his need of the Savior. Jesus put his hands on Simon's shoulders and looked down, deep in his eyes. He said, 'Simon, don't be afraid; from now on you will catch men.'

"The next week, Jesus came to us while we were casting our nets from the seashore, and he said, 'Follow me.' We left *everything* and have followed Jesus since."

Andrew sat silently looking out at the sea. Matthew couldn't speak, lost in his own experience of admitting sin and answering the call of Jesus to "Follow me."

Andrew broke the silence as he said, "I've thought many times about those words, 'You will be fishers of men.'"

*****

"Come," Jesus said, "we must visit other villages to carry the word to them." So each disciple packed his bag as he had before. Each included a blanket for cool nights, maybe an extra tunic or pair of sandals, favorite pieces of fruit, and a loaf of bread. Some brought vegetables and others pans to fry fish. Sometimes a few women would come along with them to cook. Such a different life than what Matthew had previously known.

Philip came up behind Matthew as he pushed one more handful of figs down in his bag. "Are you ready to go?" Philip asked.

"I believe so," Matthew answered. "It's a different life, isn't it?"

"Yes. I think about that teacher of the law who told Jesus he wanted to be a follower and go wherever Jesus went."

Matthew smiled. "Foxes have holes…"

"And birds of the air have nests," Philip joined in.

"But the Son of Man has no place to lay his head." Matthew finished quoting Jesus.

"That fellow went away very quickly," laughed Philip as he elbowed Matthew and walked along with him.

How good to feel that I belong to this group. Only a couple of men still hold "the tax collector" at arm's length—Peter and Thomas.

As before, Jesus and the twelve journeyed from village to village teaching about God's love, the call to repentance, and what he expects of those who are his children. Some towns had heard of Jesus' fame, others had not. Jesus asked the disciples to baptize those who had repented.

Matthew relished the way Jesus prayed and noticed when he went off by himself. He mentioned that to Andrew one day. Andrew nodded. "Yes, he goes for solitude to meditate and pray. We still have much to learn from him."

When they returned to Capernaum, Matthew felt glad to be in his own bed. His heart was full and running over, but his body felt numb. His dreams were a whirlwind of memories from the last few months—faces of joy, frowns of doubt, sounds of praise from those who were healed, and newness of life for those who repented. So many people, so many needs.

The next day, they gathered again, waiting to hear what would be next. Some days Jesus told a parable or laughed with the men or gave instructions on the next venture punctuated with teasing someone, but on this day, he looked serious.

"My brothers, we have been in many places, teaching in the synagogues, preaching the good news of the kingdom, and healing every disease and sickness," Jesus said. "The people need great compassion because they are harassed and helpless, like sheep without a shepherd. The harvest is plentiful, but the workers are few. We must ask the Lord of the harvest, therefore, to send out workers into his harvest field."

So very naturally, Jesus began praying to the Father, asking for workers, pleading for the disciples to have wisdom as they shared the good news with people. Matthew closed his eyes, taking in the surge of power and determination for which Jesus prayed.

When he was finished, Jesus was silent for what seemed a long time. He studied each of the men with loving eyes. "Today you will begin a new venture. I am giving you authority to drive out evil spirits and to heal every disease and sickness. I am sending you out two by two to go in different directions. You will minister in the ways you have watched me these last few months. Do not go among the Gentiles right now or enter any town of the Samaritans. Go rather to the lost sheep of Israel."

Split apart? Not go as a unit? What is this?

"As you go, preach the message that the kingdom of heaven is near. Preach about repentance. Heal the sick; drive out demons. Freely you have received, freely give. Do not take along any gold, or silver, or copper in your belts; take no bag for the journey, or extra tunic, or sandals or staff; for the worker is worth his keep."

Peter looked at James and John with the same stunned expression that Matthew felt. *Why so restrictive?* he wondered. *And us? We are to do the healings Jesus has done? How can we possibly do that?*

"Whatever town or village you enter, search for some worthy person there and stay at his house until you leave. As you enter the home, give it your greeting. If the home is deserving, let your peace rest on it; if it is not, let your peace return to you. If anyone will not welcome you, or listen to your words, shake the dust off your feet when you leave that home or town. I tell you the truth, it will be more bearable for Sodom and Gomorrah on the day of judgment than for that town. I am sending you out like sheep among wolves. Therefore, be as shrewd as snakes and as innocent as doves."

A tinge of uncertainty climbed up Matthew's back and into his mind. Andrew stared at the ground, deep in thought. Philip took in deep breaths and pushed them out in gentle puffs. Thomas fidgeted with his robe as he looked from Jesus to the sea to the tree above.

"Be on your guard against men." Jesus went on, "They will hand you over to local councils and flog you in their synagogues."

Jesus' gaze went beyond the men as though he were looking into the far future. "In the future, on my account, you will be brought before governors and kings as witnesses to them and to the Gentiles. But when they arrest you, do not worry about what to say or how to say it. At that time, you will be given what to say, for it will not be you speaking, but the Spirit of your Father speaking through you."

After a moment of silence, Jesus fixed his attention back on the men in front of him. "I will pray for you."

He closed his eyes and raised his face to the heavens. "Father, King of the universe, lover of our souls, hear our prayer. Touch each of these men with your Spirit of truth and wisdom. Empower them with your courage and strength. Show them the way and encourage their hearts. Increase their faith, O God. I praise you for the work they will do and the lives that will be changed because of their witness. Amen."

So, with no bag to pack and no preparation to be made, Jesus pointed out directions. "Peter and Andrew, go this direction toward Magdala. James and John, go toward the mountains that way. Philip and Bartholomew..."

Matthew's heart sank. He had hoped for Andrew or Philip as a partner.

"Thomas and Matthew toward Caesarea Philippi by way of the Jordan." Matthew did not hear the rest of the names and places. All he could think of was *Thomas*.

Thomas, always questioning Thomas. How would he manage this new endeavor with one who could not get past the thought of being with a former tax collector? *Lord, I need more than a lion's share of patience and faith.*

Philip, who seemed to understand Matthew's anxiety gripped him on the shoulder. "Shalom, my friend."

Matthew nodded his head. "And to you."

Chapter 40

Going Out Two by Two

Matthew and Thomas headed north along the Jordan River. They did not talk much.

After a couple of hours, Thomas said, "I'm getting hungry."

"I was thinking the same thing. Looks like a small village up ahead. Maybe we can stop there."

They approached a well where a sheep herder had just pulled up a bucket of water. "Could you spare some water for two tired travelers?" Matthew asked.

"Certainly," the shepherd answered. "Where are you from?"

"We come from Capernaum. We're followers of Jesus of Nazareth and have come to proclaim his message," Matthew said.

"Oh, yes, I've heard about him. My nephew in Cana told me many stories about this Jesus. I have extra room since my nephew left. Would you like to stay at my house?"

"That would be kind of you. My name is Matthew, and this is Thomas." Thomas nodded.

"I am Joseph. Follow me and my sheep, and we will take you to the house."

As they approached the humble house, they could smell a stew wafting out the door. Matthew and Thomas both sniffed in the hearty aroma and let out sighs of pleasure.

"My wife is a good cook," Joseph chuckled. "I brought the sheep home for a while, so she made my favorite stew. You came at just the right time!"

The smell of sheep hung all around the house, but the stew overpowered it, at least for the moment.

The shepherd's wife was shy, but every bit as kind as her shepherd husband. The wife pulled out extra bowls for the stew and served up extra bread. They pulled two more stools to the low table and sat to eat.

When Matthew looked at the bowls, he recognized them immediately. "Your bowls! Where did you get these?"

"My nephew bought these in Capernaum and gave them as a gift to us."

"These bowls were made by my family!"

"Blessed are we to have these made by your hands."

"Oh, not me. These were made either by my father or my brother."

"Still, we are blessed by your family."

Seeing this familiar pottery in a new place was like a blessed encouragement that the Lord was with them. "Where is your synagogue in this town?" Matthew asked.

"We are but a small village, only eight families. Not the required ten for a synagogue."

"Are you able to gather the people together so that we might bring the teachings of Jesus to them?" Thomas chimed in. Matthew felt pleasantly surprised that he had finally engaged with this dear couple.

The man nodded his head. "Yes, I can tell them tomorrow that you have come to bring us good news from the prophet."

After pleasant conversation, Joseph pulled out two mats and two blankets for them. When they settled in for the night, Thomas whispered, "The Lord does provide."

Matthew smiled. "Praise be his name. You know, seeing that pottery seemed like an assurance somehow, a sign that the Lord is with us."

Thomas soon made quiet snoring sounds. Would he come to accept Matthew? Matthew's mind wandered as he revisited memories of his father molding the clay. How could someone so cantankerous produce such beautiful pottery? He rolled to his other side and thought of his brother, James, working hard and of their childhood together, but pleasant memories of his sweet mother, ministering to Susanna, finally put him to sleep.

The next day, their gracious host went about gathering up the families of his village. They came together near the well and sat to hear the teaching from "the disciples of Jesus," for many of them had heard the stories of Jesus' work in other places.

Thomas lingered back, fidgeting nervously with his robe as he had done before, so Matthew took the lead.

"Friends, we come here today in the name of Jesus. He preaches that the kingdom of heaven is at hand. The kingdom of heaven is like treasure hidden in a field. When a man found it, he hid it again, and then in his joy went and sold all he had and bought that field."

The villagers sat with rapt attention, even the children.

Matthew went on, feeling empowered by their willingness to listen. "Jesus comes to us proclaiming the good news of God's love. That is the treasure we find, but we must allow ourselves to be cleansed of the sin that drags us down. Search your hearts, find the emptiness there that causes you to be selfish, to fail to forgive a neighbor, to be prideful, to yell at your children, to yield to hopelessness."

Matthew had seen one of the farmers out in the field earlier. "It is like a farmer out in the field or the gardener planting her flowers. They plant their seeds, but the weeds grow up, choking the life out of the harvest. The weeds must be pulled up and cast away. So it is with our lives, we must ask the Lord to show us the weeds of sin and cast them aside to let the joy of the Lord take root and grow."

The people nodded slightly in apparent understanding.

"Our new friend, Joseph," Matthew gestured to his host, "is a shepherd. He takes his sheep to pasture to feed; he protects them from harm, cares for their every need. So it is with our Heavenly Father; he cares for us, and like the sheep, we must yield to him. Instead, at times, we stray as sheep are prone to do, and we get in trouble."

Joseph smiled, nodding his head.

Matthew went on, empowered in his simple preaching to these simple people who took in each word. He noticed, however, that a few would glance now and then at one man who sat looking down most of the time.

"As the proverb goes, 'An evil man is snared by his own sin, but a righteous one can sing and be glad.' Let us sing with happy hearts to our God who loves us."

Matthew chose to lead out with a well-known psalm and the people joined in.

> *To the faithful, you show yourself faithful,*
> *to the blameless, you show yourself blameless,*
> *to the pure, you show yourself pure,*
> *but to the crooked, you show yourself shrewd.*
> *You save the humble,*
> *but bring low those whose eyes are haughty.*
> *You, O LORD, keep my lamp burning;*
> *my God turns my darkness into light.*

After a prayer, the people went their way. Many thanked him for coming and for his words. They promised to meet again the next day.

*****

That afternoon, Joseph asked if they would like to help him shear his sheep. Thomas looked at Matthew's questioning face and then back to Joseph. "We have never done that before. Can you show us what to do?" Thomas asked.

"Certainly." The old man smiled.

His wife chimed in. "But first you will need to have an old tunic, or you will smell like sheep everywhere you go!" They accepted the tunics which already had a whiff of sheep smell on them. In fact, without the stew, everything smelled like sheep.

Joseph showed them how to hold the sheep as he sheared it. After fifty sheep, they had the routine mastered, then they helped Joseph gather up the wool.

Thomas carried the last bundle and laid it in the pile. "This will keep your wife busy for some time, separating the strands of wool."

"Three other women help her, and they all weave the wool into blankets and cloaks for the winter. Homer, up the road, he has goats. Provides us with milk, and his wife dyes the wool. We all work to help each other."

That night, as Matthew and Thomas rested on their mats, Thomas noted, "This is a close village. They seem to care for one another."

Matthew agreed. "We don't see so much of that in Capernaum. Everybody is busy with their own matters. I did notice one man who seemed distant today, not as open as the others."

"I noticed him as well." Thomas took an audible breath and sighed. "I'll lead tomorrow."

Matthew smiled, glad that Thomas was beginning to feel more comfortable.

*****

The next day, Thomas spoke in power, proclaiming the words of Jesus and calling the people to repentance. He taught with parables as Jesus did and like Matthew had done the day before. The people sat once again with rapt attention.

Then the man who had not seemed to be engaged before stood up. Everyone jerked their heads toward him and leaned away, frozen in fear. Thomas was not sure what to do. Stunned silence gripped the crowd.

"I have something to say," the man finally spoke. "I haven't lived here long. I did some bad things where I came from. I don't know how to fit into this village where everybody helps one another. I know I have been rough and, uh, well, unfriendly, even gruff, and I said some hurtful things. It is all because of the bad things I've done. I don't know what to do, but I sure need this forgiveness you talk about."

Touched by the man's honesty, Thomas said, "My brother, you have just done what you need to do. You have confessed your sin. Our Heavenly Father hears your words and knows your heart. He is ready to forgive you, heal you, and bring you into a new life. Is that what you desire?"

The man fell to his knees with his face in his hands. "Yes, yes." He heaved great sobs of repentance. Joseph walked over behind him and put both hands on his shoulders for comfort and support.

Another man stood. "I will have to confess as well. I harbored ill will toward this neighbor, and I have been very judgmental toward others in our village, including," the man turned toward his wife and son, "my own family." The wife lowered her head, obviously trying to control her tears.

Thomas looked at Matthew who nodded support. Thomas raised his hands in praise. "Blessed are we to have these words of confession today. God is the giver of life and the giver of new life in forgiveness. The river is not far away, let us baptize these two brothers as a symbol of that new life."

All the villagers moved as one to the river, several touched the two men on the shoulder in gestures of support. Thomas and Matthew went into the water with the two following and baptized these new believers in the name of Jesus.

They stayed one more day, teaching the people as they had been taught by the Master.

Chapter 41

On to Greater Challenges

As Jesus had taught them, Matthew blessed the village and its people the next morning when he and Thomas departed. Mixed emotions came over them as they hugged, received thanks, and said goodbye to these new friends.

Empowered by their first successful venture and laden with enough food to get them to another place, they plodded on to the next town, following along the northern stretch of the Jordan River.

The first few men they met on the road into town did not speak to them but continued in their own conversation. Women at the well were busy with their water jars, and the children in the road completely ignored Matthew and Thomas.

As they walked farther, Matthew saw a familiar sight. "Look, up ahead. It's a potter's house!" The potter came from the kiln, entered his shed, and was now carrying newly formed bowls to the kiln.

"Shalom, sir," Matthew called. "I come from a family of potters in Capernaum. May we help you carry your bowls?" The potter barely looked at them. "No, this is my last load." And off he went behind the kiln.

"Hmm, friendly sort around here, aren't they?" Thomas commented.

"We must continue to seek a worthy person as Jesus said."

"Looks like we are coming to the heart of the town."

Matthew turned and nodded as a priest walked out of a building. "Looks like they have a synagogue."

"Shall we talk to the carpenter up ahead?" Thomas asked.

Matthew started the conversation. "I see you're carving a handle for a cart."

"Do you need a handle?" The man spoke briskly without looking up.

"Well, no. We have come in the name of Jesus to proclaim that the kingdom of heaven has come and to teach repentance."

"Hmph," the man grunted.

"We were hoping to find a place to stay tonight," Thomas added.

"Arlas has an inn up the road there." The carpenter pointed, still not making eye contact.

"Thank you."

Mathew tilted his head toward Thomas then gestured toward the road as though, "Off we go again!"

"What do we do now?" Thomas asked, as they walked on. "We have no money for an inn."

"Surely there's one friendly person in this town."

They walked on through the town, but not one person even acknowledged their presence, much less spoke to them. At the far edge of town, they came upon a vine grower bringing in a basket of grapes.

"Great looking crop of grapes you have!" Matthew said, with all the enthusiasm he could muster.

"Yes, they're doing well this year. Would you like a handful?"

"Very kind of you, sir." The two quite willingly accepted the hospitality, for they had not eaten since breakfast.

"Are you new in town?" he asked.

"Yes, we come from Capernaum. We are disciples of Jesus. We have come to teach the good news that Jesus brings to Israel, teachings of love and repentance."

"Aye, well, you will not find a very receptive audience here. They are too involved in their businesses, making money, or for some, just eking out an existence."

"We would like to try, if we might find a place to stay."

"Hope you find a place," the vine dresser said, as he went his way.

Matthew and Thomas looked at each other. "I think this is one of those places Jesus mentioned that will not welcome or listen to us." They spontaneously took off their sandals and knocked them together, symbolically shaking the dust off their feet.

*****

Matthew and Thomas had eaten all their supply from Joseph and his wife. Their feet were weary, and their stomachs empty by the time they reached the next town. The town sat near the upper Jordan. Fishermen were packing up their gear for the night.

One fisherman carried a bucket of fish. "Hello there," he said. "You look as tired as I feel."

"Yes, we have traveled from Capernaum."

"Oh, I have a brother in Capernaum. His name is Samuel."

"Samuel, the tanner?" Matthew asked.

"Yes, the very one! Have you a place to stay tonight?"

"No."

"Come, you are welcome to stay at my house. We will fix these fish for our dinner."

Matthew and Thomas smiled at each other. Thomas put his arm around Matthew's shoulder. "Again, the Lord has provided," he said.

Despite his exhaustion, Matthew experienced a surge of thanksgiving, for it seemed that Thomas no longer saw him as "the tax collector" but as a friend and fellow disciple.

The two met the fisherman's wife, his eight-year-old son, Ben, and his four-year old daughter, Selina—such a delightful family. Ben was full of questions, but Selina quietly watched with shy eyes.

To let Selina have a word, Matthew turned to her. "I noticed the fine loom your mother has, Selina. Have you learned to work the loom yet?" Selina crawled in her mother's lap and buried her face in her mother's breast.

Ben quickly took over again. "Selina is shy," he provided. "She couldn't walk until this year. It happened when we went to visit Uncle Samuel in Capernaum. We met Jesus and he healed her. She could walk right away!"

"Well, you know, Ben, that is why we have come here. We are disciples of Jesus and have come to tell more people about him."

"I want to hear more about him too," Ben said.

The fisherman stood. "We are honored to have you in our home, and we look forward to all you have to teach us. But we're all tired and I think we'll hear better with rest."

*****

The next morning Ben rose early to be up and ready to hear his new friends. Fortunately, this town had a synagogue, so several came to see the new teachers in town.

They read from the Holy Scriptures and quoted prayers. The fisherman introduced his two new friends to those who had gathered. Matthew stood to face the group and then sat in front of them to begin teaching.

"Your reading today contained our great Shema, 'Hear, O Israel: The LORD our God, the LORD is one. Love the LORD your God with all your *heart*,' Matthew paused, 'and with all your soul and with all your strength.' Let us think today about our hearts."

"Do you remember what the Lord said to Samuel when he went to anoint the next king of Israel? Samuel first saw Eliab, the oldest son of Jesse and took notice of this tall, fine looking young man. 'Surely this is the LORD's anointed,' Samuel thought, but within his spirit, he sensed the Lord saying, 'Do not consider his appearance or his height, for I have rejected him. The LORD does not look at the things man looks at. Man looks at the outward appearance, but the LORD looks at the heart.'"

Matthew had their attention. "Just as a good tree brings forth good fruit, so a bad tree brings forth bad fruit. Jesus, the Promised One, says, 'Out of the overflow of the heart, the mouth speaks. The good man brings *good* things out of the good stored up in him, and the evil man brings *evil* things out of the evil stored up in him.'"

A man came shuffling into the group of attentive listeners. Matthew felt an uneasiness as the men frowned at this intruder and shifted nervously on their stone benches.

Matthew moved on with his line of thinking. "We are careful to eat only foods that are clean, not unclean. But remember, 'what comes out of a man is what makes him unclean. For from within, out of men's hearts, come evil thoughts, sexual immorality, theft, and murder, adultery, greed, and malice, envy, arrogance, and folly.'"

Just then the intruder stood up waving his arms and bounding toward Matthew.

"What do you want with us?" the man cried. "We know who you represent—the Holy One of God!" he screamed as he continued waving his arms frantically.

The crowd shoved away from the man. Matthew's emotions hit a fearful crescendo, but he had seen this before. He knew immediately that this man was possessed by evil spirits. A sudden calming power filled Matthew's spirit. Jesus words came to him.

"Be quiet!" he declared in a stern voice. "In the name of Jesus of Nazareth, come out of this man!" As Matthew had witnessed before, the man shook violently, and evil spirits came out of him with a shriek. The man sank to his knees, hanging his head in exhaustion.

Gradually, he lifted his face to Matthew. "Thank you." The words came slow and weak. "Thank you," he said again, a tear slipping down his cheek.

Thomas stepped forward to help the man stand and take him to the bench where Thomas had been sitting earlier.

Matthew continued to speak in great power. The people were amazed with the teaching and the healing before their eyes. Many promised to bring others with them the next day.

After the evening meal, Matthew and Thomas took a walk together to have time to talk privately. "That was amazing today, Matthew."

"Just as Jesus said, the Spirit would give the words. Thankfully, I remembered many of Jesus' words, not only in speaking to the people, but also in dealing with the possessed man. Thomas, I felt the Lord's power welling up in me as I spoke the demons out of the man. I tell you, though, I felt scared out of my mind for the first few moments. Praise be to him who gave the power."

The next day a greater throng of people came. Thomas took the lead and brought forth compelling words that obviously touched many people. Matthew smiled as he listened, remembering the power the Lord gave him the day before and now sensing it in Thomas as well. Matthew had come a long way from dreading his time with Thomas.

Seven spoke up to confess their sin and asked to be baptized in the nearby river. What a day for rejoicing. Matthew gave a friendly slap on Thomas' back. "Well done, my friend," he grinned.

Then, just as they came out of the water on the shore, a husband approached Thomas with his wife. "Sir, my wife has had no use of her right arm for ten years. She manages with the other arm, but could you help her?"

Thomas glanced at Matthew who smiled and nodded encouragement. Matthew saw the look of hope in the man's eyes and the shyness of the wife whose arm dangled at her side. She clutched her good hand around her withered arm and lowered her head in embarrassment.

Thomas gently held her withered arm. Power swept over him as he lifted one hand to the sky. With eyes closed, he lifted his face to the heavens. "Oh, Holy God, maker of all things, hear my prayer today. In the name of Jesus, heal this withered arm."

The woman gently pulled her arm away and gripped *his* arm. "Praise God," she cried out despite her timid nature. "I have feeling in my arm. I can lift it. I can grip and hold. I will be able to stir my stew and wipe away tears!" She lifted and gripped and stirred her arm in all the ways of which she spoke and grabbed her husband, sobbing into his chest as he held her. Others came to rejoice with her.

It took a long time before the crowd finally departed from this time of rejoicing.

That evening as Thomas and Matthew talked, Thomas said, "I know now what you mean. The words just rose to my mind and poured out of my mouth today, and I sensed the Lord's power moving through me to that woman."

"Jesus trained us well and empowered us to follow in his ways."

"Yes, he did."

Each day the people came before they started their day's work. They listened and learned, confessed sin, and were baptized. And they came with needs of healing.

A few men were willing and able to spend extra time with Matthew and Thomas, so they taught and trained the men further.

Chapter 42

Confrontations to Come

After several days, Matthew said, "I think the time has come for us to move on to another town."

Thomas' face fell a bit for they were having great success with the people of this community. Finally, he admitted, "Yes, I know you're right. It will be difficult to leave these friends."

A bath and clean tunics felt refreshing before they said their good-byes to the fisherman and his family. They gave a blessing over this household and the community and continued north along the Jordan.

Mid-morning they stopped by a well to quench their thirst and munch on the bag of good food the fisherman's wife had prepared. Up ahead they could see the tops of houses and businesses among the trees. "It looks like a sizeable city," Thomas mused.

"Perhaps as large as Capernaum. So many more trees in this area."

"It makes for cooler air. I like that." Thomas smiled.

*****

As they came on the outskirts of the city, Matthew heard the familiar whirl of a potter's wheel. Soon he spied the potter's house, the shed, and kiln. By the time they drew close enough to speak, the potter came out of his shed with a tray of bowls to be fired.

"Let's see if this potter will be more receptive than the last one," he said to Thomas. "Do you need help carrying more of those bowls?" Matthew called out.

"They must not be dropped," the stern potter commented.

"Oh, I know all about that," Matthew said. "My father was a potter."

"Hmph," the potter paused. "There is another tray in the shed."

Matthew took that as approval and went into the shed to find the newly formed bowls lined up on a tray. The smell brought back unwelcomed memories. He carried the tray with great care, knowing the labor involved and the potential wrath of a frustrated potter.

"Set them there." The potter pointed.

Matthew and Thomas waited with patience until he finished loading the kiln and firing it up a bit more. A potter at work is serious business. As Matthew watched, old feelings of hurt and anger stirred in him. Would this potter be like his father? Maybe they should have walked on by.

The potter completed his task and brushed his hands off, then wiped the sweat of his brow with the back of his hand. "Your father was a potter, you say?"

"Yes, from Capernaum."

"And you are a potter as well?"

Matthew smiled. "No, the clay and I did not get along well together. My father made the pottery and I sold it."

"Hmm," the potter nodded his head. "Sounds like a good arrangement. Hey, are you here to sell pottery?" The old man looked around behind Matthew to see if he had a cart.

"No sir, my father died two years ago. This is Thomas and I am Matthew. We are here to share good news with the people of your city."

"What good news?"

"We come sharing the teachings of Jesus of Nazareth. Perhaps you have heard of him?"

"No."

"Jesus comes in the name of the Lord to tell us that the Kingdom of God is at hand. He has been teaching the people the ways of the Lord and healing people not only in their bodies, but also healing their souls."

"Hmph. I suppose that might be good news. Are you priests or something?"

"No, we're disciples of Jesus. We have come to share the love of God with your people."

"Where are you staying?"

"We just came into town. We have no place yet."

The potter twisted his mouth sideways and rubbed his chin. "Well, I don't have much, and you might have to cook for yourselves, but I have room for you to stay here. My wife died a few years back, and our daughter married last year and moved out. It's not much, but you're welcome to stay."

Matthew looked at Thomas who shrugged his shoulders then nodded his head.

"We appreciate your kindness. We have no money to offer you. Our Master told us to go town to town without coins or extra tunics. We are to depend on the Lord to provide for us as we preach."

"My name is Pildash. Means 'flame of fire.'" He looked at his kiln. "My father was a potter. I suppose he thought that would be a good name for a potter's son." Pildash chuckled at his own thought. "Well, we will need more food." He walked toward the house. "You can go into the market and buy what you need."

Glad for an offer, Matthew and Thomas raised their eyebrows at each other and followed Pildash into the house. The dark room was not so clean and rather messy as one might expect from a lone widower.

"Here are some coins and a basket for you to bring the food back. I'll be in the shed."

Thomas picked up a smelly blanket full of dust. "What have we gotten ourselves into?"

"We will definitely have to spend a little time cleaning this place, but he's willing and we are in need. Besides, he seems generous." Matthew turned to the kitchen area. "Looks like he could use a new pan or two. I think we'd better start by cleaning. We may find other things we need before we go to the market. You get some water and work on that stack of dishes. I will get the broom and sweep."

It took a while, but the place looked somewhat better after they worked on it.

"We are going to the market now," Matthew called into the shed.

"Shalom," Pidash answered back.

*****

"This brings back memories of taking pottery into town to sell," Matthew commented, as they walked along.

"Yes, I remember when you set up your displays. They always looked attractive."

"Why, thank you, kind sir." Matthew took a slight bow.

"They were impressive enough that I remembered them."

"One of my many tactics of being a salesman, I guess."

They walked on in silence for a bit, then Thomas asked, "What did you do when you were away so long?"

Old memories came to the forefront. Matthew looked sideways with a nervous glance and moved his basket from one hand to the other. "Well, I did more selling and ended up keeping records for the business."

"What business?"

"The balsam trade. It is a big business in Jericho."

"You went to Jericho?"

Matthew grew more uncomfortable with all these questions about the time he was away.

"Oh, look! I see the marketplace up ahead. Do you still remember your list of things to buy?"

Thomas thought. "Let me think. Uh, a pan, two blankets, and three spoons."

"I'll be in the fruits and vegetables. You can meet me there. Here's some coins for you."

Matthew watched Thomas go the other direction, relieved to quit talking about Jericho. He hurried on to the vegetable stands. Right away, the girl behind the lentil bean stand spoke to him.

"Do you have need of lentils?" she said, in a sultry tone.

Matthew glanced up at her heavily made-up face. She raised one eyebrow with a sensuous look and an alluring smile. He immediately thought of Susanna. Not to be taken in, he quickly asked for three cups of beans and fumbled with his coins as he asked, "How much?"

He moved on to the olives and found a similar woman. Again, he worked quickly, refusing to make eye contact. Even the fig lady appeared beguiling. *What is this?* he thought. *Are all the women of this town like this?*

As he looked up ahead, he saw a simple older woman busily unwrapping bread. Heaving a sigh of relief, he approached the bread stand. "Your bread looks delicious."

"Right from the oven."

"I'll take three loaves."

"You must be hungry."

"Yes, my friend and I have been traveling. Pildash has invited us to stay with him."

"Ah, yes, the potter. He so misses his wife, rest her soul. I imagine that place needs a good cleaning, though."

"You're right. We have already attended to that. Tell me, do you have a synagogue in this city?"

"Well, kind of. Do you see that row of houses?" She pointed down the street. "Just beyond the last house you can see a roof up higher. That's the synagogue."

"My friend and I will be speaking there soon. We come bearing the good news from Jesus of Nazareth."

She folded her arms across her pudgy frame and sighed. "Hmm. We could use some good news. We have little of it here."

"Well, thank you. You've been extremely helpful."

When Matthew turned around, Thomas came loaded with his shopping items. "This is a busy place," he said. Matthew was about to respond when an old man down the way let out a yell as he went chasing a boy who had two apples in his hand, evidently a thief. The boy easily outran the old man. No one seemed ready to help him.

About that time, Matthew noticed a very rotund man with a lavish robe and fancy headpiece. The man stopped at each market stand; his mission appeared to be talking, not buying. Every owner frowned as he left their stand.

Matthew and Thomas lingered where they were and leaned in, listening to what the wealthy man had to say at a stand nearby.

"Your rent for this stand will be raised to one denarius tomorrow."

The merchant grimaced as his head hung to the side. He took a deep breath and his shoulders humped. Obviously, all the merchants felt the same about this unwelcomed news. Pildash and the bread lady had it right. This town needed some good news.

Matthew fixed the evening meal, and Pildash declared his delight with the soup and the looks of his house.

The next morning Thomas and Matthew made their way to the synagogue. Sadly, it was empty and a bit disheveled. Leaves had blown in on the floor; the benches were pushed this way and that, a rickety table sat askew toward the middle of the room. Obviously, the synagogue had not been in use for some time.

"I think the people of this town have lost their Jewish roots. Now I see why the bread lady said they 'kind of' have a synagogue."

"Looks like we are to start from the beginning," Thomas sighed.

"I guess we will have to clean up this place too."

Thomas found an old rag and dusted off the benches. He pushed the benches back in order and straightened the table. Matthew discovered a broom of sorts to sweep leaves away. Thomas heaved a big sigh. "Now what?"

"I guess we have to go where we find the people—in the market."

By then, the market area flourished with morning activity. No one seemed in the mood for stopping to listen to two strangers. Matthew elbowed Thomas. "I have an idea. Let's find the one lady who treated us with some degree of friendliness."

"The bread lady?"

"Yes. I think she was over in that area." Matthew pointed to the left. They found her in the same spot as yesterday.

Matthew started the conversation. "We ate pieces of your delicious bread last night."

She smiled. "Oh, yes, I remember you two young men. Did you want more bread today?"

"No, we have plenty."

She sorted and arranged her goods.

Matthew rolled his eyes at Thomas and tried again. "We went to the synagogue this morning, the one you pointed out to us yesterday."

She glanced up at Matthew but went on with her work.

"It did not appear to have been used in some time."

"No, probably not. The rabbi left to go to another town a while back. No one has led the study or worship since. Quite a pity."

"Is there a place where your people meet for town business? A gathering place?"

"Well, no." She leaned in to whisper, "We have the town judge, as he calls himself, but he mostly meets with other businessmen at the town gate."

"Is he the one who came through yesterday telling the merchants that their table rent was increasing to one denarius?"

She nodded her head and pursed her lips in disgust, "The very one."

"May we share the good news I mentioned to you? You see, we are disciples of Jesus of Nazareth. We come to bring the gospel to other towns. Our holy God wants to bring inner joy to His people and to cleanse them of sin and disobedience in their lives. The very fact that your people no longer worship together in the synagogue is a sign that they have left Him out of their lives. We come to encourage a renewal, a change of heart."

The merchants on either side of the lady began listening and were soon joined by ones across the way and down the row. Some were attentive as Matthew continued, even repentant in their demeanor. Others asked quarrelsome questions or made degrading remarks, but others tried to subdue them.

Soon, all eyes turned down the street as the judge strode into view. The crowd parted for his entry.

"And what have we here? Strangers stirring up our good merchants, keeping them from their honest work? We will not have this disturbance in our town. Lock them up!"

He turned to three strapping young men who had found their place in the judge's reign. The people hastened back to their tables; eyes lowered as if they had done wrong. Meanwhile, the largest of the young men moved between Matthew and Thomas grabbing each arm, while the other two men gripped the other arms.

"We have not come to disturb, sir. We want to share God's love with your people," Matthew explained.

The threesome hastily jerked them this way and that as they escorted the two down the way to a building with a dark dungeon of sorts. They practically threw them in, causing each to lose balance and fall to the floor, which prompted three mice to scatter.

"We'll see if the judge decides that a lashing is needed later," the big one grunted.

Matthew and Thomas promptly stood to get off the filthy floor. Matthew ran his fingers through his hair. "Whoa, how did that happen?"

"And so quickly."

"The forces of evil are so prevalent in this town."

"But some of the people were starving for the good news we bring," Thomas reasoned. They were silent for a moment as the reality of their condition sank in. "The Master told us that if anyone will not welcome us, we are to shake the dust off our feet," said Thomas.

"He also said he was sending us as sheep among wolves and to be as shrewd as snakes and innocent as doves."

"I think we found the wolves," Thomas moaned. "It's like a Roman dungeon in here."

That night, they dare not lay on the floor. They decided to sit up back to back and lean against the wall with the tail of their cloaks against their heads for cushioning.

"Do you think they will use the whip on us?" Thomas asked, as he tried to adjust himself into a more bearable position.

"Who knows?"

Neither slept much.

The next morning, they stood and stretched trying to work out the aches in their bodies. When they heard footsteps coming, they froze. Matthew's face grew flush as heat rose from his chest. Their eyes stayed fixed on the tiny bit of light from a small window in the door. Then came the clanging of a chain, and the door opened.

The judge stood in the doorway, the plumes of his headpiece standing high. "Well, visitors, perhaps you have seen that we have rules in this town. No one is to cause a disturbance that keeps the workers from doing their jobs. You have disobeyed the rules. Now, I am a very merciful judge," he said, with affected innocence, "so if you leave without return, you may have your freedom. Can I count on that?"

"Yes, sir," they both agreed at once.

"My men will show you out."

As the judge left, Thomas mumbled, "Oh, great. His *men.*"

*****

Both traipsed faster than their usual pace, then gave huge sighs of relief when they were well out of town.

Catching his breath, Matthew was finally able to say, "With the time Jesus gave us to be gone and with the time it will take us to return, we better be heading back to Capernaum."

"I agree. Perhaps we could stop at the potter's house to get some food for the road."

"Good idea."

"Oh wait," Thomas grabbed Matthew's arm. "We have one more thing to do." Thomas reached down to take his sandals off. Matthew grinned and joined him in shaking the dust off their sandals.

After biding good-bye to Pildash, the potter, they traveled back through the towns they had visited. What an encouragement to see the progress many were making and the stories the people had to tell them!

Chapter 43

Feeding the 5,000

With Capernaum in sight, Thomas and Matthew's pace quickened. When they saw Philip and Bartholomew, they raced to meet them. Arms spread wide, they all embraced each other with hearty hugs.

Their stories lapped over one another when they poured out their experiences. Soon James and Thaddaeus joined them, and the stories multiplied.

Matthew laughed and listened to the experiences of the other men. He identified with their joys and frustrations. A union had formed with these brothers in following Christ. Finally, Matthew felt accepted.

Peter and Andrew were the last to return. Once again warm greetings were given all around.

While Peter warmly greeted each one, it was not lost on Matthew that Peter did not speak to him or even give visual contact. Matthew still felt the sting of being *Matthew the tax collector* to Peter.

It occurred to Matthew that he had not seen Jesus in this gathering time. "Where is the Master?" he asked.

Philip spoke up, "Yesterday, we received the news that John the Baptist was beheaded by King Herod. Jesus wanted to be alone, and he pushed out in a boat early this morning."

The group was silent for a moment. John broke the silence. "Jesus loved him very much." Then Andrew spoke up. "Perhaps, by now, we should go to him." The others agreed and walked down toward the shore to wait for his return. Shortly, they saw him coming in. He opened his arms to them and gave each one attention, asking specific questions and rejoicing in their stories.

Finally he spoke to all of them. "Come with me by yourselves to a quiet place and get some rest." They filled the boat and pushed out. Matthew relished this time with his fellow disciples even if it was in a boat.

When he glanced toward the shore, several people were eyeing their boat and rushing along the shore to keep up with it. The farther they rowed, the greater the crowd.

"Where's everyone going?" Thomas asked.

"Looks like they're following us," Matthew answered.

"We can get ahead of the crowd," Peter assured them. "Row faster, men!"

What he did not know was that a huge crowd had already gathered on the hillside right around the bend where Peter was headed. "We can turn back," Peter said, a question in his voice.

Jesus held up his hand. "No, Peter. The people are like sheep without a shepherd. I must go to them." Reluctantly, Peter guided the boat toward shore and jumped out to pull it in.

By the time they all climbed out of the boat, Jesus had begun talking with the people. He gathered several in a group and sat to teach them. Moving on to another section, he healed those who came to him and spoke in parables during his teaching lessons.

The disciples moved along with him, bringing those who wished to be healed and grouping people together to sit and listen. And so it went on throughout the day.

Matthew had heard these teachings before, even taught them himself, but they were ever fresh from the Master's lips along with new thoughts and parables.

Many had been there all morning, and now it was mid-afternoon. The disciples were concerned that the people had gone all day without eating.

"You feed them," Jesus told them.

"But there are so many," Philip responded.

"Where shall we buy bread for these people to eat?" Jesus urged him on. Was that a smile in Jesus' voice?

Philip frowned as he seemed to be figuring something. Finally, he said, "Eight month's wages would not buy enough bread for each one to have a bite!"

Meanwhile, Andrew was bent over, talking to a young boy. He often paid attention to children who were in the groups, and now he brought the boy to Jesus.

"Here is a boy with five small barley loaves and two small fish, but how far will they go among so many?"

Matthew stood close by when Jesus knelt by the boy and whispered, "Thank you for sharing your food. It will feed many." The boy's eyes opened bright with wonder and anticipation. When Jesus stood, he told the disciples to organize the men to sit in groups of about fifty. "Matthew, help them. You're good with numbers."

Overwhelmed with Jesus' confidence in him, Matthew sprang into action as he gave instructions to the other disciples.

"Put the people in groups of fifty before they sit down. Think five groups of ten. Leave space around each group. James, Thaddaeus, Simon, go to the back of the crowd over there," he pointed to the left.

"Philip, Thomas, Judas, take the group from there to there in the back." He pointed to the right. "Bartholomew, James, and John, help the group toward the front half on this side. Peter, Andrew, and I will take this half of the front, plus the women and children over there. Go quickly!"

And just like that, off they went to their assigned areas.

Peter was not quite ready to be so cooperative. "Why does it have to be fifty? Do we have to count people all day?"

Matthew reminded him, "You used to count more fish than that. Jesus said *about* fifty in each group."

"But fish are small."

"Just think five boat-loads of people," Matthew told him.

"Hmph," Peter grumbled, but he soon went into action as he saw the other disciples working away.

Once the people were seated in their clusters, the disciples returned to Jesus, who had accumulated several baskets. Jesus stood. All eyes toward the front of the crowd were fixed on him which prompted the ones sitting behind them to be less noisy.

All grew quiet as Jesus spoke. He raised one of the barley loaves up high. "Father in heaven, O Mighty one of Israel, Creator of the heaven and earth, we give you praise for providing this bread. Bless it to nourish our bodies and our bodies to serve you."

He broke the loaf over the first basket, then broke it over the next basket. Somehow in the process, twelve baskets were filled from just five loaves. Each disciple took a basket to his area, those in the back areas and those toward the front. The baskets were passed from one man to another.

Matthew passed his basket to the first group of fifty. When they had their share, they handed it back to him. He could hardly believe that the basket was still full. How could this be? He took it to the next group, who passed it and ate, but when they handed it to him, it was still full. When it happened with the third group, he could see the miracle that was taking place.

Matthew glanced over at Peter to watch him examine his basket. Peter looked at Matthew, puzzled. After he examined his full basket the third time, he smiled and hurried to the next group. *Hmm, these groups of fifty worked well, didn't they, Peter?*

The people chatted with pleasure. The disciples caught each other's eye and laughed out loud with delight. Word began spreading from one to another of the miracle that was happening before their eyes. Laughter and joy replaced their weariness.

Later, Jesus blessed the fish as well, which fed the crowd in the same way.

As the crowd gradually dispersed that evening, Matthew turned to Thomas. "What a day."

Thomas shook his head. "I'll never forget when I looked in the basket the first time to see that it was still full,"

"About the time we think we've seen it all, heard it all, and experienced it all, Jesus surprises us with one more thing."

Chapter 44

Leaving Galilee

Matthew lay on his pallet thinking about the experiences that had flooded his life these past two years.

He rolled over to see if Andrew was still awake. "Yes, just thinking." Andrew yawned.

"Me too. So many things Jesus has taught us; so many adventures we've had."

"Like the feeding of that huge crowd yesterday."

"I'd say we had about five thousand men," Matthew had calculated.

"Plus, the women and children."

Matthew rolled on his back. "When I think of all the experiences we've had, I believe I grew most through the experience of going off with Thomas and having to put into practice all Jesus had taught us. Not only that, Thomas finally came to see me as one of the group."

"No longer in the tax booth?"

"Right."

After a pause, Andrew asked, "And Peter?"

"That's another case." Matthew smiled. "But I think he's beginning to come around. I purposely put him in my group with the bread and fish."

Andrew chuckled. They both lay quiet for a while. Then Andrew rose up on his elbow. "Jesus said we will go to Jerusalem for Passover. I have some concern about that."

"About Passover?"

"Not the celebration. I worry about the relationship with the Pharisees and teachers of the law. In fact, all the Temple leaders. They are very opposed to Jesus. Jesus keeps saying, 'My time has not yet come.' I am not sure what he means by that."

Matthew rolled over on his back and interlocked his fingers across his waist. "We must trust that he knows what is to be and what is the timing, but you are right, it is like Isaiah said, 'These people honor me with their lips, but their hearts are far from me. They worship me in vain; their teachings are but rules taught by men.'"

"Yes, you are right." Andrew looked up at the stars. "You always seemed to be able to memorize many of the words of the prophets."

Finally they both drifted off to sleep.

*****

The twelve arose the next morning to pack their bags, eat a quick breakfast, and begin their journey south.

On the way, Jesus mentioned that they would be stopping in two towns in the Decapolis area—Gentile territory, the area where they found the demoniac. Matthew and Andrew glanced at each other in concern. Matthew noticed the same furrowed foreheads of the others.

They sailed along in light chatter, but as the boat drew near the shore, just beyond where they had been with the demon-possessed man, the men became quiet.

Three fishermen sat mending their nets from their night's catch. The fishermen glanced over at the boatload of men coming near. One slapped another on the back, pointed at the disciples, and burst out with a loud comment. Matthew could not quite make out what he was saying, but the man jumped up and went running to a house near the shore.

A woman stepped out of the house when she heard all the commotion and stared in the direction the man pointed as he flailed his arms about.

The woman, in turn, ran to the next house with the same animation to share with her neighbor.

By the time Jesus and the disciples brought their boat into shore, ten people came running toward them with more on the way.

Thomas turned to Matthew. "I don't know if they are coming to chase us away or welcome us!"

"Looks like they are excited and smiling. Must be a good sign."

By then the people greeted Jesus, all talking at once.

"Welcome."

"Master, you have come to us."

"Rabbi, teach us."

"Come stay with us."

One man turned to his wife. "Wait till we tell Marcus that the healer has come."

Jesus touched all the outreached hands, his face reflecting their smiles and acceptance. He raised his hands for them to settle and sit on the grass. He sat as well and began teaching. Their eyes stayed focused on him as they clung to every word.

Later, one man stood holding his four-year-old son. "Jesus, my son has never been able to walk. Would you have mercy on him and heal his legs?"

"Your faith is great," Jesus said. "Bring him to me." Jesus smiled at the boy as he stroked his forehead and hair. Then he placed his hands on the boy's legs. "Today you shall walk." Jesus lifted the boy from his father's arms and gently set his dangling feet on the ground. The boy stared at his feet. The small group leaned forward in anticipation, while the boy timidly rolled his eyes up at Jesus.

Jesus knelt beside him and smiled. "Walk to your mother." The boy put his hand on Jesus' shoulder as he gingerly turned around. When his mother stood, the group breathlessly watched and waited in silence. Slowly, the boy took two steps then tottered a bit. Jesus reached out, and the boy grasped his hand for balance. Then he looked at his mother's outstretched arms and walked to her. She cried out in praise and thanksgiving as the people clapped and joined her praise. "Just like Marcus," one said.

The people insisted that Jesus and the disciples eat with them and share fellowship. After they ate, Jesus led his disciples back to the boat to go farther down the way.

When they stopped at the second town in the Decapolis area, the same thing happened. Enthusiastic people came from all directions. Again, the crowd gathered and sat to be taught. Though the disciples were delighted with this kind of response, they shared glances with each other, shaking their heads in astonishment as if to say, "How did this happen in this pagan territory?"

Suddenly, Jesus paused, his attention drawn toward a man who slowly approached the crowd. Everyone turned to look at the large man.

"It's Marcus," several whispered to each other.

Matthew gasped. He leaned toward Andrew, "I think that is the demon-possessed man Jesus healed months ago."

"I believe you are right."

By then, Jesus had stood to greet this man with open arms. They embraced; the man standing a head taller. Then he kneeled before Jesus.

"You have been obedient, Marcus. I left you to share your experience with the people and everywhere we have been, we have seen the results of your testimony. Well done, good and faithful servant."

A joyful time ensued as friends greeted Marcus. Matthew turned to Andrew. "Now we see why Jesus told Marcus to stay here and share what had happened to him!"

*****

When the disciples continued their trek along the Jordan River, they stopped to eat lunch from the bounty of food the townspeople had given them.

Andrew sat next to Matthew. "I can hardly get over seeing the demon-possessed man."

"A gentle giant."

"And a powerful influence."

"Indeed. Just think of all the lives he has touched. A lesson for us all of God's miraculous power through his people."

As they rested there beneath some shade trees, Jesus began teaching them again, new things he had not told them before, parables to understand life's circumstances. Such a flurry of teaching as though he was running out of time.

Matthew noticed the others deep in thought. *Perhaps they feel like me, desperate to try to remember all these things.*

Then Jesus told them, "We are going up to Jerusalem soon, and the Son of Man will be betrayed to the chief priests and the teachers of the law. They will condemn him to death and will turn him over to the Gentiles to be mocked and flogged and crucified. On the third day, he will be raised to life."

Jesus said this before, the last time we went to Jerusalem. The others had heard it, but no one seemed to be able to take it in. No one asked about it. The next thing they knew, James and John were making selfish requests. *Their requests have no place after we have just heard Jesus' declaration.*

Just then, a messenger came in the middle of their discussion with word from Mary and Martha that Jesus' friend Lazarus was extremely ill. Jesus seemed concerned, but he said, "This sickness will not end in death. No, it is for God's glory so that God's Son may be glorified through it."

Thomas leaned over to Matthew. "What does he mean?" Matthew shook his head while Jesus talked further with the messenger. Thomas went on. "I'm worried about going near Jerusalem. The religious leaders tried to stone him last time we were there."

"Yes, I remember. It's becoming quite dangerous for him," Matthew admitted.

"That means it is also dangerous for us, his followers."

Matthew did not respond. He sat staring at the river. He sat in a bit of a stupor the rest of the afternoon as Jesus went off to pray.

Nothing was said about leaving to see Lazarus the next day. Matthew questioned Andrew, "Don't you think it is strange that we're not going to Bethany to see Lazarus?"

"Very strange," said Andrew.

"They are such good friends. You would think he would have more concern for him than this."

Andrew looked up from frying a pan of fish. "Jesus said Lazarus wouldn't die. I guess he knows best the timing. Besides, it is quite dangerous for him and for us to go near Jerusalem."

On the third day, Jesus announced that they were leaving for Bethany. "Our friend Lazarus has fallen asleep, but I am going there to wake him up."

Peter said, "Lord, if he sleeps, he will get better."

Jesus lowered his head. "I tell you plainly, Lazarus is dead, and for your sake I am glad that I was not there, so that you may believe. Let us go to him."

What does this mean?

Chapter 45

By way of Jericho

On the way to Bethany, Jesus led the group off the usual route. Thomas turned to Matthew. "Why is he leading us to Jericho?"

Matthew shrugged his shoulders. "I was wondering the same thing."

The group of disciples maneuvered around the row of wagons and traders who had lined up to make their way through the city gate, an all-too-familiar scene in Matthew's memory. He hung his head, glancing up only occasionally to see if anyone around might recognize him.

"What a busy place," Thomas commented.

Matthew did not respond.

"Didn't you say that you came here for a while?"

"Yes." Matthew said bluntly.

"Do you see anyone you know?"

Matthew gave a huffed "No," and walked on ahead of Thomas. When they were in sight of Caleb, Matthew pulled his headpiece a little farther over his bent head.

Finally, when they were past the busiest part of the marketplace, Matthew gave a big sigh, but then he looked up to see that Jesus was headed straight toward Bartimaeus. Matthew could hear people in the crowd whispering Jesus' name.

"Yes," someone said aloud. "Yes, it is Jesus! It's him, I know it is!" The comments grew louder as each one passed the word to the next. "And there are his followers, his disciples!"

Soon a large contingency of merchants and townspeople, along with two rabbis and a priest gathered around them. Matthew heard Bartimaeus' familiar voice. "Jesus, Son of David, have mercy on me!" The townspeople who were close by rebuked him and told him to be quiet, but he shouted even more, "Son of David, have mercy on me!"

Matthew moved forward to the front as Jesus stopped.

"Bring him to me," Jesus called.

Peter and James walked over to him and helped him get up. They brought the blind man to Jesus.

"What do you want me to do for you?" Jesus asked him.

Bartimaeus turned his face toward the sound of Jesus' voice. "Lord, I want to see," he said with sincerity.

Matthew's eyes filled with tears for his old friend because he knew what Bartimaeus was about to experience. Matthew was overwhelmed with the guilt of trying to hide himself earlier. He had experienced cleansing of his sin by the Master, but he had not reconciled his Jericho experiences of the past. As he sensed the power of healing about to take place, he threw back his headpiece to his shoulders.

Jesus placed his hands on Bartimaeus' head. "Receive your sight. Your faith has healed you."

Matthew beamed when he saw the clearing in his friend's eyes. He had seen this before when those healed of blindness began to see figures until everything grew clearer.

Bartimaeus slowly stared from face to face, taking in the color and shapes. "People's faces," he said, looking from one to another. He gazed up. "Trees. The sky. I can see."

He looked across the crowd, "I can see," he said louder.

The crowd gasped.

"I can see!" he shouted as he flung his arms up to the trees.

The crowd burst forth with praises. Everyone knew blind, begging Bartimaeus. Word spread quickly down the streets of the town as people rejoiced with him and came out of their homes and shops to see Jesus, the one they had heard about.

Matthew caught Bartimaeus by the arm. "Bartimaeus, my brother. I rejoice with you."

Knowing the voice, Bartimaeus studied his face. "Levi? Levi, is that you?"

Matthew smiled hearing his old name again. "Yes, my friend, it is me; I am now a disciple of Jesus the Christ." Matthew hugged his old friend.

The crowd began pushing them along as they followed Jesus. Matthew caught up with the others and realized Jesus was heading toward the street where Zacchaeus lived.

When he caught up with Jesus, he shouted over the crowd noise, "Lord, you're headed toward the street of the tax collector, Zacchaeus."

"Yes, I know," he shouted back with a smile.

What more must I learn today? Matthew sighed.

It appeared that Jesus was leading the joyful crowd right to the house of the man they hated most. *What is he thinking?* Matthew followed along in disbelief.

Just then, he noticed someone up in the sycamore tree ahead, the place where he used to meet Lily. When he spied a shimmering cloak hanging down and an expensive headpiece, he knew who it was.

"Jesus!" Matthew tugged at Jesus' elbow and nodded up to the tree. Jesus nodded back with another knowing smile. When he reached the tree, he looked up and spoke. "Zacchaeus, come down immediately. I must stay at your house today."

Zacchaeus gazed down, a bit embarrassed to be found in the tree, but he was soon caught up in the frivolity of the occasion and the attention Jesus gave him. He climbed down and gladly ushered Jesus and the disciples to his house and into the courtyard.

Matthew saw the look of surprise and disgust on the faces of the priest and rabbis. "No doubt *they* expected to be eating with Jesus," he told Thomas.

Thomas looked in the direction of the leaders. "Hmm, they don't look happy."

As they moved toward the house, old memories flooded Matthew's mind. He stood frozen, unable to move farther into the familiar area. What if he were recognized? What if Lily suddenly came into the courtyard?

Thomas turned back to him. "Are you coming?" Then he saw the terror in Matthew's eyes. "What is it, Matthew? What's wrong?"

He had been caught. What should he say? Thomas pulled him under a tree, and Matthew took a deep breath. "Thomas, I have been here before. I visited Zacchaeus, made deals with him in the name of my employer." He looked intently at Thomas. "I *knew* his daughter." Matthew turned his head away, unwanted tears welling up in his eyes.

Thomas put his hand on Matthew's shoulder. "My brother, whatever has been, is behind you. Your past is forgiven. You are a new person in the Master's care. If Jesus can change the heart of one tax collector, he can change the heart of a chief tax man as well." Matthew smiled at the simple words of assurance from his friend. As they slipped in to join the others, they heard Zacchaeus talking.

"Jesus, I have heard so much about you, the miraculous healings, changed lives, sin forgiven. I heard that the tax collector in Galilee turned from his trade to follow you. I thought a lot of that young man. In fact, I had recommended him for the position. That made me do some thinking." The disciples looked around for Matthew. He stopped in his tracks before they caught sight of him.

"When I heard you were in town," Zacchaeus went on, "I had to hear you, but with all the people crowding around, I couldn't even see you; that's why I climbed the tree."

The servants brought in fruits and vegetables while other platters of food were being prepared. Jesus began teaching. Zacchaeus hung on each word, uncharacteristically refraining from doing all the talking.

Matthew noticed out of the corner of his eye, a young man holding a baby wrapped up tight. Odd, he thought—a man holding a baby. Then a young woman walked to one of the tables, carrying a vase of beautiful flowers. When she turned, his face flushed. Lily!

Gracefully moving from the table, she appeared content and as lovely as ever. She walked to the man, and he smiled into her eyes as he handed her the baby. They stood close together while listening to Jesus.

Matthew stared at this scene, trying to put it together. Apparently, she had married this man and had the baby she had longed for. She seemed happy. Instead of being jealous, this scene gave Matthew a sense of relief.

Just then she looked his way, examining each of his friends who stood by listening to Jesus' teaching. Her pleasant expression suddenly changed. *She sees me.*

Matthew turned his face away, sure that she was staring at him. He let out a loud breath and nervously moved from one foot to the other.

Thomas noticed. "Matthew?" he whispered.

But Matthew stared at the ground.

Thomas looked about the courtyard and saw the young woman staring directly at them. He lowered his head and whispered, "Is that the daughter?"

"Yes."

Matthew dared not turn her way again, but he could not help himself. Thankfully, she had engaged once again in the things Jesus was saying. Her striking dark hair fell along her shoulders as it always had. To see her content made Matthew breathe easy again.

Zacchaeus and all his court listened intently to Jesus' teaching. Matthew sensed Jesus drawing them into his final point.

"Whoever can be trusted with little can also be trusted with much, and whoever is dishonest with little will also be dishonest with much. No one can serve two masters. Either he will hate the one and love the other, or he will be devoted to the one and despise the other. You cannot serve both God and Money."

Jesus stopped to let the words soak in.

All eyes turned to Zacchaeus. His head hung as he stared at the floor, unable to speak, humbled to the core. No one moved in the dramatic silence.

Finally, Zacchaeus rose to his feet. "I have been the man who is dishonest with wealth, whose god is money. I want to be the man who is trustworthy, the man who believes your words and trusts you." He faced Jesus. "Lord, here and now I give half my possessions to the poor, and if I have cheated anybody out of anything, I will pay back four times the amount."

Murmurs of surprise came from around the room as the visitors and household members buzzed with chatter over these declarations.

Jesus stood to respond. "Today salvation has come to this house because this man too is a son of Abraham. For the Son of Man came to seek and to save what was lost."

As they prepared to eat, many spoke to Zacchaeus. Matthew waited for an opportunity to speak to him when others were not close by.

"Your life will not be the same, my brother."

Zacchaeus looked at him questioningly, and then his face lit up. "Levi, it is you! Oh, my friend." As he embraced Matthew, he kept saying, "It is because of you."

He released him and looked him straight in the eye. "When I heard you had given up your position in Galilee, I was angry. But it caused me to investigate further about this man, Jesus, who had stolen you away. The more I heard, the more I wanted to hear. It is you Levi, *you* who brought me to him. I understand now." He hugged Matthew again.

When others came to speak to Zacchaeus, Matthew walked away smiling and grateful that even with his own failures, the Lord had used his life to touch this man.

Matthew noticed Peter standing not far away. Peter locked eyes with Matthew and looked as if he were about to comment but quickly hung his head, staring at the floor, then busied himself talking to someone else. *It seems hard for him to let go of his bitterness. An apology will not come easily for him.*

Chapter 46

Lazarus of Bethany

As the group left Jericho, Jesus told them they must go now to Bethany.

"That was certainly an eventful stop," Thomas said.

Matthew sighed. "Indeed. I rejoiced with my friend Bartimaeus and of course with Zacchaeus. He was once quite the scoundrel."

"So I hear." Thomas waited for Matthew to finish his thoughts. Finally he said, "But?"

Matthew wiped sweat from his brow. "But…" he rolled his eyes over to Thomas. "But I felt a lot of confusion about Lily. I dreaded seeing her, uh, more than that, *being seen* by her."

"She is a beautiful woman."

"Yes. I'm glad that she seems happy and has found a new life. I'm sure she will give herself to the Lord as well, with her father's influence."

"But?"

"I'm still processing it all."

"I understand."

As they approached Bethany, they saw a woman almost running to meet them. "It is Martha, Lazarus's sister," Jesus said.

She panted, out of breath, as she met them. "Lord," she said, taking big gulps of air, "if you had been here, my brother would not have died." She took one more big breath.

Jesus said, "Martha, your brother will rise again."

"I know he will rise again in the resurrection at the last day."

"Martha, I *am* the resurrection and the life. He who believes in me will live, even though he dies; and whoever lives and believes in me will never die. Do you believe this?"

"Yes, Lord," she told him, "I believe that you are the Christ, the Son of God, who was to come into the world."

Jesus embraced her.

"I'll go get Mary," Martha said and ran to get her sister. As Mary and the others came weeping, Jesus was deeply moved. "Where have you laid him?" he asked.

"Come and see, Lord."

As Matthew and the others walked along with these mourning friends, he looked over at Jesus and saw that he also wept. He overheard someone whisper, "See how he loved him."

Then another said, "Could not he, who opened the eyes of a blind man, have kept this man from dying?"

They were within view of the cave and the stone-covered tomb. Jesus looked up the path, slowing the pace. He seemed so deep in thought and deeply moved. Jesus stopped and spoke to three men up ahead. "Take away the stone."

"But Lord," Martha blurted out, "by this time there is a bad odor for he has been there four days."

Peter whispered, "Lord, this has been hard enough for them."

John touched Jesus' arm as if to hold him back. "Master," he cautioned.

Not to be deterred, Jesus said, "Did I not tell you that if you believed, you would see the glory of God?" Jesus nodded to the men who had paused, and they began the arduous task of pushing and rolling the stone away from the tomb.

Jesus raised his eyes and both arms toward heaven. "Father, I thank you that you have heard me. I know that you always hear me, but I say this for the benefit of those standing here, that they may believe that you sent me."

Then in a loud voice, he cried out, "Lazarus, come out!"

A collective gasp from the mourners could be heard as all eyes turned and stared at the tomb. All was dark at the entrance, but in a moment a white figure stumbled to the opening.

Another gasp from the crowd and they soon realized it was Lazarus with the linens still wrapped about him.

"Take off the grave clothes and let him go," Jesus told the men. Having never done such a thing before, they hesitated, but slowly they approached the bound body and unwrapped him.

Many fell to their knees in gratitude and belief in the power of God that was demonstrated before their eyes. Others shouted praises of thanksgiving while Mary and Martha ran to their brother.

"I didn't expect this," Philip told Matthew.

"He told us we would see the glory of God. I guess we did not pay close attention." They both shook their heads in disbelief as they rejoiced in this great miracle.

One group of men drew Matthew's attention away from this joyful scene. Their faces held angry, disapproving glares as they watched the crowd. They turned to each other in clusters seeming to plan something—maybe plotting, Matthew imagined. He poked Thomas and nodded toward the men.

"Looks like more danger brewing."

"Probably off to tell the Temple leaders," Matthew surmised.

"Yes," said Thomas, "most of our time has been spent in Galilee and the countryside where people were amazed with Jesus, but after our last festival in Jerusalem, it seems like the very ones who should welcome his coming are the ones who are critical."

Sure enough, that night they received word that the religious leaders were indeed plotting against Jesus, so Jesus led the disciples to the village of Ephraim near the desert where they stayed for a while.

*****

While Jesus and his twelve men were off to themselves for the first time in a long while, Matthew noticed that Jesus seemed to be making intentional time to talk with each man individually.

Matthew drifted away from the group and found a rock that reminded him of his "thinking rock" from back home by the sea. He smiled and sat with elbows on knees and chin in his cupped hands. He had not had many quiet, lone moments like this in a while. Life had been busy, active, on-the-go. He had watched Jesus go off by himself many times. Is that how he gained his spiritual strength?

Matthew sat up straight, gazing out at the vastness of the desert. His mind wandered back to that day when he discovered Susanna's secret lifestyle. Oh, the shame and bitterness he felt. "But I didn't charge *you*," she had said, as though that made it acceptable. It was comforting to see Susanna happy with the women who served in the ministry and knowing her faith would be growing stronger with Mama's help.

He recounted the bad choices he had made with Lily and Zacchaeus and Ariah. However, the recent trip to Jericho gave some closure. He smiled, thinking about Bartimaeus' healing and Zacchaeus up the tree and that he received salvation for his soul that day. Even seeing Lily with a husband and child gave him relief to know she was happy.

Yet, Papa's words, as always, thundered in his head, "You broke the plates!" Had his father still been alive, the height of disobedience would be to know his son had been a tax collector. Bent over, running his fingers through his hair, the scenes of childhood and Alphaeus' angry words and temper played over and over in his mind.

His eye suddenly caught a desert lizard. It scuttled into plain view, then jerked its head around, scampering this way and that. It finally stopped and arched its head as though finding what it wanted and dashed away.

Have I found what I wanted, what I needed? Indeed, cleansing, forgiveness, and a new life with Jesus. He thought of Jesus' words of conviction and the effect they had on him when he sat at his tax booth that day. His mind was flooded with

Jesus' heart of love reaching out with the invitation to "Follow me." Oh, the joy, the victories he had experienced in these months, the comradery he finally felt.

Just then, Matthew heard a slight rustling sound around a rock formation to his side. It was Jesus. "May I share this thinking rock with you?" he asked.

"Certainly," Matthew smiled and slid over.

"This place has given us opportunity to pull aside to meditate and think."

Matthew nodded his head with an audible breath. "Yes."

Jesus looked out at the desert in solitude for a moment as the sun began to set low, casting purples and yellows across the horizon. "You have followed well, Matthew, and learned to use your gifts to organize and teach, to heal and minister. Your past is forgiven. Our recent visit to Jericho has offered you closure. You must accept that."

"Yes, Lord, I realize that. I do accept it with gratitude."

"Your *Heavenly* Father has taken you in with love. He has much work for you to do and will equip you for the task."

Jesus paused for a long time. Matthew wondered if Jesus was waiting for him to respond, but he sensed Jesus had more to say.

"Your *Heavenly* Father," he emphasized again, "has forgiven you and expects you to forgive as well. Harboring past anger and pain only holds you back and weighs you down. You must let go of it. Do you understand?"

Tears filled Matthew's eyes. "Yes, Lord." He lowered his head and when he closed his eyes, the tears trickled down his cheek. "Yes, I understand."

Jesus stood and placed his hand on Matthew's shoulder. "Talk to your Heavenly Father, Matthew." Matthew could not speak; he only nodded while Jesus slipped away.

Matthew sobbed a long while as all the pain and anguish of past years with his *earthly* father erupted in his emotions—the hurt, the feelings of being discounted, and the brunt of his father's temper. Jesus' love and acceptance and encouragement had become nourishment for his soul. Yet, he had continued to rehash his bitterness and hatred toward his father, his only way of retaliating. What good did that do?

Jesus is right. Harboring past anger and pain has weighed me down. It hinders a forgiving, loving spirit.

Matthew knelt beside his rock and for the first time, he began to pray audibly.

"Oh, Holy Father, creator of the universe, lover of my soul, I fall before you in humility. I have allowed the relationship with my earthly father to impede my life. I have held tight to my anger and hatred and left only partial room for your redeeming love. Thank you, my Heavenly Father, for showing me your love and acceptance. Help me to see your desire to cleanse all of me. Perform a miracle of healing deep in my soul."

As Matthew knelt with bent head, a calm sense of peace swept over him. He slowly slid back on his rock and watched as the glowing sun set at the edge of the horizon, ready to make its descent. The fiery red rage in his heart had also made its final descent.

*****

Two days after being in the desert, they returned to Bethany to share a dinner in Jesus' honor at the house of Lazarus.

After the meal, a messenger came running to report that word had spread about Lazarus. The messenger talked so fast about the people's reactions that he could hardly get his breath.

"All the pilgrims coming into town for Passover are talking about it," he gestured with arms spread wide. "They want to see Jesus! People in the city are ready to greet him too. They're gathering palms." He babbled on and on until he was practically dancing. Matthew and Thomas glanced at each other and could not help but smile with delight at the messenger's enthusiasm.

At the edge of town, Jesus arranged to have a donkey to ride into town the next day on the first day of the week.

Chapter 47

Jerusalem

Peter and John led the young donkey to Jesus, the donkey's mother trailing behind. Philip and Bartholomew laid their cloaks across the back of the young one, and Jesus sat on it.

As the faithful troop of twelve set out beside and behind their leader, they walked down the path that wound around the mountain, then opened to the full, breathtaking view of Jerusalem with the Temple towering triumphantly inside the stone walls that surrounded the city. Each paused to take it in, as did most travelers who approach the holy city this way.

To their amazement, pilgrims who had come for Passover lined the path through the Kidron Valley all the way to the Eastern Gate. They had spread cloaks of many colors on the path for Jesus. A cheer of jubilance rose when they saw him.

"Hosanna to the Son of David," they shouted. They joyfully waved palm branches through the air to welcome him to the city. Smiling faces greeted him all along the path.

As they proceeded farther, more people were ready to begin the wave of branches. "Blessed is he who comes in the name of the Lord," they sang. "Hosanna in the highest." On and on sounded their voices of praise, their palms continually waving in victory.

"Where have they all come from?" Thomas shouted over the cries of adoration.

"From all the places we have been, I suppose," Matthew yelled back with laughter.

Looking on up ahead, they could see another crowd gathering. "Look, the people of Jerusalem must have heard the word about Jesus too!"

Over and over they heard the phrases, "Hosanna in the highest!" "Blessed is the King of Israel!" As they paraded on through the streets of Jerusalem, Roman soldiers stood in various locations, ready to keep the crowd under control. Matthew saw Lucius with another soldier. They made eye contact and Lucius gave a slight nod as Matthew passed by with the group.

*****

In the next few days, Jesus began teaching just as he had done from town to town throughout his ministry, but each time the Pharisees, Sadducees, and teachers of the law stationed themselves around the listeners like a pack of wolves ready for the pounce. Looks of disdain and hatred filled each face. They stared at the attentive faces of the crowd with scorn and mumbled to each other in their small clusters.

No doubt, they plotted to rid themselves of this infiltrator. Over and over they questioned him, trying one trap after another but failing miserably. Jesus stood his ground.

Andrew commented, "Even after they have seen or at least heard of all his miraculous signs, they will not believe."

"Their minds are closed," Thomas added.

Matthew turned to them, "It is as Isaiah wrote, 'He has blinded their eyes and deadened their hearts, so they can neither see with their eyes, nor understand with their hearts, nor turn— and I would heal them.' In our travels we have also seen those who will not accept him. But here we see the bitterness of Pharisees who have great influence and control."

"But look at the people," Andrew nodded. "They are coming in belief. They are learning to love him as we do."

*****

Later in the week, Jesus had arranged for an upper room in a house where he and the twelve could have their Passover meal together. They climbed the steps and gathered around the low table provided for their meal.

As they reclined at the table, Jesus stood, took off his outer garment, and wrapped a towel around his waist. He picked up the pitcher of water by the door and poured it into the basin.

It dawned on Matthew that they had not washed their feet when they entered the room, but a servant had not been hired.

Jesus lifted the basin and carried it to the table. "You call me 'Teacher' and 'Lord,' and rightly so, for that is what I am." He knelt beside John.

Surely he does not plan to wash his feet! Matthew thought.

That is exactly what he did; then pulling the towel from his waist, he dried them. Jesus moved the basin toward James to wash his feet and then to Philip. *Does he intend to wash every one's feet?*

"I am setting an example that you should do as I have done for you." Each man who was next sat up to be ready. One by one, he washed and dried and spoke as he made his way around the circle. "I serve you even as I expect you to have an attitude of service to each other and to the ones you meet."

I cannot believe that Jesus would do such a thing. If anything, I should be washing my Master's feet. It came Matthew's turn. He sat up and put his foot in the basin. Jesus continued. "Now that I, your Lord and teacher am washing your feet, you also should wash one another's feet."

When he came to Peter, Peter drew back, "Lord, are you going to wash my feet?"

Jesus answered, "You do not realize now what I am doing, but later you will understand."

"No, you shall never wash my feet," Peter protested.

"Unless I wash you, you have no part with me, Peter."

Leave it to Peter to always be the one to speak out. Jesus finally persuaded him that he must humble himself to receive this very lesson of humility.

After Jesus had finished the task and the lesson, he laid the towel aside, put on his cloak, and sat down with the group. "The kings of the Gentiles lord it over them, but you are not to be like that. Instead, the greatest among you should be like the least, and the one who rules shall be like the one who serves.

"When a man believes in me, he does not believe in me only, but in the one who sent me. When he looks at me, he sees the one who sent me. I have come into the world as a light, so that no one who believes in me should stay in darkness. To reflect that light, to serve; that is the goal."

Jesus lowered his head for a moment, looking troubled in spirit. "I tell you the truth, one of you is going to betray me."

Matthew caught his breath and heard the others muttering under their breath, "Not I. Surely, not I."

Jesus went on. "I have eagerly desired to eat this Passover with you before I suffer. For I tell you, I will not eat it again until it finds fulfillment in the kingdom of God."

What does he mean?

Jesus took the bread, blessed it, and broke it. "This represents my body which will be broken for you. Eat this always in remembrance of me."

Broken? Does he mean broken in humility?

He passed the bread to Judas Iscariot. As it passed around the table, Jesus spoke softly to Judas, "What you are about to do, do quickly." Matthew heard and wondered where Jesus was sending him. Judas left. The others did not seem to notice. *Perhaps it has something to do with the fact that Judas takes care of the money.*

Jesus took the cup. He reminded them of their faithfulness to the old covenant of the law, then he declared, "This cup represents the new covenant in my blood. As often as you drink it, do it in remembrance of me." The cup started around the table.

New covenant in his blood?

When he spoke again, they stopped passing for a moment. "A new command I give you; love one another." He looked intentionally at each man, "As I have loved you, so you must love one another. By this all men will know that you are my disciples if you love one another." When he paused, they continued passing the cup around until it came back to Jesus.

"My friends, I will be with you only a little longer. Where I am going, you cannot come."

Peter asked, "Where are you going?"

"Where I am going, you cannot follow now, but you will follow later."

Peter asked, "Lord, why can't I follow you now? I will lay down my life for you."

"Will you really lay down your life for me, Peter? I tell you the truth, before the rooster crows, you will disown me three times."

Stunned, Peter could not respond.

Jesus turned to the rest of the men who looked about as shocked. "Do not let your hearts be troubled," he said. "Trust in God, and trust in me. I am going to my Father's house and will prepare a place for you. You know the way to the place where I'm going."

Thomas blurted out in frustration, "Lord, we don't know where you're going, so how can we know the way?"

"*I* am the way, Thomas, and the truth and the life. No one comes to the Father except through me. I am in the Father and the Father is in me. When I am gone, he will send you another Counselor to be with you forever—the Spirit of truth. He will teach you and guide you and remind you of everything I have taught you.

"My brothers, you will weep and mourn while the world rejoices," his eyes brightened, "but your grief will turn to joy, for I will see you again and you will rejoice, and no one will take away your joy. You can expect persecution, but the Spirit will comfort you, counsel you, and guide you."

Jesus led them in singing a traditional Passover song, but Matthew's mind could not get past the strange things Jesus had said during the meal. *New covenant in my blood? Where I am going you cannot go? Your grief will turn to joy? What does it all mean?*

After the song, Jesus stood. "Come now, let us leave."

The eleven men followed Jesus down through the Kidron Valley just outside the walls of Jerusalem. They trudged up the incline to the familiar Garden of Gethsemane where they had been other times with the teacher to pray.

As they knelt, Jesus prayed. He prayed for himself; he prayed for the disciples and for all believers. "Stay here and keep watch," he told them, and he went farther into the garden, taking Peter, James, and John with him.

Matthew felt drowsy and slumped against a large root in an olive tree. He could hear Jesus' voice from afar but could not make out the words. He soon drifted off to sleep.

Chapter 48

Anguish

Matthew's eyes popped open when he felt the pounding of boots. He heard voices and saw the lights of their torches swaying this way and that, casting foreboding shadows among the tree branches. The others roused and all stood, then crept back behind the bushes. Soldiers from the Temple guard came marching into the garden.

Matthew peeked around Peter and saw some of the chief priests and elders from the Sanhedrin among the throng who had come to take Jesus. Then Judas stepped forward. *What is he doing with this group?* Judas walked to Jesus and greeted him with a kiss.

"Can you believe that?" Thomas whispered in Matthew's ear.

Immediately, Peter jumped in, sword in hand to defend Jesus. Unfortunately, a man was in the line of Peter's swinging sword.

"Peter, that's the servant of the high priest!" John warned.

Jesus' voice reverberated through the grove, "Put your sword back in its place, for all who draw the sword will die by the sword." His voice dropped lower. "Do you think I cannot call on my Father, and he will at once put at my disposal more than ten legions of angels? How then would the Scriptures be fulfilled that say it must happen in this way?"

Matthew's face grew hot with fear, his heart throbbing in his chest. *What will they do with Jesus? What will they do to us?*

Jesus knelt, even as he was talking, to help the young man who had cried out in pain from the sword. The man kept screaming, "My ear, oh my ear." Jesus talked to him in gentle tones, but Matthew could not understand him. Evidently, he was healing the man. *Just like Jesus, even when he is in danger, he tends to the needs of others.*

When Jesus stood again, he spoke to the crowd. "Am I leading a rebellion, that you have come out with clubs and swords to capture me? Every day I sat in the temple courts teaching, and you did not arrest me." He paused. "But this has all taken place that the writings of the prophets might be fulfilled."

As the soldiers lunged forward to arrest Jesus, Matthew and the others pushed back further into the garden. Squatting perfectly still, they watched from the darkness as the mob ushered Jesus back to Jerusalem.

When all was quiet again, the disciples, all in shock and bewilderment, slowly found each other and trudged back to the city and the upper room where they had been before.

*****

The terrified men cowered in the dark room, each trying to process what had just taken place. No one spoke a word, just an occasional sniff from crying or breathy heaves of anxiety.

Someone finally found the lantern and lit it. At first, the light stung their damp eyes, but they soon adjusted. Matthew asked if anyone had injuries.

"Just a bruise, I think."

"A few scratches."

Matthew made an immediate mental count to see if they all were there. Seven, eight, nine. Three were missing. Judas, of course. He ran the list in his head and reported that they were also missing Peter and John. All gazed around the room to confirm it.

Andrew spoke of his brother, "I imagine Peter is embarrassed that Jesus chastised him for drawing his sword and injuring the man. He doesn't like to admit he's done wrong."

"I suppose he was trying to show Jesus that he would defend him," Matthew offered. They quietly thought on those words.

Thomas asked about Judas. "What was Judas doing with that crowd? And why did he give Jesus a kiss?"

All were silent, then Bartholomew spoke. "Jesus said one of us would betray him. Judas must have been pointing Jesus out in the darkness with his kiss. And he would have been the only one to know where Jesus might be found."

The silence was deafening as each man came to grips with the thought that one of their own had betrayed their Master.

James finally broke the silence as he tried to account for his brother, John. He told how his family had known the family of Caiaphas, the high priest, and perhaps John had gone to see what was happening.

Matthew noticed that James was not as boisterous as usual. *Maybe he is thinking his brother John had been braver than he had been.*

All of them hunched against the wall. *Are the others trying not to think about what might be happening to Jesus?*

Several laid over in a heap of exhaustion since they had not slept all this long night, yet many shifted restlessly.

******

The next morning, the clouded sun drifted in and out of a small window in their room. One by one, the weary followers of Jesus sat up and stretched, still paralyzed by the unsettling events of the late-night hours in the garden. What now?

Philip went out to get some food at the market.

Then Peter burst through the door, his face drawn and filled with gloom, his hair disheveled, a strange, distant look in his bloodshot eyes. He stumbled in, glaring around the room, but not really seeing, breathing heavily as though he had run for his life. He fell in a heap against the wall, his arms wrapped around his legs, his forehead against his bent knees.

No one dared speak a word, but stared at the floor.

When his heavy breathing subsided, his shoulders began shaking with heaves of anguish and deep guttural moans that made it evident he had experienced severe emotional pain.

Matthew looked at Thomas, who shook his head in sorrow. Andrew stared helplessly. When Peter finally seemed to be breathing quietly, he straightened his legs and leaned the back of his head against the wall. Andrew slipped over to his brother.

"Peter," he said quietly, "do you have word for us about the Master?"

Peter took a deliberate breath and let it out. "They took him to the house of Caiaphas. John told me that they were holding him in a pit." Peter's voice broke for a moment. "Supposedly they were going to have a *trial*."

"Did you see him?" Andrew asked.

Peter turned his head to the side. "I was in the courtyard," he managed to say. "I think they have taken him to the Sanhedrin for another trial." All sat in silence as the realities crept into their minds—a pit, a trial, another trial with the leaders who were bent on killing him.

Peter lay on the floor and soon began to doze from total exhaustion.

Philip returned with bread and fruit—and news from the city. "I overheard some men talking about the arrest. They said that the Sanhedrin had a so-called 'trial' and have sent Jesus to Pilate. They are holding him in the dungeon at the Antonia Fortress."

"Why Pilate?" James asked.

"They likely want the Romans to do their dirty work," Matthew answered.

Several grunted their agreement.

Little by little the men ate bits of bread, their minds churning with the news. After a while, Thomas huffed out his thoughts. "This is like a bad dream. These events keep rolling over and over in my mind."

*****

Shortly, John staggered into the room, as bleary-eyed as the rest of them. "They've taken him to the dungeon at the Antonia.

311

The Pharisees and Sadducees are stirring up the crowd, poisoning their minds with lies and hatred. They're pushing for a public trial with Pilate."

James stood and walked to his brother. They embraced and John released the pent-up emotions he had held inside. Deep groans and heavy heaves caused his body to shake uncontrollably. The others sat numb, unable to know how to help him. James finally got John to sit, but he did not want to eat.

"Did you see Judas?" someone asked.

"No," John answered.

"Do you think he was working with the Pharisees?"

"No! He despised them. He knew their devious hearts." John lowered his eyes. "Or so I thought." John glanced over at Peter, who stared at the floor, and then John lay on the floor in exhaustion and drifted to sleep. The men talked quietly among themselves.

"Judas may have thought he was pushing Jesus to declare himself and bring an end to Roman domination," one said.

"That isn't the Messiah of prophecy," Matthew emphasized.

"I can just see Caiaphas and the other leaders in a frenzy of conniving."

"While acting so pious."

"Pretending their actions are for the good of the people."

"They'll spew lies to tell Pilate."

"Acting as though they care for the people."

"They only care about themselves."

"And their positions."

Some of their frustrations released, they sat in silence. But all Matthew could think of was his own lack of support to Jesus. "And what about us," he spoke quietly. "Other than Peter and John, none of us dared, or cared enough, to stay with him. We abandoned him. We cared only about ourselves."

Peter had awakened and heard their discussion. He breathed heavy, mumbling, "No, no, no," as though he would explode.

"No!" he shouted. "Don't set me apart as a devoted follower. Yes, I followed at a distance to the house of Caiaphas. I was right there in the courtyard outside the house of Caiaphas, but then someone accused me of being one of Jesus' disciples."

Peter took a deep breath.

"I denied it. I denied my Lord! Then another said, 'You are one of them.' I said I did not even know him." Peter's face grimaced. "A third time someone accused me, and I swore with an oath that I didn't know him. And that's when…" Peter's voice broke. Tears streamed down his face. He took in huge gulps of air. His head in his hands. His shoulders shook.

As his breathing finally settled, he continued. "After the third denial," his voice caught again. "After the third denial, the cock crowed. It happened just as Jesus said it would." Peter hung his head in shame. He had no emotional energy left.

All sat in silence. What could they say? How could they comfort this brother?

Somehow John slept through the whole ordeal. When he did rouse, he was determined to return to the Temple area and see if the soldiers had brought Jesus out of the dungeon.

No one offered to go with him. They sat frozen in fear.

They waited and questioned and wondered what was happening. It became more than they could manage. One or two at a time had to go outside to breath the air, see the full light of day, all the while covering their heads and dodging direct contact with people who might pass by.

Later that morning, John returned, deep furrows in his brow. Through his gloomy eyes, he seemed to stare into space, making no eye contact. "The Romans have flogged Jesus, and the leaders are inciting the crowd to cry for crucifixion." With eyes closed, he turned his head down to the side. "I could bear it no more."

The men sat stunned and helpless, unable to respond.

John looked up as though he just remembered something. "I must go to be with Mary, his mother." And out the door he went again, leaving it slightly ajar.

Matthew stood to close the door and paced back and forth. "The leaders pushed it to the end." He paced some more. "They wanted the ultimate punishment and knew they couldn't command crucifixion, so they persuaded Rome to do it."

"The leaders are no better than the Romans," Thomas added.

"And the people who demanded it," another said.

They all chimed in with criticism. "Where are those people who shouted praises and hosannas just a week ago?"

"Why would they give in to the leaders?"

"Fear, my brothers. Fear." Matthew's quiet words stopped further discussion. Perhaps they realized fear had been their own reaction as well.

Minutes seemed like hours as they waited for further news. Bits of food lay untouched at the noon hour, then suddenly, what little light they had from their window disappeared.

One of them went to the door to let in a bit of light, but it was darker than a cloudy, starless night to match their emotions. Pitch black. No one cared to try to find the food on the table. What little appetite they had, completely vanished.

Everything they had left to follow Jesus, everything they had gained in their life-transforming time with him, everything they had hoped for, everything they had expected for a wonderful future—all lay shattered. And none of them had any idea what to do about it all.

By midafternoon, a bit of light seeped through the window. Thomas touched Matthew who had drifted to sleep. Matthew looked up to the window, then to Thomas, and around the room to see his friends once again. They all commented as it brought the only relief they had felt in several hours.

They tossed around ideas as to what had happened, but no conclusions, merely a diversion to talk about. Was it only last night that the leaders and Temple guards came to the garden to arrest Jesus? It seemed like days ago.

Late into the afternoon, John staggered into the upper room. He slumped to the floor, obviously depleted. Elbows on knees and forehead in the palm of his hands, he sat, breathing heavily. He cried. He wailed. He ran fingers through his hair. Nothing would ease the excruciating pictures in his mind.

The men patiently gave him time to unload his anger and suffering.

At last, he gave bits and pieces: the weight of the cross beam on Jesus' shoulders, the lashes from soldiers prodding him to get back up, nails pounded into his hands, his bloodied face from a crown of thorns, the belittling accusations from the religious leaders, the agony, the darkness.

John hung his head, emotionally spent. Someone folded a towel and helped him lean over to rest. He had hardly slept since the arrest. They all slept fretfully that night.

*****

The next day hardly felt like a Sabbath. It seemed unending as they considered what might lie ahead for them. Questions and doubts crept through their minds and slipped into their conversations.

Matthew longed for the sea. Oh, to be sitting on his rock by the shore, a place of quiet and reverie with waves lapping onto the sandy stones.

He would not go back to his life of sin, but what was he to do now? Were these many months to no avail? He looked through the window at the top of a lone fig tree to distract his thoughts, but nothing could take away the anguish of envisioning Jesus on a cross. John's words played over and over in his mind.

The day dragged on. Questions hung in the air like restless leaves fluttering in the wind with no place to land. *How had this happened? Why was the Master tormented in this way? Will we suffer as he did? What do we do now? Where do we go?*

Chapter 49

A New Day

Early the next morning, the first day of the week, a slight earthquake jarred most of the disciples awake. After they had finished a meager breakfast, Matthew left the room early before shopkeepers were busy for the day. He had to get out of that room and into the fresh morning air. He ventured farther than he had gone since being in the upper room.

Only a few people milled about the streets, totally unaware of him. Then he saw Lucius sitting on a ledge with two other Roman soldiers who sat across from him. Lucius was facing Matthew and their eyes met. Matthew quickly lowered his head, but he could tell that Lucius had stood and was walking his way.

Lucius stood close, pretending to look at some apples that had been left in a bin from the day before. In a low voice, he said, "They crucified him, you know."

Matthew turned away but was able to speak just loud enough to respond. "Yes, I know."

"The Sadducees were afraid someone would steal his body and that the believers would claim he had risen from the dead."

"No, we did not know that."

Lucius turned to see that the other soldiers were still talking and oblivious to his actions. He went on, "The guards at his tomb were shaken with that little earthquake earlier this morning. When they woke up, they saw that the tomb was empty. They were afraid the centurion would have their heads on a platter, so they reported to the chief priests that some being or man in bright white clothes frightened them so much that they had fainted."

Lucius noticed the soldiers getting up. "You want an apple?" he called to them.

"Sure," one responded.

He carried two apples and gave one to each. "Hmm, I think I'll get one too. You go on ahead and I'll catch up." The soldiers tromped away, apples in hand.

Lucius walked back to the apple bin. When his fellow soldiers were around the corner out of sight, he continued. "When the chief priests met with the elders, they devised a plan to give the soldiers a large sum of money. They told them to say that his disciples came during the night and stole the body while they were asleep. They told the soldiers that if word got back to the governor, they would satisfy him and keep them out of trouble." He reached for an apple. "Thought you might want to know."

"Thank you, Lucius. We knew nothing about this. We have been together in a room all night. I'm the only one out this morning."

As Lucius strolled away, Matthew paused with gratitude for this one Roman whom he had befriended and whose centurion friend had been touched by Jesus.

He hurried back to tell the others.

*****

Matthew's voice quivered as he revealed the news from Lucius. It provoked the disciples to criticize the Romans and denounce the religious leaders once again.

"But, what about his body?" Thomas asked. "Who would have done this?"

Just then, Mary Magdalene, Salome, and Mary, mother of Joses knocked on the door. They poured out an amazing story of what had just happened to them.

"We went to Jesus' tomb to anoint his body this morning." Salome lifted her basket of spices.

Mary joined in. "The stone had been rolled away, but when we looked in, it was empty!"

"An angel came to us," Mary Magdalene continued. "He said that Jesus wasn't there, that he had risen just as he said he would."

The women's faces fell when they saw how the men whispered among themselves in doubt, even derision.

"Go, see for yourselves." Mary Magdalene said.

Peter and John looked at each other. "Let's go," John said. Mary Magdalene went with them.

Matthew thought to go with them but was still stunned by Lucius's words.

*****

When they returned, they reported that the tomb was indeed empty. "When I went into the tomb," Peter added, "I saw strips of linen lying there, as well as the burial cloth that had been around Jesus' head. The cloth was folded up by itself, separate from the linen. It is as they said. The tomb is empty."

"Where is Mary Magdalene?" someone asked.

"She stayed at the tomb," John said.

Shortly, Mary Magdalene came to the upper room again, beaming with her good news. "I have seen the Lord!"

She told how she had tarried at the tomb, doubting herself that he had risen. As she knelt weeping, she caught a glimpse of a man in the garden. He asked, "Woman, why are you crying? Who is it you are looking for?"

She said she thought he might be the gardener. "I pleaded with him through my tears, 'Sir, if you have carried him away, tell me where you have put him, and I will get him.' Then I realized the man had a familiar voice. 'Mary,' he said, and I knew at once it was Jesus!" She clasped her hands to her chest and closed her eyes with a smile of ecstatic joy, a tear slipping down her cheek.

When she opened her eyes and looked at the silent disciples, her joy turned to despair. "You don't believe me." Her soft, disappointed voice hung in the air as she made a quick exit.

After Mary Magdalene was gone, they were left not knowing what to believe. Their discussion was as jumbled and chaotic as their troubled hearts and confused minds. They could barely sort out all the reports in the last hours, much less understand and believe them.

Thomas stood. "I'm going to see what I can find out." And he left before anyone could respond.

Toward evening of this odd day, they heard a knock on the door and the familiar voices of two friends from Emmaus. Philip unlocked the door to let them in. "We thought you had returned home," he said.

"We did," Cleopas answered.

"But we met a stranger on the way," the other interrupted with excitement. They proceeded to tell about a man who summarized all of Scripture to them, warming their hearts with its truths.

"But it was when we arrived at our house and sat to eat with him that we realized he was Jesus!"

Just then, Jesus himself stood among them. They froze in shocked silence.

"Peace be with you," he said.

"It's a ghost," one of them whispered.

Jesus reassured them. "Why are you troubled, and why do doubts arise in your minds?" He held out his hands. "Look at my hands and my feet. It is I myself! Touch me and see; a ghost does not have flesh and bones, as you see I have."

Their expressions still showed doubt.

"Do you have anything here to eat?" he asked.

They gave him a piece of fish, and while he ate it they looked at each other with a mixture of fear and joy, as if to say, "I cannot believe it!"

"This is what I told you when I was with you: Everything must be fulfilled that is written about me in the Law of Moses, the Prophets, and the Psalms."

Dizzy with delight, Matthew watched him as he ate and opened their minds so they could understand the Scriptures. Jesus said, "This is what is written: 'The Christ will suffer and rise from the dead the third day, and repentance and forgiveness of sins will be preached in his name to all nations, beginning at Jerusalem.' You are witnesses of these things."

It was as though the veil was lifted from Matthew's eyes. He knew these Scriptures. Jesus had been telling the disciples on more than one occasion that he would suffer at the hands of the religious leaders, be crucified, and be *raised again on the third day*. How could they have been so dense? He had told them plainly. Why did they not grasp it?

Matthew realized that Thomas had still not returned. *He is missing this blessing of peace from our teacher.*

In the same way Jesus had come into the room, he slipped out again.

John summed up their feelings as he laid his hand across his chest. "My heart is throbbing with joy. Oh to be in his presence again. Cleopas, I understand now what you were trying to tell us. His body was not stolen away. Our Father has raised him up just as Jesus told us." Deep groans of assurance and nods of agreement came from all around the room.

Just then, Thomas slipped in. He looked at them, realizing something had happened. "What?" he said. "What has happened now?"

They all relayed the bits and pieces of what took place earlier, but Thomas would have none of it. "Unless I see the nail marks in his hands and put my hands into his side, I will not believe it."

Matthew tried to reason with him and tell him again what they saw and what Jesus said, but Thomas held firm to his unbelief. *Is he just angry that he was not here? Who knows?*

*****

A week later, all were gathered, and Jesus appeared to them a second time with the same words of comfort, "Peace be with you."

Yes, peace is what we need.

Matthew looked at Thomas, thankful that he was here this time. Jesus turned to him and said, "Thomas, put your finger here; see my hands. Reach out your hand and put it into my side. Stop doubting and believe."

Thomas knelt in humility, then looked up with tear-filled eyes. "My Lord and my God," he cried.

Jesus helped him up and told him, "Because you have seen me, you have believed. Blessed are those who have not seen me yet have believed."

Jesus smiled at his followers. "Remember how I told you that you would weep and mourn? I also told you that your grief would turn to joy. Now you understand. Go back to Galilee, and I will see you there."

After Jesus left, Philip said, "Thomas I'm glad you were here. Now you understand the joy and victory we have all felt."

Philip took a deep breath as though he had more to say. He glanced around at the others and then spoke as though talking to himself. "I have been wondering. Well, I have been struggling with why Jesus had to go through the crucifixion. Why that horrific death?"

In the next few moments of silence, Philip's words hung in the air like a dark cloud over their joy.

Finally, John spoke. "Philip, I understand your struggle. When I stood near the cross, watching his agony and hearing the cruel words of the religious leaders, I felt distress and confusion. I wanted to say along with them, 'If you are the Son of God, come down from the cross.' Oh, not in a tone of derision, but in a sense of pleading."

John stared at the floor. "But then I remember his telling Peter in the garden to put down his sword and that if he wished, he could call on ten thousand angels to protect him. Or even in his own power, I knew he could come down from that cross. Then I realized, he *willingly* hung there."

He looked around at the men. "John the Baptist spoke of Jesus as the Lamb of God who takes away the sin of the world. That is what he was doing, bearing our sin. Just as we take our lambs to the altar to bear our sin, he became that lamb. Once, as he hung there, he cried out, 'My God, why have you forsaken me?' I believe it was at that moment that he felt the weight of the sin of the world. Later, he said, 'It is finished.' It was intentional. He did it for us, for everyone who would believe in him."

Everyone sat in thoughtful silence.

Matthew spoke softly, "I remember now, the words of the prophet Isaiah.

> *'Surely, he took up our infirmities and carried our sorrows,*
> *yet we considered him stricken by God.*
> *But he was pierced for* our *transgressions,*
> *he was crushed for* our *iniquities;*
> *the punishment that brought us peace was upon him,*
> *and by his wounds, we are healed.'*

It is as John says, he bore *our sin* on that cross."

All heads bent as these sacred words settled in their minds.

Chapter 50

Go Forth

The disciples returned to Galilee. One evening, seven of the men set out in a boat to fish.

While they were gone, Matthew visited his mother to tell her all that he had experienced in Jerusalem. She mourned and rejoiced as he told each part of the story.

She shared with him about her work with the other women who were believers and how they had ministered to people in need, just as they had ministered to Jesus and the disciples when they were in Capernaum a month earlier. She told how James had talked with Amos about Jesus. "Amos asked lots of questions after you had that dinner for your friends. James was able to talk to him, and finally he became a believer!"

"Oh, Mama, that is such good news. Jesus told me that seeds were planted that day. Now I find out my own brother has watered those seeds and God has brought them to fruition. Blessed be his name! Thank you for telling me." He stayed that night with Mama and James.

Early the next morning, he dressed for the day, and suddenly jerked his head toward the sea because he heard a familiar voice. When he looked out the door, he saw someone shouting to the boatload of fishermen who were returning from their night's fishing. Soon he heard loud voices and a lot of commotion from his friends as they pulled a net-full of fish into their boat.

Matthew laughed when he saw Peter jump out of the boat and swim to shore. "It's Jesus," he told his mother. "Jesus is on the shore." Matthew ran over to meet everyone.

The fishermen talked of how they had caught nothing all night and then Jesus told them to cast out one more time. That is when the net bulged over with fish.

He remembered Andrew's account of a previous catch when Peter first fell in submission to Jesus. *Hmm, a reminder that we are to be fishers of men.*

Jesus had a fire going and told them to bring some of the fish they caught. They all ate of their catch for breakfast, basking once more in his presence.

He talked with them and encouraged them. Jesus paused and looked over at the piles of fish. "Now, go about your work."

While the fishermen sorted their fish, Matthew tended the fire, gathering a few rocks to snuff it out.

As he worked, Jesus drew Peter aside, but Matthew could hear them talking.

"Simon, son of John, do you care about me more than these?" Jesus gestured toward the boat and pile of fish.

"Yes, Lord, you know that I care about you."

"You must feed my lambs, those new to the faith." Jesus studied the waters washing in, then looked back to Peter. "Simon, do truly love me?"

"Yes, Lord, you know that I love you."

Jesus watched the men as they were cleaning up, then turned back to Peter. "Then take care of the lost sheep of Israel."

Jesus looked him straight in the eyes. "Simon, son of John, do you willfully love me?"

Matthew, who had been observing this encounter from the side, could see the grimace of frustration on Peter's face. His eyes moistened. "Lord," he said with passion, "You know all things; you know that I love you."

Jesus put both hands on Peter's shoulders. "Then you must feed my sheep, all my sheep."

Jesus lowered his head with a sigh and dropping one hand, he turned to the sea. "I tell you the truth, when you were younger, you dressed yourself and went where you wanted; but when you are old you will stretch out your hands, and someone else will dress you and lead you where you do not want to go."

Peter frowned, as he knew that "stretch out your hands" meant he would die on a cross. When Peter saw John nearby, he asked, "Lord, what about him?"

"That is no concern of yours."

Shortly, Jesus was gone from their midst, just as he left when they were in the upper room. While the other men were cleaning and counting fish, Peter sat by himself staring at the sea.

Matthew approached him. "Peter, you told us about denying the Lord three times. He now gave you the opportunity to confess your love and devotion to him—three times."

Peter stared at the ground, then slowly nodded his head. "You are right," he spoke softly. He raised his head. "Yes," he said, "yes, you're right."

Matthew leaned over and placed his hand on Peter's shoulder. "I know the Lord will use your life in powerful ways."

Peter looked up at him with sincere, caring eyes. "Thank you. Thank you, Matthew."

Matthew nodded with a smile. It was the first time he had *not* heard "the tax collector" in Peter's voice.

*****

Jesus had told the disciples he would meet them the next week as he pointed to a mountain beyond Capernaum.

A few days later, the men gathered supplies. "Why do we have to go all the way to that mountain? Can he not speak to us here?" one asked.

"I'm sure he has his reasons," another disciple answered.

"And where on the mountain? He didn't say," another complained.

As they finally began their trek north, Matthew made a mental count to be sure they had everyone. Yes, eleven, since Judas was no longer with them.

When they arrived, they set up camp for the night. The next morning, they trudged up paths that took them higher, a few

326

grumbled about feeling a bit lightheaded, but they pushed on into the cooler air.

At one point, they all turned around to see from their elevated spot. All of Galilee and beyond could be seen in this view. Each man remained quiet, awestruck by the beauty and vastness of the land spread before them.

They saw a few mountain dwellers down the way and one animal chasing another. "How do we know if we're in the right place? This is a big mountain," Thomas asked.

"Oh, I'm sure he will find us," Matthew answered.

They stirred around, unloading their packs and gathering their food supplies. Then Peter pointed down the hillside. "I think it's Jesus!"

"No, just another mountain man," Philip sighed. Each man stretched his neck this way and that and strained his eyes as they watched the man come closer.

"It is," Andrew whispered, "it is Jesus!"

"I think you're right," another said.

"Yes, yes, it's him!" one shouted, and they all started waving their arms about so he could see them. Jesus waved back.

Several fell to their knees, uttering praise to God at the sight of their Master again. They sang a joyful hymn as Jesus climbed toward them. He joined in as he came nearer.

"Hello, my friends, Shalom." Jesus greeted them all.

As they sat in an open area, he began teaching his followers just as he always did. Then Jesus moved to the side so as not to block their view of the scene before them. "From this vantage point, you can see all of Galilee and beyond, toward Judea. As you look to the left," he motioned, "you see other nations and to the right, more people who need to believe in our heavenly Father as you do."

It became evident why Jesus wanted to meet them in this location with its grand view.

Jesus paused until all eyes turned back to him. "All authority in heaven and on earth has been given to me. Therefore, as you go, witnessing in my name, I want you to make disciples of *all* nations, not just the Jews as you did before. As they become believers, baptize them in the name of the Father and of the Son and of the Holy Spirit. Then teach them to obey everything I have commanded you, both being and doing, giving attention to the inner person, the desires of the heart. Teach them acts of serving, loving both God and man. As you go you will face many challenges. So remember, remember always, that I am with you to the very end of the age."

Jesus sat gazing across the land beyond them. They also surveyed the scene, each one with his own thoughts of the enormity of this commission.

When they looked over again, Jesus was gone.

Chapter 51

Pentecost

A week later, Matthew stopped by his mother's house. "We are heading back to Jerusalem for Pentecost," Matthew told his mother. "Will you be going as well?"

"Yes, we are planning on it. We'll stay with my sister, of course."

Matthew traveled with his family, the disciples, and other followers who tagged along with them. He no longer had to hide himself as before. *How my life has changed!*

Along the way, others reported times when Jesus had appeared to them in these last forty days since his resurrection.

When they rounded the Mount of Olives, the full panoramic view of Jerusalem lay before them. Matthew turned to Thomas. "The last time we stood here, the people spread their cloaks out for Jesus and sang their praises with palm branches waving."

"Yes, it was a beautiful expression of their praise. Little did we know all that was to come. Nor the price he would pay for them on the cross."

The eleven walked through Jerusalem and met again in the upper room. Though it was practical and affordable, the place brought back all the bad memories. At least the bad was mitigated by the wonderful things that happened after that.

As they were eating, Jesus again came to them just as he had done before. This time he told them to meet him near Bethany at the Mount of Olives.

After they ate, they traveled through the Kidron Valley, past the garden of Gethsemane, and over toward Bethany. They saw Jesus standing higher up the mountain beckoning to them.

When they caught up, they sat before him. "Stay in Jerusalem and wait for the gift my Father promised, which you have heard me speak about. John the Baptist baptized with water, but in a few days, you will be baptized with the Holy Spirit."

Philip spoke up and asked, "Lord, are you at this time going to restore the kingdom to Israel?"

Jesus responded. "It is not for you to know the times or dates the Father has set by his own authority." He paused and repeated with emphasis. "As I was saying, you will receive power when the Holy Spirit comes upon you."

He gazed north over Judea. "Two weeks ago, we scanned this view from the mountain in Galilee. Today, we look from this mountain to see all of Judea and beyond toward Galilee."

They looked out over the vast area before them. When they turned back, Jesus stood and smiled at them and said, "You will be my witnesses in Jerusalem and in all Judea and Samaria." He spread both arms out, "And to the ends of the earth." He paused as he lowered his arms. "Remember, I am with you always."

After he said this, he raised his arms and was taken up before their very eyes, and a cloud hid him from their sight. They kept staring, craning their necks to try to see him around the clouds, when suddenly, two men dressed in white stood beside them.

"Men of Galilee," they said, "why do you stand here looking into the sky? This same Jesus, who has been taken from you into heaven, will one day come back in the same way you have seen him go into heaven."

Overwhelmed, they stood there for a few moments trying to take it all in, feeling the finality, stunned by his words of challenge "to the ends of the earth."

They walked together back across the valley to Jerusalem, each man speechless.

In the next few days, they remained constantly in prayer with one another. Other followers joined them, along with the women and Mary, the mother of Jesus. Matthew rejoiced that Jesus' brothers, who had been so opposed to Jesus, had now joined them as well.

*****

When the day of Pentecost came, Jews journeyed, as usual, from near and far—Parthians, Medes, and Elamites, residents of Mesopotamia, Judea, and Cappadocia, Pontus, and Asia.

"So many nations here," Matthew remarked to Andrew as they passed through the city.

"It seems like more than ever before."

"Many must have heard about Jesus and all that's gone on here in Jerusalem." Matthew looked to the left. "I think those men are from Egypt or maybe Libya."

Thomas looked at him in surprise. "How do you know so much about these people?"

"I used to see them in the trading business."

While Matthew, Thomas, and Andrew were still in the marketplace, they purchased oil for the lamps, then rejoined the other disciples as they waited for the promised gift of the Holy Spirit.

They sat together in one large circle as they had been doing the last few days, praying silently at times, and at other times, one led in prayer, then another and another. Matthew gave thanks for these fervent times of prayer.

Peter had just led in a passionate plea for the Lord to dwell with them, when suddenly, a sound like the blowing of a violent wind rushed in and filled the whole house. The sound of it roared in their ears, and the power of it whipped their hair around, pulling at their clothing.

Everyone looked at each other, startled, questioning. Matthew closed his eyes against the pressure of the wind. When he opened them, he saw what seemed to be something like tongues of fire that separated and came to rest one by one on the men across from him. Around the room this blazing glory went until it touched him.

The fear of being burned disappeared. Instead, an indescribable warmth filled his being, his very soul. *This must be the Holy Spirit Jesus talked about.*

He heard the others speaking in languages he did not know. Then someone spoke to him in an unknown language and he was able to answer back in that same language with great fluency.

"We must find people who speak in these languages and share the news of Jesus Christ with them!" Matthew shouted.

With excitement speeding them on their way, they went into the Temple area, proclaiming the Gospel. If they spoke in a language that someone understood, the listeners were amazed, attentive, and often responsive.

But if others did not hear their own tongue, they made fun of them and said, "They must have had too much wine." But more and more people groups gathered listening to one of the disciples speaking in their own tongue.

After a time of sharing in this way, Peter brought the disciples together and stood up to address the people in their common Greek language. His strong voice rang out, and the people listened attentively.

Peter quoted the prophet Joel:

> *In the last days, God says,*
> *"I will pour out my Spirit on all people.*
> *Your sons and daughters will prophesy,*
> *your young men will see visions,*
> *your old men will dream dreams.*
> *Even on my servants, both men and women,*
> *I will pour out my Spirit in those days.*
> *I will show wonders in the heaven above*
> *and signs on the earth below."*

Peter's powerful message moved on to include the wonders and signs and miracles of Jesus. He revealed the wickedness of those who had crucified him. Peter quoted words of David about the coming Messiah and how this Messiah would be resurrected. He proclaimed that Jesus was raised from the dead and that he and others were witnesses to his resurrection.

The people, touched by his effective message, asked, "What shall we do?"

Then Peter spoke the message of John the Baptist and of Jesus. The message they had all been preaching in the last three years—repent and be baptized.

Three thousand became repentant believers that day with the power of the Holy Spirit working through Peter and the other disciples.

Armed with the power of the Holy Spirit and charged with the commands of Jesus to go into all the world, Matthew was struck by the fact that the language he had spoken that day was the African language of his friend, Rabomba.

Chapter 52

Into All the World

Matthew traveled back to Jericho and checked in with his friend, Bartimaeus, who recognized Matthew right away. Bartimaeus had learned the art of drawing balm from the balsam bushes and proudly declared that he earned his own money now and had witnessed to others of Jesus' healing and saving power in his life.

As Matthew sat by the road that led into Jericho, he smiled at the thought of his encounter with Bartimaeus. He had previously said his good-byes to his family and friends and now he held all the possessions he owned in this world.

He smelled a whiff of myrrh and was delighted to see Rabomba's caravan approaching. He ran over to speak with Rabomba then returned to his spot on the side of the road to wait.

In his mind, he pictured faces of the many he had led to the Lord and the dramatic miracles in these last days with Peter and John's public preaching, as well as their imprisonment for preaching about Jesus and their miraculous freedom from prison. His eyes had beheld many wonders in these past years, not the least of which was his own confession of faith. Truly, like Bartimaeus, he had been given eyes to see.

And now the words of Jesus rang in his ears: "Go and make disciples of all nations, baptizing them in the name of the Father and of the Son and of the Holy Spirit, and teaching them to obey everything that I have commanded you."

Matthew gazed up at the blue sky, then closed his eyes. "And I am with you always." *Thank you, Lord.*

Matthew watched one line of wagons and carts going into Jericho with their goods and other caravans coming out, many loaded with the balm of Gilead.

He studied the faces of men from around the world, faces like the ones on the day of Pentecost when he and others spoke their languages.

Jesus' words came to him again. "You will be my witnesses in Jerusalem, and in all Judea and Samaria, and to *the ends of the earth*."

Just then, he saw again the familiar face of his friend, Rabomba from Ethiopia who had finished his trading in the city. As Rabomba's caravan came to a stop where Matthew was waiting, Rabomba jumped from his wagon with a broad smile.

"LeVi-Matthew, are you ready to go to my country?"

Matthew picked up his bag. "Yes, my friend, I'm ready to go!"

Final Thoughts

Was Matthew's father, Alphaeus, an angry, cruel potter? Did Matthew go to Jericho, meet Bartimaeus and Zacchaeus, and work with the balsam trade? Did he fall in love with a girl named Lily? Did he return to Capernaum to find his mother and brother destitute and shunned by the community, which led him to accept a position as tax collector, recommended by Zacchaeus? We don't know.

However, we are told that he was named Levi, son of Alphaeus and that he became a tax collector. Whatever sins he had committed were forgiven when Jesus said, "Follow me." We know that he became known as "Matthew" and that he wanted Jesus to come to his house and speak to his "sinner friends" as we read in his gospel, Matthew 9:9–13.

For Matthew to become a real person to us, I have attempted to give a possible scenario that might depict how this good Jewish boy became a despised tax collector. Knowing human nature, I surmised that he likely continued to face non-acceptance even from some of his fellow disciples until he proved himself.

From the point of his conversion, I was able to follow much Scripture, seeing it through Matthew's eyes. Though we hear very few words in Scripture directly from most of the disciples, we can be assured that anytime we see that the "disciples" did this or that, or heard or saw this or that, it applied to them as individuals.

Worthy of note is the fact that in his gospel account, Matthew uses the term "Heavenly Father" seventeen times, while the other gospel writers use the term only once or not at all. Matthew's gospel contains one of the genealogies of Jesus as well as numerous Old Testament quotes (more than the other gospel writers), leaving us to believe that he had had some formal training to share with his Jewish audience.

We are told that Jesus sent the men out two by two, but we have no description of their encounters. I enjoyed trying to envision the possible adventures they might have had.

Most of the apostles were eventually martyred in the various countries where they ministered "to the ends of the earth." Legend has it that Matthew ministered and was martyred in Ethiopia. Thus, I included the development of a friendship with "Rabomba."

We have so many in our country as well as the rest of the world who are illiterate when it comes to the Bible. Often, those who have been raised in the church lean on their third-grade level of knowing Scripture. Even the best of us who attempt to grow in our study of the Scripture can fall into stale thinking. I believe the Lord led me to dig a little deeper into the lives of Bible characters to bring them to life, characters like:

Nicodemus in *A Heart for Truth*
Malchus in *Ears to Hear*
Matthew in *Eyes to See*

Matthew's story concludes this series of "Lesser Known, Unlikely Believers."

May these real characters of Scripture become real in your mind and heart. I pray you will be blessed by the growth and vision that came out of their struggles.

And, my friend, if you have never known of Jesus, our Savior, he stands ready to forgive you of the sin that separates you from God. He can cleanse you, set you free, and give you eyes to see just as he did for Matthew.

~ Joyce Cordell ~

Scripture Resources

Jesus' teachings
   The Beatitudes – Matthew 5:2–5
   Salt and light – Matthew 5:13–16
   Fulfillment of the Law – Matthew 5:17–20
   Adultery – Matthew 5:27–28
   Love for enemies – Matthew 5:43–47
   Giving to the needy – Matthew 6:1–4
   Prayer – Matthew 6:5-15
   Fasting – Matthew 6:16-18
   For where your treasure is… Matthew 6:21
   The eye is the lamp of the body – Matthew 6:23
   Do not worry – Matthew 6:28–34
   Love one another. By this all men will know… – Luke 18:34–35
   Pharisee's prayer vs. tax collector's prayer – Luke 18:9–14
   The Shema (Love the Lord your God) – Deuteronomy 6:4
   Even tax collectors and prostitutes come to believe – Matthew 21:32
   I am the way, the truth, and the life – John 14:6
   Jesus' last words to his disciples – John chapter 15–16

Jesus' miracles
   Jesus calms the storm – Matthew 8:23–27
   Healing the demoniac – Matthew 8:28–34
   Healing the leper – Matthew 8:1–4
   Healing the woman of bleeding – Matthew 9:20–22
   Raising Jairus' daughter from the dead – Matthew 9:18–19, 22–26
   Healing blind Bartimaeus – Mark 10:46–52
   The death and raising of Lazarus – John 11

Jesus' warnings
   "An evil man is snared by his own sin, but a righteous one can sing and be glad." – Proverbs 29:6
   "You cannot serve God and money." – Luke 16:10, 13

Balm

Balm in Gilead – Jeremiah 46:11
Balm for pain – Jeremiah 51:8
Balm, perhaps from Queen of Sheba? – 2 Chronicles 9:9
Is there no balm in Gilead? – Jeremiah 8:22

Matthew quotes the prophets

He has blinded their eyes… Matthew (Isaiah 6:10)
"These people honor me with their lips, but their hearts…
Matthew 15:8-9 (Isaiah 29:13)
John the Baptist (fulfillment of prophecy) – Matthew 3:3
(Isaiah 40:3)
Peter's quote in his great sermon Acts 2:17–18 (Joel 2:28–32)

Jesus' actions

Calling of Matthew – Matthew 9:10–11
Restoring Zacchaeus – Luke 19:1–10
Washing the disciples' feet – John 13:1–17
Predicts the betrayal – John 13:18–30
Predicts Peter's denial – John 13:31–38
Words at the Lord's Supper – Luke 22:19–22
Prayers for himself, the disciples and all believers – John
chapter 17

Jesus' parables

Prayer of the Pharisee and tax collector – Luke 18:9–14
Parable of the Sower – Matthew 13:1–23
Parable of the Weeds – Matthew 13:24–30
Parables of the Mustard Seed and the Yeast – Matthew 13:31–
35
Parables of the Hidden Treasure and the Pearl – Matthew
13:44–46

Jesus commands

The Great Commission – Matthew 28:18–20
"You will be my witnesses in Jerusalem, in Judea…" Acts 1:8

Listings of the twelve disciples

Matthew 10:2–4 and Mark 3:16–19

Simon (who is called Peter) and his brother, Andrew
James, son of Zebedee and his brother, John
Philip, Bartholomew, Thomas, and Matthew the tax
collector
James, son of Alphaeus, Thaddaeus, Simon the Zealot
Judas Iscariot, who betrayed him

Luke 6:14–16 – Thaddaeus is listed as "Judas, son of James"
John 1:40–50 – Only lists five and lists Bartholomew as
"Nathaniel"
Acts 1:13 – James, son of Alphaeus is listed as "James, the
younger"

(Mark 15:40 also mentions both names for James)
Thaddaeus is listed as "Judas, son of James" (like
Luke)
Judas is deleted, but Matthias is added

Other references

Song that Matthew might have led at his first sermon – Psalm
18:25–28
A psalm that Matthew thinks about – portions of Psalm 42
The triumphal entry into Jerusalem – John 12:12–19
The arrest – Matthew 26:47–56
Jesus taken to Annas (the previous high priest) – John 18:13
Trial before the Sanhedrin – Matthew 26:57–68
Peter's betrayal – Matthew 26:69–75
Jesus before Pilate – Matthew 27:24–26
Crown of thorns – Matthew 27:29–31
The crucifixion – Matthew 27:41–43, 45
Darkness – Matthew 27:45
Guarding the tomb – Matthew 27: 62–66
Report about the guards – Matthew 28:11–15

Other Resources

Partnering with the King: Study the Gospel of Matthew and Become a Disciple of Jesus, by John L. Higel.

Twelve Ordinary Men: How the Master Shaped His Disciples for Greatness, and What He Wants to Do with You, by John MacArthur.

The Training of the Twelve by A. B. Bruce.

Expositor's Bible Commentary. General Editors, Tremper Longman III, and David E. Garland.

Jesus of Nazareth: Background, Witness, and Significance, by Gerald L. Borchert.

All the Men of the Bible by Herbert Lockyer
Meaning of men's names, etc.

Strong's Exhaustive Concordance of the Bible
James Strong, John R. Kohlenberger III, and James A. Swanson.

www.historicjesus.com
A copper coin called an "as" was worth one-sixteenth of a denarius. Sometimes translated as a "farthing" or a "penny," the value of two sparrows sold in the market.

www.bible-history.com/isbe/P/POTTER;+POTTERY
Descriptions of potter wheels. The wheels used in Israel today probably differ in no respect from those used in Jeremiah (Jeremiah 18:1–6).

www.christiananswers.net/dictionary/capernaum
Information about Capernaum: citizens, Via Maris highway, custom taxes, fish sales area, synagogue, biblical events in the city, etc.

www.Chabad.org
Discussion with Rabbi Malkie Janowski.
Public Yeshivas (schools of learning the ancient Scriptures with student/teacher classes). They were not as readily available until later in the first century. Individual lessons were given by the father or a hired teacher.

www.BalmofGileadwikipedia.com
Balsam appears as an ointment that was a highly praised product of the Jericho plain. Its main use was medicinal, but it was also used as perfume and to anoint kings. It comes from an evergreen bush no taller than two cubits.
A slight incision in the rind produces drops, which are collected with wool into a horn and preserved in earthen jars. It is at first whitish but becomes hardened and reddish.
Medicinal properties include expelling menstrual flow, being an *abortifacient*, assisting breathing, antidote for a poisonous plant, treating pneumonia, cough, epilepsy, asthma, *stomach aches or cramps*, etc.

www.biblicaltraining.org/library/jericho
Herod the Great's winter capital was south of Jericho, where the climate was warmer than in Jerusalem.
The Wadi Qelt provided a stream with reflecting pools lined with fifty statuary niches in a sunken garden. Had a grand stairway 150 feet long looking down on the garden.
Considerable taxes were levied on the balsam groves nearby.
Many blind beggars were in the vicinity of Jericho. Wherever wealth exits in the Middle East, a multiplicity of beggars can be found.

Vine's Expository Dictionary
It is unlawful to receive riches from a tax collector (Sanhedrin 25, Section 2).

It is unlawful to receive alms in the synagogue box from tax collectors (Baba Kama 10:1).

One tax collector in a family disgraces the whole family. Do not keep promises with murderers, thieves, or tax collectors (Nedar 3:4).

Jesus saw nothing inherently wrong with paying or collecting taxes. He opposed extortioners, yet he opened the door to repentance and salvation.

Matthew was a *dounier*, a custom house official who charged for axles, wheels, pack animals, and opened every bale and package, customs on import and export taxes.

Fausset's Bible Dictionary
Rabbis said, "Like one robber disgraces a family, so with a tax collector." The synagogue would not accept the alms from tax collectors nor allow them to testify in court.

www.bibletools.com
The resurrection of Jairus' daughter

About the Author

Joyce Cordell, a graduate of Georgetown College, makes her home in Louisville, Kentucky, with her husband, Jim.

Through the years, Joyce has taught public school music and directed children's choirs, while writing scripts, Bible studies, and short works for publication.

Now in retirement, she has turned in a new direction to fulfill the passion God has given her to write full-length novels about lesser-known Bible characters.

Joyce's desire is to help readers see these characters as the real people they were—facing challenges, struggling with their vices, striving to follow God's will, and rejoicing in his blessings just as we do.

Her first novel, *Ears to Hear*, was published in 2007.

The book tells the story of Malchus, the servant of Caiaphas the high priest. It was the first in this series of Unlikely Believers.

The second novel, *A Heart for Truth*, published in 2014, explores the life of another Bible character, Nicodemus.

Eyes to See is now the third book of the series.

A novel provides license for an amount of fiction, but Joyce's goal, as before, is to discover what might be the rest of the story for these men and to tell it with as much authenticity as possible, staying true to the culture and to Scripture.

Joyce loves to hear from readers.

For more information about Joyce Cordell:

www.joycecordell.com
joyce@joycecordell.com

www.ingramcontent.com/pod-product-compliance
Lightning Source LLC
Chambersburg PA
CBHW050916250626
47155CB00001B/258